Daughter Dusk

Book 2 in the Myrk Maiden Trilogy

Alyssa Charpentier

Praise for the Myrk Maiden Trilogy

"Charpentier writes with a potency that is thrilling and smacks of a seasoned, accomplished author."

—**Mark Justice, author of** *Gauge Black: Hell's Revenge* **and** *Death's Head: The Eye of Samedi*

"It's grand, grim, gory, and gruesome... not for the faint of heart, but very skillfully written and involving. A remarkable achievement!"

—**Peter H. Brothers, author of** *Atomic Dreams and the Nuclear Nightmare: The Making of Godzilla (1954)*

"Sinister and very entertaining, Daughter Darkness has everything you wish for in a thrilling coming-of-age story of a powerful protagonist. I love this book."

—**Rabia Tanveer from Readers' Favorite**

"Daughter Darkness is a slow-paced, character-driven read, packed with adventure, secrets, agony, deceit, and more."

—**Keith Mbuya from Readers' Favorite**

Author's Note

In 2021, my paper family was brought to life. *Daughter Darkness,* Book #1 in this whirlwind of a series, became my firstborn. For normal people, children come with fuzzy heads and cute little cries, but my "first child" came in the mail with pages, a fully furnished vocabulary, and a sweet gloss finish. Note: it is also quite silent.

Daughter Dusk is the continuation of my debut efforts as an author. It is the "middle child" of the Myrk Maiden Trilogy and the blossoming of another bloom of hope for my writing future. Because of this book, I discovered that writing sequels is challenging in a way beginning a story from scratch is not. Additionally, I am baffled that in just one year (2021-2022), my first series is already two-thirds complete! The loveliest and ugliest things take the longest time to make. The Myrk Maiden Trilogy certainly isn't a pretty read, but it is my hope that, with the second installment now in readers' hands, they will find some sense of beauty—even truth—among its pages.

~Alyssa Charpentier, 2022

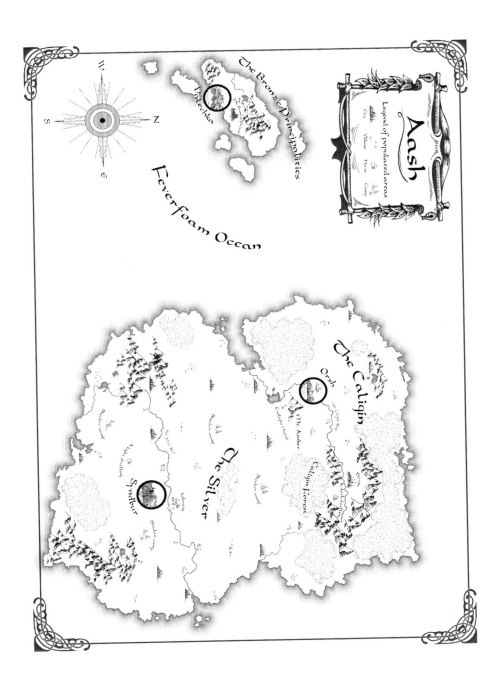

For my "Little Broth," the grandmother I never knew, and those still seeking their purpose.

THE PEOPLE'S AGENDA

*Those who lack a purpose
will be given a purpose by the powers that be.*

DAUGHTER DUSK

CHAPTER ONE

D EATH HOWLED ALL AROUND US.

   It hurdled through the trees with jaws wide and fangs piercing, claws scoring the earth as it slashed toward its prey. The stench of it was madness. Every strand of black saliva dribbling between its fangs sharpened the air, its biting scent gnawing my senses.

   Worse than the smell were the screams of the innocents clinging to me for life as we fled from Death. Hearts drummed against me, their blood flowing fast inside them, and the vibrations mingled with the sound of my own life fluid throbbing in my ears.

   The little ones pleaded with me to go faster!

   Faster!

   Before Death ensnared us in its many talons, talons it would use to tear irreparable gashes through our flesh, so the blood inside us poured hot and thick, and—

   Twilight...

   I turned and saw Death launch itself at us. Its gaping mouth with rows of curved teeth stretched into an open grin as its forepaws sliced forward. Death's claws pinpointed on us, and its body sailed through the wind. I forced myself to twist away just before the inevitable impact.

   The children screamed.

   My soul did, as well, understanding the narrow brush with Death we had just encountered and the grim knowledge that it was directly behind us—

   Twilight!

   Golden magic burned the air. I smelled charred flesh as it made contact with my assailant, and I witnessed the feverish gleam in the blonde woman's eyes as she wielded the light power against shadowy Death. My muscles locked into place at the sight, and my surroundings melted into the past.

   Death's wrenching scream contorted into a wail from the Dark Days, and in Death's place were eyes.

   Black, stark, and depthless, void of humanity.

A frigid finger scraped my soul as those eyes never left me. A man's stern lips withered into his eternal scream, and he began to die anew. The falling flesh. The melting eyes.

His cry for a god who had forever forsaken him...

"Twilight!"

Cobi hovered over me with his hand on my wrist and a wild look brightening his blue gaze. His mouth drooped with concern. "Twilight," he whispered, "You were... your magic... look."

I looked. My trembling hands, the palms pink and raw from reignited scar wounds, glowed faintly purple beneath the skin. I glanced at my bed and saw that I had singed it. Cobi must have been the one to extinguish the flames while I wrestled with my... remembrances.

"Another nightmare?" He asked.

He perched on the edge of my bed and smiled tentatively at me, trying to reassure me I was well, even though I knew that I scared him. I frightened everyone who had escaped with me from my "family" of shape-shifting cannibalistic sorcerers who called themselves Shadows. It was impossible to enjoy gentle sleep when visions of violence danced in your head.

"Yes." I sighed. "The dreams are worsening. I don't know if I'm capable of progression, Cobi. I mean, look at me."

Cobi frowned and drank me in, noting my sunken-eyed, sleep-deprived visage and my matted tangles of dark hair.

He shrugged. "All I see is a nice girl with a crooked nose. The rest looks good to me."

I rolled my eyes. He knew, as all of them did, that I was anything but nice. The Shadows had ensured that.

"Okay, Cobi. You should probably go back to your room. I don't want to wake the kids. And since they saved our lives, I would prefer not to anger Il and Norva. I'll be fine... at some point."

Cobi was not convinced. Neither was I.

But he nodded, wished me better dreams, and returned to his bedroom, where his memories would only be spotted with gore. Mine were drowning in it, and the crushing realization that much of the death I had witnessed was my own design.

I sighed the kind of sigh that scooped into my soul and dropped back against my pillow, gazing up at the ceiling of the inn we had all taken respite in for the night. We were still long miles away from our destination in Syndbur, capital of the wintry Silver, where our Akristuran escorts Il and Norva had promised to take us, but at least the worst appeared to have been left behind us.

In broken pieces, I remembered our flight two days ago from the society of the Sharavaks. I had to wonder if Solshek was still alive. Had he been torn apart by Sharavos? Or worse, sentenced to a gruesome demise by my father, Damion, who had of late inherited the sovereign position of authority over the dark magic abusers?

I ran fingers over my veins.

Blood. So much blood had stained the streets of my hometown, Orsh, painting the buildings in the fluid as it fled from severed limbs and heads divorced from their bodies...

Screams. There'd been too many. Innocent people had perished at my will.

Because of me.

My fault entirely.

How could I do such things? And to enjoy them as if savoring a piece of candy?

I wept. I buried my anguish into my pillow, allowing the hot tears to engulf me in their tidal wave and let the guilt consume me. I was a destroyer of innocence. In taking others' lives, I had ruined my own, and now I was trapped with this weight sinking my heart down into my toes.

I wished I could never breathe again. That I could unwind time and unwrite my brutal history, erase myself entirely from existence so the dead would still live and I would never have this cold, ugly tarnish marking my heart.

It was not remorse in the completest sense, because coupled with the grief was a distinct vat of anger boiling below the surface. Rage and conflicting thoughts clashed in my head and heart.

What was right? Wrong? Any of it?

You monster, I thought to myself. *You are no girl; you are unforgivable. Inhuman.*

But the little girl in me, who had yet to grow up and become calloused and tired of living, begged, *No, please, no! Can't I try again? I don't want to be a monster! I don't desire any more screaming. I know the good is still within me!*

The Sharavak in me sneered at this.

Fool. You commit abominable acts most adults have never dreamed of, yet you are stupid like a child. Naive, wasteful fool! End yourself already! Do this world one favor...

And I did try. If Cobi had not knocked me unconscious, I would have burned myself to death with my magic. I deserved that, at the very least. I deserved so much more than a quick flight from the tangible realm into nothingness.

Afterward, of course, the Akristurans gave me their hope speech. Though their intentions were pure, Il and Norva's words rang hollow in my heart. Norva assured me it was because I wasn't ready to hear them yet, but I knew I was simply beyond redemption.

No one, not even the supposedly merciful Akristura they worshiped, could ever look favorably upon me after what I had done.

"Twilight. It's time to go, love."

I roused from a gripping sleep, blinking my eyes open to the female Akristuran, Norva. She stood beside me in her white robes with the gold spiral symbol and its seven arrows painted on the front.

I slithered out from my sheets and began gathering up the few items I had been given by the Akristurans. Il, the man, had provided me with a worn leather satchel that doubled as a waterskin, and Norva's donation of a jeweled hair brush was her silent message to me that I would function better with my curls under control.

Norva watched me with her lips hugging each other too tightly as she took me in. With the whites of my eyes looking like poorly glazed pottery and strands of my hair strangling each other in a never-ending feud, I was probably a sight to behold.

My eyes alone were spectacles. Their blooming black color burned hot as Void fire and punctured cold as an ice pick, depending on my mood. Suspended like celestial bodies within the depthless black space of my irises were little sprinkles of silver, a welcome pop of brightness amidst the swallowing shadows that surrounded them.

Perhaps their most intriguing element was the single violet ring that encircled each pupil. They bled forth a promise with their soothing purple color; there was more to existence than existing. I had a purpose beyond my current situation and a life worth living on the other side of my self-loathing and crippling mistakes.

Rather, crippling *choices*.

Something else was there, too. Married to this desire to know myself was a desire to know... something else. What it was, I could not define. It dwelled above, beyond, and forever out of my reach. I liked to think I would find it in Syndbur, the capital of the Silver region where my mother had grown up, but I doubted I would.

This "something" was a something out of reach. It had no form, no definitive existence. It beckoned to me at the twilight when darkness warred with the day and scattered the colors of their mingled blood across the atmosphere: orange, violet, pink, yellow, and depthless blue.

It tugged on the string of my spirit at the blackest plunges of night when I viewed the stars overhead pulsing silently with promise. With signs and wonders I was yet unaware of.

With purpose. The sky seemed to say that I, Twilight Urik, had a purpose.

But I would not find it where I was, and my eyes, which were once a source of pride and now a prodding of shame, could not be seen by normal humans. As if she read my thoughts, Norva set my disguise item at the foot of my bed and left the room.

After placating my hair's temper tantrum with Norva's brush, I swept the flag of defiant black waves behind me and clumsily pinned it up in a bun. I ached, remembering that this hair was distinctly my mother Aubri's. When my magic had first begun budding, she had visited me in my sleep, a token of the realm of the dead. Since my power's progression, though, I had lost sight of her. Only the white stone necklace nestled above my collarbone remained to remind me I had ever had a mother at all.

I slipped back into my traveling clothes, a spare pair of plain, cream-colored robes from Norva, and wondered if I would ever see Aubri again. Perhaps I wouldn't.

Those thoughts could wait, though. I needed to focus on my un-Twilight-ing. The final touch was a pair of color contacts for my eyes. The plain dark brown masked my more eccentric features, so I appeared like any ordinary girl.

After placing the things on my eyeballs, I beheld myself in the mirror. With a simple set of robes, regular mud-splotch irises, and my hair a beast of the past hidden under my hood, I was a new person. My skin, though unnaturally unpigmented, would not be an issue for others to see since my face and the rest of my body were concealed by cloth, and my hands were mercifully gloved. No *zyz*, or non-magical person, would think much of me now.

I gave my cozy space with its rustic furnishings a final long glance, then stepped out of my room into the upstairs hallway. I was immediately greeted with the scent of sizzling meat. The innkeepers below were cooking breakfast. My mind glimmered with flashes of human blood and the sparkling flavor of their *saas,* or spiritual residue, as the aroma wreathed around me.

I was hungry again for a moment, itching to scratch someone's throat and feed on their insides...

"Twilight?"

I startled, realizing the sudden warmth in my hand was magic, and let it die down into my skin as Il approached. He gave me a knowing look.

"What were you thinking about?" He asked.

Norva appeared from her bedroom behind him. "Ready, girl?"

I nodded. Il repeated his question, and I averted my gaze. I didn't want him to read the hunger there, blushing brightly in my eyes like a hastily lit candle.

"Twilight," he prompted.

I choked on the dark feeling as it strangled me in the back of my throat. Something about being around the Akristurans resurrected the long-dead whispers of "the voice" that had once told me what was right and wrong. Father Sein and the God of Myrk had denied the validity of this voice, claiming its intent was backward and even evil.

Now who was the evil one? It had never been the voice; it was me, and I loathed the Akristurans for reminding me of it. I wanted to rage about it and scream to the high heavens, but instead, I settled for, "Can I please just not talk about it?"

I kept my eyes centered on the floor as though the scuffed slabs of wood could absorb my wicked dreams, Il's uncomfortable questions, and perhaps me. Il was about to tell my feelings off when my stepmother Marcia emerged from her room with my siblings.

My stepmother looked dazed and disheveled as my seven-year-old brother Josha held her arm. My eleven-year-old sister Aullie shot me an unsettled look, hovering behind Marcia and a curtain of neck-length red-gold hair as she stepped out.

Il and Norva greeted them. Marcia returned the greeting with lackluster enthusiasm before she looked back at me. I didn't know what to say or even to think. How did anyone perceive me anymore?

Her eyes were still somewhat caustic, but they were warmer than I'd ever seen when looking at me.

"I didn't get a chance to properly thank you the other night," she told me, "For keeping my babies safe during our departure once those creatures started chasing us. So thank you, Twilight."

Yes, the departure, the bulk of the previous night's terrifying dreams.

Marcia's tone was genuine, but it came out a bit forced. Regardless, I appreciated the gesture.

"Of course, you're welcome. After all," I said, stooping to my brother's eye level, "I love them just as much as you do."

Marcia shook her head. "I wouldn't go that far; I *am* their mother. But I know you care. You risked your life to save theirs when we escaped."

Indeed, I had, and if not for Norva's healing, I would have likely bled to death from the slash wounds I'd amassed. I hated to feel indebted to her, but I supposed there was no alternative. It had been that or bleed to death.

I smiled at Josha and ruffled his soft brown hair as I put these bloody thoughts behind me. Sometimes, at the right angle or with a certain facial expression, he looked very much like my father. *Our* father, unfortunately. It was the way his lips tucked themselves away when he smiled, giving him an irresistible, almost smirk-like grin that would be devastating when he was older.

On the bright side, Josha acted nothing like Damion. His sweetness was genuine, and his heart unpolluted. I had failed him in the past months and could never do so again. My brother would have to be preserved and loved more fiercely than ever.

"Twi," Josha cried, throwing himself into my arms. "I missed you, seester!"

Josh and I liked to say words incorrectly sometimes for fun, and instead of calling me sister, he changed it to "seester" because it made him laugh. In return, I would call him "Little Broth," which progressed into a series of bizarre nicknames like "Soup Boy," "Noodleson," and so on. I had forgotten the comforting normalcy of returning to such phrases. Tears pricked my eyes at hearing them again and knowing how deeply children could love, even when wronged.

"Twi, you gotta look at what I found!" Josha exclaimed. He beamed at me as he gently removed something from his pocket and held it out for me to see.

In his hand rested a massive golden-white spider. I heard Il and Norva gasp, Aullie squeal, and Marcia cry, "Oh, Josha, what in the name of all things sacred are you *doing* with that?"

Upon seeing the spider, I was reminded of the enormous mutated ones I had encountered living with the Sharavaks. The spirnyx was a ferocious pest that lurked in the tunnels running beneath the compound, and Solshek had protected me from one once...

"Twi?" Josha prompted, his excitement dulling into sadness at my hesitation.

When I saw his drooping face, I quickly fussed lovingly over the arachnid and asked him where he'd found it.

"From the depths of the Abyss!" Marcia yelled. "Get it away from me, Josh! Right now!"

Josha's face started to cave into a whimper. I tugged my brother down the hall and away from the commotion to reassure him.

"Hey," I said, smiling at him as I guided the spider onto my fingertips. The sluggish creature must have liked Josh because it didn't want to leave his hand. "Look," I said, nudging the spider forward, "There's nothing wrong with liking spiders. Some of them are gross—even I'm not a fan of them all—but as long as you learn to keep them away from other people, you can enjoy them. And don't feel bad about it," I told him, making an exaggeratedly serious face.

Josha giggled. In that giggle, I felt another tug on my humanity.

"I'm not kidding with you, young man!" I said. I frowned even more deeply. Josha laughed harder. "Liking spiders is seriously cool business. You are a fan of one of the world's most interesting creatures. That is no laughing matter. Okay?"

"I second that," spoke a familiar voice as the door behind Josha opened.

Out stepped Cobi, grinning broadly, into the hallway. No darkness or hints of last night lingered on his face.

"Wow," he said when he beheld the spider in my hand. "Nice monster. Thought you had enough with monsters, though? Is it your pet?"

I told him it was Josha's discovery, and Josha informed him, much to my stepmother's distress, that he had found it behind the headboard of her bed.

"Oh, goodness," she chanted, "I am *so* done here. I'll take the Shadow things over that any day."

Il frowned. "Careful what you say, lady. Now that everyone's here, are we ready to leave? We should reach Syndbur by sundown if we clock this right."

Everyone expressed their approval.

"Excellent," said Norva. "Then we leave now."

CHAPTER TWO

"**A**REN'T YOU ALL GOING to eat before you leave?"

Everyone paused at the inn's front door as the innkeeper's wife's voice grated behind us.

Norva grit her teeth. She turned and smiled charmingly at the middle-aged woman standing at the counter with a plate of steaming eggs and undercooked meat. The woman smiled back.

"Uh, we're on that new no-meat diet," Norva replied slowly as she eyed the pink meat strips. "The one that's blown up in Syndbur recently. Thank you, though."

The innkeeper's wife, Lorai, shook her head and muttered, "Weird folk *and* fad followers." She sighed. "Ladies, gentleman, and..." She squinted her eyes at Cobi. "Boy? I can't, in good conscience, let you leave this place without a meal. This is a bed-and-breakfast!"

Norva and Il exchanged an exasperated glance. Il looked slightly irritated with Norva, probably because she had told Lorai a lie when she claimed to be honest. Il explained that we were on a tight schedule, but Lorai would not hear it.

"A man as strong as you needs to keep his strength," she insisted, scouring Il up and down with too-curious eyes. She looked at Cobi and added, "And the young boys need to eat to grow into men! Same with the little one." Lorai beamed at Josha. Josha smiled back, and Cobi shook his head.

After enough arguing, though, we had all spent more time trying to avoid the innkeeper's questionable breakfast than we would have if we had simply sat down and eaten it in the first place.

I avoided the meat, keeping it far from my plate. Beyond its unsettling pink hue, the thought of eating flesh churned my stomach. I had had enough of it for a long time. Maybe forever.

Lorai looked pleased with herself as she scraped eggs onto our plates, chattering about her love of chickens and how the eggs we were about to eat were fresh from that morning.

"Now, where are you all going?" She wanted to know as she sat with us at the dining table.

Norva told her we were heading to the capital, as we had crossed over into the Silver region from the Caligin the night before. At this, Lorai blanched.

"Syndbur? What a terrible city it's become," she remarked, shaking her head.

Norva agreed with her, and Marcia asked to know more at this mention of her birthplace.

"Well," Lorai began, "What can I say except to see for yourself? It was once such a proud and prosperous place, but then..."

"Then what?" Marcia prompted gently.

Lorai sighed. "Then it... devolved. A new administration took over after the Devastation, and the decay Syndbur had already been experiencing became an expedited process. New policies were implemented, awful policies..."

"Like what?" I asked.

Lorai shuddered. "It's not fit for discussion, least of all at the table. But," she said, glancing at Marcia, "I must caution this; keep your children safe." She gazed mournfully at my siblings. Aullie's green eyes had opened wide. "It's not safe for them there anymore. Keep them with you at all times."

Marcia's mouth gaped, and she cried, "What do you mean, "not safe?" Syndbur has always been a family-friendly place!"

Lorai gave my stepmother a look so dull and tired that she looked well beyond middle-aged. "Syndbur," she replied quietly, "Does not know family anymore."

With Lorai's ominous words casting a pall over us, we began loading up onto the Akristurans' horses outside. I shielded my eyes when I stepped into the sun and pulled my hood tighter.

While looking at the horses, I remembered Aunt Carleigh was no longer with us. After the Sharavak confrontation that stole my step-aunt's life, her sister Marcia demanded that we return her body to her birthplace in Syndbur. However, it wasn't long before Il became agitated with this plan, and against Marcia's tantrum, we buried Aunt Carleigh as soon as we crossed the Caligin border into the Silver.

"She is on her home soil now," Il had told her. "Besides, she is only flesh anymore, not the woman you once knew. I will also not carry a *body* on my horse any longer than a day. Say your goodbyes, please."

Marcia was too stubborn to say farewell aloud, but she did glower at Il often. If Il noticed this, he ignored it and kept his eyes on the untamed forest in front of us as we traveled.

"So," my stepmother commented as she climbed onto Norva's mount behind her, "You have no qualms about telling my daughter she's a failure and will forever grieve not saving my sister, yet you sit there and tell foolish lies to a woman in a bed-and-breakfast? You interest me, lady, and not in a pleasant way. Always honest, my ass."

Norva blanched. "I did lie, and I am sorry for it. It was a foolish thing to break my word over."

Marcia smirked. "Am I expected to believe you? I don't."

"Norva," Il called from inside one of the horse stalls, "I know you regret it, but remember the example we need to set for people. I'm sure you've already considered it. Just don't forget."

I didn't see much wrong with Norva's somewhat amusing lie she had told Lorai. Where I came from, the concept of not eating meat was outrageous for anyone but my salad-obsessed stepmother. It would not have been problematic to *me* if Norva hadn't labeled herself unwaveringly truthful, but the Akristurans were very particular about things like that. Things that didn't, if *I* was truthful, matter.

With Norva's insensitive comment about my little sister, who was discovered to be growing into magic of her own as Aunt Carleigh had been dying, I did not blame Marcia for being angry. Aullie's healing tears were not enough to undo a mortal wound, and she had not deserved the Akristuran's comment as she wept over her fallen loved one.

"Twilight," Il said, "I bought this horse from the innkeeper last night, so she's yours. She wasn't cheap, either, so she better make for a sturdy ride. Horses can't be weak in this terrain."

I breathed a sigh of relief as I beheld the massive black mare pawing the earth next to Il. Her soft coat rippled with hardy muscle underneath.

She reared away from me when I approached her with a sudden whinny. I sensed her charging pulse. It reminded me of my sister Susenne's old horse, Star. After my magic began developing, none of the animals from my humble farm life wanted anything to do with me. They understood a predator's sickness when they smelled it.

"Um," I began, sending Il an awkward glance, "What am I supposed to do with that response? Animals aren't fond of monsters riding them."

Il sighed. "You're not a monster, Twilight. Let me communicate something to her, though, since your lumensa has gone dormant."

A thorn pricked my heart at that phrase, *gone dormant*. Il hadn't wanted to call me a monster, but that was what I was. Even as an Akristuran, his honesty had its restraints.

Il managed to soothe my mount by giving her a smooth washing-over of his lumensa. Light magic could heal wounded spirits as much as injured flesh. The sleek black mare would finally tolerate me.

As I settled into her saddle, I noticed a small white marking on her neck behind her mane. It was minuscule, but I swept my fingers over it anyway, hoping that speck of light, like my lumensa, would remain brilliant despite its shadowy surroundings. Light found a way.

And Marcia found a way to complain about our seating arrangement on the horses. She pestered Norva about having a mount to herself with at least one of her children.

"Let me take Josha," she demanded. "I don't want to sit with you."

Cobi laughed. "No offense, ma'am, but this isn't school where people squabble over desks in class. How old are you again?"

Marcia sent dagger eyes Cobi's way, then looked at me. "I want your horse," she stated flatly.

I felt a familiar fire stirring at her behavior. My stepmother and I had never known good terms, and her resentment of me for being the daughter of her former husband's first love only deepened her bitterness.

"You want to ask politely, Mother?" I replied. "Or better yet, do you want to stop acting *my* age so we can get to Syndbur sometime this week? Because *in case you didn't know*," I snapped, my capped anger uncorking, "*No one* is having a good time right now. I know you're used to everything going your way, but the world doesn't orbit around *your* needs!"

As soon as the ugliness showered out of my mouth, I knew I had probably overdone it. Maybe.

But that savage rage the Sharavaks had cultivated in me, which had become lethal blooms of violent magic, was a power I was too fond of.

The Marcia from my ranch-hand life would have pummeled me for my outburst. It would have been three days locked in my room, at least two without either breakfast or supper, and perhaps a kitchen ladle taken to my backside. There would have certainly been an increase in my chores amount, which was already baffling.

But the Marcia of my dead youth did no such thing. She didn't even part her lips to retort. The fire in her gaze quickly dampened under my words, and the slightest flutter of that low feeling settled in my guts as I watched her extinguish.

"I'm sorry," I offered sheepishly. "That, um, came from a dark place. I'm actually trying to lighten up."

Norva watched me from her mount, her azure eyes bright and calculating. "Apologizing is a good first step toward healing," she told me gently. "I hope your remorse is genuine, Twilight." She faced Marcia. "Now, who do you want to ride with, and will you, for the *love* of Akristura, ask like an adult this time?"

Marcia flushed scarlet. "It doesn't matter," she answered quietly.

Everyone knew that it clearly did for her to have made such an issue out of it in the first place, but I let my stepmother take my mount so she could ride with Josha in front and Aullie in back.

I ended up riding with Norva, and Cobi rode with Il. After a few more fusses and prayers for patience uttered by our Akristuran escorts, our party resumed its trek through the frost-dusted Silver forest.

The transition from the Caligin into the Silver was not abrupt, but neither was it entirely subtle. I'd always been under the impression that the sun seldom shone in that bleak wasteland known as the Silver, but the region was thus far only mildly bitten by winter. The fluff of white studding the leaf carpet beneath us in some places looked frail as if one weak sunray could render it all nonexistent in a blink.

Balding heads were the trees, barren in some parts and lush in others. The overhead sky loomed like a silt-laden seep; ugly clouds congregated together to keep out the prying sun, an unwelcome guest upon a land that was trying to throw itself into full-fledged frigidness.

I shuddered away a growing shivering fit as I drew my robes about me more tightly, taking care to avoid the sun's glare. Norva asked if I was all right, and I was not, but I said I was.

The sting of the chill cutting through my clothes was nothing compared to the cold inside me. I wondered if my soul could warm again and blossom into a promising spring instead of dying in its winter state.

These were not ideas that one voiced aloud, however. They were the core thoughts, the mind mingling with the blood and the bone and the spirit to produce the most intimate monologue within a person. To speak them to another human being would be folly.

I both loved and loathed these thoughts because they were so *me,* yet so *other.* Something grander than I was allowed me to conceive of my own evil, tenderness, and soreness.

How I hated the knowledge that I was weak. That I needed something not within myself to live. Damn my father and Father Sein for crippling me. And quite literally, I thought, as I glanced over my charred palms.

Wounds never truly went away. We could find loopholes to evade their pain, but forgetting a destruction zone didn't piece it back together. It, like my palms from the time my magical mentor and grandfather had taught me a lesson in insubordination, remained burned and scarred.

"You're not okay," Norva commented, slicing into my brooding mind.

"What? I am," I answered sharply.

Norva sighed. "And I'm the commune idiot. Twilight, you have to start opening up about things. Listen, if you—"

"Shh!" Il hissed.

Everyone halted their mounts, and the chatter died away. In the place of silence came a thumping sound, like the thundering of... hoof-steps?

Il and Norva exchanged glances, communicating in their minds via hursafar. Il and Norva both readied their hands with lumensa. The golden-white magic burned steadily in their palms, and for a moment, I forgot about the approaching rider and was instead pricked with envy. I missed my clean magic and the ease with which it obeyed my summons.

These thoughts were quickly drowned when an enormous white horse stomped around a bend toward the side of us. Il and Norva's hands collapsed when they realized who commanded the proud beast and the person sitting behind them. Even I was flabbergasted.

Could it really be...?

"Korbin?" Il cried incredulously.

"Susenne?" Marcia and the kids exclaimed together.

So it was. The leader of the Akristurans had escaped alive from the Sharavaks, though barely, judging by his charred and tattered robes soaked crimson in some patches. Susenne also did not look well, but the sparkle in her eyes suggested she felt well despite this.

"My word, what happened?" Norva wanted to know.

She and Il dismounted their horses and ran toward their leader. Susenne flung herself into her mother's arms.

"Sweetie, what happened to you?" Marcia demanded. "Are you not part of your... your father's people anymore?"

Susenne shook her head. "No. I... Korbin got me to leave."

"Oh, my sweet Suze," Marcia wept into my sister's hair. "I'm so happy to have you back, where I know you're safe." Her weeping dissolved into sobbing. "I worried day and night about you. Your siblings, safe with me, and yet you, far away..."

I had feared for her, too. My sister had been sent to kill me in her Sharavos form during our escape, but I had prevented this and her own death by keeping Il and Norva from destroying her. I had hurt her badly living with the Shadows, and I never liked her, but I hadn't wanted her to die.

That was not fair. That would have been too far.

Like many things I did.

Susenne bit back her own tears as she nodded, then embraced Josha, Aullie, and finally me. Her hug was quick, and her smile when she pulled away was equally fleeting. Regardless, I was glad to have her back.

"I'm happy you're okay," I told her. "What happened? And... did Solshek or anyone else make it out with you guys?"

Susenne's eyes darkened. "Don't know, but he's not with us. Korbin and I barely got out alive."

I glanced at Il and Norva embracing their lost friend and leader; it was a moving sight. But more moving than this was the absence of a third person who should have escaped with them. Solshek, born Sharavak, converted to Akristuran, a soul wise beyond his time, and my best friend... was gone.

I took the blow like it was a Sharavos burrowing into my intestines. The more seconds that passed with nothing more said of my friend, the wider my insides were strung out, bleeding, steaming, and cooling in the bitter cold.

"Twi," Cobi said gently nearby, "You don't know if he passed or not. Maybe your Dad just captured him—"

"*He's not Dad!*" I screamed. "He's not her dad!" I jabbed a finger in Susenne's direction. "Not their Dad!" I gestured to my younger siblings, and then I pointed at myself. "He's not *my* dad! He's not anything but a *monster!*"

I shrieked at nothing, at anything, my anguish raw, and a ripple of power discharged from me.

"Twilight!" Someone yelled.

I didn't know who it was. I didn't care. How could I, with Solshek dead? *Dead* because my despicable *father* had to make his point by taking his life, one that meant more than his ever would!

Another magic flare erupted from me, and the valdur scratched inside me. I laughed, then shrieked at the churning power to issue forth and devour everything in its path.

Let all things burn, and let things *hurt* as they rightly deserved! Nothing tasted as savory as pain inflicted on anyone in return for anything.

Maim and kill, I blindly commanded my magic. *Rise and hurt!*

Hurt as I have been hurt.

I screamed. The anguish poured so thickly from my core that I felt myself floundering. My head was too far under the surface to realize that hands were grasping me, and my numbness was filtering into harsh agony, then... silence.

"Twilight."

No, not again.

I had suffered another fainting episode. By the scalding sensation seething inside my skin, it had happened after a magical occurrence known as a blight.

What had I done? I could never seem to remember what brought these things on until someone informed me. By the glint of blue eyes overhead, it appeared that Cobi would be the one to deliver the news this time. He had never seen these instances of mine before.

With blatant horror flooding his gaze, Cobi repeated my name, then helped me sit upright. I mopped my palm across my forehead to sweep away the sweat that had gathered there. When I looked at my friend, it was with such burning shame that I wished my blight had reduced me to cinders. He did not deserve to suffer with me.

No one did.

"You, um..." He frowned. "You had a moment. It wasn't a good one, either."

Norva, Il, and Sir Korbin stood before me. Norva looked at me with compassion, and Il with mild disbelief edging into anger. Sir Korbin, however, was stone. His warm brown skin, a few shades darker than the summer mountains, suddenly looked cold on his expressionless countenance.

"Stand up," he ordered.

His nostrils flared slightly, and his dark brown eyes hardened from liquid into tree bark as he watched me rise.

I don't know why I stood for him. Maybe it was the otherworldly essence about him and how he could wield authority with such striking sureness. I would not have risen for any other person.

Sir Korbin's jaw sharpened, and he glared at me for a moment before launching into his speech. "I understand the loss you feel right now, Twilight," he began.

Thoughts were born anew of Solshek, my friend who had not escaped with this Akristuran.

"It's a feeling I'm afraid to say I am all-too-familiar with." Sir Korbin's gaze softened for a moment. "I have lost many good souls. Friends, family, and the non-blood family for whom I'm responsible."

Sir Korbin's eyes sharpened again before he continued, "But these episodes of yours must absolutely not happen anymore. What you did today almost took your friend's life."

He gestured to Cobi, whose robes were blackened as if by flames.

The flames of my valdur.

"And that," Sir Korbin said, "Is nothing to say of your sister Susenne, who also caught fire when you exploded. Fortunately, the rest of your family was far enough away. Twilight..."

Sir Korbin gestured for us to speak privately. "You are responsible for these lives," he said, nodding at the rest of the group. "Cobi is a Non, a non-magical person. He would have died by your hands had Norva not shielded him from your explosion. Young lady... it's time for you to grow up and move on from your tantrums. Life with the Sharavaks is over. You are *free*. Free yourself from this behavior for everyone's sake, and I can promise you there is goodness waiting on the other side of this journey if you are willing to embrace it."

Stinging, I looked away from the man and dropped my gaze to the forest floor. Around me were the remains of fallen leaves turned to ash by my blight.

All I was good at, it seemed, was destruction. Whatever redeeming qualities I might have once had were like the ash that surrounded me, scorched by my evil and degraded into dust.

Now this man hated me. Well, he could join my steadily growing fan club, then.

Sir Korbin took my silence as compliance. Despite the rage fluttering inside me, married to the even harsher shame, I accepted his speech. I hated it, but then no one liked the truth.

"Get her something to drink, please," Sir Korbin told Il when we rejoined everyone. "She needs rehydrating. Fortunately, she didn't burn to the point of injury. Anyway, Twilight," the Akristuran continued as he eyed me with concern, "You'll need your strength for the remainder of this journey. Tonight, you will see what the rest of the world has become since the Sharavaks attempted to destroy all we once held dear."

CHAPTER THREE

NOTHING MORE WAS SAID of Syndbur or my life-threatening magic as we resumed the journey to the Silver's capital. Unfortunately, the Akristuran leader wasn't finished with me. Far from it. When he wasn't regaling everyone with stories—to which my stepmother responded with more than polite attentiveness—he was milking information from me.

"I hope you don't mind the question," he said quietly, his horse sidling up to mine, "But we need to know Sein Leidyen's status. Is he healthy, ailing, or no longer here?"

Such delicate phrasing for a decidedly brutal man.

"He's dead," I muttered. "As he should be."

Sir Korbin's lips pursed, and he nodded. "Thank you. If it's not too much trouble, would you be willing to tell me how he passed, if you know? Was it age or something else?"

I grimaced. "My father killed him."

Hurry up and ask the question: why?

"Very interesting. What was their relationship like?" He paused when he realized he might be aggravating me and quickly apologized. "I don't want to push you or open old wounds. However, let's look at this like a crime investigation; I'm a law enforcer, and you're a witness. I need to gather facts to assess the situation and make better-informed decisions, especially while they're fresh."

I sighed. "I get it. Let me just show you the memory."

I focused on establishing a hursafar connection, but the Akristuran beat me to it. I sluggishly accepted his invitation and forced myself back into the darkness where ugly memories had permanently branded themselves on my mind. I found the memory of Father Sein's death in this place, shivering as it played again and passed into Sir Korbin's consciousness.

When it ended, and the Akristuran withdrew, he shook his head in the anticipated amazement. "How strange... and terrible. Sein Leidyen is your father's father and your *grandfather?*"

"That's right," I mumbled.

Sir Korbin touched my shoulder. "I am sorry." His brown eyes deepened. "This introduces a dynamic none of us ever expected, and it complicates things for you and your siblings. Twilight?"

I looked at him with some reluctance. When would this interrogation end?

Sir Korbin's gaze softened, its curious sheen quieting. "How do you feel about all this?"

I gnawed my lower lip and considered. The scars twisting over my palms still ached if I thought about them, and every spark of valdur recalled the day Sein Leidyen had carved his canyons into them. He'd shown me little kindness in the brief time we'd known each other. He'd always beheld me, his own flesh and a quarter of his being, as a tool to kill with and then discard.

I had been his token for redemption with the Dark God. He'd never needed me beyond utilitarian value. As an asset.

Sour liquid seeped over my tongue. I'd bitten my lip too hard.

Sir Korbin's mouth drooped with understanding, and he ran a quick hand over his horse's mane. "I'm very sorry, Twilight. I truly can't imagine what it's like, having such a family." He exhaled. "These people are who you began with, but they aren't the end. I promise to work with you if you let me."

To this, I said nothing, for there was nothing good to say.

Several hours passed. When we tired of traveling, we dismounted our horses and set up a little picnic of sorts beside the sluggish pace of a half-frozen river. Norva handed out tea cakes she had collected from the bed-and-breakfast, and Sir Korbin offered pieces of cheese and dried meat he had purchased along his journey to find us.

He had found us by following the lumensa messaging trail Il and Norva had left him on the trees every few hundred paces. It explained the glowing white marks coating some of the trunks. We had taken the unbeaten path because of the Sharavaks, in fact. Il and Norva had deemed it unsafe to travel by the main thoroughfare that snaked through the Silver, but the Akristurans seemed to know the way, regardless.

Sir Korbin was not keen on sharing the details of his escape story with us. I assumed this was partly because he did not want me to lapse into another episode, and he didn't want to relive those moments himself. Whatever had happened had been gruesome, judging by the marks on his robes. I hated thinking of what this implied for Solshek, left behind at my father's mercy.

Conversation gradually shifted to what should be done about the Sharavaks. Should some of them be spared? Killed? Should we prepare for a major conflict? No one had the answer. They expected their sky father to explain it all to them in time.

My face must have displayed my scorn, for Sir Korbin thought, *Are you all right?* as he passed me a lump of cheese.

I didn't answer him for a moment, but when I did, it was as bland a response as I ever gave to that sort of question.

I'm fine.

Sir Korbin regarded me with silent disbelief but communicated nothing more. He chewed his cheese quietly, falling as voiceless as the rest of us.

"Are you going to eat that last piece?" Cobi whispered, nodding at my remaining cheese slice.

Despite being preoccupied with my thoughts, I *was* rather famished. I glanced at the cheese and back at Cobi. He seemed to need it more than I did, though, if that extra sparkle in his eyes was any indication.

"Here."

I handed him the cheese, noticing his gaze straying to the little wedge of bread beside it. Chuckling, I passed that to him, too, and patted his shoulder.

"Have at it. I think I'm done growing."

I couldn't handle the silence anymore, so I padded off to relieve myself in the bushes. As I picked my way through the tangled undergrowth, I sensed another presence. An offbeat one, quite literally, judging by the irregular heart rhythm.

Snuffling and snarling erupted ahead of me. I paused, tensing at the noise. That didn't sound like a deer. The smell, too, was not one of a prey-thing.

Not seconds later, the entity in question appeared, sweeping out from the undergrowth on trembling legs. I had my palms out before I could stop myself, searing in pain as I burned the creature before me with valdur.

A sick wolf. It had the same sickness as the one that had tried to kill me months ago before Father had stopped it in his beast form.

The tall beast released a thundering, savage roar, spreading its lips until its thick teeth caught the filtered sunlight. Spittle flung at me as it parted its narrow jaws to roar again. I yelled and blasted the animal in the mouth with my valdur, sputtering from black to violet the more it released.

Before its infected saliva touched me, I sprinted back to the others.

"*Wolf!* There's a wolf; get the kids and go!"

Marcia seized Aullie and Josha and hauled them off the way we'd come through the trees, with Cobi following. Susenne remained behind with the Akristurans and me, lumensa at the ready.

Lumensa?

"It's coming!"

The wolf tore out of the undergrowth and barreled toward us across the river. As it dropped onto the ice-veiled water, Sir Korbin waved at it to get its attention. The wolf snarled and weaved its way toward the Akristuran through a labyrinth of rocks and scattered tree branches, its muzzle shedding foam.

Sir Korbin heaved a line of golden-white orbs at the animal. The wolf slowed to a crawl, looking like it was going to collapse in the river. Everyone breathed heavily as it stood trembling from the magic.

Suddenly, though, it started to gather momentum again as it surged toward us. I unleashed a massive shower of valdur on the beast, causing it to yelp as it went skidding back onto the other side of the river into the undergrowth.

Dead.

I had just killed an infected wolf with my hands.

"Twilight!" Sir Korbin exclaimed as he turned on me. "Did you not trust me? Did your faith in lumensa falter?"

"What do you mean?" I asked. "Are you trying to tell me *healing* magic could have taken *that* thing out? Please, you're joking!"

Sir Korbin shook his head. "I don't joke about serious matters. Lumensa is the magic of restoration, but it isn't limited to this when you're protecting yourself. It is governed by moral properties and will not harm an innocent person or creature."

"So, the wolf wasn't "innocent," then? Can they be evil like people?" I said scornfully.

"No. Of course not," Sir Korbin replied. "I'm saying lumensa will protect you when it senses you're in danger. Valdur, on the other hand, will destroy any and everything, regardless of your safety. Lumensa is inherently benign and linked to Akristura. It cannot exist without Him."

I rolled my eyes. "You and Akristura. I'm so tired of all you religious maniacs! So what if I used my magic? It's mine, and I should be able to use it when I'm being attacked by a *wolf!*"

Norva stepped in to say her piece. "You misunderstand what he says, dear. We aren't suggesting that you not defend yourself; we *are* insisting that you use the right magic to do so. Your lumensa wants to protect you as the wielder and restore things as much as dark magic seeks to destroy. The difference between the two magics is that one will always destroy and never heal, and the other is a restorative property that has... well, it's like a conscience."

"What's that?" I asked.

"The conscience is the voice inside people that tells us what is right and wrong," Norva explained patiently.

The voice? The voice of right and wrong? This conscience must have been the thing Aaksa Aadyalbaine warned me against.

"I see," I said, understanding now. "Lumensa is like a person. It knows who to mark for destruction and who to not. Meaning it won't hurt a person of the light or a person of darkness if they aren't trying to hurt us first, but it becomes harmful to evil people or harmful things in combat. Did I actually learn something for once?"

Sir Korbin cracked a smile. "That you did. But there is a greater reason for not using valdur, which is why I'm cross with you right now. Things happen in the moment, but you're too governed by your feelings, girl. It will get you into a lot of trouble if you don't learn to master your mind."

He explained, "Every time you use valdur or shapeshift, which harnesses that power, you maintain and strengthen your ties to the Sharavaks. Please *try* to keep your head clear and summon the right magic from now on. Neither your father nor the others can continue to track you if you cease the summoning of the magic that tethers you to their world. Their world isn't yours anymore."

No, I supposed it wasn't. But then, what was my world? Nothing felt like home anymore.

Like a bittersweet note in a forgotten melody were Father Sein's words as they drifted back into memory.

"You do not belong with humanity, and you never will!"

Tears began to burn behind my lids. The children I had played with when I was little had despised whatever was different about me; that had been long before my magic started developing. My family had hated me for years, and so had their friends. So had some of the Sharavaks. The only person who had understood my existential predicament had been Solshek.

Where did I belong?

"Wow," my stepmother panted as she walked back toward us from the woods. "You really know how to cast away fear in the moment." She smiled at Sir Korbin. "I know Damion would have never done something like that for us."

Sir Korbin thanked her but told her the true thanks belonged to me.

"Even though she did conjure enemy magic," he added with a small smile, "She's growing, and we'll give her room and time to do that. Shall we get moving? Just a couple hours left now."

Marcia nodded. "Yes, please, let's leave this awful woodland behind. I miss home something fierce."

Sir Korbin's eyes darkened with a mingling of sorrow and resentment as he replied, "And you will probably miss it for the rest of your days, ma'am. But let's worry about getting back there before anything else."

"Wait," Marcia said. "I feel safer riding with you. If you don't mind," she added hastily.

I nearly laughed. Marcia's request to ride with the Akristuran leader was as good as a love confession in my eyes. Sir Korbin didn't refuse her, either.

Susenne and Aullie saddled up with Norva, Josha rode with Il on his mount, my stepmother and Sir Korbin took his beauty, and Cobi and I were left with the remaining horse.

It was nice to speak as freely as I wanted with Cobi as we plucked our way across the landscape, reminiscing on our first encounter in the Caligin woods and all the madness that had transpired since.

"You are different," Cobi remarked as we treaded slowly behind the others.

"In a bad way," I muttered.

"Yes," Cobi replied. "In some ways. But you're no longer in that situation. It's going to linger. It'll never go away, but..." He touched my shoulder. "At least you're out of there. That by itself is pretty huge."

I cringed inside at the truth. I was out of there, but *there* was still very much in me.

As long as I lived, I was sure my self-loathing would strangle me enough that I could never breathe properly. Every inhalation would invoke a wince, a blistering reminder of my wasted months, and darker still, a waste of my innocence.

"What are you thinking about?" Cobi asked gently.

I was suddenly uncomfortably aware of our close proximity to each other and his body's warmth against the stark chill pinching through my robes. Human contact. I would never understand it.

"Not much," I answered blandly.

"Be honest, please," Cobi said. "You've been talking to me all afternoon, but you haven't said much. You've sure been insulting my jokes, though. Again."

I cracked a smile against the breeze billowing against me, and I knew Cobi was grinning, too.

"Well," I said slowly as we began to incline on a steepening hillside, "I've been thinking... I don't know. What am I supposed to do with myself now? It's like..."

"Like your purpose has been taken?" He said softly.

I lowered my head against the gathering wind and tucked my hair tighter into my hood. "Yeah."

"You can still have redemption, Twilight. That's not beyond—" he started to say, but I cut him off.

"Sorry, I just don't want to have this conversation right now," I muttered.

Cobi's voice seemed deflated as he replied, "Fair enough."

"Hey!" Marcia called from the peak of the grade. "We're coming up on a view of the city! It's incredible!"

A thrill surged through me and washed away my cold feelings, and I whispered, "Here we go."

As our mount traipsed through the last stretch of swaying grasses and we stopped at the top of the hill, I nearly fell out of the saddle. Marcia had not overstated; the view was majestic.

Before us, in the distance like a jeweled veil, stretched a glittering city.

Though it was still miles away, its thousands of coruscating colored lights threw themselves across the darkening heavens like spirits frolicking in the freedom of moonlight. The assortment of colors was so vast and intoxicating that it was difficult to fathom.

How? How had mere mortals managed to marry all these dancing visuals together and force them into a tireless performance?

No amount of clever words could describe this. No poem, no matter how musical its phrasing or magnificent its stanzas, could adequately capture every color and every sudden emotion it created in me.

"Is it always this lit up?" I breathed, my eyes never abandoning the scene.

"Yes," Il answered, though his enthusiasm was considerably lesser.

"Let's keep going," Sir Korbin said quietly as he motioned us to follow him. "We'll be arriving in half an hour. I hope you're ready."

CHAPTER FOUR

W E DESCENDED AT TWILIGHT.

Blood had begun its beautiful spillage across the clouds as the sun's reluctant retreat stained them in color and shadow. However, being directly outside Syndbur caused the appearance of the cloaking evening to fall threadbare as it was washed out in the much brighter, bolder rainbow of the twinkling neon lights.

Overhead, violent strikes of color lashed against the sky, producing a tang in the air as sparks spiraled down around us. Fireworks. My first actual show, not a product of valdur like what the Sharavaks had given me long ago.

The memories of the valdur display recalled a certain friend.

Shi.

The young Sharavak girl had been an artist among the ranks of the blood-lust-driven society, whose bold maneuver with posting up murder accusations against my father had saved our lives when we'd fled the compound.

It had only been a few nights ago, yet it felt like another lifetime. I hoped that she was safe and escaped with our older female friend, Mirivik, after the orchestrated diversion.

These remembrances slithered out of my mind as we began our entrance into the city of Syndbur. Ahead of us on the paved path that marked true civilization, the kind depicted in movies, at least, was an elaborate gate guarded by two sentries.

As soon as Sir Korbin rounded the bend, the sentries tensed and shared a mutual look of disdain with one another. I smelled their fear from several hundred paces off. The ripe odor produced an involuntary seepage of saliva.

Stop, I warned myself.

This wasn't the time nor place for my monster to emerge.

As we approached, the taller of the two sentries asked Sir Korbin why his party was bigger than it usually was and if the Akristurans were plotting any "unsavory business" within Syndbur's walls.

"Dear brother," Sir Korbin replied coolly, "I am not the one who searches for trouble around here. You know this. Please let us through."

The smaller sentry called, "Wait! I recognize the three of you Children, and the red-haired woman and her kids look like natives. But what about you two?" The sentry motioned to Cobi and me as we waited behind the others on our mount.

I opened my mouth to concoct a lie when Sir Korbin explained, "They are weary travelers who have been through a lot as of late. They are good people, I can assure you."

Who are not too far gone like one of them may think, he thought to me, sending me a quick smile.

Warm gratitude, coupled with surprise, prodded me at his words. No hint of a lie or even exaggeration was in them.

The larger of the sentry pair grunted, "Do either of 'em practice magic?"

I wondered if Sir Korbin would lie in this instance. Though Akristurans were apparently called to truth-speaking, there was only so far that could get a person, and by the way the question was asked, I sensed the sentries of Syndbur were not keen on the concept of more magic-wielders in their city.

"The young lady does," Sir Korbin answered simply. "She is a healer like us. Now, please, let us through so we can go home. We're very tired."

"And apparently fresh from a war zone, I'd say," commented the smaller sentry as he surveyed Sir Korbin's bloodied robes. "Were you converting more lost souls, and it didn't go so well, Cleric?" He laughed. "All right, then. You can come through."

The massive gate separating us from the complete immersive experience of Syndbur's "life celebration" shows parted for us, and Sir Korbin ordered his mount forward as lights were suddenly thrown over our party. I had to shield my eyes as we entered the city; the pulsating prism of color was that intense.

Thick in the air was a shroud of aromatic smoke and the throbbing of strange music all around us. As we proceeded inside, we were immediately greeted with the source of all the noise, colors, and vapors; dozens of businesses, all aglow in shimmering lights, had the aggressively paced songs spilling out of speakers along their walls. Thousands of people congregated at random alongside the businesses with tall, dark bottles in their hands and vapors pouring out their mouths and noses.

I probably sneezed more in those first few minutes in Syndbur than I ever had before. The sour stench of fermented drink in such quantities and the fruit-scented vapors and profusion of sweat—along with other body odors I instinctively recoiled from—had me doubled over on my horse.

"Are you good?" Cobi cried.

I'm fine, I thought back. *Too many smells.*

I sensed Cobi's confusion and wondered how he couldn't be picking up on all of this, too. Aromas and stenches frolicked together, clinging to one another like soap on filth. When soap touched dirt, though, it became soiled, making every scent an assault rather than offering any reprieve.

I will not throw up on this horse. I will not throw up on this poor horse's head.

Every vapor had its own distinct, false flavor. Some underlying bitter note gave them all a commonality. The people also had their scents. I scratched at my collarbone and doubled over again, clinging to the small insistence of the voice that told me not to kill.

When I dared to look at some of these people, I saw how different they were from the people in Orsh, the small city I had grown up near. Everyone dressed plainly there, never revealing as much skin as the actors in the movies my family watched.

In Syndbur, the citizens' attire was even more outlandish than anything I had glimpsed on television. Some of them didn't wear clothes at all. Everything I did not wish to see on a stranger was bare before me, and only a few of them had painted these body parts to conceal them.

As soon as our horses made contact with the fresh pavement that marked Syndbur's main street, Sir Korbin, Norva, and Il erected magic barriers around us. Our party became blanketed in a soft golden sheen, and I would have asked why when the answer immediately became apparent.

"It's the terrorists!" Someone screamed from the throng on the streets.

Terrorists?

Immediate shouting and cursing erupted as we passed by on our mounts. Many of the people of Syndbur had interrupted their activities to gather around us and scream abuse, uttering language so filthy and hatefully spoken that I wondered how the Akristurans could keep neutral expressions on their faces.

But the words were allowed to pierce the barrier. The empty bottles of fermented drinks and rocks were not. I yelped when one bottle came sailing at my head, only to be deflected by the lumensa shielding our party.

"Don't fear them," Il told me calmly. "Fear is what they thrive on."

I frowned as I looked at everyone and considered the writhing masses of curse-slinging mouths, the harshness glaring from their painted eyes, and... yes, there was a looming presence of darkness clawing out from each heart.

I swallowed, sensing a familiar churning in my stomach at the sickening yet enticing feeling of those black shadows.

If I peered closely enough, I could actually discern the faint outlines of incomprehensibly ugly things hanging onto the people. Void presences crowded around them. Baines, the Myrk God's otherworldly servants...

Everywhere.

I shuddered, remembering how they had almost killed me a few nights ago, and I asked, having to shout above the shouting around me, "Why are baines here? I thought only the Sharavaks were connected with them."

I could nearly hear Sir Korbin's grimace as he answered, "Every dark heart is connected with them. Don't pay them mind, even if they are clamoring for you."

I glanced behind me but could no longer see the baines. Instead of yelling again, I thought to Sir Korbin, *Are they here for me?*

No, he replied. *The baines were already here. They've been here for a long time. But don't think they aren't watching you. If it weren't for Norva and Il, you would already be dead for denouncing them back in that compound.*

A chill slithered into my guts.

And why is that? I asked.
Because you still belong to them.

Not five minutes after hitting the main thoroughfare, Josha decided he needed to go to the bathroom.

"You're going to have to hold it, buddy," Il said. "We'll be home in another twenty."

"I really have to go now, though," Josh whined.

"Now, really, Josh—" Marcia started, but Norva interrupted her.

"If he has to go, Il, he has to go. We can find someplace for him, can't we? Korbin?"

Sir Korbin sighed and clenched his reins. "Is this an emergency, son?"

Josha nodded. No one outwardly groaned, but the feeling didn't need vocalization.

"Alright. I can't let the kid soil himself," Korbin said. "Let's..." He surveyed our immediate surroundings, his gaze darkening. "Let's try asking one of these folks up here if they'll let us borrow their bathroom for a second. I don't like asking, but the alternative is probably worse."

He narrowed his eyes at the crowds swarming around each of the businesses before steering his horse onto a broad, dark alley scantily clad in weak streetlamp light. The rest of us followed.

In the distance, the few Syndburians who did not care about us watched us pass with blank eyes. One man was preoccupied with carving up a corpse in an alley. Blood coated him, sending its tang my way. Again, I ground my teeth and had to avert my eyes.

I was beginning to think the other citizens would keep up their attacks when the law enforcers suddenly descended on everyone. A dark purple stole through the air and clouded around the protesters screaming at us, causing their fiery voices to die down into embers, then quiet moaning as they fell slack-jawed.

"What is that?" I cried as the purple substance swarmed around our shield, unable to penetrate through.

"An airborne serum," Norva informed me. "The enforcers use it when the crowds become too rowdy. It placates anger."

I marveled at its effects, as we were no longer being pursued by a caterwauling mob. It was like our party ceased to exist to them.

"I'm surprised the government doesn't gas you, instead," I said. "Considering how the public thinks of you."

"Well," Sir Korbin replied, "We're not in their good graces, that's for sure. Eminent Simpario despises us. However, he can't exactly remove us. He's not fond of angering a large group of people armed with magic he knows has won wars, so he lets us exist outside the city limits and tries not to provoke us."

A leader who was too fearful of evicting his pious neighbors. Interesting.

"Wow," I heard Marcia say. "It really is so different here."

After this, she was at a loss for words, and I was with her in disbelief. Even the kids had fallen silent, drinking in their surroundings with breathless awe.

"Got any jokes for what we just witnessed?" I muttered to Cobi.

He grimaced. "It's difficult to tease something that makes fun of itself."

I agreed. "Have you ever seen anything like this before?"

Cobi laughed weakly. "No. I never realized this was how the Silver was. They always said this was where the educated people lived. Almost makes me want to go back and brave the "backward" Caligin."

"Well," I said, "I'm not quite at that point, but I know what you mean."

The Caligin. Home.

How I missed it. I longed for the solitude and silence of my homeland, not fond of the current strobing lights and pulsing visuals tugging for my attention all around me and the pressing feeling of the many bodies clumped along the streets. In the Caligin, nothing was ostentatious, and there was no clamoring.

"We're going to stop—very quickly—at one of these houses up here," Sir Korbin told everyone. "No more detours after that. Please."

Moments after he said this, a group of children, nude and holding the hands of much older adults, passed us. My throat began to burn. As much as I didn't know right and wrong, I didn't feel anything celebratory about young children parading around like that. It wasn't my choice, though. They weren't my own.

Marcia seemed to feel the same as she beheld Josha, Aullie, and Susenne, and Lorai's words blared in my mind; *"I must caution this; keep your children safe."*

There were no further comments from the Akristurans as Sir Korbin led the way along the dark road winding up into another set of streets. Businesses were scattered along the way. One strip featured a colorful inn, the Bed of Roses, tucked into a nook beside several other buildings. Men, women, and a few children congregated outside.

I breathed deeply. Musty scents drifted from them and numerous others through the inn's windows. Noises I didn't like, some indicating pain, trickled through the walls. I wrinkled my nose and looked away.

More buildings lined the path: Paradise Place, Daysleep Drugs, Merch Madness for the various television shows and movies currently hot in Syndbur, and others. There was even a face alteration store, Better Version Beauty, plastered with posters of too-symmetrical women who were all curiously straight-haired.

"Just so you know," said Cobi, "You don't ever need to make yourself look like that."

I chuckled. "Queen Crooked Nose doesn't need "adjusting?" Are you sure?"

"I mean it," he replied softly, causing my cheeks to warm.

Syndbur did seem to revel in beauty. It was also very fond of TV if store names like Eternal Entertainment and Merch Madness were anything to go by. We continued through the maze of businesses until Sir Korbin swung left onto another narrower street. A rough assembly of decrepit tract houses greeted us there.

Throngs of people still walked these streets, though their condition was much less colorful and eccentric than those along the main street. Instead of animosity, the ragged groups who passed us watched us with interest. As Marcia, Josha, Norva, and I dismounted, their gazes drew to the kids and me.

With their deplorable quality of life reflected in their hunting eyes and sharply drawn mouths, I wanted to feel moved for them as human beings. Ultimately, we were all but flesh and spirit, and we each required certain things to survive.

But the thirst burning in the eyes of the crowd caused my compassion to steam away into wariness, wariness edging into disgust. I did not appreciate being groped by gazes, especially not when those gazes descended on my siblings. They appeared to want more from us than money.

"Come on, Joshy, let's try this house. It looks inviting enough," Marcia said quietly as she took his hand.

We followed Marcia, Norva flanking her and keeping an eye out for the gathering crowd, and all waited in tense silence as she rapped on the door of the house in front of us. After several knocks, it became apparent no one would answer.

"Do these people not like us, Mama?" Josha whispered.

"No, honey, they're probably just—"

Locks ground against the wood, and the door was drawn open, revealing a young girl behind it. At least, I thought she was young, but by the severe disproportionality of certain aspects of her body and the makeup coating her face, I wasn't sure.

She narrowed her eyes at us and stroked her hair before snapping, "What? You here for the goods?"

"What?" Marcia cried. "No, of course not. My son here just needs to use the bathroom. Would you be willing to let us use yours very quickly?"

The girl laughed. "I've never heard *that* one before. I don't do stuff with kids, but those guys out there might be interested." She nodded at the throng wandering in our direction.

Marcia looked at them and hissed, "Listen, kid, either let us use the pot or turn us away, but don't be making sick jokes like that."

The girl shrugged. "Whatever. Mom!"

A cracked voice shot back, "What? You have customers?"

"No, just some freaks who want to pee or something. Are they good to come in?"

The mother stepped out to inspect us. She looked only a few years younger than Marcia, and like her daughter, she had an exaggerated figure. The daughter, however, was somewhat attractive. This woman's enhancements drooped with expiration.

She glared at Marcia, Norva, and me before looking at Josh, breaking a smile. "Aww. You're kinda cute. What's your name, kid?"

"I'm Josha," my brother proudly informed her. "Can I go to the bathroom now?"

Everyone laughed at this, including the woman. She sighed and motioned us into the house. As we passed the threshold, she fired nervous glances at the crowd outside, which continued to gather closer.

"Best if you hurry," she told Josh. "Go past the kitchen and into the hallway. You'll see it."

He skipped off, leaving the three of us with the woman and her young daughter. The daughter paid us no mind while her mother bounced on her heels and kept her eyes on us.

"You a native?" She asked Marcia.

"Yep. Born and raised here."

The woman nodded. "You look the part. Where were you during the whole Devastation thing?"

Marcia grimaced. "Underground, in a bunker. You?"

"Same here. A lot of my friends didn't believe the Akristurans were telling the truth when they was warnin' us, and most of my friends who survived don't even remember that they *did* warn us. Now..." She trailed off into a sigh.

"I'm sorry." Marcia's whole face seemed to slide down. "I was a caretaker then, and many people I knew also died. Wish we knew what caused it—"

Thump, thump, thump.

Someone was knocking at the door. By the horror on the woman's face, whoever had come calling was far from benign. She swallowed as the thumping became harder and more persistent, and when a third round came, the door seemed to rattle on its hinges. Hollering sounded outside. The woman's already pale face flushed a new shade of cooled-over death.

"Get your son and go," she told Marcia.

Marcia gaped. "Who are those people?"

"Hey!"

Sir Korbin. What was going on out there?

"Oh, gov," the woman muttered, wringing her hands.

Gov? I wanted to ask what that meant, but—

"Open up!" A raspy male voice screamed outside the door. "We want to talk!"

"You don't want to *talk,"* Sir Korbin snarled in the distance. "Get away from there!"

"Shut up, savage."

It was silent for a moment before the same harsh voice called, "Open this door before we break through the windows and have our way with *all* of you!"

The woman swore, running her fingers through her tangles of hair. "I can't protect you if they break in. They've done it before."

Her eyes widened further, if possible. Bile began to creep into my throat again. What had these people done to her to cause her such fear?

"I'm back," Josh sang, but he immediately quieted when he saw our agitation. Marcia grabbed his hand and gripped it.

"On my count," Norva whispered, "We barrel through these people and run. Twilight, have your magic ready."

I conjured it and felt the warm flames fill my palms with a sting, but it was–

"Valdur?" Norva scowled. "You can't use—"

"Just go!" The woman snapped, her mouth dropping at our magic.

Norva reluctantly un-slid the locks. I could hear every shifting of impatient boots on wood and every muttered conversation as the door was slowly opened to the crowd.

There they stood, a mix of the impoverished and the glamorous crunched together on the small porch with hunger in their eyes. They craned their necks to glimpse the rest of us better. Marcia hissed between her teeth at them, and one smirked in response.

"Good," one of the men spoke.

I noticed he was largely toothless, his mouth a jigsaw puzzle of empty shadows and mismatched pieces where the remaining teeth stabbed from his gums.

"Good girls. Now, give us the little boy. That's all we want right now. We won't come back for seconds unless we're really hungry."

The toothless man licked his lips as he devoured my brother with his eyes, and Marcia snarled, "To hell with you people!" She clutched Josha tighter.

"All of you are about to get hurt!" Sir Korbin threatened behind them. "Let them pass!"

"How old is the kid, Champ?" A much cleaner-looking man wanted to know, ignoring Sir Korbin's comment as he scrutinized my brother. "Can't be younger than seven or eight. Ain't he a bit old?"

"Shut your damn mouths!" Marcia roared. "These are *my children,* not your toys!"

"Ain't much of a difference these days," Champ chuckled. He turned his eyes on me. "Well, look at you!" You've got a nice face, don'tcha, cutie? Not the best, but certainly ain't the worst." He scoured me up and down in my robes, his smile wilting into a frown as he added, "Though you could stand to gain some weight. You look sickly. Not a womanly curve in sight."

I slapped him. He stumbled back into his friends, who began to laugh and whoop with excitement at the sudden turn of events.

"Whew!" The toothless man exclaimed as he staggered back to his feet. "Nothing gets me riled up like a hot little mama who can throw a good hand! Oh, gov, do it again," he begged, his mouth drooping with lust.

"I will, and with more than just my hand if you don't get out of our way. Go!"

"Careful, Twilight," Norva whispered.

I caught her locking eyes with Sir Korbin past the crowd.

The toothless man grinned, bearing his ugly mouth, a mouth as ugly as his mind, for all to see. "Sure thing, cutie," he chuckled. "As soon as you can prove you're made of something other than skin and bone and a real bitchin' attitude."

More laughter ensued.

I hissed between my teeth, clamping down on a wave of snarling anger scratching at my insides. Their stench, their pulses, the wild bleariness of their eyes; it all wept for destruction.

I'd gladly deliver.

A scorching pain lit in my palms. I raised them, gleaming black and violet, for the crowd to see.

"Twilight, don't!" Sir Korbin roared behind them.

"How dare you," I breathed, "Talk about my brother like he's *meat. You're* about to be meat, you damn zeroes."

Champ laughed. "Gov help you an' yer intolerance. Oh, wait. Not "Gov." It's probably "God" to you savages, innit?"

Sir Korbin abandoned his position at the back of the crowd and started blasting through them. Champ and several of his friends stormed us and went for my brother as cries and yells splashed through the scattering throng.

A shudder rippled down my spine.

"Monster!"

Upon witnessing my conversion, everyone in my vicinity, Champ included, sprang away. Curses flapped from his mouth. Fortunately, I was used to being cursed at.

Snarling, I dragged my bruised body to four feet. The potent power flooding my changed veins thrilled me, and I no longer viewed the congregation before me as a group of people. Now they were a chorus of beating hearts and blood charged with fear hormones.

Now they were something for my beast form, my Sharavos self, to kill.

"No! Twilight, *don't!*"

Sir Korbin's shout fell to nothing as golden magic illuminated the dark air. My attackers, the ones that remained, shuffled away from me on slow, uncertain prey feet while my foot-long talons clicked against the pavement after them.

Don't do it, that inner voice, my conscience, cautioned. *You were going to get better. You were going to find a way to heal.*

I hissed against the voice. My conscience be damned. I would kill my conscience, then cry myself to sleep later.

All the scents and sounds and sights had been clanging in my mind for too long, too long I'd been in that city. A fresh smell beckoned from the swarm of soil scents, faded blood, and decay in front of me.

Fear.

I snarled, sprang at the nearest pair of legs, and crunched down. The bones parted with little protest. Blood followed and splattered deliciously across my jaws. I paused with my snout hanging over the pervert's throat, contemplating; to tear or not to tear?

This isn't the way.

I growled and nipped the man's arm instead. He screamed as the wound dissolved into bone, and I threw myself at the next set.

No. Not one man.

Many men.

I slashed out at every leg in my path with talons longer than their necks. Half a dozen bodies fell. Some were mangled beyond repair.

Not my problem.

The smart ones scattered. It required everything not inhuman in me to resist chasing them.

The chase is fun and nice; kill, drink, eat!

I hissed at my own thoughts to *stop.*

"Go!" I roared at the fleeing crowd, though they couldn't understand my monstrous speech.

One man caught my eye near the front of the group of bodies as he tried to help his friend.

Champ.

I laughed and started to bound in his direction when Sir Korbin yelled, "Stop! You've done enough, Twilight!"

Pausing, I glared back at him.

"Please," he said softly, "Don't do anything else. I know you want to kill him, but don't. Remember *who* you are, not what."

Stupid.

I turned back toward Champ, who noticed I was approaching him. He started to stumble away.

Yes, I would butcher that miserable bastard and bathe in his beautiful blood, and if I kept going, this could be poetry—

Something slung into my flank. Something burning, hurting as it cast me aside, driving out my happy predator thoughts. I roared as I realized I had been struck with lumensa.

Cursed light magic!

It *hurt,* and that man...

I peered at Sir Korbin, black saliva trickling down my chin. Only I no longer saw him. All I could comprehend was a pulsing aura of faint light that scorched me inside. I wanted to tear it to tatters.

I would, I decided. I would dismember it.

I shrieked at the Akristuran in front of me and threw myself against him. He gasped as my acid-coated teeth connected with his arm and shredded down, opening a hole in his body that was quickly becoming infected with my venom.

Coriusg. It was a flesh-melting poison; if enough of it flooded a body, the victim would become paralyzed. Not forever, but long enough, from that powerful pain, to be torn asunder.

But I never got to remove the demon's throat.

My sisters... both of them were hurling lumensa at me from the porch.

No.

CHAPTER FIVE

D EATH HAD COME TO claim me.

It smelled like sugar. I expected something more offensive, like decay, but nothing like the fragrant, almost floral breeze that greeted my hazy senses.

Everything was dull when my eyes first opened. When the dust of my passing settled, I found myself home on Mt. Amber, my little mountain in the Caligin upon which my lifelong house had been built.

This dream was familiar. Why didn't I remember it? And where was my home? That neat little house on the mountain was absent, as... as it often was in these dreams...

These dreams.

"Twilight."

I turned to see the host of this familiar sequence of visions, the only one as dead as I surely was at that moment.

My mother, Aubri Leigh Delvian.

She smiled tentatively from across the sun-warmed meadow. But it was too bright there. Much too cheerful for death, for *maktas,* as the Sharavaks called it. The land of in-between.

The people in this realm did not receive slumber, nor were they embraced by paradise or summoned into torment. Maktas was only for people like my mother, who, well... I would have to ask her for clarification now that I was seeing her again.

"My sweet girl," Mother whispered, her soft voice filling the entire meadow and a fraction of the void in my soul.

She opened her arms. I felt a child-like pull in my body when she did this.

In some ways, I was a woman at fifteen, but the beckoning grace of my dead mother's ghostly arms shaved at least ten years off my life. I wanted to be a child again, if only for a moment, as her arms wrapped around me. I wanted to be hers.

I ran to her. Though only pieces in my puzzled mind, her arms were as warm and hopeful as I had ever wanted them to be in life. Father Sein had cursed her so that she would die when giving birth to me, but I would never allow the regret to completely leave me.

I had still been the reason she had passed in the end. I was born a killer, and then I evolved into one as the years passed.

The tears that ripped from my body at feeling her embrace were creatures of their own agenda. I could not control them and would not do so, anyway. I didn't want to. The cork had to be undone.

"My baby," Mother wept with me, never loosening her grip. "You've been gone from me. Yet I could still feel the shredding in your saas when you... when you would—"

"Kill," I choked. "When I would *kill,* Mother. I'm a murderer. I'm badly... broken," I hissed through tear-coated lips. "Truly broken."

Mother whispered, "And no one was there to understand you, all of you. So you were left alone..."

"To die by myself," I finished. "To watch myself fade. I never realized it at the time, but... I would see myself. The dullness in my eyes." I suppressed a growing sob, trying to choke it back down inside me where that anguish would never surface.

I realized I didn't want to be vulnerable then; maybe I never would. But I had to be if I didn't want my emotions to pressure cook me.

"I felt it, Mother. You were right." I laughed harshly. "The valdur; it got a grip on me, just like it did Sein, which made him choose *his* many dark paths, and Damion, and—"

"Wait," Mother interrupted. "Where are you right now? You became consumed by the valdur, so much so that I couldn't reach you anymore," she told me, her soft green eyes clouding. "Like your father. I've never been able to reach him. It seems there's a delicate balance with this sort of thing. I could reach you when your magic was first awakening, not yet developed, and I can reach you now, when... have you used it recently?"

Her concern was evident. I would be worried for me, too, knowing the kind of deceptive hold dark magic could seize a person with. What it could convince you was good to do.

I shuddered. "I did use it recently, but I don't entirely remember what happened. I hope it wasn't something awful." I shook my head. "But I did escape from them. The Shadows are behind me; I'm in Syndbur right now."

Mother's eyes glittered as she cried, "Syndbur! That's not far from my birthplace. I grew up a few miles outside of it, in Lokraini, where the old royal family lived."

"I see. Maybe I'll go there one day."

Mother smiled. "I hope so. And I hope we can continue talking to each other, but I don't know if we should. I can reach you if you use valdur at least some of the time, but not too much, or you'll become consumed again." She sighed. "The risk is too great, though. Inevitably, you will become consumed."

"What?" I cried. "But if it's just once in a while, so I don't lose you... Mother, I don't like this."

Mother shook her head, her waist-length crimson curls swishing with the motion. "I'm not fond of it, either. Perhaps we can manage something and see if we can strike a balance."

She smiled forlornly at me, her gentle white face beaming with tragic understanding, a compassion for my well-being she almost wished she didn't have to feel.

"Valdur is not a toy, dear. This kind of magic is sentient."

"What does that mean?" I asked.

"It lives," Mother answered quietly. "It is like a living entity in your body, and it chooses destruction. It destroys its host, too."

I blanched. I was one of its decaying hosts.

"Your gift is what you make it, though," Mother told me. "So please, Twilight, only do good things with it, and stop following in my dark path. Otherwise, you'll end up here," she added, gesturing at the meadow. "And eventually, in a much worse place."

I frowned. "That reminds me. Can you tell me why you're here again? Why just you and not other people? What truly happens when someone dies? And who is really in charge of this world, if anyone? Or anything?"

Mother smiled. "A good question. Well, many good ones. This," she said as she stood and pointed at the empty meadow and its equally empty sunshine, "Is my own personal hell in a manner of speaking."

"Does everyone who comes to maktas have one?" I wanted to know.

Mother nodded. "I would imagine so since I am alone here. When people like me die, we are sentenced to a place where our fondest memories were born to feel the regret over having ruined our mortal lives."

"And what, exactly," I asked, "Did you do to ruin yours?"

Once, she'd said her hands knew blood. How much?

Mother pressed her lips in a firm line, turning to give me the most soul-shattering gaze. "I killed a good friend who showed me nothing but kindness. I never fully expressed regret for it, either, and I let Sein corrupt me."

"What happens to you next?" I asked, nearly breathless.

Could there be redemption for her?

"I die," Mother replied flatly. "I am here to await my final death when the End comes, because the one who runs things is not so merciful." She grimaced. "Until then, I am left alone to think about things, feeling both the sting of regret and the comfort of this peaceful, albeit lonely place since I have not yet made it to the Void. And also," she added, "I believe I am here so I can communicate with you and be your guide."

She smiled coldly. I felt just as cold for her with this knowledge.

My mother would die.

Forever.

But at whose hands?

"Mother, I resent the concept of a deity at this point," I told her plainly. "After the Sharavaks, Aadyalbaine, all the schemes, and the lies..." I scowled. "I hate to think I might need to know who commands all this, but there *is* something out there controlling things. Maybe this "something" can fix me? I don't know, but... how do I get on this thing's good side? How do I escape the Void and unending death?"

Mother shook her head. "I can tell you a lot, Twilight, but I can't tell you everything. You must find the rest of the pieces on your own. I know you will."

A familiar snarl sounded in the distance. Mother glanced up, gazing at an unseen place beyond the meadow.

"It's here," she sighed. "My baine sentinel. It is instructed to keep me from speaking with anyone for too long, and I've said enough as it is."

Mother smoothed a hand down my hair, stroking the spirals so similar to her own, and whispered, "Goodbye, Twilight. Stay in touch once in a while. I love you."

A single tear dribbled down her pale cheek before the shadow of a baine stalked into the clearing, and my mother was pried from my waking mind.

I hoped it would not be forever.

Murmuring voices prodded me awake. I squinted in half-sleep while trying to discern whose voice was whose when they all melded into a single female's whisper.

Akristura.

That word. I squinted harder, shifting in darkness and clawing at the fabric of the sleeping part of my consciousness so I could escape it. No more of that word, the one that brought the pains and the heart pangs.

Akristura, heal her.

Heal who? No one was sick here in this little black realm. No one there but–

Twilight. Won't you heal her?

My eyes blazed under a stinging light. I narrowed them, and they slowly came to focus on red-gold curtain shining in front of me. A tentative smile spread across a pale, lightly freckled face.

Aullie. What was she doing, and where was I?

I bolted upright. "Why are you saying that word? I hate that word."

Not much of a greeting, but the "A" word wasn't much of a way to wake a Shadow up. Didn't she know how I felt about it?

"I was just praying for you, Twilight," Aullie answered softly.

"Stop. Why would you do that?" I snapped. "Where is everyone? Where are we right now?"

Aullie grabbed my hand, her eyes flashing with fear. "It's okay, Twi, calm down. Korbin!"

Great. Just who I didn't want to see.

Footsteps sounded down a nearby staircase, and the Akristuran came into view. Scars I didn't recognize twisted down his arm, and when I met his gaze, I couldn't maintain eye contact. Had I inflicted those on him?

Beyond him was a spacious white room with a few bookshelves and delicate pieces of white furniture in different places. Paintings adorned the walls with simple depictions of beauties: sunrises, or perhaps sunsets, flowers, and the ocean? I wasn't sure.

Nothing remarkable, but peaceful nonetheless. All of this quiet cleanliness, along with the gleaming hardwood floors and scattering of plush white rugs beneath the multiple sofas, was bathing in the unrestricted sunshine washing through the massive wall of windows directly across from me.

I first experienced such a design in the training arena Father Sein had used to hone my father and me into murderers. That one wall of glass had been comforting with its allowance of moonlight, one of the few comforts I'd had.

I sighed to clear the heaviness in my chest and asked again where I was.

"We're home," Sir Korbin answered plainly.

"And what does home mean?" I wanted to know. "You mean this is the Akristuran commune?"

I winced again at uttering the word, Akristura. He was not a fan of me, nor me of him—or *it*.

"Yes. The rest of your loved ones are upstairs. You know," said Sir Korbin as he helped me gently off the sofa with his scarred arm and to my feet, "If you want to stop being pained by that word, you can—"

"Don't," I interrupted, holding up my hand. "I don't need the conversion speech." I scowled. "I told you people, I'm *tired* of the religious suff. I don't *care*. Do you not listen? Honestly, maybe Sein had a point with wanting to—"

"Don't finish that sentence," Sir Korbin hissed.

I finally found his gaze and realized it was sparking into a dangerous fire. I didn't take great pleasure in provoking him, but he was still a fanatical fool, like Sein, and he had still left my good friend to die.

"I'm sorry," he said softly. He blinked and glanced away for a moment before looking back at me. "I don't have a good history with that man, which is an incredible understatement. He killed so many people I loved... Garvinuch, my good friend, should be here with me right now."

I remembered that name. Garvinuch had been a trophy from the Sharavak-Akristuran battle, beheaded by Father Sein's baine mate, Zemorah.

My grandmother.

I also briefly fought with him before being dragged away to fight alongside the Fadain.

Sir Korbin sighed. "But you're right, Twilight; the last thing you need is someone forcing things on you, especially after what you experienced. I admit that I become overzealous about my cause sometimes. I promise it's only because I care. I know what's at stake if I fail."

His eyes told the story I never would have needed an education to read. Some people were simply born too passionate. Too opinionated. Maybe that was all these Akristurans were, and the Sharavaks, too. Passionately misguided people in love with their ideologies.

I assured him it was okay.

"I guess it's a noble-seeming cause," I said. "I just don't care to take part in it. In fact, I'll probably need to go soon."

Sir Korbin frowned. "I don't think that's the answer."

———————❦———————

All the previous night's events returned to me like the fragments of a lost dream, reminding me of all the lights and the fights and how my own lack of light had led to my transformation into a Sharavos. This had progressed into my attack on Sir Korbin.

"I'm sorry I did that to you," I told him, somewhat meaning it.

"Thank you for apologizing." He tapped the scars and forced a smile. "Lumensa doesn't erase every trace of coriusg wounds. I'll add these to my body map."

I didn't respond.

He noticed my silence and said, "I understand you were upset and nervous about your brother last night. That's probably what contributed to your transformation. The monster in you does have uses, but only if it's controlled."

I ignored this and asked to see my brother. I needed to know he was okay.

Once he bounced downstairs and into my arms, I squeezed him and, for the first time, realized his thinness. He seemed snappable, not like a young boy should.

I caressed the shadows in his cheeks and planted a kiss on his nose and forehead. "Love you, Broth."

His smile spread, and he giggled, "Love you too, seester."

Seeing the hardness in his face reminded me that I never wanted him to grow up. I wanted him to pause at this stage in life forever so he wouldn't have to change.

Marcia and Susenne came down the stairs and joined us. Susenne stared, and Marcia watched Josh give me his biggest hug.

"Thank you for defending him again. He only shares half your blood, but even now, you don't treat him like it," she said.

I smiled and ruffled Josh's hair. "That doesn't matter. Family is family, right? I consider you family, too."

My stepmother's lips pursed, and her cheeks flushed faintly. "Thank you. Likewise."

Susenne chuckled. "Bet you wouldn't say that about our father and grandfather, though, right?"

It occurred to me that I'd never told Susenne about her heritage. None of the kids knew except me.

Who told you? I asked in her mind.

Her nostrils flared. *Silos. He spilled it because he didn't think Father ever would. You didn't tell me, either.*

I lowered my eyes. *I'm sorry.*

I surprised myself by realizing I really was.

"Well?" She pressed out loud.

I looked away and again traced my palm scars. "No," I said softly. "I guess I wouldn't."

"I don't mean to break this up, but we have some serious discussions to get to," Sir Korbin interrupted. "But before that, I have to ask... are you all alright?"

Marcia shrugged. "The kids are still alive. Don't care as much about my husband."

Sir Korbin smirked and nodded. "Susenne? Twilight? Josh?"

"I'm okay!" Josha cried. He threw his arms around my neck and laughed.

I pet his hair. "That's my soup boy."

"I'm fine," Susenne answered, crossing her arms.

Sir Korbin looked at me again. "Twilight?"

I looked around me at the cloud-colored realm I found myself in.

This was not the wakeful darkness of the Sharavaks. Sunlight was not a concept I enjoyed anymore. I was a nocturnal animal; I had a distaste for living during the day.

I looked at the Akristuran, searching for the scorn in his face, but found none. Despite his occasional briskness, he at least seemed authentic.

I still wanted to kill him, though.

"I just want to go," I muttered, tracing my collarbone and avoiding eye contact.

"You do that a lot," Sir Korbin commented. "Grab your collarbone. It's a nervous habit. But you don't have to be nervous here, Twilight. We're here to help you as best we can. If you want, you can take this day to rest, and we'll have a discussion with you soon about your past and how to move forward."

I lowered my head. "I deserve to die."

My inner Shadow objected to this, but my humanity knew this was true.

Sir Korbin sighed. "We will address all of that soon, but for now, I would advise you to speak with one of our shamans. A lot is happening in you, Twilight. You have done and been through many horrific things, and it would be best if you got some of that wrestled out now so our next conversation will be easier."

"What do you mean?" I asked. "Are you sending me to...?"

"Therapy?" Susenne chimed in. "Yeah. I did it a few hours ago."

"Would you like to see this person?" Sir Korbin asked.

After chewing on the decision for an uncomfortably long time, the prodding in my mind insisted that I go. I would either agree with them or hate them and move on from the Akristurans, go somewhere else and eke out a living.

Or...

I could take my life. What did it matter after the lives I had already taken?

If the shaman somehow found a way to stamp out this guilt, though, and worse, the looming apathy that often descended...

I nodded. "I'll go. No promises on how I'll feel about it, but take me to this shaman thing."

Sir Korbin smiled. "A wise decision."

When I met the shaman, I felt nothing.

At first, a prick of anger. Then the apathy swarmed in, and I gazed at the warm, weathered face and inquisitive gray eyes before me with as much cold as the Sharavaks had ever taught me to feel.

The only surprise was that this shaman was a woman. I had been under the impression another Sir Korbin waited beyond the pristine antechamber doors, but I was mistaken.

It was spacious inside the room, but not as much as Father Sein's quarters back in the compound. The atmosphere was also decidedly different. It was comforting and home-like in the shaman's quarters, with the many swaying candle flames lined up along the shelves and even circled around the shaman herself on the floor.

A skylight in the center of the room was cracked to vent the fragrance of the candles' spices. A sunray splashed through the glass, casting a bright curtain that separated us from the shaman who waited further in. It tingled on my neck as we cleaved our way through, and it was only after breaking that sunray that I began to feel my session had commenced.

The shaman observed me with eyes that continuously narrowed, her plump limps crushing each other as she waved a wreath of lumensa over herself. After muttering an incoherent prayer, the shaman ordered, "Sit."

It was then that the apathy spell broke, and the sight of her, her smug, crease-lined face and the rich color in her skin, color a sunlight-loathing monster like me would never know, taunted the snarling anger to rise, *rise*—

"*Sit*, baine child," the shaman hissed. "I will not ask again."

Sir Korbin was about to ask me if I needed anything else when the shaman snapped, "She needs you gone. I will contend with the baine spawn alone, Korbin. Take your leave."

Baine spawn. What a charming woman.

Sir Korbin dipped his head to her and replied, "Of course, Lady Annisara." To me, he added, "It'll be okay, Twilight. Just be respectful and cooperate. Please."

Only if this shaman woman returned the favor.

Lady Annisara watched him go with sullen eyes. As soon as he was gone, she turned those eyes on me. My breath caught in my throat at the way she seemed to dissect me. It was similar to Sein, but it did not feel malicious. Neither, however, was it friendly.

"You have many baines in you, child," she rasped.

The shaman slowly smoothed her hand down her many silver braids, and I both admired and despised the nobility of her appearance. She had even woven butterfly-shaped stones into the front coils, and also...

"Starstones," Lady Annisara muttered. "Yes. You have one from your mother. I was the one to give it to her when she was becoming a woman. I discerned the richness of her power as it was evolving."

I gasped at the knowledge, and my hand immediately fluttered to my neck, where I had stashed the gem inside the collar of my shirt. Lady Annisara smiled faintly.

"It has guided you, no?"

I removed my mother's necklace from hiding and considered it.

Yes, it had lent me its honesty before, in Toragaine. There, the stone had burned against my flesh, alerting me to the presence of the Void's true inhabitants, the forever dead. It had been this knowledgeable stone that had brought me to my own understanding.

"It saved me from the Void," I answered. "It illuminated the darkness."

Lady Annisara nodded. "Yes," she said, "The darkness in yourself. Akristura was with you that night."

Shuddering, I added, "So was Aadyalbaine."

Lady Annisara grimaced. "A bad name," she whispered. "And that wickedness has poisoned your very bones, child. The Dark One is within you."

I laughed. "Right. I ran away from the Sharavaks, so—"

"No!" The shaman hissed. She clutched at one of her braids, stroking the small starstone inside. Sighing, she said, "The Dark Children's ways are still your ways. The Dark One's mind is still your mind, and the spirits of his servants remain with you. Running does not save you. You must tell me all you have done to begin to heal."

The words echoed through my core, sending a shudder clawing its way up my spinal column.

Tell her what I did? No. I couldn't utter a single instance, let alone bare every black deed.

Swallowing hard, I croaked, "No, thank you." I rose from the floor and added, "I have to go."

"Stop," Lady Annisara snapped. "You want to heal? You want the blood and the monsters and the baines eating at you to leave? Then you sit." She pointed to where I had just been like I was a pet expected to execute swift commands.

Seething, I opened my mouth to empty out the filth simmering on my tongue when I remembered Sir Korbin's warning to keep respectful and cooperate. I didn't know what it was about those people or that place, but Sharavak Aaquaena Twilight felt muted. The Myrk Maiden lacked power for once, and I was almost grateful for that.

All that light, the visible kind, and that which manifested in human spirits, set my teeth on edge. Oh, how I wanted to dismember something...

"Your dark thoughts reek," the shaman spat.

I sighed and sat down again so she could at least berate me at eye level.

"You are a bleak presence here," Annisara stated bluntly. "And you will not be allowed to remain here if you resist your much-needed cleansing. As I told you, there are baines all over you."

"I don't see any," I retorted. "I saw them in Syndbur yesterday. And I don't feel any, either."

Annisara smirked, but it was without amusement. "Girl," she clucked, "Part of your issue is you think you know everything. Just because you can see another person's demons does not mean you are so easily aware of your own. Our own darkness is what ends up killing us if we are careless."

"But," she continued, taking my cold, pale hands in her warm brown ones, "This does not have to be your end. There is hope. We will find it after you have told me everything and asked for the Light to cleanse you. All the things you did, child. Every evil. Every wrong. Spill the darkness for Akristura, who already knows what you have done."

"He knows?" I asked.

Annisara nodded. "Akristura sees all. You aren't exempt from that. He is the good in this world, and without Good, you cannot vanquish that which is evil."

As much as I loathed to admit it, this made sense. Aadyalbaine was the evil in the world, and his wickedness was shared among his brethren. If such monstrous darkness existed, was there not also a light? The Sharavaks believed in Akristura. It was his existence that made his people, the Children, so threatening to them—and targets for slaughter.

Well, for what it was worth...

For a restful sleep at least once more in my lifetime, my family members, and my friends both near and far... I would try. It would be like choking up dead bodies from a gravesite, but all that blood and decay must be expelled.

Perhaps Lady Annisara could revive the rot to life.

Perhaps her deity, too, could... no. I refused to finish that thought.

"O-okay," I stammered, feeling a growing resistance in my mind at what I was about to speak into the light. "I'll start from the beginning..."

When the words began to pour, so did the blood. It showered out of my mouth, dribbling from my nostrils, eyes, and ears like hot wax splattered across a wall. Instead of a wall, my body was the canvas for this gruesome painting.

Worse than the blood was the convulsions. As Lady Annisara prayed over me with each shuddering confession, I felt them... the baines. Their ancient wickedness and raw, shadowed power yanked at the seams of my intestines, raging to unpiece me like a butchered animal.

I screamed.

I screamed once for the light, once more for the dark.

It was not a human scream. It was a yowl that steadily morphed into a vicious sound that scraped my throat raw, and as the roar clawed out of me, the shaman's prayers increased in tempo and volume.

I began to swim in darkness. For a moment, one torturously lovely moment, I was choking on memories. I recalled the savage pleasure in eviscerating a *filthy zyz,* such a wretched, majestic delight! Feeling the bones snap, the cartilage give way, and the blood and inner pieces spill into my mouth...

Then the battle with the Akristurans floated to mind. Wielding all the magic against them, feeling the fluttering darkness stretching out of my body to smite them all... I had even used hursafar to mind-control them into butchering each other. That final glorious explosion with Father Sein had been the richest sensation in all the world.

Father Sein. His death had been divine, literally and figuratively, as I savored his shrieking pleas. The melting flesh, his liquefying eyes, the falling mouth, the burning, sagging flesh... his scream for his precious Aaksa!

Aaksa.

Toragaine.

Arkyaktaas, the beast sleeping in the lake in the Void...

Aaksa!

Come back to Me, my old master commanded from the Void. *You are My child. I made you. I loved you first. It was Me. Your power is My power, and My will is yours. Return to Me, Myrk Maiden...*

The baines were strangling me now, seizing my hold on life and stripping it away from me as I—

"Begone, *begone!*" Lady Annisara chanted, wrapping me in a cloak of pure light magic.

When the baines writhed, so did I. I felt their predatory eyes gazing through my own. Seeing the world through multiple minds was a nauseating sensation, sharing something so inhuman with my flesh.

The lumensa took effect. As it seeped into my skin, the memories of slaughter began to die out as new memories swarmed into place.

Cobi. The meadow. Solshek. Our writing. My mother. Josha. Aullie. Susenne.

Love.

In those many familiar faces, that commitment was reflected back at me, beckoning me back to humanity.

With the planting of fresh memories and thoughts came the final aggravated wailing of my supernatural parasites. After the last tug of resistance, they fled my body, and a metallic stench clouded around my head.

The relief was immediate. So were the tears as I fell, gasping and coughing, face forward into the shaman's arms.

"Oh, child," she soothed as she embraced my bloody body, "They're gone from you now. But this isn't over. I must take you someplace. There you can denounce them forever. You will never be used like that again."

CHAPTER SIX

I WAS TOLD I wouldn't be used again. In the same breath, Lady Annisara informed me that the only way to keep more baines from latching onto me was to turn to Akristura. I wanted to be angry about this manipulation, but I didn't have the energy to respond at first. The shaman wiped away some of the blood on my face, but my robes were drenched and splattered. Never, in all my life, did I want to experience baines like that again. The bleeding, the screaming, and the extra pairs of eyes peering through my skull with malice were too much to endure a second time.

I shuddered, and Lady Annisara apologized as she steered me out the front door of the commune.

"Listen," she told me, pausing to look at me. "I understand this is sudden for you. You have experienced great trauma, and the speaking of your confessions will never quite be able to reach what is hurting here," she said as she touched her chest.

The shaman smiled mournfully. "Unfortunately, girl, those parasites will return to you if you do not reject them completely. They have savored your power. They are not happy at you denouncing them, and if you do not cling to the Light, these dark things will come to kill you. They'll attack you in your sleep and could take your life the moment you go to bed tonight. This is not a carefree matter."

Feeling the blood flee my face, I asked how that could be possible if I lived in the commune.

"Il and Norva kept me safe on our way here. The baines didn't get me then. Why does that have to change now?"

The shaman sighed. "This is different. You have been purged of your baine leeches now; I have driven them out of you so you can breathe a bit of clarity and embrace some peace of mind. These baines warp how you see the world once they have a hold on you. Now that they're gone, they're angry and will return as soon as you are most vulnerable. As for my young friends, they protected you for a time. But we cannot, and will not, support a

Shadow under our roof if they refuse to change their ways. As I told you, you are a bleak presence here."

Lady Annisara grimaced and apologized, her cutting gray eyes softening as she beheld me and all my blood-spattered glory. I was no longer charmed by her grandmotherly beauty, though.

Why call themselves the Children of Akristura, an implication of merciful and helpful people, when they refused to allow someone different from them under their roof?

"So, I can't stay with you without pledging allegiance to your religion, is that right?" I hissed. I clenched my fists and laughed. "Am I just too sick and broken for your perfect little society to handle? I thought you people were good to others regardless of who they were. That's what some of you like to preach, anyway. Maybe you should consider putting your preaching to practice?"

Lady Annisara took my hand. "Twilight, you are no ordinary person. Your magic is potent, and your former allegiance was to our greatest enemy. This makes you dangerous, to us, to yourself, and to others. You are not a normal—"

"Stop," I gasped, pulling out of her grip. "I'm so tired of the "You're special" speech! I was used before, I won't be used again! I didn't *ask* for this!"

The tears scalded my eyes. I let them stream, throwing my head back in the sunshine so the rays could make them burn hotter. The shaman placed a hand on my shoulder.

"We are willing to keep you for a few weeks," she told me. "Korbin and I will work with you to help you. We don't want to give up on you, girl."

I snorted. "Really? Why? Why go to the trouble?"

"Because Akristura can *fix* what's broken," Annisara insisted. "You've been a pawn for a higher power before; don't you believe it has a counterpart, maybe one who's not so malevolent?" She gripped my hands, her gaze bright and earnest. "Your shame won't go away on its own, young Twilight. Your monster isn't going to retread its steps for you!"

I pulled my hands back and stepped away from her again, feeling the anger flare and stinging from the idea that she wanted to force me into a new life path. These freaks—all fanatics, apparently—believed they had a claim to my life.

Light or dark, it didn't matter. When you were *special,* everyone wanted a taste of you, and you were prime for any twisted agenda.

"I had thought you people were almost noble in a way," I said, "But you're not any different from the Sharavaks. I don't want to stay here any longer than I have to; I want to *go!* I want my *own life!*"

With these truths spoken, I ran. The shaman called after me multiple times, but I heard little beyond my throbbing heart and the scuffing of my boots on the dirt and grass. I blundered down the hillside along a hoof-beaten road until I happened upon a narrow trail to my left.

Well, I could swing that way and make myself a meal for bugs in the tall grass, or I could continue stumbling down the main road like a drunk and make a fool of myself in town. The former option was more appealing, so I careened onto the trail and began my shuffle along its weed-choked path.

I scowled and strode through the grass. In the wild again, but alone this time. There was no Cobi to make me smile, my first friend and survival partner. Solshek was not nearby with his pithy life observations or poetry.

There was no one.

This, I thought as I pawed at a white butterfly in my path, was the way things had always been. The reality was that I was a lone entity, despised by family and left friendless at every moment.

I could not coexist. I would never find "my people." There were no such people for me.

How could there be a people for just one solitary person? The individual found no solace in human connection. We found no comfort in anything, including the restless churning of our hateful minds.

"Hey!" I snapped at the white butterfly brushing against my face. "Personal space, you should learn it."

I usually enjoyed butterflies, but the Twilight who liked simple things was dead. Purged of her parasites, sure, but still just as hollow as before.

Like everything on the forsaken planet.

I stopped in my path. A large lake ringed with a rainbow splash of flowers laid directly in front of me. The surrounding bank was white sand. It was so fine and clean that it almost made me think of ground bones or starstones, I thought as I clutched my mother's. To my surprise, the stone was glowing faintly.

With the sun kissing the lake, the gleaming water looked immaculate. The bottom appeared depthless, but the water beckoned me with its unusual beauty.

Fresh, undefiled water. Something to drink, bathe off my blood, and take the prickle of the sun's heat from my flesh. As I began shouldering out of my robes down to my undergarments, the boundary-disregarding butterfly floated out in front of me.

"What?" I asked the insect. "Are you here to make a statement? Well, I'm honored. Let me be your one-person show."

I chuckled, stripping off my boots and chucking them into the grass behind me. The sand was alarmingly cool under my feet. Being so sun-exposed, I would have expected to be crippled by stepping on it. Small miracles, I supposed.

The butterfly continued to circle around me until I stepped into the lake. It took its leave at this point and disappeared into the encircling flowers, leaving me to bathe in peace. The lakewater wasn't warm, but neither was it cold. Its coolness soothed my inner embers. I settled into it, raw and aching, and let the soft chill freeze my racing thoughts.

Void below, what a day. I sighed and began to float on the lake surface, ignoring the sun's prodding on my pale skin. I disliked being alone in this moment. Aloneness lent itself to uncomfortable thoughts and contemplations I'd rather not have. But maybe... I gnawed my lip as I continued to drift.

Maybe that was necessary.

I winced when images of myself crouched over the bodies of deceased Orshians seeped into my mind. Poison, these memories. I shivered, not at the water, but at the dark remembrances.

Who was I now? Not that... creature. But not whole, either. Still a slave to the Dark God, if Annisara's words held true. His ways were still my ways, and the baines were waiting for the ideal moment to attack. I shivered again when I remembered how she'd phrased it, like I could die at any moment. Perhaps I would.

Did I want to take chances and see if that would happen? Did I even care what became of me?

"Your shame won't go away on its own…"

Blood pooled in my mouth. I'd bitten through my lip.

"Your monster isn't going to retread its steps for you!"

I sucked the blood out and considered it.

No. It probably wouldn't. I couldn't control myself and I lacked the willpower to do so.

But I had obligations.

Cobi's smile washed out the memories of the Orshians. Solshek's deep eyes drove away the hollow promises of the darkness. As always, I thought of my siblings, too, and how once, I'd striven to save them from Sein and the Shadows.

Then what? I'd *become* a Shadow. *I* was the monster plotting for the destruction of non-magicals and their "kind." I snorted. "Kind." Sein hadn't seen humanity as man*kind*, but distinct groups that required careful sorting and pruning. Like tree branches.

My teeth ground. I clenched my fists and released another breath.

I will not think about my murderous grandfather when trying to relax.

The problem was that I couldn't relax. Remorse—was that what this was?—didn't allow anything to settle. My soul would twitch and spasm repeatedly until… unless… I sighed.

"Do you hear me, Akristura?" I called to the sky.

That was where their god lived, right? The sky? I'd always assumed so.

I cleared my throat. I didn't know what had come over me, but I supposed it was the necessity to fix—or attempt to fix—this monster. If I didn't…

I blinked through the oncoming tears. I might be the reason Josha passed far before his time. Or Aullie. Susenne. Cobi. Marcia. Korbin. Any number of people who firmly didn't deserve to die.

"I don't know if you exist," I whispered, my voice breaking on "exist." "But…"

I need to rein in this monster. It controls me, not the other way around.

"If you do… and if you're not bent on using me to kill people like Aadyalbaine…" I tried not to laugh at the darkness of that statement. "Please… fix me. Save me from myself." My eyes stung. "Because I can't live my whole life wanting other people to die. I can't…" I let the waterworks come, suddenly crippled by everything I'd done.

My senses demanded me to kill. That was just the nature of things, of *me,* and I was powerless against it now that I'd been so thoroughly trained. So skilled in the art of slaughter. And this was wrong, I realized. My mind opened, and clarity entered where there'd been only smug satisfaction before.

You were wrong. Everything you were taught was evil.

Evil.

Evil was me, and I was it.

If I could have lowered my head, I would have.

"I can't fix myself. I don't know how."

These last words sighed out of me like the final breaths of a dying person.

I deserved to die. Like Sein, I should have been reduced to a bleeding, crumbling mess, carrion for the baines. Without Akristura's protection, I apparently already had that waiting for me.

But it wasn't protection I sought. I raised one hand from the water and stared at the burnt palms. The jagged cuts, sealed in scar tissue, remembered what it meant to be a Shadow. They spoke of my monster's bottomless appetites and how much my magic lusted for control.

They remembered how unrighteously wonderful it felt to pillage a man's blood and flesh and plunder his psyche's deepest thoughts. Shadows were puzzles. As people, we weren't completely darkness, but we certainly weren't light. Stealing the residue, saas', from our victims supplied the necessary pieces to make us whole. The picture of our personhood was incomplete without ravaging the parts we needed from others.

Murder made a Shadow a proper monster. Even the smell of it, the mere suggestion posed in the scent of blood, reminded us of our purpose: to maim and kill. We were nothing if we didn't fulfill these tasks.

I loosed a shaky breath and attempted to keep floating. The sunlight had somehow strengthened, and it was starting to burn. Another thing about Shadows was we had awful skin.

I decided it was time I actually bathed and removed the blood on me that for once wasn't someone else's. I'd attacked Sir Korbin last night in my Sharavos form and probably covered myself in blood then. Someone had had to wash it off of me.

Planting my feet on the soft, shallow lake bottom, I began to scrub the blood from my skin, letting the clothes simply soak. This outfit was ruined, and everyone would have to accept that. The blood shaved off and hit the water in clotted clumps. I gaped at it when I saw how they fizzled in a spot of foam and disappeared upon hitting the lake.

It was as if the blood hadn't ever been there once the foam went away. The lakewater dissolved it, and the more I thought about the feeling creeping over me, the more I was convinced that my remorse's harsh pain was fading, too.

Did I dare think this sensation was peace?

I squinted at the sun-bathed clouds, reeling from the bright light. I didn't recall them being so bright before. There were many things I could have dared to think, and I found myself too afraid to consider them.

Once finished, I dragged myself up from the water and groaned when I remembered how I'd chucked my footwear into the grasses. Now I was going to have to step on the sand, and it would coat my feet like powdered sugar on pastries.

Sighing, I waded ashore and made my way to where my boots were. I started to work my feet into them when I had to gape for a second time, this time at my soles. No sand was stuck to them.

That's not normal.

I started to worry that this lake might be much more than it seemed—as if it hadn't already proven that—when the same white butterfly I'd seen earlier bobbed my way. I watched it flutter closer, its gentle movements enviably calm, before it landed on my head.

Gasping, I swatted it to brush it off. It nudged my hand before taking off to the flowers where it had gone the first time. Breathless, I watched the sun shine increasingly bright through the clouds, certain I wasn't imagining it this time, and I stood up to trudge back to the commune.

Back to the fanatics.

I didn't have the heart to laugh at the nickname. It felt wrong all of a sudden, like my heart was too heavy and soft to want to mock anyone.

How strange.

I frowned, moving through the swaying grasses back toward the path that led to the Akristurans' dwelling. The words I'd uttered in a moment of desperate vulnerability to their deity trailed behind me like the sigh of the breeze.

CHAPTER SEVEN

"TWILIGHT?"

Sir Korbin met me halfway back to the commune road, startling me before I could begin to process things.

"Are you okay?" His dark eyes searched mine.

"I..."

Where to begin?

"I cleaned off in the lake," I muttered. "And while I was there..."

He frowned. "You look shaken. Did something happen?"

I nodded. "I... talked to your god. I didn't get an answer, not that I expected one, but it happened." I shrugged, ignoring his narrowing eyes. "Then, when I was washing off the blood, it turned to foam in the water and disappeared."

The Akristuran's eyes flashed. "How interesting. I've never had the nerve to touch that lake myself."

I raised my brows at him. "Is something wrong with it?"

He shook his head. "On the contrary. It's very sacred. That lake, Lake Silvera, is the first place Akristura stepped when He first descended to our world to fight Aadyalbaine."

I looked back at the lake. It was beautiful, but otherwise, it appeared quite normal.

Sir Korbin touched my shoulder. "I am glad you reached out to Akristura. I can assure you He received your words. What exactly did you say, if I may ask?"

Chills gripped my spine. "I asked him to..." I hesitated, burning with shame. "To fix me. Because I don't think I can go on like this." I gestured to myself.

Sir Korbin nodded. "He will accept you as you are, Twilight. You made the correct decision, and I'm very happy you did. If there's one thing I can tell you, it is this; do not worry. You're in good hands. The very best hands. If you went to the length of setting aside your inhibitions and pride to ask Him to save you from yourself, He will do that. We want to help you, too, Twilight." His smile turned firm. "Will you let us help you?"

It was all so sudden, but when would it not be? No one spent any length of time with the Sharavaks and recovered quickly. Theirs was a worldview so upside-down and backward, so defiling of nature, that exposure to such madness was permanently branding. I touched my palms again and met Sir Korbin's eyes.

"I guess I don't have much of an alternative. I was going to leave, but that's not fair to my family."

"It's not fair to you, either," Sir Korbin added gently.

"Sure." I shrugged. "But even after asking Akristura to help me," I said, looking back at the lake, "I'm still myself. I don't need baines to help with that. I kill. I attack. I don't just have a monster that shows up once in a while; I *am* one. You really want to deal with that?"

Did *I?*

The dark thoughts remained, though something—this deep and permeating sense of "otherness"—had shone a light through them. Something new had joined my spirit when I'd made my plea to the Light God.

Hope. It was a desperate kind, clawing for my attention. It was a softness I missed in myself, giving me longing again for wholeness. Had Akristura really just... given that to me? So freely, after one miserable string of whispers?

And when will this not *war with my other nature?*

Because that still existed, too, in a confusing juxtaposition.

Sir Korbin seemed to understand. "It's true that I've never worked with a Shadow before. You'll test me, but I think that's for the best. For both of us." His gaze locked onto mine. "We *can* turn this around, Twilight. I accept that you'll always wrestle with wrong desires. I accept you'll have difficult moments, emotional outbursts, and other things along your developmental journey. That is part of the process. More importantly, it's *human*. As long as we can keep you from committing more crimes, I consider your growth useful and exciting. Do you want to grow? Do *you* believe it's time to move on?"

My Shadow self snarled, *No.* My other self, who had woken up just minutes ago in a sudden puncturing of the soul, begged my tongue to form a "Yes." Now I at least knew which parts of myself were wrong and which pointed to healing. Before, it'd been so unclear. That lack of clarity had gotten me into trouble.

"I do," I answered softly. I thought of Josha, Cobi, Aullie, and Solshek. Even Susenne and Marcia. "I really do."

It was the first decision in a long time I'd made for myself. No domineering deities or family members had ordered it to be.

"Good. We can begin lumensa training soon, then. We'll need to build it back up after what you've been through. It has quieted."

I winced. "Right."

Sir Korbin started back to the commune, promising we would begin training the next day.

"We also need to address your time with the Shadows. Since you've accepted Akristura and will live with us, we must assess your crimes against humankind and confirm that you were used and forced into some of these situations. It was the Fadain who trained you?"

"Yes."

He nodded. "No doubt you didn't have much choice when it came to some of the things you did, but we'll see. You still need to take some level of accountability for what you did. Do you agree?"

I shivered. "What's the punishment? I'm sure I deserve the worst you could throw at me, so..."

He frowned. "We're not going to kill you, child. Not even imprison you. I believe we need you." He glanced back at the lake. "But we will have something lined up for you. How does tonight sound? It should give my counterparts and me enough time to think things over."

I considered it. No death? No jail?

What, then?

"Sure," I finally replied. "Trial me."

Morbid curiosity was the name of the game.

Sir Korbin nodded and went ahead of me. I followed, not quite believing I was treading this man's same path. Back to another faith.

I sincerely hoped this one would give me the clarity and wholeness I needed to change from the beast I'd become.

The entire family was waiting for me when we got back. Their faces echoed their expectation, and even Il and Norva whispered something to each other when they saw Sir Korbin and me coming up the hill from the lake. Sir Korbin pulled them and a few other Akristurans aside down a hallway where his office was.

"Give us a few hours to compose our trial for you and decide on an appropriate sentencing for your circumstance. The law of the age cannot be trusted, and we don't want you in the government's clutches, anyway. They would take advantage of you or, worse, turn you over to your father."

"Okay," I said quietly. "I'll see you then."

Sir Korbin patted my shoulder, as did Norva before the three Akristurans retreated to decide my fate. As I turned from them and gazed at my hands, I decided this was more than fair. My darkness snarled at the thought of being tried like the vicious criminal it was. Its reluctance against accountability was almost righteous in its own twisted way. My mind was expanding, though, especially when I was forced to look over my family members.

I'd almost forgotten who they were. Weeks of unraveling my soul and sanity had colored them differently in my head. Half of them didn't have magic. My inner Shadow sneered at this.

They're nothing if they have no magic. They're liabilities you must take care of because they can't protect themselves.

I ground my teeth and snapped at these thoughts to go away. Little Josh didn't deserve the bones pushing against his flesh. Nor did Aullie or Marcia. Even Susenne.

Susenne.

I looked at her and my chest stirred with longing. She avoided eye contact, but the moment wasn't allowed to grow awkward when the questions came.

"Where did you go?" Aullie asked softly.

"Did you meet an angel?" Josha cried. "Did you *become* an angel?"

"No." I chuckled. "Actually, I... I think I just traded religions." I smoothed my hair down and ignored the prickling of my ruined hands. "I've chosen to follow the Light God."

That sounded right coming out, my decisiveness. So did the lift in my heart when I said it. But the Shadow in me disagreed. I looked at my family members and decided it could go to Toragaine with its nonsense.

Marcia laughed. "You're not serious."

Josha looked at his mom, then at me, and said, "I believe you, Twi. I always have." He smiled and ran to me to give me a hug.

"Thanks, buddy," I whispered, squeezing him.

"It's like when you told everyone about the monster and the wolf. You weren't lying then!"

"Good memory, Joshy." I fluffed up his hair and watched Marcia's face redden.

"I suppose it's not the strangest thing to happen." She chuckled weakly. "But why?"

"I guess a lot of it boils down to guilt." I fumbled awkwardly with my hands, a surge of affection warming my chest. "I love you all. What the Shadows plan to do to this world I cannot allow. It's disgusting, and... so am I."

My eyes strayed to the red and white lines on Marcia's body. Scars and half-healed wounds. There were a few on Susenne's face, too, and fortunately, none visible on the other two.

"They hurt you," I hissed. "Let me... try to heal those." I pointed at Marcia.

Marcia shrugged. "I won't object. I've got a few nasty ones on my legs. Go ahead and use your freaky magic on me. It can't be worse than the kind *they* used."

She dropped into one of the living room recliners and propped her feet up. I knelt before her and peeled back the cloth to reveal crusted cuts and blushing bruises. The other wounds had smoothed into cold white scars.

I had to bite back tears while I placed my hands on the scabs. "I'm so sorry. None of you deserved this."

I meant that. It was one of the first glimmers of remorse I'd felt since... whatever had just happened at the lake.

Marcia sighed. "The kids don't, certainly. I do, though."

"What do you mean?"

She shrugged. "I wasn't good to you. And look at the man I married! You call that a good decision?"

I contemplated while trying to draw out lumensa. It wasn't budging, and I felt none in my internal realm. "I do, actually. We wouldn't have the kids otherwise. That's not a mistake."

"That's true."

"And as for you and me," I said, "I don't hold that against you, either. I get it. You saw me as the kid you couldn't claim as your own. I was the outsider."

Marcia huffed. "It doesn't excuse my behavior, though. I want you to know something; *I'm* sorry. I could stand to act my age."

I smiled. "Me, too, though acting fifteen isn't really a good thing."

She laughed. "You're not so bad, kid. Thanks, by the way. Are you getting them?"

I paused, gnawing my lip. "Nothing's coming out." I held open my empty palms.

She frowned, nodded, and said, "That's okay. Or maybe not. I don't know, but don't sweat it. Maybe I can ask that woman, Norva? I do want to show you something, though. Follow me."

She took me to the bathroom and closed the door so she could safely remove her shirt. She made a face at herself in the mirror.

"Sorry you have to see this." She ran rough fingers over her stretch marks.

"Why are you ashamed of those? You're a mother."

Marcia snorted. "Wait till you pop out a few. Then you'll know."

I shook my head and smiled before she lifted her arm, exposing the rest of her wounds. I kept my gasps inside as my eyes roved over everything that had been hurt. They'd carved the myrk symbol all over her, the crude, arrow-headed spider forced on with aggressive care. I swallowed my revulsion at this display of apparent enjoyment.

"Sorry I can't erase those," I said softly. "I'd sure like to."

Marcia threw up her hands as if to say, "What're you going to do?"

"I'll see what can be done about them."

"I appreciate you trying, kid." She fixed her shirt and opened the bathroom door.

A rush of affection swept through me, and I found myself desperately wishing I *could* remove her scars and every other ghastly mark. She hadn't earned them. She'd been tortured, and in ways I hadn't.

I reached out a hand to touch her but drew it back. "Of course... Mother."

Both our faces heated. We laughed through the moment, and Marcia pulled me into a quick side hug before letting me go. I approached Susenne next and asked if she wanted anything fixed so I could tell Norva or someone about it.

Her arms remained firmly against her chest, and she answered, "No. I'm good."

I frowned. "Are you? What about that scab on your forehead?"

Who gave that to you? I thought.

Susenne's eyes darkened. *Father. Who else?*

My stomach sank.

"I'll keep this for now, thanks." Susenne poked her wound.

"Ouch! Don't do that, Suze," Josha cried.

"You don't have anything like that, right, Josh?" I asked. "If you do, let's see."

"Nope! I'm okay, Twi. I'm better now that I'm with you." He grabbed my hand and twirled me around before dashing up the stairs with Aullie.

"Well, those two are clearly good," I said, smiling and shaking my head. "Cobi?"

Cobi stepped out of the kitchen, his eyes lowered. "I have a wound. Right here." He touched his chest.

Oh, no, not something wrong with his organs.

Flutters of panic set in.

"I'm sorry," I blurted, "For leaving you down there for so long. I have no idea how much damage that caused to your–"

"My heart," he interrupted, "Breaks every time you roll your eyes at me. You might want to watch that."

I paused to process his words. When they sunk in, I crossed the space between us and pushed him in the sternum.

"That's not funny!" I cried, only half-joking.

My push was harder than I'd anticipated. He started to slip into a fall when I caught his shirt collar and pulled him back against me. We collided in laughter, and he hugged me, assuring me he was okay.

"You'll be okay, too. Don't worry about your magic. It'll come back. And don't worry about the outcome of this trial they've got planned for you."

"It's hard not to," I replied. "With the things I've done? The Myrk Maiden's been a very poor lass."

"It's true," Cobi said, "That, uh, murder and all that isn't very ladylike. But everyone understands what you went through, Twi. They shouldn't hold that against you too hard. And if they do?" He pulled back, gripping my shoulders and focusing his warm blue eyes on my cold black ones. "You'll always have me on your side."

The Akristurans came for me at sunset. Their gazes were dark as though the subject matter of their conversations—me—had filled them with shadows.

Appropriate.

"Come, Twilight," Sir Korbin said gently.

Norva didn't miss my concern. "You will be fine," she tried to assure me. "Into the study."

Il said nothing. I choked down some of the mad moths flapping in my throat and stomach. When I flicked nervous eyes at Sir Korbin, I saw compassion in his own and firm resolve.

So, this was what all the murdering and messing around had come to. I was in the old enemy's clutches and about to be tried for what I *thought*—what my "family" had told me—were noble actions.

I followed Sir Korbin into his private study and filed in behind Il, Norva, and Lady Annisara, who joined them from the next room. Each of them took a seat across from me. I collapsed onto the sofa and tried not to fidget, especially when Sir Korbin withdrew a paper and a writing utensil from his desk drawer.

"I apologize in advance for the relative... informality of this trial," he commented, looking me over on the sofa. "As we briefly discussed, you were under Sein Leidyen's control during your time with the Shadows, and we all suspect that without his influence and that of his followers, you wouldn't have done the things you did. Would you agree with that?"

I nodded and struggled not to shake at the memories pouring in.

Yes, I had been used... at first. What of the dark and hideous delight I enjoyed *after* succumbing to my role as the Sharavak Aaquaena?

"Fortunately," said Lady Annisara, "You have memories to help your cause. We will use those in this trial to decide what must be done with you." She sighed quietly. "Before we begin asking questions and poking around in your mind, please give your account of what led to the crimes you committed."

Chills. Not those. I didn't want them, didn't welcome the way they glided over my body and took me over, like valdur...

"Twilight?" Il prompted.

"Father brought me to them," I whispered, clenching one fist in the other. "In the beginning. And I ran from them. I swear I didn't want to be one of them!" I cried.

"It's okay," soothed Norva.

"Continue," Il said.

Shuddering, I shared the details of my loose escape plan with Cobi.

Sir Korbin nodded. "We have already spoken to the young man and investigated his memories, and your story matches the events we found. Of course, we will still be checking *your* recollection, but we know that everything to do with Cobi is probably true. Now... what about what happened *after* Cobi was cursed and locked away? What happened to you?"

What had happened to me was...

I was gripping the sofa arm too hard. Something popped in the frame. Sir Korbin's eyes flashed disappointment, and I looked away, hoping my hair would hide my face.

"S-Sein," I said so softly I was asked to repeat myself. "Sein made me his monster. His *pet.*"

Heat sizzled in my palms. Lady Annisara warned me to watch my magic.

"You need to compose yourself," Sir Korbin said quietly. "I sympathize with your feelings, Twilight, but now is not the time to choke up. It is time to speak out, confess what you have done, and explain what the Shadows did to you."

Nodding, I closed my eyes and recalibrated my mind, forcing myself to detach my emotions from my words.

"I trained every evening. Worked on my magic until Sein was happy because he'd threaten me otherwise. He hated my initial resistance." I smirked bitterly. "He told me I was a fool for so many reasons. One of them was because I wanted to know what morality was, but he said I was too young to know anything about it. He hated me."

After the words hung in the air for a few moments, Sir Korbin asked, "And what about when you stopped resisting? What was the turning point for you in all this?"

The misery was brewing again. I had to order it away, but I couldn't. It wasn't an obedient dog at my heels awaiting commands, it was a menace, this misery, and they had to understand that.

"It was when we raided my hometown," I gasped. "Sein had us shift, and we killed Orshians. I've never... never been so disgusted with myself, and yet I was enjoying it, too."

Sir Korbin waited to be sure I was finished, then nodded. "Thank you for telling us. We would now like to investigate your memories. You cannot fabricate those."

Please, no, I thought miserably.

But it was the only way. They had to be sure I hadn't wanted to partake in all this straight away.

Lady Annisara came to me and settled across from me, closing her eyes. Her hursafar prompting came seconds later. I accepted her request and bit down on a shrill scream when she dove into the dark realm of my rotten memories, streaking across the landscape of slaughter and hazy feelings back to the beginning.

The memories began to play. It was not unlike when Annisara had purged me of my baines, though there was less agony considering otherworldly beings weren't involved. Regardless, reliving the same heinous acts again and again was scarring.

Relax, the shaman ordered when I started to twist in my seat.

I had killed the shopkeeper. How could I kill him, the sweet man? How could I? *How?*

How many times would I have to relive all this death and destruction?

You deserve it, my critical side sneered.

I deserved it and so much more.

Lady Annisara mercifully pulled away minutes later, dragging our connection with her. It died, and I slumped in my seat, sweat dripping down my temples. She looked back at Sir Korbin.

"She was definitely used," she said quietly. "I saw her resistance and felt her conflict. It never fully left her."

Sir Korbin agreed. "I remember. When I met the lass, she was quite the storm of internal struggle."

He smiled at me, a half-formed smile that didn't want to commit to fully-realized warmth.

"I remember it as well," Norva chimed in. "And as you saw from when we fled the compound, Twilight did not want her sister to die, nor did she want to be on the Shadows' side anymore." She nudged Il. "We remember."

Il nodded. Sir Korbin cleared his throat and said, "Good. We have strong evidence on your behalf that will spare you from any too-harsh punishments, Twilight."

I blanched, and he glanced at his jury members, then asked me to step out of the room. He would call me back when they agreed on what to do with me. If not death... what?

I stroked my scarred palms, searing from the memories, and fell into a chair in the living room. All the white space was too bright for a dark creature like me. I shouldn't have sat on any of it. I was a stain.

"Hey."

Cobi came around the corner and dropped next to me. Everyone else had gone upstairs. He was silent for a few moments before he said, "I know you've done some terrible things, Twilight."

No one could argue with that.

My friend sucked in a breath and added, "But you will move past this. It isn't over."

I sighed, dropping my chin onto my chest. "Easy for you to say. Sorry, but... you don't understand."

Cobi shrugged. "Maybe not personally. But I never gave up on my parents. They've done not-great things themselves."

I watched his eyes when he said this. An earnest shimmer of pain reflected from them. There we were, two young people from dysfunctional families, seeking lives apart from them. I shook my head and looked away.

Cobi took my hand. "These same hands *can* be used for good. A gift is what you make it, remember?"

I sighed and crawled inside my flesh, knowing this innocent boy was touching the same hand that had neglected him and murdered others. "Is this a motivational seminar, Cobs?"

He chuckled and let go of me. "Only if you want it to be."

Josha's laughter echoed somewhere upstairs. Cobi noticed me flinch.

"He doesn't hate you, Twi," he said softly. "Nobody here does."

I blinked away oncoming tears and whispered, "And that's the worst part. You *don't* hate me. But don't you think you should?"

Someone *tsked* nearby. Sir Korbin stepped out of his study, looked at me, and said, "No one ever got better by throwing a pity party, my dear. We have determined a sentence for you. It is time to move forward."

I stood slowly from the sofa. The Akristurans gathered around me.

"Well," I said cautiously, "What is my sentence?"

Sir Korbin removed his paper from his robes, unfolded it, and read the contents aloud.

"We, as the Akristuran jury, under the authority of Akristura and High Cleric Sir Javari Korbin, do find you, Twilight Mavericc Urik, guilty of numerous accounts of murder."

My chest caved. Of course, but what next?

He paused to let me process this before continuing. "However, due to complex extenuating circumstances and the defendant's initial resistance to such actions, we as the jury hereby sentence you not to death—or imprisonment—but to extensive service with the Akristuran people. This may include magical education, mandatory counseling sessions, and compliance in any actions that may be taken to combat Sharavak influence on scales both grand and small."

So... enslaving me to an undetermined purpose?

Sir Korbin saw my confusion and elaborated. "I have received indications from prayer and consideration that the Light God is invested in you, Twilight. You have a vital position in things to come, and we intend to nurture that. What this sentence entails is that you have no choice in the matter anymore whether you want to serve or not; you *will* do all you can to prevent as few losses as possible, and—"

"Losses?" I interrupted. "From what? A war? The end of the world?"

All the Akristurans' faces fell.

"Possibly," Sir Korbin answered gravely. "Take a look outside. And from your memories..." He steeled himself, clenching his fists. "This is what the Sharavaks want, as well."

I nodded slowly, digesting the terrible truths. Our planet was undoubtedly in peril, but the other worlds could save us.

"What about the realms Sein spoke of?" I asked." Can't we move there?"

"What realms? You mean the spiritual dimension?"

I shrugged.

"If that man saw realms," Sir Korbin muttered, "Then he was seeing things baines wanted him to see. This is our world, Twilight, the only one there is. It's possible it won't be here for much longer, but that's a discussion for later."

Maybe I'd signed myself up for more than I'd ever wanted with this sentencing. Then again, I'd always wanted adventure. Perhaps this was the fulfillment I'd sought so desperately as a younger girl. More importantly, following Akristura might be the cleansing I needed from the past's filth.

"Anyway." Sir Korbin cleared his throat. "Please enjoy the rest of the evening to yourself. Tomorrow, we'll begin training."

I thanked him and asked where I'd be sleeping. Norva seemed to know, so I started to follow her when Sir Korbin called me back.

"I know you probably feel you deserve much worse than this." He paused, looking at the floor. "And perhaps you do. But all of us are guilty of the misdeeds of our nature, whether we're baine-blooded or not. No one is innocent, Twilight. Bear that in mind."

He gave my shoulder a reassuring pat and turned, leaving me to my business.

I padded up to the second floor of the commune to see what my family was up to after glancing at my bedroom. Josha beamed when he saw me. I tickled him and kissed his forehead, moving on to Aullie. She was trying to kill a wasp in the window—with her magic.

"Don't!" I cried.

She whirled on me, tiny sparks of purple-edged magic in hand. Fear burned from her eyes.

I gently took her wrists and guided her away from the window.

"Do *not* use the dark magic," I warned her. "Otherwise..."

Aullie's green gaze bloomed wide, and she stepped back, whispering, "I'll turn out like you."

I lowered my head and nodded. "That's right. You don't want to be who I was, honey. Please be careful with your power."

Aullie jerked her head up and down and stifled her magic, then pointed nervously at the wasp repeatedly slamming against the glass.

"It's evil," she hissed. "Kill it!"

I looked at the creature in its ugliness as it strained for the waning sun, disgusted by the gangliness of its legs, its too-long torso, and the offensive colors under its wings. It wasn't beautiful by any means. Its barbed behind and aggressive buzzing it made didn't make me like it any more.

"Twi!" Aullie whined.

Cruel and mean. Like Sein. Like Father.

Like me.

The weapon of the insect world.

"Please kill it!" Aullie begged, tugging on my hand.

I gave the wasp one final glance and then pushed open the window, letting it sail away into the evening light.

CHAPTER EIGHT

I ENJOYED MY FIRST normal night of sleep in months. Maybe years.

Nightmares had plagued me long before they'd become real. Dreams running with restless things tormented me when I was younger, but the dawn of my new life warmed with light and fresh purpose. There'd been no darkness skulking in my mind. My body, and soul, seemed to have gobbled a breath clutched long past its due.

For my first morning as Akristura's own—how strange to form that thought in my mind—it felt good to wake with the sun. And in a small way, it even felt good to be alive.

"Hi," came my little sister's voice from inside my room.

I peeped at her from my blankets. "Good morning, Aullie."

And it *was* good. I was tired, as this was not my schedule, but I hadn't dreamed of death and endless murals of gore, so the day was already promising. Aullie maintained a certain degree of distance from me that did throw a taint over the morning, but I ignored it and asked her if she had something else to tell me.

She nodded. "Sir Korbin and everyone is downstairs. They're reading the Akristuran books together and want you to come, too."

Religious studies. Of course. I could only hope it wouldn't be like reading the Sharavak texts...

"I'll be down," I promised.

She turned to leave, but I called her back.

"Wait. Stay awhile. Don't be a stranger."

Aullie's brows raised. "I'm not a stranger."

"Then don't leave so soon. Don't you miss me?"

Please say yes. I can't bear a no.

Aullie paused. I saw the consideration cogs clanking in her mind while she considered how to respond. Finally, in a hesitant tone, she spoke the truth.

"It's hard to miss you when you left us to die."

Now it was my turn to pause. What could I do for her? How many hugs, apologies, and promises could I give to ease the hurt?

"You're right," I said quietly. "I did. But Aullie, I wasn't in my right mind. I was being used by people, and I lost my way."

Her eyes narrowed. "You *chose* to do what you did. You didn't have to be evil."

I stroked my collarbone, taking comfort in its valleys. "That is true. However, I originally intended to grow my magic so I could free you and the others. My plan didn't go as I'd hoped." I lowered my eyes, unable to face her.

Why were children so gifted at cutting people to nothing?

Aullie sighed. "Just come downstairs when you're ready." She started to pad off when she was intercepted by Josha.

"Seester! Good morning!"

He threw himself onto my bed and bounced into my lap. I laughed and pulled him to me, giving him a quick pinch on both his cheeks.

"Morning, Soup Boy. How are you?"

"I'm good. Everyone's waiting for you, Twi. What are you and Aullie doing?"

"I'm leaving," Aullie answered quickly.

Josh peered closer at her and asked, "You aren't mad at Twi, are you?"

Aullie shook her head. Josha looked at me.

"She's mad at you. I don't like it."

I shrugged. "She's allowed to be mad, Josh. So are you."

"But I love you."

"I'm sure Aullie loves me, too."

I didn't wait for her to affirm this. I doubted she would, and that was okay. Hurtful but acceptable.

Josha tugged my hand and "helped" me off my bed so I could get changed before leaving to go downstairs. Aullie lingered for a moment before joining him, and I didn't call for her again. Part of this new path was going to have to be contending with unpleasant reactions from the people I loved.

I found my dressers stacked with neat bundles of white, gray, and light-colored clothing, a welcome change from my wardrobe with the Sharavaks. After slipping into a plain white blouse and pants, I tentatively descended the steps into the living space. When I reached the main level, all eyes were directed at me.

"Good morning, Twilight," Sir Korbin greeted.

In my mind: *How do you feel?*

Fine, thanks, I replied.

Norva patted a spot beside her and Il in the crowd of white-clothed people assembled around Sir Korbin. I dropped beside her and made myself comfortable, and then she handed me a thick book and navigated to the right page for me.

"We're going over the full Story, in brief, today," she explained in a whisper. "Consider this your overview introduction to Akristura and what He has done in this world."

This had to be interesting. Would I learn the worthlessness of non-magicals in this lesson? Or that some sacred beast was waiting to be summoned and released on a rampage? I supposed I'd find out.

"Most of you here are familiar with the story in front of you," Sir Korbin began, "But it never harms us to remember."

I squinted at the words and tried to piece together this story. Some of them evaded my understanding—only the Aadbaineos texts from the Sharavak library had been fully discernible—when Sir Korbin began to read them aloud. I clutched the book and attempted to follow along as he did this.

"In a time of growing wickedness, when mortalkind's grievances against the Sacred and the natural order could be tolerated no longer, a great Light descended from the sun. Its brilliance surpassed all understanding; none could bear to look at It and live."

I tried to picture this light being so immense that it killed. The mental visual alone spun my mind.

"When the Light made landfall, It condensed, taking the form of a man clothed in similar brilliance. With His arrival came the quivering and parting of the earth; through its split mouth, a beast emerged, filled with darkness and fueled by the evils of the age."

Shuddering, I envisioned Arkyaktaas slashing its spindly limbs through the ground and jutting its twisted neck above the ceiling of the Void. I swallowed quietly and hoped this portion of the story would finish soon.

"So, darkness and Light declared Their war for all to see. But the darkness would not be defeated with ease."

No. It never is.

"As a battle between darkness and Light ensued, the man sought the face of the darkness, which had retreated into hiding. Every conceivable wickedness assailed Him as He passed through the Valley of Death. With no food to consume and no water to sustain Him, He could only march forth and share His message with every mortal in His path. He would not stop except to heal. He did not accept offerings of food, drink, or pleasure. Though games and comfort called Him, He resisted, for the dark beast awaited its sentence."

This was the point where the memories began to spill into my mind. Though they were hazed in age, their content was too mesmerizing to notice. It was as if the memory's quality was fully and crisply contained in the shape of human light passing by on an empty forest road.

The Valley of Death.

Somewhere in the Silver, by the looks of the trees.

I watched this lone man, whose features were too radiant to study, lay his hands on a prostitute. She had wanted to seduce him, but he hadn't seen her for this. Instead, by his relaxed stance and forward speech, he appeared to have *seen her.*

After murmuring something too quiet to make out, he passed the woman and continued through the woods. At a certain point, there were no more towns. The people had thinned out, leaving a final shadowed path ahead... out of which roared the beast's voice.

I recognized the tongue. It was speaking Aadbaineos, a language I could no longer understand. The alien phrasing and its dark, seeping drip was my only indication that this was what it had elected to speak.

Did accepting Akristura, something I still couldn't quite believe I'd done, sever my ties to the Sharavaks already? It must have. Strangely, I liked this, grateful I couldn't comprehend Aadyalbaine's slick speech. It didn't strike me as a loss.

In reply to the beast, the man passed into the darkness. It seemed to devour him in the way it pressed around him. Sir Korbin's words had to describe the following details, as there were no memories to display.

"Upon entering the dark realm where death resided, Akristura engaged the Dark One in combat with the magic He gifted to mortalkind, but which Aadyalbaine had corrupted for his own purposes. Light and dark clashed until Akristura's shape changed into that of a butterfly no larger than a child's thumb. Patterned in pure white, Akristura confronted the Dark One in his monstrousness. The Dark One easily dwarfed His humble form and size, and the small white butterfly was reduced to ash in minutes. As the dust settled, the Dark One emerged from his realm and gloated for all the world to see."

A fresh memory faded in. I tried not to gape at something a thousand years removed from me captured in another person's recollection, but Aadyalbaine's twisted form was not something to look upon lightly. Rather, darkly.

There goes my peaceful sleep.

Something more grotesque than Arkyaktaas—an accomplishment I hadn't known was possible—stepped out from the darkness Akristura had descended into in the last memory. My pulse accelerated at the gruesome marriage between humanity and baine-like, corrupted spider parts.

This beast looked larger than its Void-dwelling cousin. Twelve spine-smothered legs arched from a sleek abdomen, and each was tipped in clawed, human-like hands. Two tails waved behind it, black flags of war, but I would have rather looked at this end of the creature than its front.

The front was disastrous. The beast's neck was thick and short, flared with veins. Its face was none other than Sein's treasured Ulysyg mask, from its black bone spurs encircling its six pale eyes to the insect shape of its visage and pinching mouthparts. It was not an exact match, but Sein and I knew it was close enough.

Aadyalbaine, in his hideous and deformed majesty, shrieked his victory in Aadbaineos. His roar rippled over mountains and fields—and directly across a plain writhing with war.

Another memory filtered in, centering on two distinct groups engaged in combat. I recognized the pale robes of the Akristurans, their golden symbol shining across blood-spotted backs. Familiar, too, were the black cloaks of the Sharavaks hurling dark magic at their opponents.

Metal clashed against metal. Bones and arrows clattered into torsos. Great gusts of snarling, spitting magic detonated in midair, scattering men from mounts where many were trampled below.

One figure was apparent above the others on the Sharavak side. I wouldn't mistake those broad shoulders or obscene height. The face was young, but the eyes and energy were ancient.

Outside the memory, my heartbeat stuttered.

It shifted once more into a new image of Aadyalbaine. A tiny white butterfly—Akristura—was soaring at him from out of the dark realm, gleaming and whole. Aadyalbaine's distorted head turned. The cries of warmongering men echoed below.

Then, as if it was nothing...

A sharp light stabbed through the atmosphere. Its rays washed out the memory, forcing everyone viewing it back into the present. All of us collectively groaned and massaged our temples.

"Akristura's rebirth marked the Dark One's demise," Sir Korbin stated passionately. "He was crippled and forced back into the Void where he could no longer menace the world in the flesh. Instead, until the Hour in which humanity's wickedness once again reaches its peak, he will remain spirit."

"Excuse me," I said, "What does that mean? Do your prophecies indicate Aadyalbaine will rise again, but not in spirit?"

Sir Korbin's eyes brewed storms. He sighed and asked everyone to turn to the last chapter in our texts. Once there, I frowned and squinted at the title: "The End." Only there was no following text. I flipped back to the previous chapter, discovering a dissatisfying conclusion there.

"The End?" What does that mean?" I asked. "Is this really the end of the book?"

Sir Korbin shook his head. "That," he said gravely, "Is the title of the Lost Chapter. It was wiped out several hundred years ago during a Shadow raid. It's funny because they didn't bother burning or tampering with the rest of the texts, but they destroyed our conclusion. Now, we do not know what the future holds for this world. We only know that it will end at some time in an evil age."

Il narrowed his eyes. "No doubt that was the point. They wanted us doubtful to impair our faith."

Norva smiled softly at him and then at me. "Which has made us *more* faithful. We can rely on Akristura's history for everything but the future, which must be pieced together patiently. You can help us sort out the future part, actually, Twilight."

Sir Korbin agreed. "We'll speak more about that later. Let's close out this story with the final memory."

Everyone hushed again, and he introduced us to this concluding vision, which showed... no...

My heart bolted inside me as if it would tear through my chest. The broad-shouldered man I'd seen earlier was looking at me—*me*—as he rode directly toward us. The monster supporting him sneered, and when its lips slithered back, so did his.

His eyes burned. A flame of the nightmarish Void roared inside him, and it had been kindled to consume. To maim and kill. I reared back in the real world and struck someone's shoulder while he drew ever closer, prepared to smite me with the magic in his hand.

Then the light came. He was never able to finish me because I knew, in my bones, that *it* was over as the brilliance spread its power over us.

My wickedness. That of my friends. And even Sein Leidyen's, if he so desired. But he didn't desire it, so he and all his cohorts went toppling to the earth when the wave washed our darkness away.

Wailing followed. He'd struggled long to destroy Akristura. We'd seen him hunting the Light God in His vulnerable form, in the flesh and tendons He'd elected to clothe Himself in. Sein was always ready. We'd been prepared, too, hence the horrors draping the plains.

Blood. Heads. Other body parts no one wanted to see severed from their rightful places. It was all there, and Sein... his cries were the loudest. It was as if he no longer cared who heard him or respected him because Aadyalbaine—the Shadow deity—did not.

Not anymore.

In my own mind, I thought with a shiver, *Never again.*

Shaking, I pulled out of the memory before the others. Norva shot me a worried look. "Are you okay, love?" She asked gently.

I couldn't answer. Sein's screams had joined his others, and in witnessing his failure, I'd seen what might have been my own. Those hadn't been the cries of a man who believed he'd recover or that his god would smile upon him again. Nay. He'd lost, well and truly, when he'd failed to kill Akristura in the flesh.

"Twilight?" Sir Korbin prompted, joining Norva's side.

"I'm okay," I assured them. "I just... can we train now? I'd rather do that and—"

"Let those memories air out a bit," Sir Korbin said. "I understand. Thank you for watching them as long as you did."

I nodded. "But before we go, I do have one question."

It had bothered me throughout the story's unfolding.

Why?

"Why all of this?" I asked. "Why was this necessary, this wild story? Can you answer that?"

Sir Korbin smiled. "She asks good questions, doesn't she, Norva?" Norva agreed. "The reason," he explained, "Is because of what the Sharavak High Father did two thousand years ago, long before he forged his status."

"Was that giving himself to Aadyalbaine?" I asked, recalling Sein's own memories.

"Even before that. Our texts indicate his was the first heart to turn against Akristura when he was just a boy. Sein's mental and emotional rejection of Akristura began humanity's depravity and cast a shadow over us that would only darken in time. His curse lingers to this day in every human being, magical or not. It's why you will never be perfect. Because of Sein's choice, this is now impossible."

I shook my head at how my grandfather had shaped, rather, *un*-shaped, the world's fate. Had it really been that one decision that had turned the Light God against us?

"That isn't the end of the story, though," Norva promised when she saw my visible discomfort. "What you just saw *is* the conclusion of it."

"How so?"

It was a lot of lore to digest at once. I wondered if it would be easier for someone who hadn't already been put through the proverbial wringer with a former religion to grasp it all. And yet, between the memories and explanations, it was beginning to make sense. This story stirred me in unseen places where I knew my spirit must dwell.

"What you saw," Sir Korbin said, "Was the blotting out of the consequences of Sein's curse."

"What were the consequences?" I wanted to know.

Sir Korbin's mouth tightened. "The Forever Death. A one-way trip to the Void, but it's no vacation down there."

I shuddered, remembering. "No need to tell me twice."

And Mother's going there, too.

My stomach twisted.

"Anyway," he continued, "This was done because man alone cannot salvage himself. Akristura endured His trials and fought the living manifestation of death, Aadyalbaine, and perished for His efforts so that you and I might not die in that place the Sharavaks affectionately call the Void. There have been memories suggesting that His ministering to humans wasn't always pleasant, either. Some tried to kill Him along His journey. Sein was one of those people."

"Of course he was," I muttered.

"But the Light God was successful. He died and returned to life, promptly smiting the Dark One. At that moment, when that tiny, unassuming little butterfly touched that hideous beast, everything changed. Aadyalbaine's physical form withered, and his broken spirit was banished to the dark realm where he lacked a body. He still does, and we pray he still will for the foreseeable future." Sir Korbin grimaced and crossed his fingers.

"But if you still have questions later, as I'm sure you will, we can address those," he said. "I believe you wanted to train?"

He took me to a field past the commune. Its grasses were carefully clipped and cleared, and the thick Silver woods fenced off its perimeter in the distance. It was then that I saw the commune was not alone. It had brothers.

Sir Korbin waved to a couple on the porch of another large house-like structure, and beyond it, dotting the even, grassy terrain like white butterflies on a wildflower field, were several more.

"How many of you live on this land?" I asked, taken aback at the size of the Akristurans' people.

"Over a thousand," Sir Korbin answered. "When the Silver government began taxing us heavily for living in the city, we moved out here and gathered under eleven different roofs. If you notice, we use horses and carriages instead of automobiles."

I did notice, as several horse stalls surrounded each residential building.

"Why did they tax you so much?"

Sir Korbin chuckled awkwardly. "I think it's safe to say they don't care for us. We can't afford their fuel prices for transportation, nor a lot of their food. We mainly visit town to minister to the citizens or invite them to our congregation sessions like the one we had this morning."

"I see," I said. "Do people usually come?"

His faint smile wilted. "Not usually. Anyway." He gestured to the field. "Let's focus on something we *can* change for a bit; you and your magic. How do you feel right now?"

I shrugged. "Like death. That's normal, right?"

Sir Korbin's easy smile returned. "Sometimes. But it's not advisable to approach life with mourning and scorn. You can, but what good does it really do you?"

"Not much."

He nodded. "Right. Extend your arms, please. Try to draw out some magic."

While I did this, he asked, "Do you know the history of your power?"

I began the familiar scraping process. Breathing. Sipping in my intentions and feeding them to my cells.

Light magic, I coaxed internally, *Please come through.*

"I don't know," I finally answered when my palms refused to warm.

"It comes from Akristura. All magic was once light magic."

This surprised me. I couldn't focus while thinking about it.

Sir Korbin's palms instantly lit, and he raised them to display their flares of golden energy. "In the beginning, Akristura granted a select few human beings the ability to wield just a smidgen of His power. This magic was much like the kind you see here: benign and gentle." He tossed it at me. I twisted out of the way, and the orb dissolved on the shorn earth.

"Don't be afraid," he said softly. "Remember, lumensa won't hurt you if you're not trying to hurt its wielder."

I nodded, attempting to draw more out while he continued his story.

"He gifted this ability originally so that humans could create with it. As the builder uses materials in construction, the blessed human used this creative power to make his own beautiful things if he was chosen to receive it. But, of course, Sein Leidyen listened to Aadyalbaine's hateful whisperings in his heart and set his mind against Akristura, and the Dark One, well..." Sir Korbin paused, staring at me.

The only magic I'd been able to summon was black, swinging wildly into purple. I swallowed hard and clamped my hands shut to extinguish it. My scars burned when the skin met.

"He, in his corrupted form, discovered the new nature of *his* magic. He'd once been so lovely. So... pure."

I bit down on a scream at the heat searing my hands. I wanted the valdur *gone,* and I needed lumensa in its place, but still, the dark power burned.

"But he wasn't those things anymore. He changed when he was banished to the Void. Devolved, you could say, him and his supernatural friends. Aadyalbaine was the most powerful magical being in existence. That didn't stop when he was thrown from high."

Lumensa, please, lumensa, I begged myself, moisture pricking my eyes.

"It simply changed. The power to create that had been inherent to him reversed into the power to destroy. And the Dark One shared this power with humans. He got them drunk on it after corrupting those who were already magical and poisoning bloodlines with bainic interbreeding. Aadyalbaine is the true High Father of the Sharavaks."

My heart feathered against my ribs in panic. When the sweat broke, I knew the awful truth.

I can't summon light magic anymore.

It was with this thought that I turned, half-blinded by tears and the pain scratching through my palms, to hurl an orb of pure, crackling valdur at the nearest tree behind me. It struck with a savage thud, causing the trunk to tremble uncertainly. Neither of us said a word. Moments passed, and the tree, with a soft, shuddering sigh, descended to its demise on the forest floor.

Birds and insects cleared the area in droves. I watched with an empty horror in my chest until I finally wept, "I can't do it anymore."

"Do what?" Sir Korbin asked gently.

I gestured to myself and my hands with frenzied desperation. "This! The magic! Everything. I can't... I don't have lumensa in me anymore."

I lowered my head, seething and shivering with a despondent rage. That valdur had felt *right* soaring out of me. My Shadow self wanted to chuckle at how that tree had snapped like a matchstick or a finger. Yes, a human finger, crunching in my mouth—

"Twilight."

Sir Korbin drew me into an embrace. I didn't believe I'd ever enjoy human affection, but I was too shattered to refuse him.

"You have not lost lumensa. I promise." He straightened back out with his deep eyes evenly meeting mine. "It was never yours to lose. It has gone dormant. You know the nature of dormant things, right?"

I shrugged.

"They can be awakened. Will you let me help you stir Akristura's gift again? You belong to Him now. He will let you reclaim it."

I looked away, still wrestling with violent imaginings. Perhaps He would. But would I? Me, with these filthy hands and the bloodier mind that possessed them?

"Twilight. Please look at me."

I looked.

"Akristura very much disapproves of dark magic. It is not His desire for anyone to use at any time. Do you know how He refers to its practitioners, both magical and Non?"

"What?"

The Akristuran's gaze softened until it was a liquid of rippling sorrow. "He calls them abominable because the power they seek is not His. He refers to dark magic as a "perversion" and condemns the use of it—whether it be the consulting of constellations or the butchering of whole societies with it—as gravely perilous for the soul. If it is not of the Light, then it is of darkness, Twilight, which is why you must not practice it anymore."

I started to protest, "But I hadn't wanted to use valdur on that tree," when he stopped me with a raising of his hand.

"What happened, happened. I don't want you under the false impression that this will be easy. Frankly, I don't envy your position. You'll have to deny yourself more than anyone I've ever known. I'm not angry about that." He nodded at the fallen tree. "All I'm asking is that you try. Just *try*. And please, girl, let me help you."

You don't need help, Shadow me sneered. *You are a beautiful and vibrant abomination. Whatever esteemed deity calls you that as an insult merely envies your freedom.*

"What freedom?" I whispered.

"Pardon?"

I shook my head and removed my fingers from my collarbone. "So, I'm pretty far gone, right?" I closed my eyes and drove deeper into my magic. I'd drill and sift and search until I identified it: at least one meager speck of light, like the one that had protected me in my dream with Aadyalbaine many moons ago.

If that had existed during the ripest season of my undoing, then surely it existed now. I would pick it and savor it. Sweetness. The blooming, yearning tug of hope.

"I didn't say that."

I smiled through the last trickle of tears. "You did, kind of. You said you'd never met someone who'd have to "deny" themselves as much as me. That's hardly a compliment."

Sir Korbin opened his mouth to elaborate. I stopped him with my own raised hand.

"That's okay." My voice splintered on, "okay." I gulped down the tears coating my throat and whispered, "Because that's true. I am pretty... far gone."

I spread my arms and called for the magic again.

Lumensa... Akristura... if you hear me, why aren't you responding?

I raised my chin to the sky and let the sun spray over me. It tingled on my too-pale skin. It seemed I'd never flee my weaknesses.

"I am a monster," I croaked to the clouds. "Bloody, filthy, and savage. I've killed people." The words choked in my throat. Louder, I cried, "And I'm not the girl I once was!"

"Twilight?" Sir Korbin prompted.

I didn't hear him. I couldn't through the blood throbbing in my temples, spreading down to my scorched hands. Speaking my evils almost seemed to shake them loose like dirt packed into a hole. Like cakes of chicken excrement uprooted from a coop floor.

I smiled through a fresh wave of tears and wept, "But if this feeling I have right now is true..."

Loss and disrepair. A mangling of the mind. Tarnishing of the soul. And yet, a disquieting and strangely comforting sense that things hadn't *ever* been okay—

"Then I was never much of anything to begin with."

Warmth blasted in my open palms. I let my grin grow as wide as it wanted. It could consume my entire face if it wished. Why should I deny it this simple bliss?

I was broken. I always had been, hadn't I? Why was the girl before Shadowhood so different from the one trying to escape it now?

She wasn't. Sure, she hadn't been the sort of predatory horror that usually graced her family's nightly news, but neither had she been content. Old Twilight. What was she? Kind but naive and occasionally snarky to an unlikable degree.

Her peers hated her. Adults feared her, and her parents—nay, her entire family except for one very forgiving little soul—had wanted her gone.

And what had this made old Twilight?

Very.

Very.

Angry.

Laughing, I allowed these truths to breathe and take their leave from my spirit. I popped open an eye and observed my magic.

"It's..."

I could have cried again for all the purple lighting my palms.

Not fair. This is—

"Progress," Sir Korbin said quickly. He pointed to a faint glimmer of gold I'd missed, waving delicately amidst its shadowy counterpart.

There it was. The speck of light in the darkness.

My heaviness dropped, and I met Sir Korbin's eyes. He smiled with every ounce of warmth I had yet to conjure and said, "Well done. The sleepers rise."

"And the dead live."

I laughed, and the sound twisted into a newborn sob.

CHAPTER NINE

WE RETURNED TO THE commune. My training was finished for the day. Breaking back into my light magic was all Sir Korbin wanted from me for the time being, but as we walked, he asked me other things.

"I'm sorry to ask you more troubling questions, but it's imperative to know; what are the Shadows planning? Or what *was* on their agenda before you left them?"

My earlier heaviness settled back in, weighing in my torso. "They wanted me to usher in Myrkraas, the "Dark Hour." They made it sound like this would be the end of the world."

Sir Korbin smirk-grimaced. "Naturally. Can't have a story without planetary peril, eh?" He shook his head. "What was your role supposed to be in all this?"

"Maybe I should show you the memory," I offered weakly.

It was one of the many that graced my nightmares. Arkyaktaas's disfigured form reared in my mind, and I passed it along to Sir Korbin, who witnessed its horror secondhand. I let the memory play out until my blackout moment when the Void took on an equally frightening form, with shattering stars and curse-laden screams melting through a stifling heat.

I felt Aadyalbaine's rage anew.

"Silence!"

He'd shouted at me, and that had broken my mind. I'd never tasted such fear before. I'd experienced it plenty of times with the Sharavaks, but there were echelons of emotion, and Aadyalbaine had topped the charts.

Sir Korbin removed himself from the memory and apologized. "You've really *been there.* And that monster..." He sighed deeply. "I'll be frank; this doesn't bode well for us. Not that giant monsters usually do, but this looks like it came from Aadyalbaine. He must have taken a piece of his twisted form after the Absolution War and molded it into something else."

"What do you think we should do about it?" I asked.

He swept his hand over his brief black curls and groaned. "Don't know. We'd have to kill this thing, but there aren't enough of us to achieve that and fight off the Shadows protecting it. We're plainly outnumbered."

"Could the Silver be of any use? Surely we could appeal to them and enlist their help?"

Sir Korbin chuckled darkly. "The Silver and the Shadows serve the same master. That's a bust. The Bronze, on the other hand..."

I gnawed my lip and considered things. "The Silver is seriously on their side? How? And how will the Shadows fulfill their plans when I'm not around anymore? Sein and Aadyalbaine made it clear I was instrumental to waking the Void beast."

Sir Korbin nodded. "I'll tell you about the Silver sometime. There are things the world doesn't know about the Silver, and maybe it never should. Their faith in government would be rocked forever." He lightly clenched his fists before adding, "But at least the Silver should know something about Myrkraas. You bring up a valid point; what will be done now that the Myrk Maiden is gone? I believe someone in that horror house they call a capitol building will know, and we already have a good lead."

"Is it a lead I could follow?" I asked.

I needed to be useful. I had to fade the dark deeds of my past by painting over them with light ones. Benign ones that benefited the world and my new purpose if I was bold enough to pursue it. I had to be, didn't I? The alternative was unacceptable if my memories of Aadyalbaine and the Void were anything to go by.

I clenched my own fists and savored their residual burn.

"How sharp are your senses?"

I frowned. "What do you mean?"

"I mean," he said, "Have you generally had a sensitivity for light, sound, taste, and smell? Heightened sensory perception?"

I sniffed the air and tasted several flavors at once. Pollen from nearby flowers, faint smoke trailing from the commune chimneys, and even a very soft pulsing of horse heartbeats greeted my inquiry. I hadn't ever given it much thought—it was simply how I'd always been—but if I dwelt long enough on the horses, I might taste their blood. Everyone knew what happened when I got a whiff of that.

"Yes," I answered. "Even as a child. Light and sound and even being around people have exhausted me much more quickly than I think it does others. Little light flickers, small noises, all of them bother me. When we came into Syndbur, I felt assaulted. It was difficult to breathe. Don't even get me started on what I was thinking of doing to the citizens." I blew air out of my mouth.

Sir Korbin nodded. "It's as I thought, then. Your Shadow senses remain. I don't think those will ever go away, either; like your shape-shifting ability, it's inherent to your composition. However, shape-shifting harnesses magic. Smelling blood from a hundred paces away does not. Do those horses smell to you?" He pointed to the stalls.

"Yes, and I don't want to think about that right now," I admitted. "They, uh, smell a little too much."

"Fascinating," Sir Korbin breathed. "You really ought to use this to your advantage, Twilight. You may be able to "hijack" this part of your nature for benevolent purposes.

The challenge will be resisting the urge to *indulge* your physical traits. You will need to work the rest of your life to keep your appetites in check."

I agreed. "I'll add it to the mile-long list."

Sir Korbin grinned. "I imagine you'd be a good tracker. Well, we've got someone for you to track, but we'll save that for a later date. Right now, I need to train you, and you need to hone your skills. I don't think Akristura would fault you for using what you've been naturally given."

"That makes sense. When you're ready for me to get this person, I'm on it," I said.

"I like your ambition." His smile turned serious. "I'll be helping you, though. This individual isn't one to trifle with."

"Neither are most of my relatives," I replied, "But I've survived this far."

Using valdur had felt like using my life force. It stripped me of energy and sunk me into a lethargic low, forcing me to retire earlier that evening than I would have liked. I wanted to ask how everyone was doing to prove that I was willing to detach myself from my barbaric identity, but my body cried against this.

So, with reluctance, I vanished into sleep.

Upon first entering the dream realm, I was relatively at peace. If anything, my mind yawned surprisingly empty. This blissful nothingness did not remain.

I had forgotten one of the principal side effects of valdur.

"Hi, daughter."

That was not a feminine voice. I spiraled to face the speaker.

My imaginary breath caught. I hadn't expected this. But when confronted with that knowing smile and the dark eyes that simmered above it, I remembered the regular consequences of using dark magic.

Yes, it had gifted me the ability to connect with my mother.

Now it granted me access to my other parent.

"Father," I whispered.

My dream heart chugged a little faster.

Damion was no small man. Like his father and mother, he possessed a striking height and equally brilliant eyes. If possible, they'd darkened since I'd seen him just nights ago. His lips coiled into a satisfied smile.

"How interesting to find you here."

I inhaled quietly. "Yes. In my mind, where you don't belong."

Father smirked. "I must because I'm here. It's funny, really. There I was, minding my business. Then, I got this sudden flash of surroundings that weren't my own. Your emotions—every one of them—came pouring through."

I didn't answer.

He cocked his head as if determining my prey status and asked, "So. Where are you?"

"Like I'd tell you that," I snapped.

Father cracked a broader smile. "You don't need to. I already know. Your outburst yielded enough to piece together. Well, how do you like being the Light God's lickspittle?"

"Shut up!" I hissed. "Get out of my head. You call me names, yet you run around trying to end the world for *your* "god?" *I* just want to save it!"

"No, you don't." Father started to pace around me, his black, patterned robes gliding over the fog. "You know what you are. An abomination. I told you months ago that I knew your desires. I did not lie." He paused, outstretching a hand to touch me. I flinched away, and he shook his head.

"I've lost many things in my life, Twilight. Why must I also lose you?"

I cackled and stepped back, growling, "You are not trying to manipulate me right now."

Father shrugged. "I suspect I won't have to. You give me everything I need to work with. That I'm even speaking to you is confirmation that your inability to control yourself will be yours and everyone else's downfall."

"No. I am on the right path now, and—"

"Why?" He interrupted.

"What?"

He gestured to me. "Why are you on the right path? You Akristurans are awfully self-righteous." His eyes narrowed to black slits.

"Okay," I hissed. "Rich coming from the High Father. How high are you right now?"

"Oh," Father chuckled, letting a gust of black magic unfurl on his palm and seep into his nostrils, "Very." He closed his eyes briefly. "Don't pretend you don't also miss the high."

I did. He had me there. The thrill of valdur did not outpace the swiftness with which it destroyed lives, though. I knew this intimately. Shadow Twilight knew but did not care.

Father didn't care, either.

But do you know the path you're on?

"Why," I asked softly, "Are you doing this? Why do you insist on following in your father's footsteps?"

He flinched. It was nearly imperceptible, that crease in the corner of his eye, but I'd struck a nerve.

"I'm sure I'll be seeing you soon," he replied before vanishing into the mist.

Morning came, bringing decisions with it.

I hadn't slept soundly since the dream with Father. The mere knowledge that that man could access my mind stilled me with fear for the rest of the night. I'd drifted through shallow gasps of sleep, never quite able to settle down until dawn.

Now I had to decide what to do about it. Tell Korbin?

I might have. But it was Mother who held me back. Why hadn't she appeared during my sleep, the parent I wanted to see?

"I can't lose you," I whispered to my starstone.

It wasn't prudent to keep exercising valdur, but sacrificing my mother, who was to perish in Toragaine forever, for a little more security didn't seem like a fair tradeoff. I didn't want to think further about what this might entail for my tentative new relationship with Akristura or His people.

No, it was best to keep the Father dream to myself.

"Twilight."

Aullie again. I sat up in bed and threw a smile her way, and she shot a shy one back.

"Come downstairs. Lady Annisara is waiting for you with Suze and Josh."

"Okay. Thanks for letting me know."

When she turned this time, I clenched inside at the slope of her nose. It was strikingly resemblant to Father's. His haunted face floated to mind, and I called out, "Wait. Come here. Please."

Aullie's mouth fell. "Did I do something wrong?"

Breaking my heart, that's what you do wrong, but how could I ever complain about that? I thought desperately.

I opened my arms. "Can I have a hug?"

Aullie shrugged. "Don't really want one right now. See you downstairs."

If my heart was breaking before, this sentence spelled its doom. It shattered, and tears sprinted over the fallen pieces down my cheeks.

"Is it always going to be like this?" I asked.

My sister's gaze fell. She shrugged again and answered, "Maybe."

I touched my palms. "I don't want to rush you. I just wish..." I looked away and realized my following words would be foolish. "That things could be as they once were. Minus, you know, the fighting and everything. I don't miss that."

I missed my family, though. Family meant fighting sometimes, but I could live with this. I couldn't live with my little sister or anyone I loved hating me.

"I'm sorry, Twi," Aullie replied. "It's hard. You really scared me and Mom and Josh. I don't want to be scared anymore, but I still am. Will you forgive me?"

Would *I* forgive *her*?

"That's not even a question, honey. There's nothing—absolutely nothing—that I need to forgive you for. *I* need forgiveness, but I won't force it from you," I said.

Aullie nodded. "Okay. I'll think about it, Twi. Maybe I'll forgive you someday, but right now, I'm hungry!"

She dashed downstairs, where the scent of eggs and meat hovered, enticing and repulsing me simultaneously. I didn't enjoy wrestling with opposing parts of my nature. Humanity and Shadowhood did not combine well, and traumatic memories didn't help my case. I swallowed, trying to blot out the tang of the meat in my nose, and descended to join Lady Annisara and my siblings in a small circle by the window wall.

Lady Annisara dipped her head. "Good morning, Twilight."

I nodded back. "Morning."

Her silver eyes scoured mine, narrowing with her growing frown. "You seem tired. Too tired. I don't like the energy around you. Did you sleep okay?"

No.

"Yes."

Ah, there it was. The sting of a lie.

As I suspected, she wasn't convinced. I ignored her gaze, and mine strayed to the pulse in her neck. How musical. The way it thumped was—

"Please sit." The shaman pointed to the floor.

I settled beside Susenne at the end of the group and tried to meet her eyes. She didn't look at me, so I sat back and let Annisara introduce the purpose of this grouping.

"We have another lesson today. My spirit tells me I should explain what makes the Sharavaks evil and why their ways defy Akristura's wishes for the world." She sighed. "I must also tell you the Dark One's role in all this. First and foremost, we need to establish something; Aadyalbaine is not a god."

Somehow, this wasn't terribly surprising. Aadyalbaine and his people seemed almost desperate to "win," but if they'd already been defeated and were simply allowed to run their course for a while, they probably didn't overpower Akristura. In any case, what was darkness when the light was turned on? It had to acknowledge its superior counterpart and retreat.

"Aadyalbaine," Annisara continued, "Is a creation like you and me. When humans came to being on Aash, he despised us, thinking us filthy and lesser. In his rage, he wanted to kill us. Obviously, that didn't go according to plan, but even now, he lives. Twilight, I believe you've had the displeasure of meeting him?"

"That's right," I muttered.

"How was that?" Susenne asked with an edge of scorn.

"It sits comfortably at the rock bottom of my list of favorite life experiences," I replied quietly.

Her lips twitched in a smirk, and she looked away. The shaman's eyes sharpened again.

"Aadyalbaine came to "maim and kill." It is why this phrase is oft spoken by the Sharavaks, a race that he corrupted into existence. He wanted to defy Akristura and spit in His face by taking His favorite beings and warping them into beasts."

"Ouch. I'm right here," Susenne mumbled.

Lady Annisara ran agitated fingers down her braids. "It is the truth. But, as you will continue to learn as you live here, your genetic composition does not have to define you. Each of you has responsibilities to Akristura and your fellow man. Your grandfather did not realize this at his tender age. It was Sein Leidyen's resentment of Akristura that first began the seeping of the human curse. He'd introduced something dark into us, opening unclosable doors to the Void. Aadyalbaine saw him for his potential to serve Akristura greatly, so he tainted and destroyed him in fear and spite." Her eyes centered back on me.

I shifted uncomfortably and looked at the ground. Susenne chuckled.

"Is something funny?" Annisara asked. Her voice had its own edge now.

Susenne shrugged. "Is being the granddaughter of some old maniac funny? I find it sad."

"That old maniac," Annisara said carefully, "Caused irreparable damage to millions of souls. I would not be surprised if he single-handedly filled most of the seats in Toragaine." She shook her head. "The good news is that the curse he brought upon us, while it continues through all generations, is not final. This is what Akristura was killed for.

Twilight here is not the same person she once was, and I would advise all of you to support the lifestyle change she's made. It is major. We are proud of her for taking this crucial step." Her face finally broke a smile.

"What step was that?" Susenne asked. "She just asked the god thing to save her, and booyah, she's golden?"

And just like that, the shaman's smile fell.

"Perhaps it's best if you go train," she responded gruffly, her face burning scarlet.

"Susenne is right," I said quickly. "That's basically how it went because... can you elaborate, ma'am?"

"Because Akristura, despite any egregious action or tongue-wagging, loves," Annisara answered. "Some seek Him. Others don't. Twilight didn't realize she needed Him until she gave her life some serious thought. Most people choose to live apart from Him. That is their choice, and they are free to make it, though at the expense of the Forever Death. So, yes. She asked for Akristura and..." She blinked. "Booyah. She's golden."

"Wow." Susenne sat back on her crossed legs and thought for a moment. "That's really it? You guys don't do any rituals, hunts, sacrifices, or anything for His favor?"

Annisara shook her head. "Anyone who earnestly reaches out can make contact with the Divine. Akristura is never far. Anyway."

"On to what makes the Sharavaks evil," Susenne grumbled.

"Do you miss being evil, Suzy?" Josha asked.

My sister looked at him, and her eyes briefly softened. "I don't know."

"Everyone likes evil, child," Annisara said, her voice finally warming with compassion. "You don't have to be bainic to understand that. But there are boundaries in this world that should not be crossed. Can either of you girls tell me something the Sharavaks made or encouraged you to do that felt wrong?"

"How about everything?" I mumbled.

Susenne said, "They glorified murder."

Annisara nodded. "No doubt. They're a society of death. Twilight?"

I reflected on my closest friends in that compound. They hadn't been the elites. Little power pulsed through their blood. This had humanized them, in a way, as they'd never been able to drug themselves on their own magic.

Mirivik. Shi. The other Zyvienkts.

Solshek.

I winced. "They had rigid power structures. Treated the less magical like cattle. They also broke up my family." My eyes slid to Susenne, who stared straight ahead and said nothing.

Aullie stood from her spot. Moments later, arms circled around my neck. I smiled and patted the tiny white hands.

"Thanks, kid," I whispered to her.

"Sorry I didn't do it earlier," she said sheepishly. "I'm still scared of you, though."

I chuckled softly and told her this was okay. She returned to her seat, and I noticed Lady Annisara processing the exchange with approving eyes. As soon as Aullie sat down, Josha hugged me, too.

Susenne glared at him and snapped, "What am I, chopped organs?"

Josha paused, his gaze widening with fear, and I urged him to hug his other sister. Susenne sneered and hissed, "No, don't. If neither of you wanted to do it at first, I don't want you doing it now."

"Honestly, Susenne, you're being too much," I said, but Annisara cut me off.

"I see what you mean about the family part," she muttered. "While you're here, please abstain from using dark magic. Additionally, you are not to value your physical senses above your consciences. Translated: if it seems wrong, don't do it."

"Define wrong," Susenne pressed.

Annisara snapped her fingers and pointed to the front door. "Outside. Train, both of you. We'll continue this discussion later."

Susenne looked like she would stay put until the shaman fixed her with such a sharp stare that she finally cried, "Alright!" And stamped away. Annisara dismissed my other siblings, telling them she'd be with them and their mother shortly, and then she pulled me aside.

"I don't need to tell you your sister is struggling," she said quietly. "She's very young, even younger than you, and is understandably taking all this differently. I sympathize with it, but I don't have the patience for her behavior right now. I need some time to adjust." Annisara sighed. "Will you train with her, please? She clearly has unresolved issues with you that some together time may mend."

"Yes," I said. "And you're not wrong there. She's always hated me. It's dumb for me to think it would change now. Even Aullie doesn't trust me, and she's right not to." I massaged my collarbone and whispered, "But maybe I can get somewhere with them through magic. It's a point of common ground."

Annisara patted my shoulder. "Try it. Your relationships matter more than you realize."

CHAPTER TEN

S USENNE WAS JUGGLING OSHKAS—NO, *orbs*—when I joined her outside in front of the commune. She didn't look at me when I positioned myself across from her and beckoned my magic. Hers, as expected, was black.

That was okay. So was mine.

"I'm surprised he trusts you out here with me," she said sharply before letting her magic die down.

"Who?"

She nodded at the building. "Korbin. Didn't you almost kill him yesterday?" Her thin lips twisted into a cruel smile.

"No, that was a tree," I replied, "But I see your point."

I dove back into myself, straining to find what I'd identified yesterday. It intoxicated me to search for it, as it had ages ago when I'd first learned I could heal. Such a wholesome, warm, enveloping feeling, like a hug from a parent. Akristura had manifested that in me. It hadn't come from myself because the only thing I was capable of producing was—

"More dark magic? You couldn't get it out of your system yesterday?" Susenne challenged.

I glared at my blackened palms and their tingling burn before dropping my hands in frustration. "I just started this. So did you. We won't be perfect, but we have to improve. Do you want to?"

"Want to what?"

"Improve."

Susenne shrugged and rekindled her magic. She tossed it at the nearest bush, reducing it to cinders.

"I wouldn't do that if you can help it," I said softly.

"You're not Mom, and you're not Sein," she snapped. "I don't take advice from you, Myrk Maiden."

She spat "Myrk Maiden" like coriusg and probably hoped it'd eat away my dwindling patience. She wasn't wrong.

"What's your issue?" I demanded. "You don't get to talk to me like that, *Zyvienkt*. Yeah, I said it. You want to use their terms? I'll call you what you are, then. Learn your place."

I shook my head and started to reignite my magic again when she opened her fist and chucked her own at my head. I dodged the swirling black sphere before it sank into my skull and snarled, "What. Was. That?"

She opened her mouth to snap something back when Sir Korbin came charging out of the commune, his face blooming crimson and his nostrils flaring worse than Susenne's ever could. He pointed a finger at Susenne and growled, "How dare you, young lady."

"What?" She cried. "I wasn't going to—"

"Kill her? Paralyze her? What was your intent in aiming for the head if those things weren't it?" He yelled.

Susenne's brows lifted almost into her hairline. "W-what? I didn't... that wasn't what I was trying, I swear!"

Sir Korbin's jaw softened, and he asked, "You really don't know?"

Susenne tried and failed to stammer a response. He nodded to himself and stepped back, his thick brows drawing together in contemplation.

"I see. So he never told you about aiming for the head. Figures. He probably thought it'd be a cheap, no-account way of killing someone. Not interesting enough to pass along, perhaps. Or maybe he was afraid it'd be used against him."

"Sir Korbin?" I prompted.

He looked at me and explained, "Striking an opponent's head with magic is one of the easiest ways to finish them. Yes. Finish for good. Even lumensa can do this in a combat setting. Neither of you," he hissed, glaring at Susenne, "Shall ever perform such an action on each other, or anyone else you love, again. The mind contains the essence of a man's being: his thoughts, choices, emotions, and personality. That is sacred. It should never be aimed for unless you intend to kill or severely disable your opponent. Is that understood?"

At first, Susenne looked like she would give her assent. But then she glanced at me, and her green eyes hardened to cold, dull jewels.

"I hear you went easy on *her* yesterday when she misused her magic," she accused.

"Not the same scenario," Sir Korbin replied. "Twilight wasn't aiming for anyone's head. She aimed for a tree. But let this be a lesson to you both to guard your heads in combat. Araveh forbid you perish because of something you didn't know."

"Araveh?" I questioned.

"Yes. It's the paradise Akristura has created for His people when they pass. Aadyalbaine has his Toragaine. Akristura has Araveh. Look forward to it if and when you find yourself at death's door."

Susenne scowled and marched off, apparently over the whole conversation. I started to follow her when she snapped back and hissed, "Stay away from me." This time, I decided to respect her disrespect. If all my relatives except Josha wanted to hate me, I supposed they had a right to, didn't they?

What had the rest of us done but fight, anyway? These wounds would be raw for decades, let alone days. In my desperation, I longed for someone to accept me, but it seemed the people who were supposed to wanted nothing to do with me.

"It's not new, is it?"

I turned to Sir Korbin. "What isn't?"

"The family issues."

I shook my head.

He nodded. "I see that. Enmity like that doesn't breed overnight. I hope you'll learn to forgive her, even if she never forgives you, Twilight." He smiled dolefully, and the smile reminded me of the secret I'd stashed inside me that morning.

"Before I go in there," I said, "I need to tell you something. It happened last night."

His brows raised, and he motioned for me to continue.

"When I used valdur yesterday, it opened a mental door to my father. He was able to visit me last night in a dream. He said he knew where I was, and I can't bear the thought of that. What if he comes by here and brings a band of Shadows? What if, since you suggested they're friends with the government, they send the Silver after you?"

Sir Korbin's lips twitched in amusement. "I appreciate you telling me this, Twilight. That is an alarming ability and another reason to take your magic seriously. Your father can't know where we are just by your surroundings, though, because *you* don't know where you are. By that, I mean that you don't remember the journey up here because you were unconscious. Something like a shape-shifting moment and all that." He grinned. "As for the Silver? I don't feel your father has the time or energy right now to move them on his behalf against us. We'll consider that more carefully if things get worse, but I sense we are reasonably secure for now."

I loosed a relieved breath. "That makes me feel a little better. Thanks. And I'm sorry about yesterday." I gestured to the front door. "No one's really taking that well, clearly."

He waved me off. "Your sister has a personal problem. You do, too, and yesterday was us beginning to work through that. You're a bit keyed up right now, so why don't you do something else today and take your mind off that?"

I decided I would. Inside, I found Aullie and asked her if she'd like to learn more about her magic. I could help my sister if I couldn't exercise my own.

"I guess we can," she mumbled, fidgeting with her hands. "Do you promise not to be mean if I mess up?"

"I would never," I assured her. "Why don't we find something to heal? We can start small and go slow, okay?"

She nodded. "Okay. I guess I can trust you."

"Well," I said, "If you decide that you can't, you don't have to continue. I'll go do something else. Susenne didn't want to practice magic with me, so I thought you might."

"I have wanted to," she admitted, "Ever since Aunt Carleigh died."

The last word choked out of her in a wisp. I gently pulled her close and wrapped an arm around her, melting at her tears.

"Honey..."

What could I say? No one could tell me something that would erase *my* pains and regrets. This tiny girl hadn't even tried to do something wrong. It had simply happened with all the inevitability of the sun rising and the war between dark and light intensifying.

"There is no way," I began slowly, "That you could have saved her if it was her time to pass. I believe that it was." Her tears scampered faster. She dug her face into my front and shared her liquid warmth, chilling my heart.

"I did something wrong," she wept.

"No. You did nothing wrong, sweetie. You did your best. And you know what? I couldn't have saved her, either. I was stuck, trapped in that beast body," I told her with not a little bitterness.

I'd failed my aunt, who had killed a Sharavos with impeccable prejudice. Aullie hadn't failed anyone. She hadn't even been aware of her power, nor were the rest of us when it briefly manifested.

"I really wanted to save her, too, sis," I said quietly. *"I failed. But maybe I wouldn't have been able to make it happen, either. Whatever happened, we can't blame ourselves for it. We tried. We both know that much."

Aullie sniffled. "Is trying okay? Even if it doesn't work?"

It certainly didn't *feel* okay.

"It does count," I told her.

"And Carleigh won't be mad at me wherever she is now?"

I shook my head. "Of course not. I'm sure she'd be very proud."

I guessed it depended on where she'd gone. To Akristura's Araveh, or to the horrors embracing the dead in the Void? Her final destination couldn't be dwelt on. No one had the answers, and what was done was done.

"Let's focus on happier things, like developing your magic. You weren't aware you had any before, right?"

"No," she whispered.

"Okay. Nothing wrong with that. It's not like I knew about mine, either."

If I had, maybe I could have planned better.

"I want to heal Norva's plant," Aullie said.

"A plant? Interesting. Lead the way."

She took me upstairs to hers and Josh's bedroom and pointed to a small, wilting white flower on her nightstand. She cupped its drooping head and looked to me for instructions.

"Uh..." I paused, and my heart skipped at her sweet, expectant half-smile. "Sometimes, it helps me to close my eyes. Try that. While you have them closed, calm your mind by letting any bad or scary thoughts leave. Focus on the feeling of goodness. Think about healing and light."

Aullie nodded vigorously and squeezed her eyes shut, taking her own dive into the magical realm within. No matter how often I used lumensa or witnessed it, it never ceased to amaze me how different the summoning process was. Valdur taxed a person. It felt like a withdrawal. Lumensa was challenging when smothered in shadow, but otherwise, it lent itself easily to selfless motives. I wondered if Aullie, with her nascent, chaotic magic, would experience that now.

I watched her closely and studied her hands. Gentle energy began to beam from her presence before sparking in her palms. She was doing as I'd suggested, and it worked.

So why won't it work for me?

It seemed simpler to give advice than to follow it.

A full minute passed before my sister's magic revealed itself in gilded fingers that closed around the flower. She peeked when she felt the warmth pouring through, and a smile almost as bright as the magic lifted her face.

"I did it!" She cried, urging more of the magic forth.

"You did! Good work," I congratulated her. "But don't get too excited while handling it because it can change on a whim. Be mindful of that, okay?"

She barely seemed to hear me in her awe, but she nodded and coaxed more lumensa onto the flower. As it was with lumensa and whatever it touched, the withered plant began to change. In place of its sagging petals were perky, verdant scoops lapping up the golden power. Aullie finally stopped and clapped her hands in delight once the restoration was complete. She turned to savor my reaction.

"I did good, right?" She gasped.

I smiled and stroked her hair. "Very. You'll have made Norva so happy. Shall we go tell her?"

"Yes!"

As she scampered away from the nightstand, she collided with me and gave me a quick hug.

"Thanks, Twi," she giggled, fleeing just as soon as she'd gifted me her affection.

Josha trailed in moments later and gaped at the new flower adorning the table.

"Wow! It's so pretty now. Is that a new one, or did you fix it, Twi?" He wanted to know.

"Actually, your sister Aullie healed it," I informed him proudly.

Josh's cheeks filled with a smile. "That's so cool! I wish I had magic."

"Maybe you will someday, buddy," I said, kissing his forehead. "Maybe you will."

I was content with my deeds for the day despite the earlier incident with Susenne. Aullie, in her forgiving youth, was discovering herself. Hopefully, she'd learn I didn't intend to be her enemy.

Not anymore.

There was one person I hadn't spoken to much since coming to the commune, though. He was alone on the balcony, overlooking what could be glimpsed of Syndbur from his vantage point.

"Hey."

Cobi's blue eyes flicked my way, and he broke a grin. "What's up?"

"Not much. I wanted to see how you're doing. How are you taking all this?" I asked, gesturing to everything at once.

"Well," he said slowly, "Akristuran lore is kind of fascinating. I'm having fun with it. You?"

I didn't have an answer. I supposed I shouldn't have asked a question that was commonly turned on the other person. Cobi seemed to understand because he waved it off, but I didn't want it dismissed so easily. Honesty pleaded for release.

"I don't know how I'm doing," I blurted. "I asked for Akristura, and that changed something in me, but I'm still me. The difference is I'm aware of what "me" *is* now. It's kind of screwed up."

Cobi's answering smile sagged with a touch of mourning. "You're not wrong. But you feel like moving forward now, right? You can tell me the truth if you're not."

I paused. My spirit had been irreversibly awakened as if its peak understanding and breadth of wisdom were now fully unfurled. That had to be the Light God's doing. Before, my understanding cramped and ached like a muscle that wanted to stretch but couldn't. It didn't know how.

The voice. Sein had preferred me pained and unaware of myself.

Aadyalbaine had liked it, too, and so had I. It felt *good*—not right, but grotesquely satisfying—to maim and kill. To chug another's blood and feed on their pain. Void below, my broken appetites *treasured* that feeling.

I looked over my hands and vaguely appreciated the brutal scars and what they symbolized. They remembered my suffering. They'd mapped my brokenness and celebrated what I'd endured for my former dark purpose. It was strange, but I didn't miss it upon reflection. What composed my unseen being rejected and recognized it for the horror that it was, but my flesh...

It wouldn't mind taking a bite out of you, I thought desperately as I looked at my friend.

"Twilight?" Cobi said softly. "Do you not want to move forward?"

I parted from my sudden physical longings and answered, "Yes! I mean, no, I don't not want to move forward. I mean, I *do* want to move forward." I sighed and pulled my fingers through my hair. Cobi watched with faint amusement.

"I know you do," he replied. "Know how I know?"

"How?"

"Because." He turned around to face me fully and leaned against the balcony railing. "I remember who you were before we were separated."

I winced at that word.

Abducted, stolen, and stored away like canned food is what you wanted to say.

"Who was I?" I asked.

It was a serious question. Sometimes, I scarcely remembered.

His smile softened with the precious few memories he had of us. Some of them, I thought, recalling how I'd almost killed him, weren't so precious.

"You were a girl who was adventurous but afraid. You were willing to throw away your entire life to escape the people who enslaved you. And don't make that face; they did enslave you. You can't be blamed for everything that happened."

I swallowed a rising throat lump. "Is that really what you believe?"

He nodded. I bit back tears and a growing smile.

"You're all too kind. Honestly. Don't think I'm radically different now, though. I don't want you under any false impressions. I murdered a whole tree yesterday. Did you hear about that?"

Cobi shook his head and stifled a laugh. "Yes, I did. Doesn't seem like a proud moment, but actually, it is. You were trying to bring out light magic and do the right thing. I don't know the mechanics of magic." He threw his hands up. "But it seems pretty emotional. It's gotta be tough on you."

"It is," I admitted. "Is living here and everything tough on you?"

"I'll be honest, I didn't see my life going in this direction," he said. "You know, being stolen by sorcerers, unconscious for weeks, and finding myself in the middle of a huge mess like this. I'd no idea what would happen when I decided to run away with you."

Memories frolicked through our minds once more, coruscating with the brilliant force of a forgotten sunny afternoon. Sweetness dusted the former days, but terror had also injected them with an inescapable poison. We'd been people with lives before the Shadows. When they'd forced us to run, the former things were thrust into disarray, not unlike the dazzling noise and lights scattering haphazardly across Syndbur.

The boy would have to become a man. Perhaps he, with his delicate, blushed cheeks and soft eyes, wasn't ready to mentally cross the adolescent threshold. And I, with my dark desires warring against a newborn spirit, wasn't prepared to become human.

"I hope you don't leave," I said suddenly. "I hate to endanger you. I really do. But I can't lose you, either. Is that selfish?"

He lifted his eyes from their preoccupation with the ground. Their blueness punctured me, and their pure tone constricted my heart. How was his a face I'd once wanted to kill?

"I don't plan on leaving. I can't. Part of it is because I can't forget you. Don't ask me about the rest of the experience because I can't quite remember that." He cracked a grin. "Being unconscious does that to you. But no, I don't think I'll leave. There's nothing for me to go back to, anyway. No, my purpose is here. I get the feeling I'm supposed to be part of all this, too. Whatever "this" even is."

I chuckled and said, "Look at that. Being a stalker has given you access to world secrets, and it's made you instrumental to the plans and schemes of world leaders."

Cobi loosed a nervous laugh. "Yeah, well, I kind of hope I'm never *that* important again. I'll stay on the down-low if I can. Still, I'm gearing up to do something useful. Just haven't figured out what it is yet."

I crossed the distance between us and spun into his side to put a hand on his shoulder. "You're already useful—as my friend. That's as much as anyone can ask for, especially me. But that's enough heaviness for now. I like to brood, but—"

"You, brood?" Cobi snorted.

I rolled my eyes. "Yes, I know. Shocking. Really, though, let's do something fun. How about..." I thought for a moment, wondering what harmless entertainment we could get up to. "How about we look for butterflies in some of these fields? There are bound to be some pretty ones."

Cobi's eyes flashed with shadows, and the memory of the beautiful black butterfly we'd found in a meadow running from the Sharavaks slithered to mind, bringing its horror with it.

"This time, no butterfly gets hurt," I told him. "Promise."

CHAPTER ELEVEN

"**G**OOD MORNING, HUNTRESS."

Sir Korbin's resonant tone filled my bedroom early the next morning as a rooster's crow signals dawn's light. I roused quickly and sprang up from under my blankets, drinking him in from a distance.

"Sorry to get you up so early. I had your little sister come peek in on you to ensure you were decent, and it seems you are. How do you feel about an adventure today?"

His suggestion sliced through my sleepy stupor, and I shrugged. "Okay. Where to?"

"Oh." He grinned. "To a place that indulges the senses. They call it Syndbur. Ever heard of it? It'll be a fine place to fine-tune yours." He withdrew from the threshold and pulled the door toward him, whispering, "I figured we could get out of here as the city's waking up. It'll be in full swing in another hour or so. I'll let you get ready."

The door snicked shut, leaving me to wonder what devious errand the Akristuran leader was planning for me. Fine-tuning the senses? I hoped he didn't have too much faith in me. If he exposed me to certain sweet-smelling liquids, I'd be swinging more to the indulging side rather than refining.

Unsophisticated people did not simply adopt sophisticated actions overnight.

I let my curiosity guide me into my clothes and out the front door, where Sir Korbin waited in a small carriage.

"Climb in. The trip's not too long. We can watch the sun rise."

Indeed, morning's blush was beginning to warm across the horizon. Dawn carried an almost sugary promise, whereas the cold glow of sunsets ushered in a sense of sadness and a curious reminder of death. I rubbed my collarbone and wished my brooding thoughts away. It was not the time for them.

"How are you today? Feeling especially sensory?" Sir Korbin asked.

"I guess. Don't let me eat too much bread, and I should stay sharp all day," I answered.

He grinned. "Noted."

So jovial today, I thought.

He noticed my expression and said, "Twilight, I'm excited to work with you. I believe your senses and intuition may yield good information in time. I pray Akristura watches over you in this."

I nodded, still under the sluggish grasp of sleep, but dawn's stirring scents and sounds expanded my awareness. I captured and tasted the earthy aroma of slain forests in the chimney smoke, which had sprawled over the commune and fields. A sweetness of waking blooms eased the heavy scent while sap, the brittle odor of grasses, and bursts of pollen shimmered beneath.

Yes, it was a good day for the senses.

I, too, prayed, asking, in my tentative way, that no harm befall me or others while I danced to the prompting of my physical insights. My spirit asked that there be no more if there should be blood. The Shadow paced and snarled at this thought. Well, it could make a fuss if it wanted as long as it wasn't fed.

"Aren't you worried about me?" I asked Sir Korbin, clenching increasingly sweaty palms.

He considered for a moment before replying, "I am always concerned about you. A human with an addiction is one trouble, but a Shadow is nothing I've experienced before. Yes, you will try me, but I'll be ready. I believe you can control your urges."

"And if not?" I pressed.

"If not, then Akristura is a liar, and He has forsaken one of His own who most needs Him."

I shivered, teetering into a thought crisis, when Korbin added, "Which I have very little reason to believe will happen. I have a long, storied history with Him, as thousands of others do, and He has yet to abandon this stubborn old fool." He beamed and urged the horses forward, beginning our descent into town.

The billboards became apparent the closer we drew to Syndbur's heart. On them loomed many faces, most of them random except for one. The recurring individual appeared to be a man because of the breadth of his shoulders and domineering green gaze. However, his smooth, feminine face, lightly puckered lips, and dangling ear piercing indicated otherwise.

"Who is that?" I asked of the man.

There was darkness in Sir Korbin's voice when he answered, "That is Eminent Yesah Simpario, head official over the Silver."

"And is this Simpario a...?"

Hopefully, he'd fill in the blank.

"He's a man."

I sat back, taking him in again. "I see. A very unusual man."

Sir Korbin grunted in response.

On almost every billboard, the Eminent was striking some kind of pose. What interested me were the frequently used hand gestures that also appeared on other unrelated billboards. Models and advertisers of every sort imitated the Eminent—or was he copying them?

"Do these hand signs have a meaning?"

I had to raise my voice as our surroundings were cluttering with buildings and noise. The safety of out-of-town lingered helplessly behind us.

"They do, and I'm glad you asked about them. If you see or meet someone making any of these gestures, assume they're ignorant or deeply serious about their faith."

"Faith? Are these religious gestures?"

Sir Korbin pointed to the nearest billboard, which featured a man in a suit and tie with both hands held level with his shoulders. The left hand's middle and index finger pointed straight up, while the other two fingers were pressed together with the thumb. On the right hand, the other three fingers kissed the thumb while only the index finger was raised.

"The Salutation," he said. "It's a greeting for the non-magical society associated with the Dark One. Yes, Aadyalbaine consorts with "normal" people, too."

I was beginning to understand how the Silver could be evil. The Shadows had mocked alternate religions and paths zyz commonly followed, but what about this one?

"They call themselves the Brethren of Myrk. "Myrk" is a widely-known term for people who run in these spirituality circles," Sir Korbin explained. "And they run this city. With these taunting gestures and symbols, they flaunt their associations to the public, who are largely unaware of the supernatural crisis around them. I'm sure they do it for Akristurans, too. They are aware that *we're* aware we're in a tough spot with the people."

"I'm sorry," I said, meaning it. "That's not fair."

"As the old adage goes, "Life's not fair." You come to live with things, but we mustn't surrender these people to the wolves. The Under Market is no joke."

"What's that?"

Sir Korbin's jaw hardened. "You'll see. It's part of the mission I'll be helping you with. The person we need to find works directly for it. In fact, they're the market's primary supplier."

I didn't like to think of what materials might be selling in this "Under Market," but if Sir Korbin's tight tone was any indication, it was probably not tea and cakes.

I asked him about a few other hand gestures and their representation. One of them, Enduring Fate, featured the true left hand curled inside the right hand and positioned at the sternum. The "swirl" pattern that the left hand made represented myrk, dark magic, and Aadyalbaine's command to continue his will on Aash.

A third sign belonged solely to women. Both hands' fingers interlocked with the knuckles facing the maiden, and the thumb pads pressed together beneath them to form a teardrop shape.

"Dark Lady," Sir Korbin said. "Used by high-ranking priestesses to display that they are Aadyalbaine's concubines. It is considered an honorary position, and that teardrop formation with the thumbs is supposed to symbolize the female anatomy."

"Lovely," I muttered. "Now I know Aadyalbaine sleeps with humans, too. How like his baines of old."

Sir Korbin chuckled darkly. "He gets around. He doesn't rest, that's for sure. Though the final chapter in the Akristuran texts is missing, Akristura's fix at the Absolution War spelled the Dark One's defeat, so he must be concerned his time on this planet will end soon."

"Will it?" I asked.

With a small, satisfied smile, Sir Korbin's voice finally lifted above a dragging tone when he said, "He will be destroyed in time. Who and what he ruins during his reign here is unclear, but Akristura will not allow him to rampage forever. We don't know how and don't know when, but we do know *what* is coming, which is Aadyalbaine's eventual damnation. Be certain of that. Anyway, we're here."

We'd arrived in a cluster of decaying businesses and tangled side streets. Colorful banners and decor acted as bandages to the wounds of time afflicting the decrepit structures. Hundreds of men, women, and children swarmed the storefronts, marching in droves through the doorways while just as many others chattered outside with their goods.

Around these businesses, missing persons flyers were posted up. A man looked at one of them and scoffed. Children, to my quiet horror, vastly outnumbered the amount of missing adults.

The area wasn't devoid of scents, either. Candied aromas gamboled with jarring stenches as the smell of burning sugar cloaked the bitter expulsions of body fluids I couldn't remove from my nose. Sir Korbin noticed my discomfort.

"Are you okay?"

I nodded. "Yeah, but it's a lot at once. How many people threw up in this square?"

"Too many, my dear. I'm happy you can smell all that, though, because I can't. I feel unfortunate with an occasional whiff. What else are you picking up on?"

Honey's faint, seeping warmth softened on my tongue. Hot bricks yielded the filling scent of baking bread, and in the puffing breaths of certain groups, there fogged that artificial sweetness. Some mouths stung with fermented drink's bite. And in a forgotten corner lurked the bright but slowly dulling flavor of a fluid I had no business savoring ever again.

You sure you're okay? Sir Korbin thought.

I swallowed nervously, my hand fluttering to my collarbone and scaling my throat. *I smell blood,* I thought back, *In one of the alleys.*

Akristura could condemn me to the Void without further questions because I *liked* it. I was suddenly choking on a burgeoning *need* as the promise of death wafted over to me from its secret nook.

You can't eat! It's not yours. Control yourself, I snapped at my Shadow's hunger.

Maybe I could control myself if the smell left me, but it tingled relentlessly on my tongue, throat, and nostrils where it made its bed, yanking saliva from its storage. The thick liquid washed over my teeth. I ground them and looked to the seasoned Akristuran for help.

"Please," I begged.

The word dripped out of me like a—

No.

Yes, I argued with myself, *Like a fat, salty drop of blood—*

"Come on." Sir Korbin placed his arm around me and forced the horses to turn around. We retread the ground we'd covered and began a swift escape from Syndbur's throbbing temptations.

Faces narrowed at us as we passed. Sir Korbin ignored them, and I had to look away, too, for fear that I'd view the citizens as less than human. At least I had that fear because old Twilight didn't know it.

Blood's tang finally faded once we'd broken back into the outskirts of town. I dropped back in the carriage, gazing up at the sky and devouring several clear breaths.

"Better now?"

I nodded slowly and mumbled, "I'm sorry. I failed."

Sir Korbin scoffed. "Are you kidding? You exercised self-restraint. That's not failure, kid."

I said nothing. How was I meant to improve when the call of the blood sounded so loudly? Akristura above and Aadyalbaine below, it *sang,* and the melody was alarmingly sweet.

"Twilight. I mean that," Sir Korbin said softly.

Moisture clouded my eyes. I blinked and looked away, not wanting him to see. Of course, he did.

"You're okay, girl. I wouldn't let you do something you regret. You're very new to this, so you need to be a bit gentler with yourself. Okay?"

I couldn't move my lips or my head to indicate my agreement. I didn't agree. At that moment, gentleness was the last thing I felt I needed.

Sir Korbin accepted my silence and decided to change the subject. "I'm sure you noticed the state of downtown Syndbur. The neighborhoods, businesses, and everything; they're crumbling." He scowled. "That is courtesy of the Eminent. He is the human who destroyed the Silver."

I dabbed my tears away with my shirt sleeve and asked, "Human? Was he not alone?"

"Oh, no. Not in the least. Simpario owes everything he has to Sein."

I laughed bitterly. "Why am I not surprised?"

"Yes, he's responsible for many wrongs in the world. I'm sorry." He patted my hand. "But you're not going to be like him. When we get back, I'll show you exactly what happened during the Devastation and how we got to this state we're in. I'm sure the Shadows showed you their abridged version of the event, but I've got the facts."

"Were you going to tell me about that person we're tracking soon?"

I'd need to whip my mind into shape if it was a hunt. Maybe this little outing had changed Korbin's mind about that, though. I might be more of a liability than an asset.

"They call this person the Harvester," Sir Korbin explained, "And they work for the Under Market I told you about earlier. Grisly stuff. This person is infamous across the region for supplying the market with the bulk of its..." He shook his head. "Goods."

"And what do they sell?" I asked breathlessly.

His answer came with a terrible calm.

"People and bits and pieces of them. It's a highly profitable market in this place."

Sir Korbin seemed to deflate after having spoken this. I imploded with him.

"How awful," I said softly.

And it was. For the first time since the Shadows had claimed me as their own and forced their invisible crown upon my head, my heart was gripped with wrenching guilt for mankind.

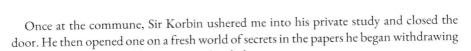

Once at the commune, Sir Korbin ushered me into his private study and closed the door. He then opened one on a fresh world of secrets in the papers he began withdrawing from a filing cabinet and laying out on his desk.

"These," he said, "Are the notes and blueprints Sein sent to the Eminent in his early days, generously copied for us by one of our former informants. I think you'll recognize one of the exploitation schemes in this one." He slapped his hand down on the first set of pages.

I scanned them briefly, stumbling over too many words, so I asked Korbin to help me. He read the relevant content aloud.

"With your partnership, the event I am hoping to bring about—what I am tentatively titling "the Devastation" for now—will eliminate many of your nuisance citizens. This will be accomplished with a coordinated magic strike between My brethren and Me. Do not concern yourself with the details; you would not understand them."

I made a disgusted noise at his condescension.

"What is relevant is this: the appropriate people will die. You have control over who perishes in this wave and who does not. My advice is to lure your targets into a single space at the southern border of town. Make the bait enticing enough to bite. Remember, our payment for this is twofold: the immediate enjoyment of the energy of those who die, and the slow burn, as it were, of the decay of this fecal nation. You have been selected for tremendous service to Aaksa Aadyalbaine. We expect your compliance in helping us help you fulfill your part in the Dark Hour."

"Ugh. Please stop. I can't listen to any more," I groaned. "Sein really said all that? And the Eminent just went along with it?"

Sir Korbin shook his head. "He didn't "go along" with anything. He wanted this. Sein simply guided him to the glory and wealth he craved, and now he sits comfortably over this dying region and milks it for what it's worth. No doubt he's biding time until Myrkraas and whatever that now entails."

I bit my lip and hissed, "We'll find out. As soon as I get my hands on this Harvester guy—"

"You won't kill him," Sir Korbin interjected. "As hideous as he is, we're not in the murdering business here. But enough about him for right now. We're still getting acquainted with the past. I think you'd benefit from a memory of the Devastation."

His eyes closed. I knew what was to follow.

In the tried-and-true manner of memory-sharing, a tinted vision trembled into my head from someone else's lived experience. White-robed figures flooded into view as they passed frantically through a cobweb of streets, begging people to heed their warnings.

"A great danger is coming! Many of you will not survive unless you seek shelter now!" One woman cried.

Another wailed, *"Seek the Light or die in darkness!"*

A bit dramatic, but it achieved an effect.

Several men marched together and chanted something about "three more days."

It took the second memory to realize these were Korbin's experiences.

"They'll keep the useful idiots," he murmured, *"And the rest will die."*

A man beside him—Garvinuch, I realized with a painful jolt—nodded.

"Yes, and this region will be flattened. Any validity to the claim that it will destroy the world?"

Sir Korbin snorted. *"Sein couldn't. He wouldn't even want to; what ties does he have to the Bronze? That's too much energy for little good reason. No, they'll do what they said in the letters we have—they will ravage the Caligin and some of the Silver, reap their energy from the mass deaths, and set the stage for the new Silver leader to sign more horrors into law. Watch. When this death wave comes, it'll prime the government for becoming a savior of sorts. The people will do anything it wants, and it wants what the Shadows want: their decay."*

Garvinuch muttered, *"How I hope you're wrong,"* and the memory melted into the next.

"They're heading out! Look!"

The memory narrowed on Sir Korbin's trembling hands propped against a familiar balcony railing. His gaze fell upon a throng of vehicles passing from central Syndbur to an icy road snaking past the outer ridge. They moved with impatient purpose, bumpers tapping bumpers toward a distant destination.

"Attending the celebration, I see," rumbled Garvinuch. *"You aren't actually surprised, right? We expected they'd do something like this. Like you said, useful idiots."* He huffed a dark laugh.

"We warned the others—" Sir Korbin protested, but his friend would hear none of it.

"Yes, we warned them. You see what they've done with our warnings. They live like no tomorrow."

"It's not them that's the issue so much," Sir Korbin moaned. *"It's our own unwitting people out there in that other meeting at the edge of town. My God, Gar... they're at the southern border. They're right where they're wanted, and I can't bear the thought that maybe we didn't try hard enough."*

Garvinuch vehemently disagreed. *"We did exactly what we were supposed to do, brother. What more was required? The smoothest tongues in the world couldn't have charmed them from destruction if their hearts were set on receiving it."*

I felt Korbin's defeat, sagging and empty in my own chest. It echoed with fears he refused to voice, washed with tears he would not spend. People would perish because he had not striven hard enough to reach them. Bodies were probably seconds from piling in the streets.

"Our barriers are good. Everyone who listened to us and is here with us is safe, Korbin," Garvinuch said.

A flash ruptured the sky.

Korbin turned. The languid motion dragged on in his mind, weighted by the screams bleeding through a thousand streets below. Fantastic clouds of shadow clambered over hill and valley, business and home, roaring and wailing as even the dead could not.

His chest had yawned empty before. Now it sank into the floor and through the earth where the dead—much of Syndbur, the Silver, and the unprotected prey dwelling in the Caligin—would find themselves when the living recovered from this horror. The Devastation had been touted as something that would affect the entire world, and in a way, it had. The only parts of the world worth destroying, whether for politics or power, were being flattened.

Valdur writhed over the lumensa barriers protecting the commune. Animals in the fields strayed from the darkness, and those inside the light magic had little but noise to fear. The beasts outside it dropped. Unfeeling energy swept over them on its vicious, devouring path, stealing their breath in its frenzy.

Sir Korbin dropped into a chair, cradling his head in his hands. Garvinuch and a much younger Lady Annisara took seats on either side of him to offer their silent support.

The entire commune felt heavy. Korbin found the air stifling and the snarling magic outside his doorstep utterly exhausting, a horrid entity he didn't want to contend with anymore. It was then that he prayed.

Give me Your strength because I've none of my own.

A liquid he only vaguely realized was tears prodded his eyes. He clenched his fist and vowed he would not let them leave their place.

Eminent Simpario's supporters would live. This was almost as terrible as the knowledge that many who loved Akristura had been deceived into congregating down in town, at the cursed southern border, for their final moment. Those who were true now stood before the Light. It was not a total tragedy, but the Silver achieving such a dark accomplishment for their political strategy burned him.

"They have won a battle, friend, but not the war," Garvinuch assured him.

"They've thinned out their opposition," Korbin groaned tiredly. *"Us. And they've kept those who hate us and love their hideous policies alive."*

"Think of the ones who didn't attend the Simpario meeting or didn't at least heed our warnings and go underground or come to us for shelter," Lady Annisara said. *"They're gone, too. We've lost many souls today, Korbin. Our own people who weren't willing to listen? They are not complete tragedies. It's the other citizens who are."*

His deep, sinking sigh was the last sound heard before the last memory played.

Fallen bodies flooded my mind, some battered and others draped peacefully over the pavement. Little blood was to be found. A few mouths trickled red, and several construction workers had toppled from high. This aside, the streets whispered of nothingness, save for the few intrepid survivors willing to brave the new world.

We came upon a square at the edge of town where death had stolen the most. It wasn't enough to speak of nausea. The sick feeling screamed and twisted so deeply in our being that it permeated our spirit. Every cell cried against the injustice.

So many friends of the faith... slaughtered.

Sir Korbin dropped to his knees and uttered a desperate prayer for the loved ones of his lost brethren, brethren who refused to believe the Children of Akristura when they'd shared the news of the Devastation before it had killed them with such prejudice.

He rose from the ground as the vehicles from the meeting in Lokraini were returning. A fresh wave of sickness touched him, and he had to scold himself for feeling this way.

Eminent Simpario's supporters were still people; as long as that was true, Korbin had to love them. But it was not a small challenge when, upon braking in the square, cheers and whoops streamed through their car windows.

This was what they'd wanted. Death. Death of the opposition. Simpario had gathered the faithful in the safety of his capitol building, leaving the Akristuran faithful—who did not believe the Devastation would happen—to perish.

Some of the regular citizens had listened. They'd taken respite in cellars, bunkers, and other places. But these people...

Korbin sprang back in disgust. The first vehicle in the pile-up suddenly lurched forward, gliding over the bodies. The cars behind it followed. Crimson mist sprayed, and more jeering laughter followed each successive jet spattering their tires and front bumpers.

"Forget these terrorists!" One of the drivers shrieked.

"Run these bastards into the ground!"

More harsh, strident, and frighteningly uncaring laughter covered the crushed corpses. Then the headlights turned on Korbin. He blasted the first line of cars angling toward him with lumensa and ran. The memory went dark.

Pain reared in my chest. My conscience spoke again, aching over the vile nature of events older than me. And yet, strangely—or perhaps not strangely—I understood the citizens' capacity for hatred. Shadow Twilight had been taught to revel in it, and she had.

I lowered my head and whispered, "I'm sorry about your people."

The present-day Sir Korbin sighed. "I am, too. Our informant got word of this just a few days before it was scheduled to happen. When we got the news, everyone in the communes took to the streets. We told the people what was going to happen. They laughed at us." He shook his head. "So did some of our own. We tried to dissuade them from attending that meeting in town where they were being lured to their deaths. Sein and Simpario orchestrated it."

His dark eyes reflected his pain in gathering tears. "They were protesting the new laws being implemented in the Silver. The people you saw in the vehicles had been invited to attend their own meeting celebrating Simpario's policies in Lokraini, the capital. That's why we called them useful idiots; the Silver government lured their loyal supporters to protection while leaving everyone else to die."

"Gross. Did the wave really cover the whole world, or was it limited to the Silver and the Caligin?"

Korbin grimaced. *"Limited* isn't the word I'd use. The wave didn't reach the Bronze—it wasn't supposed to—but it certainly caused damage here on the mainland. Two of Aash's three regions fell that day, and if that wasn't enough, they tampered with people's memories afterward. They wiped out the part where we had warned them about it and insisted there had been no warning; it was a horrible unknown thing that no one could have predicted."

I frowned. "People bought that?"

"Enough did. Simpario's supporters did, anyway. We had some citizens take respite up here with us, and they knew the truth."

"My stepmother survived," I said. "But that was because she—"

"Hid in a bunker, yep. Her father believed the crazies." Korbin laughed softly. "I'm grateful for that."

I smiled. "Me, too."

"Your mother was likely being protected by the Sharavaks at that time. Your grandparents, however, were not protected. They were among the Silver court's dissenters."

My breath caught. "What happened to them?"

"They were executed, we believe," Korbin said quietly. "I'm sorry."

I dropped the pent-up breath and nodded to myself. "I see."

"Well." He sighed. "With these revelations, I hope it's clearer now why we can't trust the Silver and why it's almost certain they know something about Myrkraas. The Harvester is close with the Eminent, and the Eminent is probably close with your father. If we find them, we find answers."

I nodded and, thinking of my deceased relatives, and my siblings who would not exist had the Akristurans not warned people of their fate, said, "Then we'll find them. I won't let what happened today happen again."

What if another Devastation came? It would be partially on my head because I wasn't willing or able to temper my urges.

"What happened today," Sir Korbin said patiently, "Was not a bad thing. It could have been, but it was not. We will continue to train your magic and senses. I have an outing for you and your sister tomorrow. Let's see if you can complete it successfully."

Chapter Twelve

I was beginning to like rising at dawn. Weeks in darkness had hidden the old treasures of day life from me. The girl in me missed the butterflies and the warm mornings spent on a rickety fence. I'd missed the chickens, the cows, and the general sense of busyness the sun bestowed on the world.

Night bloomed tranquil. It demanded little of its inhabitants but silence and stillness, and of Shadows, occasional hunts in the woods. I was on such a hunt at the moment. A smaller figure with flaming red hair crouched beside me in the undergrowth.

Smell anything? I thought to her.

Not yet.

How about the other scents? Are you picking up on the needles from the trees, the sap, and the soil?

Susenne shook her head.

I frowned and wondered how acute her senses were in comparison to mine. She was of diluted blood. Little of a Sharavak's composition existed in her to lend her its sharpened lifestyle, but that wasn't a bad thing. The higher the senses, I imagined, the deeper the cravings.

Sir Korbin was back around the commune monitoring us from afar. His task for Susenne and me was eerily similar to the first hunting mission Father Sein had sent us on. That, too, had been a mission for sniffing out blood. This time, though, it was not humans that we sought.

Other creatures moved about the forest, filling it with their aromas. My human senses were lesser than their Sharavos counterparts, but I could still distinguish the soft, varied layers in the earth and among the tree trunks. The ground beneath us shivered with bright spots of animal urine, decaying insects, and scattered bones from kills.

I inhaled and appreciated their nuances. Susenne tried the same, but her mouth fell in disappointment.

I guess I'll lead the way, I thought, and I began sliding through the bushes.

Discomfort was my first impression. This hunt cut marrow-close to my outing with Susenne, yes, but also to my prowl with Zemorah the evening we discovered an Akristuran not far from the Sharavak compound. I recalled my angry hunger toward the man in memories ripe with shame and a hint of predatory regret. How I'd wanted him pinned under my claws and shredding from my burrowing teeth.

Discarding this intrusive idea, I took another whiff of the leaf carpet and the dirt it covered. A larger animal had trodden this path, and recently. Soil had caked its feet and sprayed lightly across the fallen foliage. I continued into the shadows with Susenne flanking me, looking thoroughly unenthused.

What's wrong? I asked.

Susenne glanced at me and gave no answer. Of the many wonders I wondered, if my sister would ever not hate me frequently crossed my mind.

I paused suddenly when a new scent hit my nose. This one was sweet and somewhat warm. Its moistness prompted me to uncover the leaves in front of me. I kicked them aside and scanned the dark pebbles resting there, lurching at the realization.

Deer. Now this experience had become frighteningly familiar.

Ahead, a twig snapped. I was sure its crack was too faint for normal ears because it was nearly inaudible to me. But when I narrowed my eyes and flattened down, I saw the source of the movement about a thousand paces forward in the darker portion of the woods.

The animal moved with a delectable slowness, yet its blood burned with vigor. It was young. I listened to its steady heartbeat and wondered what it would sound like much faster, and then—

Not beating at all.

My tongue caressed my teeth. I grabbed my collarbone and dug my nails in, watching the deer pass unaware.

If I sprinted—not a difficult thing to do, minimal effort—I could have it sprawled out, bleating its last notes of terror before I buried inside it. Its flesh still had the softness of youth. It would part easily, with much steam and brilliant blood, and the leaves would darken with it as if autumn was enjoying an early arrival.

I liked red leaves as a child. Older Twilight's idea of red was brighter and harsher, a more striking hue than the kind autumn brought, but she could make the colors fall all the same.

"Twilight!" Susenne hissed. "What are you doing?"

The deer hadn't noticed her voice, but of course it hadn't. It possessed only the awareness it needed to survive creatures like me who owned *more* than I needed to have a little fun.

I grinned despite myself and enjoyed the feeling of my sharper teeth exposed in the darkness. The sun couldn't judge me in the cloak the trees had thrown over me. And Susenne—

"Stop it," she whispered. "You're being weird."

Her voice drew me from the predatory realm, and I blinked at the deer, seeing it in an altered light. That poor animal didn't deserve to die, certainly not so horribly. Why had the Shadow come over me so strongly?

"Let's go," I said, rising from my haunches.

The deer perked up and paused.

Can't look at it, won't, it's just a member of the forest minding its business—

"Why? Are you seriously tempted by that thing?"

I ignored the scorn in her tone. "You're not?"

"Um, no. I get that you're superhuman or something, but why are you having problems with this? Hasn't your soul been saved?" She sneered.

"I... I don't know. Can we go?" I snapped.

Susenne laughed. "You haven't changed at all."

Biting back a growl, I spun around and marched through the trees toward the commune. Toward Sir Korbin, who I hoped had answers. But the deer scent followed me, as it hadn't left my nose. I picked up my pace. Before I knew it, I was racing over roots and around bushes. If Susenne didn't keep up, I didn't care.

I have to get away.

The deer's smell was seducing my mind. I was like a zyz—curse that word, a *non-magical*—in a Shadow's clutches. Maybe I could have escaped by other means than running, but I didn't think I'd have the willpower to resist.

That deer's muscles had rippled!

I broke through the treeline. Gasping, I stumbled up to Sir Korbin, and he grasped my shoulders and asked if I was okay.

"Where's your sister?"

I jabbed a thumb behind me, still breathing heavily. He frowned until a few seconds passed, and she came jogging out of the woods. Her smirk stretched wide.

"What's got you smiling like that?" Sir Korbin demanded.

"When will the temptations subside?" I cried. "I know I haven't been here even a week, but if I belong to Akristura now, why aren't I getting better? The urges are just as bad as they were with the Shadows."

Sir Korbin took my hand in both of his and looked into my eyes. Surely he saw my shame and knew I was genuinely trying?

"You're correct. You've been here five days, and like I told you yesterday, you need to be patient with this. Impatience will kill your progress, Twilight. As for your urges, remember what else I told you before? This will be a *lifelong struggle.* You are safe in Akristura's hands. He is working within you and will lessen these burdens over time as you grow, but they will never fully leave until *you* leave this world. One's soul is not one's flesh; the two have separate desires. You will always war with your body."

The weight of this statement brought me to tears. I tried again to blink them away and pretend they didn't exist, but Sir Korbin saw them and rested his hand on my shoulder. Golden light began to leak from his fingers and pass into my being. I gasped at the soothing warmth. My distraught thoughts were fading.

"Relax," he said softly. "I see you returned from your task unscathed. It doesn't appear that anything died. You did see animals, right?"

I nodded. "Yeah. There was a deer. I wanted to kill it."

Susenne rolled her eyes. "Maybe just get stronger? It can't be that hard."

Sir Korbin's gaze narrowed. He took his pointer fingernail and scraped it across his hand hard enough to draw blood. The scent thrilled and terrified me.

"You can walk away if you need to," he said to me.

He approached Susenne, scarlet threads welling up in the cut, and put the back of his hand in her face. "Breathe in," he snapped.

Susenne moved her head, and he repeated, "Breathe. In."

Finally, she listened. She bent over his hand and inhaled. Her lips drew back seemingly of their own will, and Sir Korbin dropped his hand, nodding. "You like it. It tempts you. Don't worry, girl. I saw." His satisfied expression soured. "You think you're immune because your senses are much lesser, but you're not. There's still a beast in you that you need to control. You could also stand to control your mouth."

Susenne looked away, her arms crossed over her chest.

Korbin motioned for us to follow him. "To the carriage. We're going to try town again. We'll do it every day if we have to, until both of you can figure out how to navigate the world without blood-lusting after everything that moves... or mocking those who are putting in honest effort to improve."

He glared at Susenne, who in turn glared at me.

Our second trip to town was silent. Korbin attempted conversation twice, and though I was more willing to talk than Susenne, whose lips did not shift from their pinched scowl, I didn't feel very chatty, either. The deer struggle haunted me.

Yes, I'd been with the Akristurans for five days. But the newness in me that man could not see ached. My conscience screamed when my tongue danced over my mouth. It pierced me to look at a creature otherwise so whole and innocent as something to tear to pieces.

Hunters who acquired animal meat with firearms and bows did so with a certain level of dignity. There was a separation between man and beast when man murdered from a distance. But the kind of killing my Shadow side liked required an intimate, tooth-filled encounter in which my entire face became a painting. This was only noble for animals to partake in. To a hybrid like myself—a person with a soul—it was lowly to eat like that.

I hope you don't feel too badly about the deer, Sir Korbin thought to me. I saw his eyes slip my way with concern. *I'm very proud you didn't give in and harm it. You turned away, right?*

Yes.

His smile grew. *Then you did the right thing.*

This was true on a rational, supernatural, higher-than-animal scale. According to that, I was making prudent choices. I didn't want to dwell on what my flesh made of my refusal.

Town greeted us shortly after hitting the road and lingering in awkward quiet. Susenne's gaze brightened, and she didn't bother concealing her interest when we crossed into Syndbur's heart.

"Take it in," said Sir Korbin, breaking the prolonged silence. "It's a mess, but it's never dull."

Everywhere I looked, activities jostled for my attention. Merchants, prostitutes, revelers, and stooped figures holding crystals and talismans peddled their goods and made plenty of noise in the streets. Shadow women seemed almost pitiful compared to the output of their zyz counterparts. The "night ladies," or "anytime ladies," rather, were drawing impressive lines.

I'd noticed these people yesterday, but my tiredness and general overwhelm had kept me from analyzing the full, chaotic picture. Sir Korbin suggested I take in the scents as well as the sights. I did so, taking care to only sip instead of devour. No deer had been harmed that morning, but it didn't eliminate the possibility of a fine-scented lad or lass meeting death.

"What do you think, Susenne?"

She glared at the Akristuran and shook her head. "Too weird. What are we doing here again?"

"Learning scents, or at least your sister will be," he said, "And finding out about..."

His thought projected to both of us: *The Harvester.*

"What is that?"

Sir Korbin explained to her in private hursafar, making her eyes widen.

"That's definitely too weird for me," she huffed. "And we're looking for this freak?"

"Yes, because they may know things we don't. We're coming up on one of the six streets we've narrowed them down to. They primarily operate on this side of town as it's where the families come, and they get, uh, stock for the market."

I drummed my fingers on the carriage and let myself slip into a brief fantasy of savaging this foul person after making them confess to every sick misdeed. Then again, if I was to fantasize about other evildoers, I supposed I'd need to add myself to the list. The Harvester was his own kind of monster, but so was I.

What's that look on your face? Sir Korbin inquired. *I'll be honest, I don't like it.*

I straightened up in the carriage and looked away, directing my attention back to the Syndburians.

"Having fun smelling everybody?" Susenne asked me.

"Yes, tell us what you smell. Forgive me, but I find your sensory enhancement fascinating."

"Okay," I said. "Well..."

The revelers had fermented drink's tang all over their breaths and in their blood. It caused their hearts to beat faster so that they outpaced the flocks of other hearts in their vicinity. When focusing on the sounds, I forgot about the scents and reeled from the sheer quantity of pulses.

"I'm having a hard time focusing," I admitted. "But those drinking guys have fast heart rates. I smell their breaths. Those ladies in the clothes, or lack thereof, have horrendously strong perfume. I probably couldn't be around them for very long."

"You and me both, though my younger self wouldn't have cared either way," Sir Korbin chuckled. "Good. But what did you mean by having a hard time focusing? Are you struggling again?"

"Not yet. It's just a lot at once."

Sir Korbin agreed. "It's not for everyone. These days, it's not for anyone if they know what's best for them. Look there, though, see that street? That marks the first of six our friend might be on. Take this time to absorb what you're seeing, hearing, and feeling, girls. Test the things entering your mind. Are they good? Do they feel wrong or misleading? How are you reacting to your sensory input physically and spiritually? This should be a good start for you. I'll take you around."

He ordered the horses down a side street crammed with businesses and twice as many smells. Some of them were so sweet, grainy, and pleasant that I desired to eat them as they were. Sir Korbin noticed mine and Susenne's hunger. He stopped and handed a bread vendor a few Silvons, then passed the bread pieces to us.

"Enjoy," he said. "But don't indulge."

Susenne snorted. "With this stuff? Try and stop me."

She proceeded to shove an obscenely large chunk of bread into her mouth. Sir Korbin and I exchanged looks of mild horror.

You may be the "Shadowier" one of the pair of you, but I appreciate you not eating like it, he thought with amusement when I took my own, measured nibble.

I replied, *Don't look when I'm around blood.*

"Speaking of that, how about we dare to be dangerous?" He suggested.

I raised my eyes from my bread. "Isn't everywhere in this town dangerous?"

He grinned. "You haven't lingered in the good parts yet."

I might have thought the Akristuran leader was mad. There he was, taking two unruly monster people around an environment that implored them to surrender to their every whim and want. His magic was strong, but did he really not fear us?

As if he knew my thoughts, he explained himself.

"You're probably wondering why I'm taking these risks with you both, bringing you to this den of darkness and encouraging you to take it in. I believe that when people seek to conquer something they dislike in themselves, they should start by exposing themselves to it gradually and taking opportunities within reasonably safe environments to resist what tempts them. The trouble with many Akristurans today is their unwillingness to acknowledge evil and confront it. Now, don't misunderstand me—evil is not to be underestimated or toyed with, and it does no one good to expose themselves to it frequently—but we can't hide from it, either. We need to see ourselves for what we are and respond accordingly. This isn't a method I recommend to everyone, but I'm going to try it with you. Some would call this a form of exposure therapy."

"You think exposure to whatever you're about to bring us around is useful for our growth because it forces us to not enjoy it?" I asked.

"In a way, yes," he answered. "I wouldn't want you to do this by yourselves, though. That tempts more than you; it tempts fate. No, I don't want you being exposed recklessly. In this controlled scenario, I am responsible for you and am overseeing your struggle. But the struggle has got to happen. If it doesn't, you risk repeating past horrors you'd rather not because you never strengthened your resolve against it."

It made enough sense. I didn't think it was a smart strategy for everyone to fol-low—some people could relapse quickly and viciously when the vice that tempted them was placed in their face—but I understood the idea. Sure, not everyone was designed for that, but people in my position would probably be exposed to plenty of blood and other temptations, anyway. If I trained myself to view these things in a proper light, I might begin to heal from the hold they had on me.

"I recognize this street," said Susenne.

I looked around and also realized where we'd come. "So do I. We came here when we went to that lady's house for Josh, right?"

Sir Korbin confirmed this. "I'll expose you to a few scents here, so you at least know what they are. We'll dismount, but for no more than a couple minutes at a time. I don't trust us to have a carriage if we stick around."

I dropped onto the pavement after my sister behind the Better Version Beauty clinic, wondering if any of the altered Syndburians thought I was buying my physical appeal. Faces and bodies with no logical shapes passed out of its doors. Like the woman and her daughter a few streets above, these citizens featured modifications that were extreme to the point of vulgarity. I worried for them. I feared what they may have experienced in their lives to drive them to such drastic "fixes."

"Don't pay mind to them," Sir Korbin told us. Susenne was eyeing a woman with protruding lips. "Their beauty, if that's what it's being called these days, costs more than formal education. Yours is courtesy of Akristura."

Susenne smirked. "Wonder where it could be."

"Hey. Don't knock yourself. No fake face compares to your natural one," I said.

Susenne was preparing a retort when Sir Korbin pointed out a small, scattered pile of white powder in the corner of the parking lot. "Give that a careful whiff. Don't let too much of it into your nose."

I stooped to the powder pile, Susenne beside me, to sniff it and determine what it even was. I'd never seen a powder like it before.

"Try putting a little on your finger," Korbin suggested.

I hovered over the pile with my pointer. Susenne looked at me and muttered, "After you."

I took the plunge. When I pulled it back up, I held the dust-coated pad under my nostril and breathed in.

"What do you smell?"

A bitterness crashed into my throat. I snorted and drew back. Susenne knocked into my shoulder when she inhaled, too, and Sir Korbin nodded.

"It'll do that to you. How do you feel?"

The powder settled, bringing a softening feeling to my burning tongue. My mind calmed as if preparing for rest, but the world also seemed to brighten around me. My already enhanced senses expanded further. I could taste the air, salt, sweat, and blood with richer clarity!

Bones were being sawn into inside the clinic. Briefly, I heard and smelled them crack under the metal, and around it, flesh and blood burned and suffered beneath heat appliances and other blades.

Then the numbness came swooping in. My tongue weakened, and the brief flame of sensation died into embers. Worse, a headache followed.

"What is it?" I asked.

"One of the many pharmaceutical remedies here in Syndbur," Sir Korbin answered.

I blinked. "You lost me."

"It's a drug. People take it to exist differently. It takes their pain and gives them excitement instead. Some drugs make excited people calm."

I shook my head and climbed to my feet. "That's nice. I think I'll pass."

"Same," Susenne groaned.

Sir Korbin sighed. "Many have indeed passed from using them."

He sent us on a hunt for the next new scent. This one was salty and distinctly human. We tracked it to a corner behind the popular Bed and Roses lodge.

"What do you call this one?"

Sir Korbin peered down at the fluid and nodded to himself. "It comes from human intimacy. That is what this lodge is about."

"Sounds exciting," Susenne remarked.

"Of course you'd think that," I said. "All you ever read were romance novels."

She grinned. "At least I got to read."

"That's enough from you both," snapped Sir Korbin. "We've one more stop. Let's get it done and get back home. This place is starting to drain me."

Other things were draining in another part of town, and my sister and I were immediately edgy. How I hoped Sir Korbin's "exposure therapy" wouldn't cause a tragedy.

"You brought us to a blood truck?" I whispered.

Heat was building in my chest and face. We stood a safe enough distance away, but was anywhere safe when all that blood was just... sitting there, ripe for the taking?

I watched the needles descend into veins and slowly suck out the scarlet. It spilled swiftly into vials with a dark, rich scent that caressed me even from a hundred paces back. As with the deer, my tongue began to shift restlessly against my teeth.

"Tell me what you're thinking right now," Sir Korbin said. "I need to know."

What I was thinking? Oh, no. He wasn't prepared for that. Because if I was wholly and unabashedly honest, what I wanted to do should have banished me directly to Toragaine.

With every slip of a needle as it dipped into unwitting arms, I clenched. I did not see a human being, at least not in the complete sense. I felt the vibrations of their lungs exchanging air. My ears pricked at their delicate heartbeats, and I tasted the sweet tang hovering around them.

I wanted the salt. I wanted to claw it out of their bodies and make an unrecognizable mess of it, rip, shred, tear, and eviscerate until even their mothers could not recognize them. Of course, while I did this, I'd enjoy my toys, snapping up an organ here, crunching down on some cartilage there, and wallowing in the *life fluid*.

It was disgusting. It was wrong and sick and savage, and all parts of me, Shadow, human, and spirit, agreed.

"Araveh above! Twilight, stop!"

I was vaguely aware of a pain in my collarbone and hands moving mine away from my chest. Looking down, I realized I'd cut several gashes into it. Seeing the carvings decided the fate of the blood donors for me.

I lunged. Strong arms pulled me back, but I was strong, too. A Shadow resided in me, filled with the divine rage of the Void. I'd cut more than myself to pieces if I had to.

"Stop this!" A man called, and I thought I recognized him, I really did, but no zyz's voice had an identity, these pieces of cattle—

"I call Akristura's peace over—"

I bashed the person behind me with my elbow, more preoccupied with stopping them than slaking my thirst. It was then that I caught a glimpse of the green-eyed, freckle-speckled girl in front of me, her heart sprinting with fear.

Susenne.

My flesh.

I relented. The arms around me held me fast and began to pull me away from the blood truck. I'd have killed them. All of them. And as I inspected my bloody self, I hated that.

One of the blood vials disconnected from its needle and went shattering across the pavement. This turned both my and my sister's heads.

"Susenne," Sir Korbin growled. "Don't."

I witnessed the same madness come into her eyes. The possession became hers.

"Akristura, please," he begged.

Never had such concern—nay, fear—colored his voice. It was this fear and a remembrance of the part of me that was not ruinous that made me force an arm through Sir Korbin's and grab my sister.

"Don't," I echoed hoarsely.

She had to smell it now. Her dilution could only serve her so far when still a monster roared inside her. Her scowl at me was only half-formed.

"It's... wrong," I gasped. "You know it. Turn... away."

I hardly knew whether I was talking to myself or Susenne. My warnings seemed applicable to both of us, as I was struggling against the Akristuran's grip even then.

"Susenne," he said sternly. "Let's go."

Susenne's wild look weakened when one of the truck staff vanished the blood with a cleaning solution. A harsh scent replaced blood's warm fullness. She turned, her eyes blazing anew with hatred, and hissed, "You dare try to get *me* to control myself? Pathetic hypocrite. You would have eaten those people alive!"

Gazes fell on her outburst. Sir Korbin ordered her to come with us before a scene broke out and insisted it was time to go home.

"You've been tried plenty enough today," he grunted, taking me with him.

I let him. I didn't trust myself enough to walk alone.

CHAPTER THIRTEEN

D AYS PASSED, AND TEMPTATIONS followed. I was beginning to understand the seriousness of Sir Korbin's assertions that I would always struggle with my desires. The natural had to become unnatural. Darkness had to become darkness again, and light would have to assume its rightful place in my mind if I wanted to experience pronounced healing.

As it was, I battled myself, frequently losing to some flight of filthy fancy when I smelled blood or wrestled with a strong emotion. Images of Father pressed me to keep refining myself so I wouldn't be the downfall of everyone I knew as he'd predicted.

Recalling the dream he'd infiltrated, I'd force my mind into near-silence when withdrawing magic. Sir Korbin oversaw me most days, but sometimes he trusted me to exercise it alone. Occasionally, he'd have Susenne join me.

"What plants are going to die today?" She'd taunt in the fields.

"Do you want me to fail? Is that what this is about?" I'd hiss back, clamping down on my anger.

The issue was preventing it from squirming out of its restraint. This anger had to be roped in, or else it, like the Sharavos within, would happily rampage wherever it liked and ravage anything in its path. If that was my frustrating sister, it didn't matter. A random stranger in town? It'd devour them, too.

I constantly trod the thin line. My feet were beginning to navigate it more deftly, but a chasm still stretched beneath should I ever spectacularly fail.

My little sister was anything but a failure, unlike Susenne and me, who consistently struggled to undo ourselves. Aullie and I healed many small things around the commune and outside. Flowers, bees, tiny mice, and other helpless creatures became our patients. Aullie's magic beamed brilliant and pure. She hadn't stained it or her soul. Mine had grown, but it still required diligent work.

Cobi, as the Non, was progressing in his own way. He'd taken up exercising per Sir Korbin's suggestion to strengthen himself for "whatever lies ahead." When I asked him about it, he admitted Korbin had also encouraged him to begin weapons training.

"He seems to think I'd be good with a sword or gun or both," he chuckled one afternoon when I came upon him stretching outside. "But I don't know. I don't think that'll do much good against a magical opponent, you know? Korbin thinks there's definite value in sword training, but let's be honest; if I'm up against a sorcerer, I haven't got a chance." He laughed with a trimming of nervousness, and I felt bad for him.

It had to be challenging living in a world of magic when you had none. Cobi would have to become highly adept at the sword to deflect magic defensively or offensively—something Shadows learned to do with valdur weapons—and the likelihood of that, looking at him, was...

"Zero chance," he said sullenly.

"Don't say that," I scolded him. "If I can make my light magic come back, you can take up swords and guns, or whatever it is, and become a pro. You need to take the first step, though."

And that was the thing with Cobi—he wouldn't move.

"One of my greatest fears," he said softly, "Is having to face a magical opponent. Can you imagine?" He tossed his head to the side, frowning deeply.

"I won't have to imagine anything unpleasant if you get started on training, Cobs," I told him. "Tell me you'll think about it, at least."

"I will," he promised.

One had to wonder if he actually would.

I also noticed over the passing weeks that Susenne had an utter reluctance to get along with me. Despite Korbin integrating her into my training sessions and attempting to bond us, my sister persisted in avoiding, slandering, or mocking me to the point that I'd had enough. I loathed being around her, and the newness in me recognized this loathing wasn't good. I was determined to help our relationship, even if only in some small way.

"I want to take Susenne to lunch," I told Sir Korbin one morning.

His brows raised. "In town?"

"Where else?"

He let out a breath. "I don't feel comfortable with that myself. Granted, I think you're in a much better position now with things than you were a few weeks ago, but do you trust yourself—and whatever devious citizens you may encounter—to keep this outing from being disastrous?"

I shrugged. "I really don't know. I'd like to try. Besides..." I exposed a palm full of bright golden magic. "Thanks to a good teacher, I've finally gotten *this* to come out."

Sir Korbin smiled. "That you have. You'll still be tempted, though, and it's likely you'll smell blood. You also need to keep the Harvester in mind. They enjoy prowling around that downtown area."

"Yes," I said, "But I think Susenne and I will be safe together."

"Do you think she'd protect you, from yourself or another, if something happened?" Korbin asked.

What a question. A normal sister with a healthy relationship would be offended that it was posed.

"I don't know," I admitted. "I hope so. All I know is I can't go on like this anymore. The constant snide comments, disrespect, and just... hate. It's not right."

Korbin agreed. "I like your motive behind this. It shows you're maturing. Well, I can drop you both off if you'd like. I wish Syndbur was a better city so I could do some shopping and not feel I would lose a wheel from the carriage or something, but I'll hang around town while you both have lunch."

"Okay. Let me ask her if she even wants to do this first, and if so, can we leave in maybe half an hour?"

"A half hour sounds good."

I hurried off to find my sister, who had been withdrawing to her room more and more frequently in the past week. I knocked on her door and received a tired, "Who is it?"

"It's me," I said. "Your sister."

"Which one? The one who can barely use magic, or the one who won't use it properly?"

I swallowed a retort and said, "Can I come in? Or can you come out? I have a question for you."

"Ooh," she replied. "Is it your turn to beg for *my* forgiveness?"

"Will you just shut up and come out here?" I snapped.

I regretted the words the moment they threw themselves out. My urges to maim and kill had subsided some, but my desire to throttle Susenne had worsened.

She fumbled slowly and with pronounced disinterest with the lock before sliding it out and opening the door. Her thin lips had their usual pinch, while her pale green glare met me with all the cordiality of a dose of coriusg to the face.

"Let's hear it, then," she muttered.

I straightened up, pinned my gaze on hers, and asked, "Would you like to come to lunch with me in town? Sir Korbin will drive us."

She smirked. "What's on the menu? Any street person whose blood's got you excited today?"

I gritted my teeth and forced out a restrained, "You were eating them right there with me, sister. Don't pretend you didn't enjoy it, too, or that it never happened. You are not innocent."

A wry smile crossed her face. "Maybe so. But at least I don't go around acting like I'm this perfect, sacred person now."

"What?" I cried. "When do I ever act like that? You're joking. You're sick. You know what? Lunch is off. There's no repairing this relationship."

I turned, prepared to march off, when she called, "Wait."

"What?"

Her smile had fallen. Regret shone briefly in her eyes. "I'm sorry. Let's go."

"Take back what you said. About me acting like I'm holier-than-thou."

Susenne nodded. "Fair enough. I'm sorry I said that. You're right; you haven't acted that way. Are we good now?"

What was this flash of sincerity? Had I finally gotten through to her?

I searched her gaze for any hints of fakery, and though I sensed she still hated me in her heart of hearts, she seemed to be acting authentic for once. A welcome change. Hopefully, she'd keep it, and maybe it'd stick.

"I guess," I muttered. "Meet Korbin and me in the carriage in half an hour."

Susenne didn't know what she wanted to eat. I should have foreseen her making it difficult, shifting the responsibility to me. I prepared myself to be irritated when she'd reject my next suggestion, so, in a clipped tone, I proposed the bakery on one of the famous downtown streets.

Her eyes lit. "That works. It has flavorful stuff."

"You girls sure about this?" Sir Korbin asked. "That's one of the prime streets for the Harvester, remember?"

"We've been there before and didn't die then," Susenne sighed.

"She has a point," I agreed. "Drop us off there, please. Can you pick us up in an hour or two?"

"That's fine," he said quietly. "Have a good time, girls."

In my head, he thought, *Be patient with her, kid. She needs that: someone to challenge her but still love her as she is.*

So do I, I thought privately, though I didn't think I'd ever admit that.

Besides, I felt more of Akristura's presence in the past few weeks. Though I couldn't see or hear Him, my spirit perceived His occupation. Looking at my sister, I wondered if she'd ever experience this herself.

I nodded to Sir Korbin before climbing down from the carriage. I joined Susenne in front of the bakery, letting the scents absorb into my being. If our conversations didn't yield sweetness, those pastries, exploding with richness and the cheerful blood of many fruits, would.

I frowned. I really did have a preoccupation with blood.

"Ready to go in?" I asked Susenne.

She was looking irritable again.

Great.

"Let's go," she said cheerlessly, stepping into the building.

I moved in behind her and asked her to get us seats while I ordered.

"Is there anything specific you want?"

She scanned the menu as if her happiness depended on selecting the exact right thing. "That," she said, pointing to a spiced pastry loaded with some of the most potent fruits and additives.

"Okay. I'll get that, then."

Interesting choice. It looked more like a gimmick than a food item with everything inside it. I gave my order when the time came and received it seconds later from a glass box where they stored the things, and when I went to find Susenne, I saw her.

Yes, I saw the sister I was supposed to eat lunch with.

Sitting.

By.

Herself.

She'd selected a tiny table with one chair, leaving no room for a second person. Seething, I set down her pastry harder than I should have and hissed, "Why are you at this table? I asked you to get us seats."

Susenne, with no attempt at joking, replied, "I did. My pastry and I will be sitting here. That's "us," isn't it?"

Now she'd done it.

I grabbed the pastry bag and strode across the bakery to the opposite end, dropping into one of the booths. I caught her faint smirk as I watched her go up to the order line herself to make her own purchase. Sir Korbin had paid us some Silvons here and there for odd jobs and chores. I regretted that I was stuck with a pastry she was probably ordering a second time that I had no interest in eating.

I rolled my eyes. Spitefully, I took a bite of her pastry first.

Our relationship truly was ruined. Susenne would never accept me. Something in her nature or the nurture, or lack thereof, with which we'd been raised had set her against me. I couldn't change that, I decided. Like the pastry, she was what she was... and what she was wasn't good.

I spat out the bite I took and scraped my tongue off with a napkin. Far too much sweetness! Who had made it taste like that, like candy?

Like candy.

My already sore heart took a fresh plummet. The many sugary scents recalled lost days of my youth... and people who were equally lost from it. I chose not to focus on the myriad of appealing, borderline sickening smells and instead tucked into my own pastry. As I chewed, I noticed that my senses were numbing a bit as it often went.

Good.

I took another bite, then looked at Susenne, who happily, remorselessly enjoyed lunch with her sister from fifty paces away. Some connection we had. I snorted in bitter laughter and took another bite.

More dullness. I liked this.

When the last bite disappeared, I contemplated buying another. The candy scents still pricked me with memories and guilt, each stained in blood, loss, and horrors I hated to relive. The longer I sat in that bakery waiting for Sir Korbin to come, the longer I battled relentless reminders of what I'd done. How sweet *I* was not.

Well, you don't want to kill and eat these people, and that's a fine improvement from two and a half weeks ago, I told myself. *Progress is progress.*

That had required considerable training, daily exposure to blood and people, and exposure to the outdoors to acquire, the soothing of my murderous urges. I still detected people's blood at close quarters and their breaths and heartbeats, but constantly being around Syndbur's wildest citizens had taught me a measure of self-restraint.

If someone angered me, all bets might have been off. I didn't know how I'd react in an emotionally provocative setting, but resisting the general urge to kill people was already ideal.

At that moment, though, I needed to either stuff my face again or leave. I had to breathe to clear my head of those reminders that lingered like the cold touch of death.

I counted my Silvons and decided I'd rather save them for a future awkward dining occasion, so I slid out from my booth and exited the bakery through a side door into a small street. Inhaling a quiet breath, I turned away from the bakery and ran my fingers through my hair, over my temples, and down my collarbone. How I wished I could wash those memories away.

Why had I killed him? Why any of those people in that sleepy little town?

Monster, the Shadow sneered.

Shut up, I snapped back, but with weaker force than I usually silenced it.

I loathed how present it was. It was in me and around me, like the weather. Like air. My very physical makeup boasted its horrors. I couldn't cut it out like a tumor or fumigate it into non-existence. It *was* me.

My self-control was developing at a steady pace, which was encouraging. That had to indicate Akristura's intervention. I gazed up at the clouds and muttered a prayer of appreciation for this monster in me finally being subdued.

Rough fingers closed over my mouth and chest, driving the air from my teeth. I thrashed at the sudden constriction of thick arms closing around me. Curse this man; he was strong!

"I'll kill you," I growled at my attacker, and I wasn't bluffing.

His answer was to squeeze me tighter until the air drifted from my body. I kicked wildly, but my Shadow agility was useless when I'd been pinned from behind. Who *was* this person?

My heart skipped.

The Harvester.

This wasn't how I'd wanted to meet him.

With what range of motion I had, I scraped my nails over the man's hairy arms, satisfied when they carved out blood. Dark red seeped under them, and between my fear, adrenaline, and the smell of that warm, metal flavor, Shadow Twilight sprang to life.

I shoved back with such force that I threw us into the bakery wall. My captor grunted and clobbered me in the head with the side of his bloody arm. I stretched out my neck to grab a taste when the side door opened, and Susenne stepped out.

"Suze!" I hissed between near-airless lips.

With the reflexes of a true, albeit reduced superhuman, Susenne thrust out her hand and smashed into my attacker's face with purple-tinted lumensa.

But it was still lumensa.

She's actually been practicing, I thought in amazement.

Stunned by the blow, my attacker howled and dropped me, allowing me to regain footing.

He cursed and hissed, "Magicals!" Before backing away.

In seconds, my predatory eyes had him memorized and studied. His height was above average, not terribly tall, and his frame loomed large. His face was hidden under a dark hood, and his clothes were the form-fitting sort that allowed one to move deftly.

He had an irregular heart rhythm that bounded at times and seemed to stutter at others. If I didn't kill him right then, I'd save that knowledge for later. I bared my teeth at him and lunged.

I was met with enormous hands that tossed me back. I sprawled across the pavement, preparing to light my palms, when Susenne went for him again, her hands full of magic. The Harvester retaliated to her charging attack with an elbow to the mouth. She toppled back onto me, and I caught her, putting her behind me so I could finish this. Before I could strike, he sprinted into the dark street and vanished into the small crowd ahead.

I realized no one had helped us fight him off. Many faces watched us, panting and bloodied up, but no one offered support.

"Simpario sympathizers," I muttered.

I hated to see him flee with little consequence. I swore he'd be found again, and next time, he'd have plenty more wounds to remember me by. At that moment, I needed to tend to Susenne.

I kept my face pointed in the direction the Harvester had gone and pulled her toward me to look over her wound. Blood was welling around her lips and even spilling between them.

"Curse him," I hissed, placing my hands on her mouth. "But you did so well, sis. You summoned lumensa, too. That's good!"

Susenne didn't respond, or perhaps she couldn't with the red dribbling over her. Any earlier anger I'd felt toward her vanished. My sister was bleeding and hurt. My sister, who Sir Korbin hadn't known would even defend me if something—something exactly like this—were to happen.

And she did. She attacked the Harvester for me.

My heart, steaming with frustration from before, softened for her.

I didn't care if our lead was gone. What did that matter when one of the people I loved was okay? I would find the monster later and show him what a true monster looked like.

Can't think those thoughts, my spirit warned me. *Thoughts like that create dark magic, not light.*

Susenne started to weep, prompting me to hurry my lumensa summoning. Thick tears rolled into the crimson crusting her lips, and she half-gurgled, "I can't even... taste it. It's like water."

"What?" I asked. "The blood? Suze..."

Was this her concern when she'd nearly been killed? I didn't want to be upset with her, but after she used the correct magic and had placed herself in danger to defend me, now she sought to disappoint me by lusting after her own blood and lamenting when she couldn't savor it?

"That's so not okay, Suze," I told her. "I'm sorry, but it's just not."

Susenne shook her head fiercely and pointed to her mouth. Through the blood and saliva, she managed to slur, "I can't... because my tongue is..."

And that's when it hit me.

What I'd done to her.

What, in either a complete lapse of memory or traumatic self-denial, Shadow Twilight had inflicted on her own younger sister and then *forgotten*.

The tongue wound. Of course.

Her new injury had softened me, but now, with my malleable emotions, she was shaping me back to a familiar, gnawing remorse. I broke apart in her hands, melted, liquefied, and ruined at the memory.

I'd told Sein to do it. To punish her as she'd punished me all my short life with the branding of her tongue, the part of her she never seemed able to control.

He'd done it. And if my other recollections were correct, she'd never quite been able to taste again. Sein had laughed at that. Abusing children brought him pleasure, the baine spawn. I scowled those memories away and focused back on the task at hand.

The mouth injury. One of them I could fix. The other was long since scarred, and the functionality was lost.

"Oh," I moaned, drawing my sister close. "Void below, Susenne, I... I'd forgotten. I forgot what I've done to you."

It was my turn to cry, but I didn't deserve any tears. Susenne was the victim. If only she could taste my pain... but I wouldn't do that to her. She did not need mine in addition to her own.

She continued to weep uncontrollably into my chest, and I cried with her, our tears joining into a river that washed us both. It cleansed us of the blood staining us then and the memories tarnishing us from the past.

It was no secret why she hated me! How was she supposed to even stomach me when I never bothered to apologize for the single worst thing I'd done to her?

The Sharavak Aaquaena could have spared her. Sein might have allowed that, as it seemed he enjoyed reveling in my choice. Giving me the power to make such a horrid decision—knowing full well that I, in my post-hunt high and perpetual dislike of my sister, would be inclined to accept his offer—was what made it delicious for him.

My corruption.

I tried not to seethe. It wasn't the time for seething. It was a time for soothing and uttering the apology that should have been spoken weeks ago.

"Susenne," I whispered through a throat choked with tears, "I am sorry beyond what I can express right now. I mean that. In the core of my rotten being, I mean it." I dropped my chin on her head and gently stroked her strands of brilliant red hair.

Red like her tongue was the night you let a child be punished.

I winced and attempted to say more. "Of all the things I did with those people, that is one of the worst offenses. It was disgustingly cruel of me. Like so many things, it never should have happened."

She fell limper and limper in my arms. She'd reduced me to putty inside while she sagged with similar softness.

"Susenne... it never should have happened, and I would surrender all my magic, abilities, and everything I own to take it back. That ruined it for us. It set our hatred in stone."

Another sob broke from her throat.

"What we both did in that compound will follow us forever," I said with a shiver. "And we can't take any of it back. Not you. Not me. Neither of us. We can't right the past because it's already gone. What we have now are the present and the future. Do you understand? We *can't go back.* That history's been written. In all its ugliness... it's there. Our story."

"I wish it wasn't," she replied, her words veiled in agony.

"I know," I said. "Me, too. I understand. But now..."

My fingers strayed to her busted lips. I coaxed lumensa out and bathed in its satisfying warmth. Golden tendrils seeped slowly into her mouth and began erasing the Harvester's cruel hit.

"I don't want us to fight anymore, Susenne," I sighed. "My heart can't take it. Can yours?"

She thought for a moment before shaking her head.

"You hate me," I murmured, "And you have every right to. But I truly am sorry. Unfortunately, that's all I can say right now. The rest is up to you. I don't deserve it if you forgive me, but I'm forever grateful. If you don't..." I lowered my eyes and nodded to myself. "Then I can accept that, too. All I ask is that we at least try to move forward as sisters instead of lingering on the past when our relationship was pure dislike. I love you, Susenne. I don't want to do this anymore."

Susenne's tongue passed over her lips to wipe away the rest of the blood. I stopped her and dabbed it off for her with my shirt sleeve.

"Thank you for bravely protecting me today," I told her, my shattered heart pieces beginning to rejoin at seeing her repaired mouth. "That means a lot to me. You were so cool."

Susenne cracked a smile. "You were, too. I had a feeling something was wrong. I saw you step out, so I followed you when I got the bad impression. I'm glad I did... even though you ate my pastry."

"Actually, I didn't. It was awful."

She laughed. I laughed with her and gave her another hug.

"Next time, save a seat for me, will you?" I said.

She sniffled through her last tears and nodded. "I will."

Chapter Fourteen

"How did I know you two would find trouble in under an hour?"

Sir Korbin was livid when he picked us up, firing a rapid line of questions as we returned to the commune.

"Who was this man? Anyone recognizable? How tall, how big, what were the facial features, and how did he speak and carry himself?"

I shared the memory, and he grimaced, then shouted at the horses to go faster. Susenne and I shared a bewildered expression at his loosely capped rage.

"Never again, girls," he muttered. "I'm sorry, but you probably agree now, after that. Figures. It's an off day for most citizens, so of course the Harvester would be lurking around town, prowling for more meat." He hissed a barely audible curse, surprising us further.

"It's okay," I said softly. "Actually, it helped us bond." I touched Susenne's shoulder.

Sir Korbin looked over at us. "I see. Praise Akristura for small miracles. Did either of you use valdur?"

"I wasn't able to get much magic out at all," I admitted.

"I used lumensa," Susenne said.

Korbin's brows hiked to his forehead. "Really? That's excellent. Wow. Were I in your position at your age and level of experience, that man would have been quite dead. Good work, ladies."

Not murdering a murderer *was* an accomplishment, especially when Sharavak blood polluted one's veins.

"How did you not sense the man coming up behind you, girl?" He asked me.

"Uh... I think I'm going to have to blame the pastries for that. They mellowed out my senses," I answered.

He shook his head and grumbled, "Pastries. They'll take years off your life one way or another." He pulled into the driveway. "Tomorrow, Twilight, you and I will find this man. It's time to stop this and find out what's happening."

"I was going to suggest that myself," I replied, inspecting my palms and wondering how much I'd be using them soon.

Dark red caught my eye as I observed them. Blood had crusted under my nails. I brought my fingertips to my nose and inhaled to study the sour scent that entered it. My predator mind filed away the scent for recollection, and I descended from the carriage feeling, finally, that I was about to begin fulfilling the first phase of saving the world from certain destruction.

I was woken about two hours before dawn. Sir Korbin, not dressed in his usual robed attire, waited for me outside my room. He looked awkward in his plain gray sweatshirt and pants, but not bad.

"Morning," I mumbled. "Is there a reason we're going at this hour?"

"Yes. I need you to get into clothes like mine, please, so we don't shine brightly under the lantern lights. The Harvester can best be tracked down in the early morning when he's making deals or making his rounds."

Hearing the word "Harvester" set my teeth on edge, prying sleepiness from my mind. I changed into darker attire like Korbin's, then joined him outside, where his vehicle waited.

"Can't afford much gas," he said, "But we really can't afford to lose the horses, so we're taking this today."

The vehicle aside, this would have been such a regular occurrence: hop into our transportation in the morning, go down to town, see the sights, smell the non-prey, and return, prayerfully unscathed. It carried a danger with it this time. The Harvester was much larger and stronger than me, and though we were both predators in our own right, I suspected he was more seasoned. I had the instinct, but he had that and more: experience.

"You ready for this?" Sir Korbin asked, switching on the headlights.

I nodded. "The timing's ideal. I've finally reached a point where I'm not tempted to kill everything in existence. Feels kind of nice. But I'm still not afraid to rough a creep up a little... or a lot."

Korbin chuckled. "Feisty as ever. We'll not be inflicting major damage unless we have to, though. We've talked about this: you'll track the guy down, and we'll both jump him together. Rumor has it he lives almost entirely alone. I believe that. People like him can't keep company for long." He sighed. "After that, we'll interrogate him."

"What about his operation?" I asked. "Are we not going to turn him in to the authorities? I mean, he abducts little children!"

"I know." Sir Korbin's jaw went rigid. "Unfortunately, Twilight, the Silver authorities already know about this. They've elected to remain quiet about it for money, job security, or something along those lines. Remember, the Under Market is in direct service to the Silver government and Simpario. No law enforcer would dare tempt death by speaking up about it, and besides, the Double Digit Liberty Act already allows adults to use children."

Sourness seeped into my mouth, and I had the briefest thought that maybe the Shadows were right in wanting to destroy the world.

"What's the Double Digit Liberty Act?" I asked, my throat gone dry.

"All children ages ten and up—the double-digit age—are allowed, by law, to "consent" to sexual relations with adults," Sir Korbin said with such controlled quiet that the vehicle's tires passing over the road seemed to be shouting their rage for him.

The sourness had gone to my stomach. Suddenly, all the naked children wandering Syndbur and holding reluctant hands with adults made sense. Exploiting them and marring their innocence was a *government-sanctioned practice.*

"You see why I was so hesitant to take you to town, and I couldn't leave with you two there yesterday. Had you wandered any length around it, you would have met people not much better than the Harvester. At least the Harvester has the dignity to kill children after he's robbed them."

Sir Korbin's voice closed off with tears that he fiercely swallowed back. Mine were sprouting, too. I hadn't realized we'd already made it into town and parked in one of the empty spaces behind the bakery.

Dozens of bodies still meandered through the streets, seeking additional pleasure like listless shadows searching for more darkness to justify their lack of light. They yelled obscenities at each other, giving the impression they were about to fight, but I quickly learned this was how they all talked to each other. Calling someone a "randy cat-licker" was a compliment in Syndbur.

"Keep your head down," Sir Korbin muttered, swinging his legs out of the car. I followed him, keeping to the darkness behind the bakery so the wanderers on the other side of it wouldn't notice us.

I took in a silent breath. If we were fortunate, the Harvester would be lurking nearby, and I'd be able to smell a flicker of his blood. Those with stronger blood had trackable scents. The Harvester's acrid life fluid was one of the harsher scents I'd learned.

Let's start walking, I thought to Korbin.

We'll take this first street here and make our way through each of them, he thought back. *If we find nothing, I hope you're okay with giving it another hour or two to see if something comes up.*

I nodded, and we began our trek down the street the Harvester had tried to steal me from the previous day. I shuddered at the memories and kept my head down as Sir Korbin asked while letting my nose lead the way under my sweatshirt hood.

We probably never would have come down here if not for this situation, Korbin thought. *Not that we can track like you seem to be able to.*

Several men on our current street whistled at me. I kept walking as my cheeks warmed with angry heat.

I don't blame you for not wanting to come down here, I replied.

"Who's this sweet sack of bones?" A lone man cried.

I caught his eye and tried not to glare at him.

Don't answer him, Sir Korbin begged.

"You hear me, whore? Listen when a man talks to you."

I chomped on my lip. It was that or his neck.

"Begone," Sir Korbin snapped.

The man cackled. "Want to join us, pal? Are you Dad?"

"Get out of here!" I snarled.

"Ooh." He whistled again and started to come toward us. I threw myself at him, and Sir Korbin had to restrain me.

The man found this display outrageously funny. "Man, she really wants it! What're you charging, darling?"

Sir Korbin started to drag me faster down the street. The man stayed back and didn't choose to follow us, but his laughter did.

Small miracles, indeed.

"You're going to hear a lot of that tonight," Korbin hissed, "So you'd best adjust to it now. You can't kill every troublesome man you see."

"Why not?" I groaned.

It was a joke—half of one, anyway—but Sir Korbin wasn't amused.

"Let me handle these engagements from now on," he said.

We passed along one dim, lantern-lit street after another. No promising scents presented themselves, and light was being born on the horizon. I groaned. Sir Korbin urged me not to become frustrated.

"All we've seen tonight are creeps!" I cried. "And not even the right ones. I doubt he's out here right now."

Sir Korbin whispered a prayer and begged that I keep going. It was the fourth street, and we'd already crossed half of it. Disbelief was setting in.

"Maybe we're not meant to find him," I whispered. "Did you think of that?"

An annoyed look passed his face.

Even if we did, the only way we'd get him to talk would be with death threats. I didn't trust myself enough not to follow through on them.

You're afraid.

I looked at Korbin. *Of what?*

Of doing something you regret.

Like making a hole in this guy's throat? Naturally. Someone had to, didn't they?

A tang hit the roof of my mouth. A familiar one.

I inhaled deeply and consumed the aroma, letting it simmer on my tongue. Saliva flooded in moments later. I shook my head and swallowed to wash away the warmth of that scarlet spoil's scent, but it only brought more spittle.

"Damn," I muttered, tracing my palm scars.

"You have something?"

I did, and if I could follow it without my mouth watering, that would be ideal. The blood sang with bitterness, like fluid hate. It projected its repulsive attractiveness from up ahead.

Won't surrender to these desires. I will not kill. That isn't me anymore.

Oh, but the way the crimson winked on my tongue...

It is me, I thought. *It's every bit of my monster.*

If I could just dip my finger in, have a taste—

"No!" I growled.

"What's wrong?" Sir Korbin asked, keeping his voice low.

I stopped and scrubbed my face with my hands, attempting to stimulate some sanity into my head. I was tired of this game. I was tired of thinking of *human beings* as game.

"He's up there," I whispered with strain. "Smells foul, but I like it all the same."

I gave the atmosphere a mental scan while Sir Korbin granted me some of his lumensa to soothe me. He began to pray over me in low tones. I said a prayer for myself, too, before continuing on my way.

Every stride sharpened the scent. I could ignore it, I decided. The throbbing ache in my temples and how my tongue danced inside my cheek.

No dismemberment. You're here for answers and answers only.

The scent trail was leading us to places neither of us wanted to be, but of course it was. It wasn't as if the Harvester would live somewhere with pleasant people. No. He had to make his neighbors match himself.

The alley steadily darkened as we walked. A few faces poked out of crumbling window sills, and I drew the hood on my sweatshirt tighter around me. Ignoring the shadows didn't make them go away, but seeing as I had a shadow to contend with in myself, I could resist the prickle of watchful gazes trailing my steps.

If I didn't, if this beast wasn't contained...

"Hey, kid."

I sprang back at an older man's voice behind me. He leered at me from his kitchen window and beckoned me closer, throwing a glance at Sir Korbin, too. I turned to keep walking when I caught the glint of the blade in his hand.

"Let's fix that nose, sweetie," he crowed. "All I do is make a few incisions, crush a few bones, and realign them. It's cheaper than a stuffing job." His gaze flicked to my chest.

"We'll have none of that, thanks," Sir Korbin replied evenly.

I locked eyes with the man and, in his mind, growled, *Touch me, and I'll mangle much more on you than your nose.*

The man stumbled away as if I'd turned his blade on him, and I swiveled around, back to the mission at hand. I understood the Akristurans' hesitation to investigate this place. Every alley was cobwebbed in dark characters.

A minute passed. A pair of eyes caught the faint lantern light up ahead, and I heard the erratic heartbeat that had distinguished the fellow yesterday.

Him.

He was there, his broad body overshadowing the shaking form of a tiny older woman. They spoke in hushed and hurried phrases, and the Harvester's high body heat and faint snippets of harsh sentences spelled his anger.

It's the guy, I thought to Korbin.

You're certain?

Yes. It's his blood I'm smelling. I also recognize his heart rhythm, and he has the same build as my attacker. It's got to be him.

I strained my ears to listen, catching pieces of their conversation.

... "debt. You've owed me that for weeks, and don't pretend... don't make enough from... projects."

I hoped the Harvester wouldn't kill this small woman, too. Her lack of youth probably wasn't appealing to him as a parts collector, but if she was in trouble with him...

Should we move in? I asked.

Korbin didn't have time to answer. The Harvester caught us looking, his empty eyes glaring in the lantern light.

... "watching us. A girl... I have to go. I'll see you soon."

He took off down the alley. Sir Korbin gave him a few moments to get far enough ahead for us to accost him. We stepped out, prepared to follow him when the lady stopped us.

"Please," she whispered, "I owe that man. I'm in terrible debt. He saw you, you know. He's no one to mess with."

"I'm sorry," Sir Korbin said curtly, "But we need to get going."

The woman's face fell, and she cried, "No! Please. He's a monster. I paid him once for a big project and haven't been able to pay him back since, but now my son is sick, and I can't get him medical care because that man keeps coming around and threatening me."

Her eyes shone with tears. Moved for her, I told her that I could help her son. I touched my palms, and Sir Korbin thought, *You shouldn't have exposed your abilities! That wasn't smart, especially since she knows the Harvester!*

So, it was foolish. What was also foolish, and wasteful, was letting a man die when I could very well heal him. If this woman no longer had to contend with medical expenses for him, she might even be able to pay off her hound.

Not that I intend to leave him unscathed.

"What? You have some means of doing that?" The woman's cheeks bloomed with a smile. "Oh, wonderful! But... how much would I owe you? I can't afford much more of anything right now. He already has my money tied up." She nodded at the retreating figure down the alley.

"How about we go talk to him first?" Sir Korbin suggested, giving me a knowing stare. "Before he gets away."

"Don't leave me alone," the woman wept. "He knows more people like him. I live in fear every day, and no one even knows."

I looked helplessly at Korbin. He sighed.

"Take care of her and the son. I'll go talk to our guy." His eyes narrowed at me. "Be safe."

I nodded, and the woman urged Sir Korbin to do the same. She invited me into her house, explaining that her son had been suffering for months as she took me inside.

"The doctors know it's a life-threatening illness, but they can't tell me what, exactly, it is," she fretted.

I drank in the interior of her home and appreciated its simplicity. Dark red walls. Neat, clean stone surfaces. She'd meticulously arranged her decor, appliances, and utensils so that nothing was displaced or mismatched. I burned knowing men like the Harvester preyed on people like her.

Akristura, please protect Korbin, I prayed.

I regretted not going with him. It hadn't been the plan, but I would make this detour quick. The woman needed me, too.

"If you'll just come down here," she said, flipping the light switch on a set of wooden stairs descending into her basement.

It was interesting how I could still vividly smell the Harvester despite his absence. I really wouldn't have been opposed to biting that smell. As the basement door opened, new scents met me.

Only they weren't new. Not entirely.

It was blood.

Again.

But different this time. Older, colder, and slightly masked by the more pungent odor of the Harvester... which was coming from the woman behind me.

Why did I let her walk behind me?

"So," I said casually, taking in the basement with each step, "What was the project the man was doing for you that cost so much?"

"Oh, well, I was extending the size of my basement," she replied. "In my golden years, I've taken my collecting hobby more seriously."

"Interesting. What is it you collect?"

Because it sure smells like people's life fluid to me.

"Come."

The woman—I realized I hadn't even gotten her name—brought me to a metal door with a keypad. She flipped open the keypad cover and punched in the passcode. When the door's locks hissed, she gently pushed me in front of her and let the world beyond it make itself apparent.

"There's my son," she whispered when the door exposed a freezer with a metal table upon which a young man was sprawled. "And won't you make a lovely sister for him?"

The blade came. I heard it rustle in her pocket. Before she jabbed it between my ribs, I seized her hand and forced her back, where she crumpled on the ground. A bag of red exploded with her fall. The Harvester's blood—or else not the Harvester's—screamed for me to taste it.

"You?" I snarled, ripping the knife from her hand and pressing it to her throat.

"Please," she whined, "I just take parts. That's all I do; that's it!"

"I know what you do," I snapped. "Why do you do it? What would compel you to do such a horrible thing?"

The woman stammered, "I just harvest from what I find in town, r-really. It makes good money. Some of them are already dying, yes, dying when I take them." Her eyes stretched wider. "And then... then some of them offer me their spare things when *they* need money."

I laughed. "People pay you to cut them up? Is this your favor for the noble Eminent?"

"It's only a few organs!" She gasped. "People have two for a reason!"

I pushed the knife harder against her neck. "And let me guess; you were just luring me in to stab me so you could offer me your services?"

The woman smiled hopefully. "If you want to use them, I'll gladly detach the pieces! Your eyes..." She gazed longingly at them, and I growled. "Or maybe just your hair! My work isn't always bloody."

"You're about to be bloody," I snarled.

Don't kill her. You're above that now; it shouldn't be that way anymore!

I drew my lips back and imagined burying myself into her throat. This was going to be the moment that set back all my progress.

"What sharp teeth you have," the woman whispered, trembling beneath me. "Why so sharp?"

I smiled. "The better to eat you with, I guess."

I breathed deeply of her scent. Softness. Weakness. Her very bones were decaying, as was the rest of her aged flesh. It wouldn't be much of a challenge to kill her, but all predators liked an easy meal...

"Akristura," I groaned.

"Don't kill me, child! Please don't! It's only business!"

"Shut up," I hissed.

In her mind, I thought, *What is Eminent Simpario planning for this region, and what is your role in that? You know things. I hear you're one of his favorite pets.*

The woman blinked and thought back, *A Shadow who doesn't know her master's orders? Interesting.*

"We obey no zyz," I growled. "Answer the question."

"I won't." The woman smiled madly. "I take parts for him. I help him get the children's parts, too, keeping him and his officials young, but if I told you more, you know what?" She licked her lips. "My parts would go bye-bye, too."

Every word she spoke was a call, a kiss, a beg, a beckoning. She wanted to die and fall apart in my mouth, nicely, yes, melt away like butter and salt, like the spindly muscles clinging to her little body—

"Gah!"

I blinked, keeping the knife in position. What I wanted to do was undoubtedly wrong, but was it worth it? Looking into her eyes, I didn't know.

No. I couldn't screw this up. I'd have to acquire answers another way.

An ethical way.

"What are you doing with your assistant's blood?" I demanded.

"Selling it." The Harvester grinned. "I promised him money if he'd give it to me. I was going to present it to one of the officials as a child's blood and get a higher price out of him. He's one of the dimmer members. He'd be none the wiser."

I clamped down on my rage and hissed, "Where do you hide the children? Show them to me!"

The Harvester laughed. "You came to the wrong place, Shadow. Don't you know I have a special location just for them? The Market couldn't possibly be supplied only from here."

Araveh above... if she didn't stop speaking like that, she'd find herself carved to pieces. Did she not know this? Had she no fear?

"I will kill you with my magic, with the utmost brutality," I growled, "If you do not reveal two things to me: what Eminent Simpario and the Silver government are planning for the Shadows' Dark Hour and where you hide the children. You will die."

She grinned, empty-eyed as if she did not hear or see anything but my face. "Beautiful monster," she breathed. It was the last phrase she uttered before my hands closed around her throat and began to squeeze.

Shadow Twilight commanded me. Her movements glided with all the suppleness of a moon ray washing over the world at night. Night, from which she derived her energy, bathed, played, and hunted. A creature of darkness was Twilight, who did not know the light and cared nothing for it.

Stop, my spirit ordered.

I won't listen to you, spirit, I snapped back. *I've a monster to kill.*

Oh, the battle was on, and darkness was winning. Shadows draped my mind, driving my fingers to crush and degrade the bones inside them with further disregard. The only regard Twilight had was for destruction. Like Aadyalbaine, she only knew how to ruin.

Stop.

My fingers paused, and I hesitated. The Harvester had gone limp beneath me.

Gasping, I drew back as she was no longer fighting. I looked at my hands with the same nausea I'd felt about them before. My madness was subsiding. I climbed down from the high and removed myself from the woman before it demanded me to finish what I'd started.

In the high's place settled a chilling fog. My conscience had spared this ghastly person's life, but the Shadow in me loomed. I surrendered to its next impulse.

I thrust my mind into hers and forced a connection. She couldn't stop me, and she wasn't willing to give me answers. Shadow Twilight decided on the unethical approach. As soon as the click formed, my dark magic groaned inside me and roused like a murderous beast awoken from a deep slumber. So, it *had* been sleeping. I'd unknowingly disturbed it and drawn it to the surface to fulfill my devious task.

Which is...

I sifted through her memories, committed. Plenty of useless and wretched ones passed by. I wouldn't dwell on any that weren't absolutely relevant.

Finally, after over a minute, I stumbled on Eminent Simpario's face and paused there.

"My good friend experienced a loss recently, but we're both of the opinion it's a minor setback."

Ugh. Was that him? I loathed the grace of his movements. Another floater, like Shadow men, whose delicate movements never matched their brutal interiors.

"One of your Shadow friends?" Harvester rumbled.

Simpario nodded. *"Despite the setback, we'll be proceeding as usual. The schedule hasn't changed much. We're going to rely more on your business expertise in the days to come to keep us strong, dear. As always, the paychecks will be fat."* He smiled, and I moved on to the next memory.

There, Simpario was privately discussing his next political moves with a group of men and a couple scattered women. *"We're on the brink of bringing the extremists and everyone who supports them under fire. They're the last threat to this Dark Hour my friends speak of."*

"Have we graduated to murder, eh, Yesah?" One of his companions chuckled.

Simpario considered, his feline eyes narrowing in thought. *"We're about there. Give it a little more time."*

The last memory I made myself watch before withdrawing from her soiled mind showed Simpario reveling in the coming riches of the post-Myrkraas world.

"They've brought me this far. I was nothing before, do you remember, dear?"

The Harvester nodded. *"You were practically a child. I remember thinking little of you."*

She laughed, and Simpario frowned.

"Not now, I hope?"

"Oh, no," she said quickly. *"You pay better than the others did."*

"Mm," he said, *"And I'm about to pay you more when this Dark Hour thing goes through. So exciting. Who else gets to be part of history like this? If the plunder from the people isn't ripe now, wait. We'll be drowning in it."* He licked his lips.

Disgusted, I disconnected from the Harvester and stepped away, wondering what to do with her. She hadn't stirred while I'd been invading her thoughts. While there, I'd come across the location of the Under Market's youngest victims. Surely I could put that information to use?

I sprinted back up the steps to the main floor. I had to find Sir Korbin.

Fortunately, neither of us had to wait long to reconnect. It wasn't but seconds after fleeing the Harvester's house that I collided with him, running back up the street from whence he came.

"Are you okay?" He cried. "I felt it, that I shouldn't have left you."

I shrugged, feeling disjointed from my body. "I don't know."

His gaze was only shades from being wild with fear. "Are you hurt? Where's the woman?"

I gestured weakly to the house. "Inside."

Korbin frowned. "What's wrong? You're not hurt, right?"

I shook my head.

"Twilight, please give me something to work with," he implored. "Words, preferably."

"I almost killed her," I choked. "But I didn't. She's still alive down there."

He nodded quickly. "Okay. And *you're* fine?"

"Yes," I muttered. "I'm fine."

He nodded again, processing this. "Good. That's good." He ran agitated fingers over his head. "You discovered she's the real Harvester, I assume. My man was a bust. He's just a supplier."

"I did find that," I said. "I also found out where she keeps the children for the Under Market and what Simpario and Father seem to be planning."

"Oh? She yielded that?"

I snorted. "No. I took it from her."

Sir Korbin's hovering frown descended. "You didn't."

"I did."

He loosed a sigh and crossed his arms briefly before uncrossing them again. "You know forcing yourself into someone's mind is a violation, right, Twilight? It uses valdur."

"I know."

Sir Korbin threw up his hands. "Okay, then. We'll discuss this later. Now's not the time. What did you do with the woman?"

I relayed the memory, trembling with a sudden onslaught of guilt and fear. He was disappointed in me. This only fueled my nightmarish emotional state.

"You're shaking," he said softly. "Come on. Let's get you home."

"We're not going to do anything with the Harvester?" I asked.

"Don't worry about that right now."

He took my arm and guided me back down the twisted road that had brought us there, promising he'd share my memories with people who counted: the citizens. Syndbur was waking with the coming dawn, or at least some of it was. The honest folks were.

Once we'd broken back onto the main road by the bakery, Sir Korbin projected my memories to dozens of citizens commuting to work, walking to the store, or exercising their pets, filling their minds with the location of the Under Market's operational crux. A storm against the Silver government took shape shortly thereafter.

CHAPTER FIFTEEN

I HAD WANTED TO go about the rest of my day and hear the continuing updates about the Under Market situation, but Sir Korbin would have none of it.

"You've had a long and exhausting morning. Go rest."

I tried to sleep, but slumber evaded me. I'd stoked my valdur flames. They weren't likely to quiet down anytime soon.

Who will I dream about tonight? I wondered in my bedroom. *Mother or Father?*

At that moment, I realized how much I missed Mother. She always had answers, and even if she didn't, she had a pretty face, didn't she? A pretty smile. Pretty hugs. Pretty everything.

I looked at myself in my bedroom mirror as most girls do sometimes and studied the face gazing back. Yes, something had changed there. The predatory look had softened into an expression approaching wisdom, and not a kind that usually belonged to people of my young age. So why had I acted on my Sharavak impulses and used the dark power to acquire answers?

"You told yourself you'd be ethical," I whispered to my reflection, "And you weren't. You failed."

It was the wisdom under valdur's stain in my eyes that chastised me. The wisdom was the accusing finger that frequently pointed at me, though not nearly as harshly as my own, when I scolded myself. The darkness in my eyes, I realized, was the newness, the spirit, expressing its sorrow over my deed.

I warned you, but you silenced me, it whispered. *Why did you silence your soul?*

I couldn't bear to look at myself any longer. It was too horrible to be alive and constantly subjected to temptation, yet my depravity was comfortable. What it lacked, though, was substance. When met with substance, I crumbled. I could not withstand my newness or its questions.

After an hour of restlessness, I descended to the main floor of the commune and found Sir Korbin.

"Yes?" He asked gently.

"I think it's time I did what you suggested a while ago," I said. "Something I didn't give much thought to at the time: going to the Bronze."

Sir Korbin nodded thoughtfully. "I'm in agreement with you. If the Shadows are indeed proceeding with their plan, we've no other choice. The Bronze is strictly isolationist. They don't play political games with anyone, but if they learn the entire world is threatened by this Shadow menace, they may change their tune." He took a sip of water and handed me a plate of crackers, fruit, and vegetables. "For you. Please eat."

I accepted the plate and took an uninspired nibble of a cracker. Sir Korbin frowned.

"You need energy, girl. You may not feel depleted yet, but your body does after this morning."

I cracked a smile. "Always concerned about my well-being."

"I can't help it. Someone needs to look after you. If I leave it to Norva, she'll smother you, and Il or Annisara won't be kind enough." He chuckled. "But go eat. If this is really what you want to do, we'll need to make some arrangements. Do you want to announce it when you're done?"

"Sure."

"Okay. We'll do that. Now, really, kid. Eat your blasted snack."

He smacked my arm with a cracker box and ushered me off to the kitchen table. I chewed slowly, feeling that even my mouth was weighed down with magic. The snack did not satisfy. I required more than a snack to stave off the madness that leaned into my spirit, desperately working to force my hand.

But force it on what?

I joined everyone in the living space where Sir Korbin had called them together shortly after eating. They watched me expectantly as Sir Korbin briefly explained what took place earlier that morning and what it entailed for me.

"After seeing what I saw today and learning that the Sharavak Fadain is going to continue with the original Myrkraas plan—the one where the giant monster in the Void is summoned and set against the world—I've decided to go to the Bronze to enlist their help," I informed them. "Because if all this is true, we're going to need a bigger army."

Excited and anxious chatter broke among them, faces turning to whisper into ears and eyes stretching wide with wonder and fear. Doomsday talk passed between them. Cobi stood up from the back of the crowd and said, "If you're going, I'm coming with you."

My chilled heart warmed. "I'd love that. Thank you."

Norva stood up, too, pulling Il to his feet beside her. "We'll be coming along as well. They're going to need bodyguards, Korbin."

Sir Korbin nodded. "This is true. Thank you, both of you. I'm grateful you've volunteered."

The three exchanged thoughts. Korbin concluded the meeting with, "This is the best option we have right now to combat a rising plague. It is only Akristura's light that will defeat this present darkness, so please offer Twilight and whoever goes with her your prayers. They will comfort her in a foreign land."

Numerous people came up to me after the meeting to offer me their appreciation and congratulations. No one had ever done something like this before, nor had such assertive posturing been taken to curb the Shadows' power in centuries.

"We've fallen by the wayside," Lady Annisara told me, "Because we have been giving darkness a foothold for years. Now we act surprised when it kicks us?" She sighed. "But you are doing a great service to us, child, and the world, especially if you are successful." She touched my starstone. "Be careful."

When she touched it, I did not think of the daunting road I'd just opened for myself that loomed ahead. I thought of Mother, who I was suddenly desperate to see. Annisara drifted away, and I clutched my necklace, writhing more agitatedly than I had an hour ago.

All the faces, expectations, and hopeful eyes filled me with a desire to escape. I needed to breathe.

I had to process what, in a moment, I had decided for myself. The potential fate of the world. The ruin of nations. I gazed out the window at the dips and valleys of fields and the city stretching beneath them. The fate of all those people now rested on me.

Power had made Sein go mad. Would it have the same effect on me, or would I navigate it successfully?

Massaging my collarbone, I slipped outside, away from the noisy chatter, and into the still silence of the woods. It was high morning by then. The natural world had already loosened its limbs for another full day of existence. I, however, sought a respite from existence just for a little while.

In a vague sense, I'd planned to hunt. A fog still covered my mind. It even washed out my spirit to an extent, as the blood scents still sang to me. I tasted the Harvester's assistant, the jeering men on the streets, and the Harvester's own intact fluids as I wove my way through the trees, searching.

For what?

I knew what I wanted. I could justify it by claiming it as meaningless heat-seeking and sensory enhancement practice, but my nose already knew things. I sought to mask the knowledge of my own intentions with the pretenses that my nose *didn't* know, that it required this random training that put an expectant tilt in my form and suppleness in my limbs—suppleness that also coated my mouth in the form of saliva.

Yes, my beast needed a post-mission exercise to cool down.

Flattened brush waited up around a bend in the trees ahead. I immediately dropped to a slinking position, ignoring the crackling of my knees as I slipped through the under-growth. I breathed in and let the taste of whatever made this mess settle.

Deer. Wasn't it always deer?

Maybe it was even the same one as before. It certainly had the nutrient density in its heavy scent and thick blood aroma. It was no stranger to youth.

Again, my tongue stirred, and I had to bite it back. I didn't intend to kill this deer. That's what I told myself, but every step forward was beginning to weigh less, as if I simply needed one good lunge to reach, and plunge into, my target.

"It's not a target," I growled to myself. "It's one of Akristura's—"

I paused. Heat and a motion imperceptible to ordinary people shifted several hundred paces to my left. I tensed and dropped a little lower until my palms grazed the forest floor. Yes, a thick slice of early lunch was crouching behind a tree not three strides away.

The warmth pulsing through its flesh echoed to my own flesh. I wasn't warm, though. My blood was hot—as was my temper—but the mind... I swallowed and found my throat washing wet with saliva.

That was decidedly cold.

I knew I'd already accomplished what I told myself I'd gone there to do. Sniff an animal's blood, resist the temptation to slaughter it, and seek it out using body heat. Bing, bam, boom. A success.

Only it wasn't. The temptation part remained, and if I kept staring at that thing, breathing in its blood and its weakness—

I raked my nails over my arms. The pain pried me from feverish delusions, and I wanted to flee. Myself, that was what I was running from, and the twisted longings of my flesh.

The spirit was new. The body, old and accustomed to getting its way.

This time, the animal overrode the spirit.

I was out of the bushes before I quite knew where I'd gone. The deer started to bound away. It was faster with its four legs, but I wasn't slow by any means. I was driven forward by the lure of the hunt and promises of satisfaction. My teeth ground, and the wind whipped deliciously through my nostrils, carrying the deer's sweet scent with it.

I sprang. One of the deer's hind legs caught in my hands. It kicked and nearly jostled me off, but the predator in me clung doggedly to my prey. I gave it a yank, more strength in my small body than there ought to have been, and the animal collapsed.

I didn't hesitate.

As it struggled beneath me, I clambered on top of it, thrashed around by its movements, and leaped for its throat. It wasn't the deer I saw as I dipped in, but the Harvester. Her twisted face dominated my mind. It took the shape of the squirming deer, dragging me into a mania I hadn't enjoyed in weeks.

Immersing myself in her bloodstream was as natural, as *right,* as it was exhilarating. Her life essence unraveled on my tongue. I laughed through a mouthful of it and shredded my teeth through the flesh.

The child abuser had been exposed, and the people in town were rioting. The ones who cared, anyway. I couldn't think much beyond this. Rational reasoning didn't exist, not when the Harvester had never enjoyed my mouth fitting around her arteries and stripping them out.

Wrong, my spirit screamed. *You're wrong!*

Couldn't... focus...

The taste... my newness... didn't want to spoil it anymore.

Scarlet stained everything. Akristura had patched me back together and restored my purity, yes. That had been the hopeful feeling, but the flesh still rotted.

The flesh in my mouth.

On my tongue.

Corrupting my soul.

The flesh—

"What are you doing?"

Cobi.

I snapped back from my meal, which no longer struggled, and gazed wildly into my friend's eyes. He watched me with an expression that didn't know if it was disgusted or intrigued. I smeared some of the blood off my face and swallowed the bite in my mouth.

"I..."

I had no answer, no justifiable reason except—

My flesh wanting what it wanted.

I spat, enraged. Like a child, I'd concerned myself only with my aberrant hunger. Now my friend looked at me as if he didn't know me, and worse, as if he didn't *want* to.

Cobi shook his head and took a trembling step back. "I have to tell Korbin."

"No!" I cried. A dribble of blood snaked down my mouth. "I have to be the one to tell him."

I read the uncertainty in his gaze. His posture wasn't prey-like, but neither was it confident. I wished I could read his thoughts.

Tell me what you're thinking.

Cobi accepted my hursafar message and allowed me briefly into his mind. A grip of horror met me there, and the chill of dread. Fear's pungent scent also swirled inside him. Nestled among these feelings, though, was awe and deep fondness that outshined the darker thoughts. Moisture pricked my eyes, and I withdrew.

"You don't hate me," I said softly. "That's a relief."

Cobi's eyes turned down. "No."

"No?"

"I don't hate you," he clarified.

I nodded slowly, gulping down approaching tears. "I'm sorry. I shouldn't have done this."

Cobi's gaze briefly flicked to the deer. "You're right. You shouldn't have. Why did you?"

I shook my head fiercely and pointed behind him. "Go. Leave. You're not safe with me at this moment. Let me get myself under control."

"You're thinking of killing me?" Cobi whispered.

The tears poured when he said this. I clawed my collarbone and hissed, "Yes."

There was silence as he processed this. Cobi broke it with a sigh. "I can't be afraid of you every time you're like this, Twi. You can't alter what you are. The benefits do outweigh the bad—"

"How?" I snapped. "So, I can stalk. I can track. My magic can create ungodly storms, and I was the chosen teenage savior of a death cult. So, what? Even you just standing there right now..." I shook my head and, Cobi's feelings be damned, took another large bite of the deer.

My magic realm fluttered, and I brushed off Cobi's scent like it didn't affect me, but my watering mouth said otherwise. He shouldn't have visited me when I was feeding. When he spoke to me like he knew things about myself that I didn't, I wanted *his* neck in my mouth, and no sound-minded person thought like that.

"I'm sorry," he said. I looked up at Cobi, tracing the heat in his face and the ice in his eyes. "Maybe I should stay here," he said tremulously, trying to convince himself he had the courage to. "You need to get better. You have to try harder, Twilight—"

"You know what?" I snapped. "Why don't you try to be less of a coward?"

This was what turned his eyes into searing coals and sent him whirling back to the commune.

"Wait!" I blurted through the deer in my mouth. "I'm sorry! I didn't mean that."

He didn't turn. Desperate, I spat out the meat against my animal side's wishes and ran to him. I grabbed his hand and spun him around, pulling him into my arms.

"I'm sorry. That was cruel of me. I'm not in the right state of mind right now," I babbled.

Cobi didn't hug me back. I let go of him, frustrated, and studied his scent and energy. His heart thudded to the slow pace of sorrow while his face burned with anger and shame. He looked me over in all my bloodiness. I realized I'd transferred some of that to his clothes and quickly apologized. He interrupted me.

"You've said too much, Twilight. You're too much."

I bit back my anger and hissed, "Excuse me? "Too much?" Then why did you come out to find me? You shouldn't have approached me when you saw what I was doing; you should have turned and ran!"

I licked the blood off my lips with aggressive flair and marched back toward the deer. Too much, was I? I descended on the animal and ripped a new hole in its flank.

Maybe he was too little.

Regret ravaged me after I finished my fill of the deer. Half choked with sobs, I hurried back to the commune and tried to compose myself before finding Sir Korbin. He was in his study reading when I intruded on his peace.

"Twilight?" He closed his book when he saw me and set it aside, his mouth tightening with concern. "What's happened to you, girl? Why all the blood?"

His surprise carried no disappointment... yet. The poor man believed I'd been hurt. In a sense, I supposed I was.

"I killed a deer," I gasped, "In the woods. I-I ran out there to get away from everything and process this morning, but I did more than that." I glanced guiltily at my stained clothes. Sir Korbin exhaled quietly, and he folded his arms across himself.

"I see."

I looked at him and saw his gaze elsewhere, staring aimlessly at a corner of his desk. He cleared his throat and looked back at me. "This is not a good thing to have done. I am sure you're aware."

I nodded quickly.

"How do you feel after having done it?" He asked.

"Bad. I feel awful."

"And at the time, I assume you were... enjoying yourself?"

I sighed, and he took this as affirmation.

"Your best course of action now, Twilight, is to pray about this. It will eat you up inside to keep it from Akristura. Though He already knows what you've done, He desires that you express yourself to Him. Tell Him what's happened, and pray that He will correct and guide you through your struggles with your flesh."

"Okay," I replied. "I will. I... I'm sorry."

The only consolation in this was that the victim wasn't human. I might have been ruined with fear if the deer had been a person—even the Harvester, as I'd briefly wished it was.

"I am sorry, too," said Korbin.

"For what?"

He inspected his fingers thoughtfully. "For dragging you into this Harvester mess. I never should have left you alone." He settled his hands in front of him on his desk. "But I am proud of you for not harming the Harvester. Very. It's better that you took an animal's life than a person's, even if they were as ghastly as that woman."

It was exactly what I'd thought. I suppressed a smile and said, "Don't feel bad. I'm glad I proved myself even a little today. Thank you for always looking after me."

Father never had. He'd only cared about my well-being if it impacted my chores and ability to complete them. Sir Korbin gave me tasks from time to time, too, but his expectations of me weren't those of an overseer handling their servant.

The depth of his warmth radiated from him like lumensa. He carried an almost innate kindness, which I assumed was amplified by his relationship with Akristura.

"Would you like me to pray with you?" He asked gently.

There he was, exercising his goodness again.

"Yes, please."

He nodded and had me take a seat across from him. He took my hands on his desk, closed his eyes, and said, "Akristura, thank You for opportunities to learn from personal weaknesses and grow as children under Your care. I ask that You please erase Twilight's misstep with the deer she killed today and soothe her spirit with Your peace so that she may begin anew tomorrow and continue walking in Your guidance."

He finished, released me, and asked me if I needed anything else.

"If you're too upset to go about your day right now, you're more than welcome to sit here and calm your mind. We can read more of the texts if you'd like."

"Actually, I would like that. Thank you," I said, readjusting in my seat.

We spent the better part of the afternoon reading together and increasing my knowledge of Akristura. I didn't realize until after the session ended that it was something I would miss when it came time to leave for the Bronze.

That night, after tumbling into an exhausted sleep, I found Mother. She was sitting on a log overlooking the Caligin Valley, a deep frown darkening her face.

"You're back. It's been a while. Come here," she whispered, opening her arms.

I fell into them. She pulled me close and propped her chin on my hair. We were still for several moments, basking in one another's presence, when she asked, "What's brought you here today? Are you well?"

"Well enough, I guess. I forced myself into the mind of a predator, Mother, one who's not like me. One who's somehow worse. Afterward, I was so upset that I then went and killed a deer and ate some of it."

Mother smiled somberly. "Perhaps a few moments of vigilante work and indulgence now and then aren't so terrible, love."

"I think they are," I said, "And I don't think I can afford to mess around. When I mess around, I mess up. I attacked that evil woman, and my valdur stirred. I felt it in here." I touched my sternum.

"Mm. Yes, that's troubling. Still..."

She sighed and pulled back to take me in, and I took this moment to study her face. She was lovely in a way no other person ever could be to me. Not even my grandmother, Zemorah, could attain such beauty.

Mother was the natural sort, blessed with abundant red hair and soft, ethereal features that did not require the glow of afterdeath to enchant me. Even in photos, she looked this way, effortlessly feminine, forever frozen at nineteen years old. She was also the most beautiful to me because she was my mother. No one else could ever match her in my eyes.

"Oh, come now," Mother chuckled, "I'm not that comely, am I?"

I smiled. "You are."

Mother chuckled. "And you look very much like me."

"I'm grateful for that," I said.

Mother sighed. "How I wish we did not have to part." She gazed longingly at me, wishing she had done things differently for the thousandth time, most likely.

I tried not to linger on it, instead telling her about my fears for the world and the potential coming war. Mother wished me well.

"Please be safe through all this, love," she whispered, "Because the Sharavaks—"

"What about us, Aubri?"

Mother gasped. My heart grated nearly to a halt. We turned away from the panoramic view of the Caligin and saw...

Him.

My father standing before us, as much a part of the dream as we were.

He smiled calmly, a serene look softening his expression as he beheld my mother. He was dressed in Father Sein's favorite robe.

"It's been a long time, love," he said softly.

Mother's lips tugged down into a grimace, though her eyes were brilliant with surprise and yearning. "Damion."

Father took a step toward us, and we both took a step back. He smirked.

"So, this is where you went all those years ago. Not to Toragaine, where you belong. Maktas. Aaksa must not have been pleased with your conduct, so He put you here until it was time to go Home. I will plead your case with Him."

Mother shook her head. "No, Damion. It was not your god that sent me here. I'm damned! Because I didn't fully follow your beliefs or my own, I was sent to the in-between. I wait here until I am sent to eternal punishment—your beloved Toragaine."

Father sighed. "You are lost, darling. As I said, I will plead your case. I... need you back. I miss you."

He opened his arms for Mother as he'd opened them to me before, and Mother refused him. She stood beside me, clutching my arm, and hissed, "No, Damion. You can't bring me back. I'm here now, and this is where I will remain until the Termination."

Father's eyes gathered moisture. He whispered, "I won't let you stay here. I will find a way to bring you back, Aubri. You know that. You know I couldn't not try, now that I know where you are."

He swallowed. "I felt you... after Sein died, something cleared in my mind, and I could feel some vague connection to you... then our daughter here screwed up again so that my mind opened into hers, and I followed her thoughts from there. I can connect with you now as I couldn't before."

Mother wept, "You can't," But Father would not listen. He came to her and embraced her, placing his chin on her head as he stroked her neck. The moisture in his eyes was now spilling down his cheeks.

"Come back to me," he said gently. "I might forgive Twilight if you'll visit me some-times in my own dreams. I have been dreaming again as of late. Aaksa will allow us this connection—"

"No!" Mother cried.

She pushed out of Father's arms, sobbing, and Father turned to me, wearing such bitter hatred on his face that it caused my heart to pound.

"You fool," he chuckled. "Opening yourself up to me like that when you did and then failing again? You're only proving my point."

He smiled. Mother ordered him to leave and never bother me again, but Father silenced her with a kiss that had her crumpling in his arms.

No.

There couldn't be an alliance between my parents, not with everything I'd told my mother and all I had been through. Father could take a lot from me, but my mother was the one thing he should never have.

Not ever again.

From the adoration in Mother's eyes, it seemed I had already lost her.

No! I never should have used valdur for this, I shouldn't have—

"*Run*, Twilight!" Mother gasped. She drew back her hand and slapped Father.

Father recoiled from her and roared, "Myrkraas will happen, daughter, with your cooperation or without! Go ahead and run."

The sickening sensation of darkness draped over me, my body going stiff. In a blink, my half-conscious mind opened to my bedroom. All my sheets had been pried from the bed and laid in a tangled mess on the floor. I sighed and cradled my pillow, waiting for my breathing to even out again.

Father. In my dreams. With my mother.

I wondered what else he might know.

How will we stay safe now?

Chapter Sixteen

I was going to be the death of everyone.

As I shuffled to breakfast the following morning, I couldn't help but see Cobi as a corpse. When he lowered himself to his chair at the table, I envisioned him lowering into the ground.

Though he didn't make eye contact with me, he smiled at everyone else. How could he smile so much? Optimism evaded me sometimes.

After breakfast, Norva asked me why I had been quiet throughout it.

"Does this have to do with yesterday?" She asked.

"It does," I admitted. "But my valdur use, um... opened me up to another dream with my father."

I was not willing to tell anyone about my mother. No one could know about our meetings. If I still wanted to contact her once in a while, I had to ensure no one warned me against it.

"Have you told Korbin about this yet?"

I hadn't. That would be the next step in unraveling the Father concerns.

"Take me to him," I said.

My guilt intensified when we found him outside on the balcony, enjoying a moment of solitude. How many pleasant moments of his had I ruined just being myself?

"I'll leave you to it." Norva gave me a quick hug and left.

Sir Korbin took a sip of his drink and glanced at me. "Good morning."

I sighed. "I wish it was."

"Tell me what happened."

Was that resignation in his tone?

"Well," I said slowly, "Because of yesterday, Father showed up in another dream. I'm worried about what he might know after being in my mind."

"Hmm. I see why that's troubling. I am curious about what he does or says in these dreams of yours. Does he threaten you? Give any relevant information?"

I shook my head. Korbin grabbed another sip and had me sit with him at one of the small tables on the balcony. Once he'd settled in, I explained what Father did.

"He makes broad threats, I guess. Promises Myrkraas is still on and tells me I'll be everyone's ruin. Things like that."

"Naturally. He wants to disarm you, and it seems he has a method of awakening his beast regardless of your input."

"Maybe he absorbed Sein's power when he died," I mused aloud, shuddering.

As wicked as Sein was, what a horrible thing to be ravaged for parts in your final moments.

"That's quite possible, actually. Are you worried he knows about your decision to go to the Bronze?"

"That's exactly what I'm worried about. I don't want to be the reason my friends die. One of them is already gone."

Sir Korbin knew who I was speaking of. "He might not be gone, Twilight. It's okay to have hope."

I snorted. "With Father? There is no hope. He had no reason to keep Solshek alive."

Speaking the truth was like releasing a bitter poison from my mouth. It stung coming out, but the pain didn't fester as much with it gone. Korbin's next question brought some of it back.

"Do you hate your father?"

What a question. Could I scream my "Yes!" from the rooftops?

"He's the one who dragged me into this," I hissed. "I have responsibility—I'm not saying I don't—but he's my parent, and he failed. He failed miserably."

"Perhaps," Sir Korbin said. "But what's done is done, remember. You can choose to look at this as a tragedy or as the setup—the prologue, if you will—to your necessary adventure. One is only a tragedy if they have rejected the Light."

"Father definitely has."

"Certainly, and maybe he always will. My suggestion for you about the Bronze is to keep your eyes open on the off chance he does visit. Fortunately, getting into the Bronze these days is impossible without strict authorization. Since the Silver implemented its strange new laws, the Bronze has closed its borders to casual travel. An additional note: they hate the Sharavaks."

I laughed. "Who doesn't? Besides the Silver, anyway. What did they do to them?"

"The Sharavaks made the mistake of torching their capital city during some unknown disagreement. They never attacked them again, and it's assumed the two have no ties, considering the Bronze's self-sufficiency and how it prefers to close itself off from the world. The Shadows have no reason to fear them, anyway. No, you shouldn't have a problem appealing to the rulers about the Shadow problem. Their issue will lie in getting entangled with the mainland."

"You'd mentioned that before," I sighed. "Who will I be speaking to there?"

"A prince, princess, or both. The Bronze is a sovereign state. Mind your manners." He chuckled.

"I'll do my best. Hopefully, I won't do something terrible there."

"You won't."

I looked at him. "How are you so sure?"

He smiled through another drink and said, "Because you know how to combat your feelings. You can stop yourself. What you haven't learned yet, though, is a practice I believe you may need over there. To be best equipped for this journey, I'm going to teach you how to cast out a baine."

"You mean from a person?"

"Yes. It's not complex, but it can be taxing. Here."

He stood and faced me. "What you're going to do is firmly and loudly tell the baine that you cast it out by Akristura's authority. These dark creatures can't stand His name, as they know it is the name of Light. It's something I noticed in Sharavaks. That's because they are indwelt with them."

"It made me flinch, too," I admitted.

"Yes. You, too, were indwelt, as you probably remember."

I shivered. "No need to remind me."

"Try it on me. What I just showed you."

I rose from my chair, fixed my eyes on him, and commanded, "By the authority of Akristura, I cast you out!" I laughed. "Was that good?"

He smiled. "Yes. It feels silly now, but it won't when the time comes. *If* it comes. I hope, for your sake, that it doesn't. But there's one additional thing to remember when you force these things away, which you should *only* ever do if you absolutely *must.* Do not use this practice lightly. Here is why: if a baine is cast out, this leaves a void in the person it inhabited. This void will only be filled with one of two things: Akristura's spirit or another baine, often the same one that brings back a few friends with it."

Chills laced my body. "So, if that happens, the only way to prevent a worse inhabitation later is to... get the person to accept Akristura?"

"Correct. And if you think that's easy, think again." He sighed. "We were very unsure of what would happen to you after Annisara purged your baines. As frightening as it is to say, we believed that only a miracle could turn you to the Light. It seems you received that miracle."

"I'm grateful I did," I said softly.

I'd stare my beast in the face sometimes and remember its appetites, the same ones I'd fueled the previous day. I didn't understand how those brief glimmers of predatory joy enamored me. Acting on an urge gifted intense shallow pleasure that burned for a moment and stained for a lifetime. Murder's theft and blood's burglary gave something to me, yet it also took away. The spirit's conscience was generous. My flesh had only ever wanted to steal what it didn't deserve.

What I deserved was death.

A blast sounded somewhere out in the fields. I jumped, rearing to strike something, and Sir Korbin chuckled.

"No need to do that. Go see who it is."

I looked at him quizzically. "Is it one of us?"

Korbin motioned for me to investigate. I thanked him for the baine lesson and rounded the corner of the commune to the fields. Two human shapes moved ahead, and beyond it, wooden targets had been erected.

Another bang shook the air. Gunpowder perfumed it. The first shape fading into view was Cobi's, and his assistant was Il.

"It's a start," I heard Il say.

Both their heads turned when I approached them.

"Twilight," Il said politely.

"Hi. What's going on out here?" I asked, taking another whiff of the gunpowder.

Cobi glanced at his weapon. "Just practicing."

Il saw the look pass between us and whispered something to Cobi. I thought I heard him say, "Talk to her," followed by Cobi sliding the gun in his hands into a holster on his hip. Il walked off, leaving Cobi and me alone. We stood in silence until he broke it, gazing at the targets instead of me.

"Got a few of 'em. I'm a rough shot, but Il thinks there's hope."

"Cobi..." I glanced at the wild spray of holes peppering the targets, none of them near the center. "You decided to take up shooting?"

"And swords," he added. "Though I won't be getting one until we go to the Bronze. Il says the Bronze has great swords and shields for magic deflection."

I chewed my lip thoughtfully. "That's, uh, good. What brought this on?"

Cobi crossed his arms. "Don't worry about it."

"Is this about—"

He waved me off. "Like I said... don't worry about it." His voice carried an edge I disliked.

"Well, it's good you're taking weapons more seriously now," I said. "I appreciate it. I do want to apologize, though, for yesterday and stuff. Especially when I told you I... wanted to, you know—"

"Kill me?"

I blanched. "Yeah. I know I'm a bit out of control, but I'd never want to hurt you. I really don't. I want you to know that it's not me speaking when I say things like that. Not entirely."

"Korbin says we're all depraved," Cobi said. "It makes sense. Everyone likes doing evil things. Even you, after turning from the darkness."

I nodded. "I'm the most depraved, though. I'm stuck in a flesh prison, and the guard just wants to feed me meat."

"Human is a nice, sweet meat," Cobi chuckled darkly.

I cracked a smile and said, "That's really not funny, but... yes. Anyway, I don't want to ever do anything to you again. I don't even want the thought to cross my mind, but in case it does, I give you permission to retaliate."

Cobi looked at me briefly before gazing at the ground. He kicked at the grass, smearing green over his shoes. "Noted."

His cheeks reddened slightly and he looked back at the targets.

"You're not mad at me?" I asked tentatively.

Cobi flashed me a half-hearted grin and shook his head. He then removed his gun and aimed to shoot. The trigger squeezed, and a bullet tore out, clipping the edge of the target on its path. He gritted his teeth and let his arm down.

"You'll get there," I assured him. "Know how I know?"

His brows jerked up, but his eyes remained distant. "How?"

"Because you're trying. Eventually, that leads to progress." I fashioned an orb of lumen-sa and tossed it at the sky, watching it pass as a smile touched my face. "I would know."

Cobi postured for another shot. "Right. You're not the Murk Maiden *or* the Myrk Maiden now."

I rolled my eyes. "Only with deer."

"And trees. You gave that one over there some sick burns. It never even needed to reach the fireplace." He grinned and popped off another round. Again, it missed spectacularly.

"Well," he said, blowing air, "You miss all the shots you don't take in life, and if you're me, you miss the ones you do. That's okay. It won't be like that for long." His grip on the weapon tensed and he narrowed his eyes at the target, firing once more. This shot was closer to the center.

"That's better!" I applauded him.

Cobi looked too focused to respond.

Despite our awkward encounter, I was going to watch him a little more when Norva ran up to me, beaming.

"You won't believe what you've started with your Under Market memories," she cried. "Come inside and take a look."

I followed her into the commune, where several dozen bodies congregated around a television set. It was the only one in the building, used explicitly for news purposes. Onscreen, a reluctant reporter showed footage of the outside of Eminent Simpario's residence, which was also the Silver's capitol building, in Lokraini.

"As you can see, hundreds of protestors out here are demanding justice and answers regarding the recent discovery of a "black market" in central Syndbur that has been in the service of criminals for a few decades. The details on this black market are still unknown—specifically how several hundred citizens simultaneously seemed to "know" the location of the building without any prior knowledge—but one thing is certain: the Eminent and the Silver government have a lot to answer for."

I laughed, and everyone cheered as the Eminent, looking highly uncomfortable, stepped out on the capitol balcony to address the public.

"What defense has he got for this?" I cried. "None."

"He's doomed for sure," another Akristuran said.

Sir Korbin was the only one who looked troubled.

What's wrong? I asked him.

He didn't answer, only continued to watch the screen with a tight jaw.

The cameras zoomed past the bodies clumped outside the capitol building shouting their abuse and demanding resignation, instead focusing on the feline-faced Eminent. His expression succeeded at maintaining decent neutrality, but if one dissected it, they'd see the tension in his neck and the narrowing of his eyes.

He cleared his throat. "My fellow Silverians—"

The screen cut to static. Everyone groaned, and nervous conversation started.

"What happened?" Norva asked.

Lady Annisara, who had joined Sir Korbin at his side, shook her head. "What do you think?"

Sir Korbin switched off the television to the noise of disapproving murmurs. He then positioned himself in front of it and said, "Who can tell me what likely just happened in town?"

A few voices spoke out. The last voice was the one Sir Korbin agreed with.

"Yes. Everyone outside that capitol building has had their memories tampered with. All those protestors will now disperse, believing they gathered there for some other reason, and the Silver government will escape any penalty unscathed."

I shivered at this probable explanation. If Shadows were in town assisting the Eminent, it made sense that they'd be cleaning up his messes to preserve him. I wondered if Father was in that building or if they were merely lackeys under the government's employ.

Was what we did pointless, releasing that information? I asked Korbin.

His eyes smiled, and he thought back, *Not at all. Many children and others are now free from that market because it was discovered, and it makes a clear point to our opposition and any criminals involved with that place: we know their deeds and are willing and able to expose them. They can erase their wrongdoings from people's minds if they wish, but they are not free from the unease or the knowledge that their enemies are now striking. This will make the Eminent very nervous.*

A strategic strike at the enemy's heart. I liked it. I *didn't* like knowing all those protestors had been disarmed of their information.

Can that happen to us, losing our memories? I asked.

No, actually. Those who have received Akristura's spirit are immune from mind-meddling because the essence of Truth indwells them. You should never fear memory alteration.

I pulled from his mind and chewed on this, relishing the fascination of the supernatural realm. What had my benefits from Aadyalbaine been? I'd been allowed to shapeshift. That was useful for sensory elevation on a level my human self couldn't achieve. I could speak and read the Sharavak language. I could maim and kill remorselessly and steal energy from other mages.

Brutal satisfaction. That was the gift of Sharavakhood. But it was a lie, and it had weakened me, if this fun fact alone could speak to that.

"We now know with complete certainty that Sharavaks reside in the Silver capitol building," Sir Korbin told everyone, "Which is a further indication that it's time our Twilight went to the Bronze. Don't discourage over what's just taken place; the Eminent and the dark ones know their time is short. Let them wallow in that fear."

The room cleared. Sir Korbin approached me and asked me when I'd like to leave.

"Within the next three days is best. The Eminent may create a law further restricting Akristuran activities in the city, which may include transportation. We want to get you out of here legally if we can." He shrugged. "It's less hassle that way."

I agreed. "Three days from now works for me. I'll pass that along to Cobi, Il, Norva, and anyone else who wants to come with me."

"Good. Do that. Afterward, meet me outside in the training field, please. Since you're leaving soon, I want to get in one last session with you before you go off on your grand adventure." He grinned and passed outside, leaving me to inform any company to the Bronze when we'd be departing.

I found Susenne reading in her bedroom with Aullie and Josha napping around her. She looked up from her book when she saw me, and her gaze lighted.

"Yes?"

"Hey. I'm letting you know I'll be leaving for the Bronze in three days if you're interested in joining me. Are you?"

Susenne thought for a moment. She stroked my siblings' sleeping heads and said, "I don't think I should. The Harvester incident got me thinking about these two. Well, them and Mother. I know you have to go, so you can't look after them, but I can. I have magic, and I think it's better if I use it here."

I nodded. "I respect that. Thanks again for what you did, by the way."

She smirked slightly. "What? Saving you? You saved me from Il and Norva. I owed you one."

"No. The only thing we owe each other is familial loyalty. It's not about scores, or whether we like each other or not, I'm realizing. You and I might never get along; I've accepted that. What I won't accept is you getting hurt or dying."

She made an affirming noise. "Good luck with the Bronze. Maybe you'll find a way to stop Father after all."

I shrugged. "Or I won't. It's not in my control anymore."

"Maybe it never was. Anyway, have a good time."

"Thanks," I said. "I, uh... love you. Stay safe."

She nodded and returned to her reading. I turned, accepting she wasn't going to say it back, when a thought reached my mind: *Love you, too.*

I didn't bother making it awkward by looking back. I crossed the threshold to find Cobi, feeling that that goodbye was enough of a win for me.

Cobi had returned to the training field to shoot. I told him about the date, and he accepted it.

"I'm just here for the ride right now," he said. "While I'm there, I'll improve my shooting game and everything else. I'll make myself worthwhile." He took apart his gun and set the parts in a carton, reflecting over his targets. "Yep," he huffed. "I'm awful. I'll try to remember you and your magic when I get discouraged."

I chuckled. "Fair enough. I'm happy you're coming with me, Cobs."

His blue eyes blushed with their usual warmth.

"Twilight!"

Sir Korbin waved me over to the far side of the field.

"Gotta go," I said, clapping Cobi's shoulder on my way over.

"Your lumensa's considerably better than it was," Korbin said when I met him. "That's great. Back up a little, please."

I did so and ignited my magic.

"But is it good enough to match the new High Father?"

Lumensa scurried from his hands in a shuddering cloud. Mine rose, full of their own magic, and projected against it. The storm veered away and dissipated. An easy success.

The following storm wasn't.

This one tramped fresh on the heels of the first attack, but it loomed larger, crackling with denser energy. I tossed up my barrier moments before it collided with me and let Korbin's magic and mine embrace. The effect was instant and harsh.

I bit my tongue when the cloud slammed into me, driven back several steps. My shoes scuffed the earth. I grunted and heaved back, but the storm's impetus prevented me from recovering stable footing. Hissing, I scraped for more lumensa.

Come out! I begged it as my arms started to seize up from holding their position for too long.

Sir Korbin seemed to enjoy seeing me struggle because he added a second storm to the one I grappled with. I watched it come and, determined not to be toppled, tensed my torso, threw myself forward, and shoved at the magic to heave it away. It sighed as if relieved to be defeated and shimmered into non-existence on the breeze.

Korbin didn't wait for my words.

As the storms shivered out, he leaped in front of me and nearly impaled me with a magic sword. I didn't have time to gasp. My hands operated of their own accord and fashioned a lumensa weapon, a companion sword to resist Korbin's.

We parried. Magic slashed magic, shedding energy particles with each successive strike.

Korbin forced me back. I tripped over my own foot and thrust my sword up to rebuff his when it descended on me. I wasn't in the best position... but neither was he.

Grunting, I stabbed at his torso and was met with a defensive block. I rolled nimbly to the side and back to my feet as sweat burst on my brow. This was what magic fights were made for: the delicate, dance-like destruction of one's opponent. It wasn't enough to simply kill them. By virtue of the creative force that magic was, one deserved a dignified slaughter.

My senses sharpened, savoring the sweat tang between us and how our hearts thudded with purpose. I would "kill" Sir Korbin before he "killed" me.

I advanced on him and sliced up to his growled warning of, "Watch my head!"

Right. I didn't want to actually murder him.

He responded to my slice by slashing at my flank. I blocked, but my sword crackled more than I liked. I ignored this and struck out again. Korbin met my blade and decided he'd had enough of stabbing and slicing; he determined to use his weight against me. I sensed him leaning forward before he did so and scampered back.

His answer was to attack me with orbs. Gone was the sword, and in its place flew a fleet of light spheres darting one after another from his palms. I deflected several with my sword, but its earlier crackling gave way to its sputtering ruin. I quickly threw up a barrier to withstand the coming orbs with one hand while I readied the other for an offensive.

I unleashed my orbs. They gobbled the first few of Korbin's, and the two of us started to sweep around each other to the rhythm of a sort of combat choreography. I twirled, hitting my mark multiple times, and he dodged and weaved around my following attacks. Then his orbs started pouring faster. I struggled to keep pace.

It wasn't enough to protect myself with my barrier and use the other hand for offensive strikes. Supported by only one hand, the barrier would quickly fail, and one hand alone driving off Korbin's attacks wouldn't deflect them in time.

It's all or nothing, I thought.

I let the barrier drop. Lumensa streamed from both my hands and met the approaching targets more swiftly and deftly.

And yet, it wasn't swift enough.

I couldn't comprehend how he could throw out all that magic so rapid-fire, but it was wearing me out and knocking me back. I started to burn inside. Heat surfaced in my palms where a soft warmth radiated moments ago.

Too much, I thought frantically. *Can't handle it, can't—*

And with the fear came the purple wave. Valdur, mingled with remnants of light magic, roared out to meet the orbs. Sir Korbin saw its snarling departure and responded with another lumensa storm. The cloud of chaos hugged the light... and the resultant embrace tossed me to my rear.

The lumensa had burned me in spots. I groaned at the singe stains, and Sir Korbin extended his hand to help me up.

"What just happened? What went wrong?" He asked as I settled back on my feet.

"I don't know."

He took my hand and looked over the palms, noting their heat and glowing scars. He nodded. "You know what went wrong. You let your emotions best you."

"I didn't mean to," I said. "I just... panicked."

"That's right. You lost sight of Akristura working through your magic and thought of yourself. Focusing on the self and negative emotions always leads to dark magic, Twilight, and eventually defeat. What I did was attack you like I was your father. I didn't play for prisoners, understand? No high-level sorcerer will give you the luxuries of time and mercy. Does that make sense?"

I sighed quietly. "It does."

"Good. Despite that, you did well. Promise me you'll keep regularly practicing in the Bronze?"

"I will," I said. "I'll practice like it's nobody's business."

He chuckled. "Only it is. It's everyone's business how you perform." He stopped and laid a hand on me. "I'm sure it doesn't need to be said, but for your very young age, you've got a lot to deal with, kid. I don't claim to know what Akristura is planning for this world's near future or yours, but I understand that dark times are close. Very close, in fact. You will be instrumental to them." His eyes locked on mine and softened. "Promise me one other thing, then... that no matter where you go or what your circumstances look like, you will never doubt two things: one is your assurance in Akristura's hands. The other is your age. They may call you "child," but I do not see you as such, young lady. You are so much more than that."

I blinked away oncoming tears and dipped my head to him. "Thank you. No one's ever said that to me."

"Not everyone," he said, "Is willing to look past the obvious to see the obvious."

He laughed and gestured for us to go back to the commune.

CHAPTER SEVENTEEN

MY LAST DAYS IN the Silver drifted by at the reluctant pace of clouds wanting to linger longer than they were welcome in the sky. I, too, wasn't welcome in the Silver anymore. Like the clouds, I had other horizons to scurry off to, separate skies requesting my attention.

It was with not a little pain that I began the dreaded goodbye-ing process. Aullie needed reminders to watch her magic. Josha needed hugs and play. Marcia—Mother, in a way—needed to know I didn't hate her, and I regretted what had happened. Lady Annisara didn't require much. She seemed to know most things before they were spoken. Susenne... I prayed she'd grow more into her own lumensa and use it prudently. And Sir Korbin needed to understand how much he'd done for my family and me.

What did I need? I supposed it was this very thing I was about to experience—the chance to live out my intended adventure, wherever that brought me. If it dragged me to death, I could accept that as appropriate. My friends were another issue. Cobi had already tasted death several times. I hoped to keep him from that again by any means. Il and Norva were competent, moderate magicals, and I trusted their wisdom and capabilities, but I still worried about them, too.

When departure day came, tears spotted many eyes. Akristurans I knew and others I was barely familiar with came to bid me their good wishes. The final goodbyes came as Cobi, Il, Norva, Sir Korbin, and I filed outside to Korbin's vehicle.

"Take care, you two," I whispered to my little siblings. I kissed them both, pausing in front of Aullie to share my last thoughts via hursafar: *Grow your magic, and be patient. Don't be afraid of it. Use it with good intentions only, okay?*

She nodded, her eyes lowering bashfully.

I moved on to Susenne. "Don't look down on yourself because you're not as magical as other people or me," I said quietly. "Trust me, it's more hassle than it's sometimes worth. Do what you can with what you've got, and please... find Akristura."

She smirked. "Should I go swimming in his magic lake?"

I shrugged. "It might be worth a visit. I was pretty messed-up when I went, and it did something for me."

She laughed softly. "Yeah. We're both messed-up." She looked away. "I guess I'll think about it. Korbin's pretty nice. He's nice to Mother, too."

"I noticed. Look out for both of them. Take care of the entire family like you said," I told her, "Because I believe you can. Thank you for that."

I stepped away to speak to Lady Annisara next. Someone wrapped themselves around me, and I glanced back.

Susenne smiled awkwardly over my shoulder. "Don't die."

I smiled and swallowed fresh tears. "No promises, but I'll give it the ole university try."

She nodded and left me to approach Annisara, who took one look at me and yanked me into an aggressive hug. "Don't lose sight of the light, hear me?" She gazed fiercely at me.

"I won't," I promised through a mouthful of her robes.

She pet my cheek and released me. Finally, it was on to Marcia.

She opened her arms and sighed, "One big one before you go."

We enjoyed a brief embrace. She dropped her arms and said, "Now, Korbin, you get these guys safely to the station, got that?"

He grinned at her half-threatening tone and promised he would. Il, Norva, Cobi, and I took our seats in the vehicle, and Sir Korbin got in last. Once we started off, our small belongings rattling in the back, we turned to take in one last view of what we'd be leaving behind.

Friends. Family. The place I'd found my new reality.

Redemption's name.

I waved at my siblings. Marcia waved tentatively, too. Annisara's smile was slight but deeply satisfied. Her thought reached me as we passed down the driveway: *You've made us proud; now make us prouder.*

I will, I thought back.

"We're here. Time for your new horizon."

After navigating the nightmares of inner-city traffic, Sir Korbin delivered us safely to the Syndbur train station. It would take us to the Silver coast, where our ferry waited to bring us across the Feverfoam Ocean separating the mainland from the Bronze.

Sir Korbin handed me my satchel from Il and pulled the hood on my robes over my eyes. If any prowling law enforcers wanted to inspect us closely enough, they might get ideas, considering the Under Market incident.

"Twilight..." He paused, his dark eyes glittering with purpose. "I know you fear being ensnared by the dark realm again. I sense it from you. It's an ever-present worry."

I looked away, grazing my fingers across my collarbone. Sir Korbin pulled me into a hug. Never had my own father embraced me like that.

"It's a valid concern. But the darkness cannot claim what belongs to the light. I also apologize if this is awkward," he said, "But you could use some parental affection, seeing as..."

I withdrew from him. "Both my parents are essentially dead."

Sir Korbin shook his head. "I wouldn't give up on your old man just yet. You came around."

I shrugged. "I'm me. Father is... Father."

"Just think about it," he said. "Avoid violence when you can."

He gave Cobi a quick hug and talked with Il and Norva before sending us on our way. As we boarded the train, my eyes strayed to the platform across us. Platform 6. The train on the departure board was bound for Orsh.

But not us, I thought as we took our seats. Shortly after, the train began to move.

"Look," said Cobi, pointing out the window.

Sir Korbin was running alongside it.

"Goodbye!" He called, waving. "Don't have too much fun!"

Laughing, Cobi and I waved back. Il and Norva smiled quietly across from us in our booth. As Sir Korbin's face washed into a blur among the masses, I remembered how much fun I would probably *not* be having on our journey.

But as the Akristuran leader himself had said, darkness could not claim those of the Light. My past was free, and so was my future. Or at least it would be one day. I still had to do some living in between then.

Boats were fascinating contraptions. They were like water cars as they scooted across the vast, turbulent blue that comprised the ocean. It was something I had always longed to see.

As our train pulled into the station along the coastline, I gaped stupidly at the broad ribbon of glittering turquoise, breathless at the beauty. How could it stretch on forever like that? And the way it charged at the shore with reckless abandon, writhing with unbridled energy, reminded me of myself. I smiled.

"Uh, Twi, we'd better go," Cobi said. "Before we have another train accident."

I stepped away from the window, inhaling the briny air. "Hopefully, one that wouldn't involve many more innocent deaths."

Cobi grimaced, and we made our way down to the docks where the ferries idled in the water. We were to board *The Mosura 61,* one of the faster vessels. In about twenty-four hours, we would be in the Bronze Principalities and away from a government that didn't want us alive. Hopefully, the Bronze's would be more forgiving.

"Papers, please," barked a customs agent.

"Here you are," I heard Norva say. She showed the woman Sir Korbin's abbreviated request and his letter of authorization.

The agent scoffed. "Cleric of the Children of Akristura? You cultists don't get special access."

"We do, actually," Il said a bit gruffly. "The Bronze welcomes mainland entities in the event of global emergencies. Our organization's leader is sending us on his behalf."

The customs agent glared at Sir Korbin's letter and read its contents multiple times. She then referred to her guidebook to assess the legitimacy of Il's claim. Finally, she shoved the papers back into Il's hands and huffed, "Whatever. Go ahead."

We strode past her, and her glares followed every movement until we boarded the ferry.

"Charming lass," Cobi said mildly.

When the boat departed, I took a long last look at the mainland and remembered all I was leaving behind—then reminded myself why I was doing it. The mainland would forever be my home. It was its own country, its own culture, and an unfortunately depraved one.

But it was still home.

Now, though, I looked to new horizons. The Bronze had called to me from a young age. I loved the concept of warmth, tropical waters, and an intricate population of more than frightfully pale people. The Bronze was as much a new beginning as my new religion. I embraced it wholeheartedly, but I didn't forget the losses.

It had to be done, after all. The world could not suffocate under a veil of Shadows.

The day bled into the night. Cobi and I shared a luxurious meal quite unfit for our peasant mouths, while Il and Norva had their own a few booths away. In our abounding maturity, we privately poked light fun at the patrons around us.

"Look at that one." Cobi tilted his head toward an ostentatious woman sipping from a glass. "She actually does the finger thing. Lifts it while she drinks."

I chuckled. "And you eat like flies on death. I'm sure your manners are appalling to everyone here."

"No more appalling than your dreadful sarcasm."

I punched Cobi on the arm, and the drinking woman glared at us.

"Oh, come on," I said to her, "Don't act more important than you are, pinky raiser."

The woman scowled and hissed, "I am the captain's daughter." She shuffled off, and Cobi laughed.

"You have a knack for ticking people off. I'd consider it your greatest talent, though I don't suggest you make it a hobby."

"It's no hobby; it's a lifestyle," I scoffed. "You think I exist for people to like me? I'm already an epic failure on that front."

"Well," Cobi said, "I like you."

He grinned, and I rolled my eyes.

"Maybe a little too much."

Cobi sighed. "Well, that's just cruel, isn't it?"

I laughed. "That's me."

"How do you feel, though? Is it tough to leave the mainland behind?" He asked.

"It is," I admitted. "It's all I've ever known. I hate knowing what I know about it, too."

He agreed. "I won't see it the same way again."

It was impossible to maintain a pure view of something that had been tarnished, even if it was home. I'd always love the mainland, the Caligin, specifically, but knowing of its evil prevented me from liking it.

"I wonder what the Bronze will be like," I mused.

Cobi shrugged. "We'll see. It'd be hard to be worse than the Silver."

The following day, as afternoon edged into evening, we caught our first glimpse of the Bronze archipelago. One massive slice of dark green land marked the main island, while smaller ones stretched away from it into the water. The fertility of the vegetation, luscious and abundant, and the sheer enormity of the mainland made me think of Araveh. I didn't know what Akristura's afterlife was supposed to look like, but I hoped it would resemble this.

"Would you look at that?" Cobi breathed. He released an appreciative sigh. "I already have a good feeling about this place."

"You have a good feeling about everything, Corn-on-the-Cobi," I told him.

He laughed. "I've never heard that one before. Dare I think you're developing a real sense of humor?"

"I hope you're not implying that what *you* have is humor."

Cobi shook his head. "Careful. I might have to get myself a pretty Bronze girl who appreciates me if you don't shape up."

I protested, "You wouldn't!"

"Jealous?" He teased.

"Hardly."

I rolled my eyes and gave him a little hug as the ship began to pull into port. I didn't know what I expected when we reached the mainland. In my childhood imaginings, the Bronze was carved of gleaming stone with beautiful decorative statues and monuments. It was a prosperous place flowing with music and bustling artisans, affluent, but never in a pretentious way.

Well, I was half right. The Bronze had wealthy sectors, and many artistic types crowded the streets. But then there were the less fortunate parts that made my heart clench to see. These people were not ornately dressed and lived in much smaller homes around the fishing docks, though, like the villagers in DuVon, they seemed to want for nothing.

An ideal mindset, and one no Sharavak would settle for.

We met several guards on the docks who requested our papers when we arrived. When we presented them, their pleasant expressions withered, and they scrutinized us, firing one question after another.

"What is the full reason Cleric Korbin sent you here? Why must it involve the royal family? Is it true none of you have criminal records?"

I blanched at that last part, though according to the government, I *didn't* have any such record. Il explained things to the guards until Norva had to intervene for his lack of patience. After several minutes, the guards eventually relented and allowed us to enter the country.

"We will be sending you a guide to the palace," they said with some reluctance. "Keep your noses clean, people." They glared us off in the direction of our guide.

A man with deep brown skin and a blue and gold uniform approached us, beaming. "Please wait here while we request a carriage from the palace," he said in a soft accent.

I noticed a single father with three little children watching us solemnly across the way. Their sunken cheeks and hollow eyes spoke of their suffering, and I wondered if the father was struggling to provide for them. On the mainland, giving to the less fortunate was met with mixed views. Some appreciated it, while others ridiculed it. Hopefully, the Bronze had a more favorable perception of it.

I foraged in my wallet Norva had given me and pulled out three Silvons I'd earned tearing out thistles from the Akristurans' pastures, then asked our guide, "Can I?" Nodding in their direction.

"Oh! How charitable. Thank you, but the Bronze doesn't run on Silvons. Our currency is gold."

"Oh. I don't have any of that," I said sheepishly.

The guide smiled. "Not to worry. We can exchange some of your currency for you while you're waiting. Come."

He led us to a neighboring building along a cobblestone path gilded in the late afternoon sunlight. Our passage revealed glimpses of the Bronze's culture in clay houses and burbling courtyard fountains. The less affluent homes had sheets draped over their open windows and smaller yards where they tended gardens, and beyond them was a marketplace where merchants jostled about, accosting passersby at every turn.

"Try this elixir!" One woman cooed, dragging Cobi to her stand. "It will put muscle on your bones. And for you," she added, looking at me, "I have Glow elixir to cure your pale skin. You are very sick, yes? Or is it bad breeding?"

Cobi busted out laughing, but I certainly wasn't. I *was* poorly bred. I wrinkled my nose at the thought and whisked Cobi away before he tried to become some kind of superhuman with the merchant's magic potion.

"My apologies," the guide chuckled. "They can be quite zealous about their wares. In here, please."

We entered a customs affairs office, where we handed over a good portion of our Silvons. Il watched the exchange and commented that we were getting a currency upgrade.

"With that finished, let's go back to where we were and see if the palace carriage has arrived yet," suggested the guide.

Aside from the dock guards, Bronze citizens had shining dispositions that one could see in their eyes and hear in the laughter of the children careening around the streets. No one smoked publicly, although some politely imbibed drinks. No one yelled except for the merchants and the children. Everyone else hurried off quietly to their destinations, rustling over the cobblestone in their thick, colorful robes.

"Everybody wears robes," I commented.

"The ladies do," the guide explained, "And the men sometimes do, too. Traditionally, though, they wear tunics and trousers."

I looked at Cobi. "Ready for a wardrobe change?"

He observed a woman shuffling along in quick, tiny steps in her robe. "Are you?"

We watched the woman pass. She certainly had more grace than I had in my usual, non-provoked form. Only Shadow Twilight would make that outfit work.

"Do I get points for trying?" I asked.

"Actually, the Bronze really appreciates when foreigners use their manners and customs. Assimilation into a new culture is not easy, so we respect the effort. Ah! Speaking of which, there's our carriage."

The guide waved down an elaborate wood-and-gold, lacquered carriage drawn by horses much smaller and stockier-looking than the ones at home. These creatures had a nearly reptilian point to their snouts, and their hoofed feat ended in miniature claws that clicked on the cobblestone.

Our guide spoke briefly with the carriage driver, whose brows drew together in suspicion. The guide asked for our papers and showed them to the driver, who nodded after several moments of contemplation and stepped out to open our doors.

"Please," he said, opening his palm.

"Uh..." I looked at his outstretched hand and then at the guide for answers.

"A gesture of respect," he said quickly. "No worries. You will learn." He smiled and climbed into the carriage after us.

The driver whipped the horses—or whatever they were—and we began to sweep up an inclining street toward the gleaming bronze building we'd glimpsed from the boat before pulling in. It had looked perfect sitting on its hill over the capital city, Valechka. I was sure it was even lovelier in person.

"I saw from your letter that there is trouble on the mainland," the guide said, "Which has forced you to seek the Bronze's counsel. I am sorry for any troubles that have befallen you." He dipped his head low. "I hope the royals may look favorably upon you and assist you in this grave matter."

"Thank you," said Norva.

You and I both, sir, I thought worriedly.

The houses faded into more elaborate structures the further we drifted up the hillside. At a certain point, farmland and gardens replaced them, each bursting with lively green and other colors. Another minute passed. The driver began to pull around a circular driveway.

"We've arrived," he said curtly. "Sentries will meet you now to investigate your intentions and read through your papers. If they accept you, you will be passed into their care and taken into the palace. If not, I will drive you back to the docks, and you will be forced to return to the mainland."

Norva, Il, Cobi, and I shared a nervous look.

"Let's see what we can do," said Il.

We thanked the driver and were escorted out of the carriage by our guide. At this point, we all stopped to gape at the building before us.

The Bronze Palace was the most magnificent structure I had ever seen. The ornate bronze-and-marble building was topped with massive domes, complete with spires, arched door frames, and a road leading past the outer gate paved entirely in bronze.

Numerous stained-glass windows overlooked several levels of balconies, along which the servants bustled to carry out their tasks. Outside, in the small plaza before the entrance gate, was a fountain with flowers twirling around a statue of a woman standing in the water.

As we approached the gate, we were greeted with the expected slew of sentries who inquired about our business with the Seraphina family. Il removed the complete, official statement from Sir Korbin and passed it along with the other papers. They accepted and began to read.

"There is a war coming, and you, one of the old Enemies, are here to speak about it on behalf of those who oppose your traditional faith?" They asked me.

"Yes," I replied. "I have rejected my old beliefs and embraced Akristuranism in their stead. Might we have the honor of speaking with the royal family?"

The sentries exchanged glances.

"We will inquire," one of them said.

They passed through the gate, ordering us to wait for them, and we spent the next few minutes in silence. The other sentries held their weapons ready while keeping their eyes on us.

What do you think is going to happen? I asked Il.

His lips pressed together. *I don't know. Let's pray they accept us.*

Literally, I thought back.

If war really was coming, it terrified me to think we might not be ready. Sir Korbin had urged us to keep our faith, but that didn't guarantee we wouldn't be packing our bags back to the mainland in a few minutes.

"At least it's nice here," Cobi commented.

Norva nodded. "Truly. I've never been before. I'm glad I got the chance to go. Did you see all those flowers in the gardens?"

"And the fountains," I added. "It's definitely a nice place."

"Hopefully," Il said quietly, "The leaders will be nice, too."

As if in response to this statement, the sentries who'd gone to speak on our behalf came to collect us.

"Follow us, please," they said, leading us through the gate.

We were shown into a foyer as high-ceilinged and grand as the one in the Sharavak compound. A wall of stained glass to the left bathed the room in light. Before the foyer was a pair of doors, tall slabs of gleaming wood set with gold handles that a bronze-robed man partially obstructed. He bowed deeply and dismissed the sentries accompanying us.

"I am one of the Bronze Palace ambassadors," he said, speaking as if it pained him to address us. "Prince Seraphina has agreed to meet with you, but he will not be kept long." He sighed almost too softly to hear. "As soon as you are brought before the throne, you must bow or curtsy. Answer questions clearly and directly, ending each phrase with, "Your Highness," and do not trouble the Prince with many words. Finally, do not move about when you speak, and refrain from making eye contact. You may look at his face and the face of the princess, but keep your eyes from meeting. Do you need me to repeat anything I have said?"

We each thanked him and said that we did not.

The ambassador smiled vaguely. "Good, then. I will admit you now."

Our moment of truth awaited.

We entered the throne room. Several hundred paces away from us on elaborate golden-and-bronze seats were the royals. Prince and Princess Seraphina looked out at us from their lofty positions, heavy incense and spiced perfumes clouding around them. Both were clothed in multi-colored garments, bearing jewel-heavy crowns dripping orange stones and equally gem-studded sandals on their feet.

"Welcome to the Bronze Palace," boomed the Prince. "State your name and business, each of you, starting with the Shadow."

I bowed to him, keeping my gaze on his chin, and said, "I am Twilight Mavericc, Your Highness. I have come from the mainland seeking your assistance with an issue concerning the Sharavak race."

The Prince sighed. "So we have heard. I will ask for elaboration on that in a moment. The rest of you may introduce yourselves."

Il, Norva, and Cobi gave similar remarks as I had, causing the Prince's energy to warp with frustration. I sensed his increasing heart rate and body heat when he responded to us.

"So, all of you are here—Akristurans and a Sharavak—to make a request of us on behalf of your home region?"

"Yes, Your Highness," we echoed together.

The Prince snorted. "And what request is that? You are aware we limit our dealings with the outside world almost to having no interactions at all?"

"We are, Highness," Il spoke. "We encountered some resistance reaching you here, but we were sent on this mission by our leader, Cleric Javari Korbin, as he believes you are our primary hope for preparing for what's to come."

"And what is to come, according to you?" The Prince asked.

"Highness," I said softly. "May I show you something?"

The Prince's gaze descended on me. I was careful to avoid meeting it. "Why are you here with your enemies? Are you a defector?"

I opened my mouth to speak when a female voice cried, "Father!"

Our heads turned. There, standing just inside the throne room on the other side, was a girl. Not a young one, but a blossoming lady like myself, with luminous brown skin and an intense golden gaze that trained on us inquisitively.

She donned a striking, deep blue dress with short sleeves that loosely hugged her form, delicately trimmed in lace. Her hair was like a black cloud fluffed around her head. It was as wild as mine, but it was coarser and curlier and grew upward rather than down.

Was this their daughter?

"Sakaiah, return to whatever business you were tending to," the Prince ordered gruffly. "This conversation does not involve you."

Princess Sakaiah shook her head. "I want to know why a Shadow is here, Father. I sensed her presence. There is light inside her, but she wrestles with darkness."

"Thank you, daughter," Princess Seraphina said dismissively. She looked back at me and demanded to see Sir Korbin's letter.

The ambassador handed it to her, and after reading it, she snorted. "What is this foolishness? The Bronze is not a war-fighting people! Read this, husband."

The Prince took the letter, and his brows drew together in confusion when he read a particular part.

"Surely this is a joke?"

"No, Your Highness," I told them. "It is all true, I'm afraid. The Shadows want to destroy this world and will go to war to achieve that. Might I form a hursafar connection with you to show you what I've seen? It is best for you to share my memories to truly know and understand what I've been through and what is coming."

"Form a *what* with me?" The Prince laughed. "Absolutely not. You cannot expect to march in here and start ordering me about with your magic tricks. I do not trust you or your kind."

"Wait!" The princess cried. She sprinted toward us and stopped, breathless, in front of our group to gasp, "I will form this magic connection and see into your memories. I believe you, Shadow. Show me what you've endured in your former life."

"No, Sakaiah!" Snarled Princess Seraphina. "Stand down!"

"You are being a fool again!" The Prince hissed. "This is precisely the erratic behavior that keeps you from the full privileges of the throne, Sakaiah. Need you be set back further?"

Sakaiah glared defiantly at them and said, "If what she says is true and we are to fear the Shadows, if war is coming... then you will want to know something about it, Father, so you can begin training our armed forces for a proper conflict."

The Bronze's military was weak, and Princess Sakaiah, it appeared, did not hold power in her own sovereign state. Neither of these things was good.

The Prince sighed. "If you want to die, go ahead, but you only place more distance between yourself and living up to your title."

Sakaiah scoffed and faced me. "Let us see these memories."

I bowed. She snapped, "Don't waste your time with that. Just tell me what to do."

Apparently, the princess was as temperamental as her parents.

Once I formed the link to her mind, Sakaiah closed her eyes, and I closed my own, drifting back to moments in my past life ripe with violence. I replayed my most distinct memories of my first hunt in Orsh as a Sharavos, then my memories of Father Sein speaking of Myrkraas and the subjugation of the world for the Myrk God's glory.

I then shared the monstrosity that was the Akristuran battle, revealing the devastating power Sein and I had used to erase enemies from existence, then the monster in the Void, and my friends and me escaping from the compound and fleeing to the Akristuran residence in Syndbur. I concluded with secondhand memories from the Harvester that showed Eminent Simpario's plans for Akristurans and Myrkraas.

When I was finished, Sakaiah blinked and turned to her parents. She pressed her full lips together and moaned, "It is bad, Father. Very bad."

The Prince's frown deepened. "What did you see?"

Sakaiah grimaced. "War," she told him, "And many deaths. Promises intended to be kept. Father, the Shadows have risen again."

"And how do we know that this one right here isn't deceiving you with clever mind tricks?" Cried Sakaiah's mother.

"She is not," Sakaiah assured her. "Not with this level of clarity and the emotions surrounding each memory. This is the one Shadow who does not deceive us, Mother."

The Prince laughed. To me, he said, "How many times have people been swindled by your sweet talk, little sorcerer? If I wanted to believe in the Dark God, your kind would be the most compelling evidence for such a thing. However, because I do not subscribe to madness, I have no incentive to help you. Away from me!"

"Father, no!" Sakaiah yelled. "I have some say in this! You can't keep me from making every decision we face. Let me show you the memories she showed me." She gestured to me. "There is light in her. She is more than a dark magician."

The Prince and Princess shared a look of contemplation. Finally, they ordered us to step outside the palace so they could converse in private.

"Give us a few minutes to discuss things and reach a conclusion," said Sakaiah.

We were dismissed. A few minutes after we stepped out, Sakaiah joined us.

"I showed them the memories. The rest is in their control," she explained with a note of bitterness. Her brilliant gaze trained on me. "Tell me about yourself, Twilight. I learned your name from your memories. Strange name."

I chuckled. "I have heard that a few times before. What would you like to know, Highness?"

"No need to call me that," she said quickly. "I haven't earned it. Refer to me as "Princess" if you must be formal." She sighed. "Your memories indicate you were some form of royalty to the Sharavaks. An Aaquaena or something? What was that like?"

I fumbled briefly with my collarbone before answering, "Not ideal. The Sharavaks believed—and still do believe, I think—that I am the chosen one of their "Dark God" to rescue the world from the light. I think they mean "light" in both a literal and figurative sense. They're not the nicest people."

Sakaiah shook her head, her eyes widening. "Not in the least. I'm sorry you had to go through that. What compelled you to leave? Was life as Sharavak royalty really awful?"

I noticed everyone was paying attention to the descriptions I was giving. "It was... very dark. The Sharavaks make murder a religious practice, like a sacred ritual or something. Everything was so twisted. So backward." I suppressed a shudder. "But that's over now. I have Akristura to thank for my escape."

Sakaiah's nose wrinkled. I wondered what this meant but couldn't wonder long, as the palace ambassador swept out to meet us and invite us back inside.

"The Prince and Princess have arrived at a decision concerning your situation," he said stuffily. "If you would follow me, please."

He led us back into the throne room, where we again bowed and greeted the royals. The Prince, his tone somewhat halting and quiet, said, "After reviewing your memories and discussing things over, my wife and I have agreed to allow you and your party to stay here, in the palace, for exactly one month. Not a day longer. Not a day less. One month. During that time, we will decide whether or not we wish to pledge our forces to you in the event of a mainland conflict."

All of us dropped into steep bows, thanks pouring from our lips. The Prince dismissed us with a flourish of his hand, and Sakaiah turned to us, beaming.

"Welcome!" She cried. "This is so exciting. I can't wait to show you to your rooms."

CHAPTER EIGHTEEN

"**T**HERE ARE SOME STIPULATIONS attached to your stay here."

Princess Sakaiah led us past the throne room up a flight of candle-lit stone steps into a shadowed hallway.

"I'm sure we'd be willing to meet any of those for your kindness," said Norva.

"Good, because my parents will be observing your conduct during your stay. This means you will each need to become accustomed to our ways of life. No one expects immediate perfection, but my parents will be formulating their decision to help you based on your manners, behavior, and—this is an important one—your response to public service."

"I would be happy to help, Princess," I told her. "All of us would."

She beamed, then pointed to a simple wooden door to our immediate right. "Yours," she told Cobi. "Go on in. I'll send servants your way shortly."

Cobi dipped his head and stepped inside. Sakaiah continued the living quarters tour, pointing out two rooms further down the hall.

"For each of you," she said, smiling at Norva. Her gaze hardened when it touched Il.

The pair thanked her and chose their spaces; now, it was just the Princess and me.

"How old are you, Twilight?" Sakaiah asked, pausing in front of a door between Il and Norva's rooms.

"I'm fifteen, Princess," I replied. "May I ask your age?"

Sakaiah grimaced. "If you stop speaking to me like I'm some sort of god, sure."

"I apologize. You had said you preferred "Princess" over "Your Highness" or something like it," I pointed out gently.

"I'm over formalities almost entirely at this point," she said. She sighed and pointed to the door in front of her. "Your room. And... I'm eighteen."

I thanked her for the room and entered.

The bed was a canopy type with sheer white curtains for privacy. I had several dressers, and a cold fireplace rested along the far wall surrounded by smooth wooden chairs. A chandelier dangled from the ceiling like a jewel hanging from an elegant woman's ear.

On the opposite side of the fireplace, not far from my bed, was the master suite bathroom. Its light and airy layout with a white and gold theme faded out my drowsiness.

And what a beautiful tub and shower! The window overlooking the fountain by the entrance gate was so inviting with its allowance of evening light. These quarters would do. They had the richness of bathrooms in the Sharavak compound, but warmth and light were also present, making for a lifting atmosphere.

"It's lovely," I said.

"I'm glad you like it. You're free to spend the rest of the day here adjusting if you need to. You're probably tired from your travels."

"I am," I admitted. "I'm happy to spend the evening resting if you have no plans for me."

Sakaiah shook her head. "I don't. You'll receive supper in an hour. Once you've earned Father's favor, you may eventually find yourself with us at the table, but in the meantime, please be patient with my parents."

I chuckled. "I assure you, Princess, I have no intentions of being impatient. I consider us fortunate to even be here. Thank you for speaking to them on our behalf and sticking up for us."

"Of course," she said. "I understand you're a Shadow, but you're not a Sharavak. Does that make sense?"

"How do you mean?"

She explained, "You're a Shadow in body, and "Shadow" is the word common people used to describe your sort back in the old days. "Sharavak" is the sacred name of your tongue. Isn't that right?"

I blinked. "You know more about them than I thought, uh...?"

"Sakaiah. You can call me that, but don't do it in front of my parents," she said.

"Noted."

"Yes, I know a bit about your culture. Not "your" culture, but the one you used to be involved with. Anyway, I'm rambling. If you reject the intimate phrases used in their language and reduce it to the common tongue, "Shadow," then it feels less religious."

I nodded. "I see what you mean. I had a friend once who would notice things like that about language." I trailed off into memories of our days writing. I hadn't been able to read much or write since.

"Had a friend?" Sakaiah prompted gently. "What happened to them?"

I sighed. "I wish I knew, Sakaiah. Unfortunately, I don't have any idea."

Sakaiah's bright eyes dulled. "Ah. Well... anyway. I try not to issue commands when I can help it, but here's one for you: try out that bathtub and our soaps. You'll never want to bathe anywhere else again."

I thanked her, and she stepped out, looking in both directions down the hallway as if checking for traffic before closing my bedroom door behind her. I collapsed on the canopy bed, smiling despite everything we'd gone through to reach this point, and offered my gratitude to Akristura.

The future loomed dark and uncertain. Father's schemes proceeding "on schedule" frightened me. If we had an army, though, we could better deter the forces aiming to eliminate us. I told Akristura this, though He already knew, and faded into the unconscious bliss of sleep.

Morning came. I woke to servants moving about my room.

"Miss Twilight," a stout older woman greeted, stooping into a bow. "We have come to see if you are awake."

I looked over her frilly blouse and skirt, the same uniform her companions wore, and asked playfully, "Well, am I?"

The older woman appeared confused, and I laughed.

"Only kidding, ma'am. Can I do something for you?"

"Actually, we would like to know if we could do something for you. The royal family requested to dine alone this morning. We're sorry you missed supper last night, but we assumed you were sleeping. We've been told you may eat here. What would you like for breakfast, miss?"

I blinked. Even when I was royalty, the Sharavaks hadn't served me breakfast in bed.

"For breakfast, uh... surprise me," I said.

The older servant nodded. "Very well. We will be back up shortly. Thank you, miss."

"Thank *you!*" I called as they filed out the door.

I glanced at the bathroom and thought I would fulfill Princess Sakaiah's command sooner rather than later. My muscles carried tension from the past several days preparing for and traveling to the Bronze.

Sakaiah hadn't joked about the soaps. Zemorah's soap had competition in the rows of natural, freshly-scented body washes and scrubs that lined the tub. If she could have seen them, she'd have been jealous.

After heating out my muscle woes, I was going to slip into a pair of my Akristuran robes until my eyes passed over a stack of colorful silk on the vanity. The Bronze and their resplendent attire. I smiled and shrugged into something gaudy, deciding to embrace the absurd.

"Breakfast is ready, Miss Twilight!" Sounded one of the servants outside the bathroom.

The chef's idea of a surprise was a hearty helping of Bronze-native fruits dusted with exotic spices and cream-filled, honey-drizzled pastries. To wash it all down was a pitcher of sugared tea. Looking over my multi-colored garb and the meal before me, I wondered if the Bronze people weren't a bit indulgent.

Someone knocked on my bedroom door.

"This is Sakaiah. May I come in?" She called.

"Yes!" I replied, feeling awkward that I couldn't follow up any phrases with "Highness" or "Princess" for fear of her wrath.

The princess swept into the room, donning another deep blue dress, simpler and more loosely fitting than yesterday's. Unlike her parents, she wore no crown.

"How is the food?" She asked.

"It's very good. Thank you."

She smiled. "Sterling. I thought today would be ideal for customs and courtesies practice."

I agreed. "Would you also like to practice your magic with me? I know you have it. I can sense it's there. Our leader, Sir Korbin, asked me to keep my magic sharp while I'm here."

Sakaiah's eyes brightened. "Sterling idea. We'll do that, too. I see you've found your in-house robe." Her mouth pinched into a look of mild horror as she observed me. She cleared her throat. "Not to worry. We will... fix that. Let me call my servants."

I looked at my robe and wondered what was wrong with it. I'd seen where the cloth met in the middle and tied it closed with the attached cord. Had I oversimplified it?

Sakaiah disappeared for a few minutes, leaving me to puzzle over myself. She returned with several servants whose arms were draped in robes of too many colors to count. It dizzied me to even look at them.

"These are traditional Bronze robes," Sakaiah explained. "I'll show you how to wear them properly in a bit. I ask that you set your Akristuran attire aside while you're here," she added distastefully. "It is frankly awful. Single colors for robes aren't viewed fondly here."

"Okay."

Strange request, I thought. And a bit fussy, though I'd never have told her that.

"You would also benefit from using certain gestures and phrases while interacting with locals. For example..."

She bent her knees and curtsied, sweeping her arms against her sides and out in front of her before rising.

"That is a general gesture of respect. Use it for greetings, departures, and expressing thanks. Try it."

I tried it. Sakaiah shook her head.

"Graceless. Smoother movements."

I repeated myself, and she sighed.

"So, grace isn't your strong suit. We can work on that."

You should see me when I hunt.

I chuckled. "Guess I'm not surprised."

"About what?"

I gestured to myself. "My lack of being... lady-like."

"Did the Sharavaks not teach you—oh, wait." Sakaiah grimaced. "I answered my question by asking it."

"Not manners," I said quietly. "But they taught me things."

Her eyes softened, and she had me step into the bathroom with one of her servant's robes.

"I sawthat in your memories."

She didn't want to undress me, so she had me model the new robe on top of the old one and urged me to always wear the robes with the proper undergarments. I slipped my arms through the sleeves and let her align the fabric how she saw fit. While she did, a persistent thought nagged me.

"Your Highness—sorry, Sakaiah—I have to ask something if you don't mind."

"Of course not." She adjusted my shoulders and prepared the cord that would encircle my waist.

"How, after seeing all those memories of mine, can you believe I'm any good?"

Sakaiah paused and met my gaze in the bathroom mirror's reflection. "Because I could tell you were conflicted. You had a struggle inside you in the memories." She dropped her eyes to the cord and pulled it taut around my torso, tying it to the right. "Always tie to the right. To the left symbolizes dishonor. To the back? It becomes funereal. And tying it in front of you tells the nation you're a call girl."

"Oh." I stood very still as she tied the knot in the cord. "I'll keep that in mind."

"Don't just keep it in mind," Sakaiah grumbled. "Practice it, or Father will have a conniption fit."

I didn't respond to that but kept still for the final moments she took to finish the knot.

Her arms dropped, and she sighed. "There. You're properly dressed now."

I thanked her. "We won't tell anyone about the robe underneath."

Sakaiah huffed a laugh. "Practice the bowing one more time, please."

I dropped, wobbling slightly.

She shrugged. "It will do for now. One more thing when you bow: don't make eye contact. People might not respond well to your eyes, anyway."

I blanched. "I hear Sharavaks aren't popular in these parts?"

Sakaiah snorted, patting her hair as she scrutinized it in the mirror. "An understatement. Anyway, if you want to impress my parents, try to do big things. Grand gestures are appreciated here. Bronzians like grandiosity."

"I noticed from the breakfast."

She cracked a grin. "It'll sit in you like a stone for hours. The good part is that you won't even need to eat lunch. We practically live on two meals a day out here."

"Good," I said, "Because I'm usually too keyed up to eat as it is. Speaking of which, did you want to practice magic soon?"

Sakaiah nodded. "We can do that now, actually. The Bronze doesn't have too many notable customs, but if you can master grace and wear the right clothes, you'll have done much for yourself. Try to live gracefully if you can. And remember to be extravagant and to tie your sash cord correctly." She flicked the knot on my robe tie and invited me downstairs to the palace garden.

We ran into Cobi when we stepped outside. He was overlooking the sprawling field of lush hedges and fountains that comprised the garden.

"Good morning, Your Highness," he greeted politely, bowing to Sakaiah.

"Please," she whined. "Don't. I really don't deserve it."

Cobi's puzzled look echoed my sentiments. "What would you like me to call you, Princess?"

"Just Sakaiah," she sighed. "But good morning. It's Cobi, right?"

He nodded, drinking her in with a gaze brighter than its usual shade. "That's me."

Sakaiah smiled and bowed to him. "Welcome. I'm glad Twilight brought company across the world. Is there anything you need here, Cobi?"

"Actually," he said, "There is if you know where and how I might acquire them. I've been needing a sword and shield to take up the craft. I don't want to die if I'm forced to face magical opponents."

Sakaiah pointed to the door. "We will gladly deliver. Head inside and speak with one of the servants, please. Flag one down if you have to. Tell them you have my full permission to use any swords and shields from the armory."

Cobi's eyes widened. "Really? Wow, thank you! That's generous of you."

Sakaiah shrugged. "I call it hospitality. My parents could learn it better."

Cobi and I exchanged a nervous look.

"I'll go look into those swords now," he said gingerly.

"Sterling. Enjoy them. They're magic-proof, so feel free to get creative," Sakaiah told him.

Cobi hurried off, and Sakaiah watched him leave with a smile.

"Where were we? Oh, right. *Our* training."

We descended a set of stone steps into the garden's entrance, a flat and spacious pathway that would allow plenty of freedom of motion. Sakaiah pulled back several paces and readied her hands, that familiar golden-white flame kindling in her palms.

"How much lumensa training do you have?" She asked. "I got an idea of your dark magic abilities, but I didn't get to see your whole life story."

I chuckled nervously. "That's probably for the best. I have a few weeks of dedicated experience with the light kind. Try me."

Sakaiah smiled mischievously. "As you wish."

Light exploded from her palms. I responded to it with my own detonation, and sparks split the air. The force knocked us both back, prompting us to attack again. This time, our meeting magic collided and stayed. Sakaiah tilted into it, and I did the same, biting down on my lip.

When Sakaiah pushed, a ripple of her magic smashed into mine and threatened to topple me. My retaliation produced the same effect on her. We seemed to find ourselves in a stalemate.

Magic was simple in that it required little from the wielder except for might and power. One's power indwelt them, drawing from their existential energy to emerge, whereas might derived from the mage's will.

Whose will would overcome in this scenario? Sakaiah and I seemed to be on a level playing field magically, but was she as tenacious as me? Did I want to risk my own aggression to find out?

Why are you so powerful? I wondered, meeting her stare.

Sweat jeweled her brow. Her irises burned like molten gold, and she heaved at me again.

With satisfaction, I shoved back and witnessed my beam reaching further into hers.

"Princess?"

And just like that, we were interrupted. Perhaps it was better that way. We carefully extinguished our magic simultaneously and faced the person addressing Sakaiah.

"Yes, Reysa?" She said in ragged breaths.

"I didn't want to interrupt you," an older female servant explained, "But I've been meaning to speak with you. I stood and watched, but when I saw the intensity in both your eyes..." She laughed nervously.

Sakaiah smiled at her and then at me. "We were just having a little fun, Reysa. No worries. Now, what's brought you here? I see you have some papers?"

"Yes, Princess, for the Sun Festival. These are this year's participants."

Reysa handed Sakaiah her paper stack, and Sakaiah sifted through them, nodding approvingly.

"Sterling, thank you, Reysa. It's a good crowd this year."

Reysa agreed. "Shall I begin preparations?"

"Please do." To me, Sakaiah explained the significance of this Sun Festival. "It's an art and culture celebration show dedicated to the Bronze settlement and our sovereign state's establishment. Mother and Father find it frivolous, but the people and I enjoy it very much."

"That sounds exciting," I replied. "When is it?"

"Oh." She dabbed her brow sweat away with a handkerchief. "Not for another month or so. You'll probably be gone by the time it happens."

My heart stilled. Gone as in rejected, or gone with the royals' blessing?

"Anyway, while you may not be here for that, you can begin impressing my parents—and me—with some good works out in town," she said. "But I will need more customs training from you to ensure you wouldn't make too much of a fool of yourself out there. My people are forgiving, but my parents are not. I apologize."

"No need," I said quickly. "I understand and will do what's necessary to integrate."

"Thank you." She performed the Bronze bow. When I didn't copy it, she snapped, "Always bow back when someone bows to you."

"I'm sorry," I mumbled, imitating her.

When she spoke like that... never mind. I ground my teeth and swallowed the thought.

"You're more graceful in combat than in your normal life, it seems," she said huffily.

I sighed. "You're not wrong."

"Of course I'm not. Come, let's train you up some more. Oh! Look at that; it's Cobi."

My friend, joined by Il and Norva, stood in a small training area tucked away to the far side of the garden. A blade glinted from his fist, and Il had his own that he used to demonstrate appropriate poses. Cobi took a wild swing at the air, throwing too much weight into it. He spun around and nearly sliced Norva.

I hissed between my teeth.

Sakaiah chuckled. "He'll be okay."

"I'm not so sure," I admitted. "You don't know Cobs like I do."

"Cobs?" The princess snorted. "Give the boy some time. How old is he?"

"Sixteen."

"Mm. He has time," she said.

He did. An entire month, apparently. He might make good progress if he practiced regularly.

"Let's go inside," Sakaiah suggested, "So you can try to put on your own robe this time."

She led the way back into the palace and out of the heat I was beginning to realize was oppressive. Even in the shade, it loomed, heavy and moist.

"If you can master the different modes of robe wear—oh. Karvo."

A pinch-faced man in dark blue robes strode past. He paused, greeting Sakaiah before turning his sharp, needling eyes on me. "Who is this, Highness?"

"This is Twilight," Sakaiah said curtly.

Karvo nodded slowly, taking me in. "How interesting."

"Not much is interesting about it, frankly, Karvo. She is a guest." Sakaiah's tone carried an unmistakable edge.

The longer he looked at me, the more uncomfortable I grew. His presence was off. Something in him seemed lopsided, but who was I to be the judge of character when I was what I was? He might have been enduring some emotional trial or wrestling with a difficult day.

"Pleasure, sir," I said, giving him the Bronze bow.

His mouth drew further together in something resembling a scowl. "Not the best Bronzian greeting, but grace doesn't belong to all of us, I suppose." He bid farewell to Sakaiah and sauntered off, leaving me to gape silently after him.

"Pay him no mind," Sakaiah growled.

"Who is he?"

"He," she said quietly, "Is one of the court advisors."

"I see. He reminds me of one of the Sharavak advisors, Silos."

"Why is that?"

"Because," I said, "He was always scowling."

She laughed. "That's Karvo, as well. I'm sorry for that embarrassing introduction. Let's try the robe technique again and not give him any more reason to be rude, hmm?"

A pleasant evening followed an equally lovely morning and afternoon. The young Bronze princess's fervor and optimism for our stay rejuvenated us after our travels, relieving us of at least some of our worries for the future. I settled into my bedroom as dusk fell and was visited by Cobi.

"Check it out," he said, drawing a sword from his sheath and waving it in the air.

"Wow!" I exclaimed. "Guns *and* blades! You're getting fancy. Are you sure you can handle yourself, though? I see Il's teaching you."

"I am."

He came up beside Cobi, Norva behind him, and clapped him on the shoulder. "Good work, kid. That was a clean strike back there."

Cobi lit up. "Thank you, sir. I'm happy the princess was willing to let me use the materials here."

"Well, color me impressed," I said. "You really are committed to becoming an asset."

He frowned slightly and struck a few poses, awkward and unstable, and Il tried to hide his smile behind him.

"Try not to murder my nightstand, Cobs," I laughed. "Or Il and Norva. Or yourself."

"His hands don't quite know what to make of their new extension yet," Il snickered to Norva's disapproving glare.

"So, he's a bit clumsy. That's what practice is for, Il, so be nice." She punched his shoulder, and he punched hers back. She rolled her eyes. "We are proud of you, Cobi. And you, Twilight. We saw the high-intensity training you and the princess were up to!"

"Was it really that intense?" I asked.

Il nodded. "We thought so. She's abundant, like you."

I swallowed quietly and nodded. "I guess so."

"I'm tired," Cobi yawned, "So I'm going to bed. Good work today, Twi, and thanks for the, uh... lack of a vote of confidence." Grinning tightly, he took another stab at the air and filed out of my room behind his mentors.

The embrace of my mattress was a welcome one as I tumbled onto it. I stretched out on the quilt and glanced at the canopy rearing over the bed, outside lights filtering faintly through the curtains.

What a different world I was in now. Only a couple nights ago, I had been where I believed my new home was, the outskirts of Syndbur with the Akristurans. At least I could properly grow up there and evolve into an adult. Now I was on the other side of the planet making attempts at war preparations. I laughed softly in the darkness as I pondered the absurdity of it all.

From a skeptical person to a worshiper of the Myrk God to an Akristuran in a few months. From one small sliver of the world to the next two regions. From one group of people to the opposite. As a child, I had always longed for adventure, but this was a bit excessive.

Akristura and His ways.

Despite my preoccupation with the abstract, I was not lofty enough to consider them. No mortal mind could piece together a deity's thoughts. If we were able to, would that not render the deity less... deific?

I laughed at my "pretentious" mind and how it always seemed to be floating away with me. Even my life failed at groundedness. What was I, if not entirely uprooted? Tossed around by this magical god here and this other one there, intensified, weaponized, and cast out into the world to do everyone's bidding?

First, it was killing non-magicals and consuming their flesh. Next, it was slaughtering Akristurans. Then I was commanded to make a giant monster my pet of planetary annihilation. Now I was to *save* the world from that same "god" I'd served?

Another chuckle escaped my lips. Such absurdity. I was only fifteen, yet I could swear I was five hundred.

An entire lifetime and then some had already been lived. Choices made, regrets amassed, and lessons learned. What more did my new god have waiting for me?

Please, Akristura, I prayed into the darkness, *You have given me hope. You have dulled some of my urges. Keep me on the path, and forgive me if I sometimes doubt whether I am indeed "enough" for anything. I'm young, and You and I both know I love blood.*

I sighed and rolled over onto my side, pulling my pillow out in front of me so I could hold it close, as my mother had never been alive to do for me. I liked to imagine the pillow was my life and I, being the one clutching it, symbolized Akristura.

I would not let go.

Would He?

CHAPTER NINETEEN

S AKAIAH WAS RARING TO go at sunrise. I might have been privately irritated with her if not for her effervescent enthusiasm.

"Sorry to wake you this early," she said, sweeping through my room to open the window, "But I thought we'd get a headstart on the day with some training."

I blinked through my grogginess and sat up in bed. "That's fine. Any particular reason?"

"Oh, I'm just excited. Yesterday was neat. I've never dueled with someone of my caliber before."

"I have," I muttered. "They almost killed me."

"I won't kill you. Promise." She laughed and asked me to meet her downstairs after I'd fully woken up and gotten ready.

I found her pacing outside in the garden at the same point we'd trained yesterday. She brightened at my presence and summoned her magic.

"Ready?" She asked.

I hardly had my mouth open to reply when she blasted me. The lumensa washed warmly over me, unwilling to attack a non-combative target. Chuckling, I ignited my own stream and launched it at her.

Sakaiah met it deftly. We found ourselves in the same swift stalemate, our respective magic blocking each other and creating a wall of pressure. Given the sparkle in her eye, she wanted me to challenge her. I would, then. Challenge accepted.

I forced a leap forward, causing my end of the magic to devour some of hers. Grunting, she shoved back, but I'd positioned one foot behind me to help withstand the motion. Sakaiah hissed through her lips.

I smelled her strong will, even fear and desperation like this duel counted for much more than practice. I locked eyes with her. I shouldn't have done that. My hostility kindled, and between her various scented emotions and the depth of the struggle in her eyes, she was angering me again.

No, I wasn't stupid—I wouldn't harm a royal—but my Shadow senses were stirring and asking that I do *something* to put the princess in her place.

What? I thought worriedly. *Put her in her place for training hard?*

I tried to reason myself out of it, but the more I looked at her, the greater my aggression became. Sein had told me I was special. Sir Korbin had, too. This girl—never mind that she was older than me and presumably ruled a nation—could not win. I wouldn't allow it.

Pride, my conscience warned.

For a moment, I faltered. Sakaiah seized my hesitation and used her magic to flip me off my feet. I landed on the hard stone, not remaining for long.

She'd called me graceless. She had yet to see me in peak form.

Shivering with delight, I fired at her feet. The lumensa wouldn't damage her, as she wasn't attacking me, but the force of the magic was still enough to destabilize her.

Predictably, she wobbled. I sprang to my feet and marched toward her with a barrier in one hand and offensive magic in the other. I'd only use this technique as long as I needed it.

Sakaiah attempted to barrage-attack my barrier. It wavered slightly but didn't break, allowing me to utilize my other skills on her.

Tapping into my primal prowess, I darted behind the princess and lashed at her back. She whipped around to strike me, but I'd already rolled to her side, hitting her there, too. She turned in my direction this time. I let her throw orbs at me.

Laughing inside, I danced under, around, and between the spheres of light, keeping a constant lift in my feet. Her furrowed brow bespoke her frustration.

"How?" She whispered.

I struck out again and smashed into her torso. She responded by throwing spheres at me and maintaining a steady stream. I kept my barrier and rolled toward her, watching her eyes widen with every orb I dodged while my barrier protected me from the stream.

A prey game, that's all this was. She was strong, but she wasn't me, and her blood smelled mighty salty. I breathed deeply and made my move.

When I came close enough, I tackled her by the feet. We tumbled in a tangle of legs and glowing palms, panting from the exertion.

Unfortunately, Sakaiah didn't seem to enjoy the exercise as much as I had.

"What was that?" She cried. "That... that look in your eyes, like you wanted to kill me?"

Whoops.

"Sorry, Princess," I mumbled. "I was having fun."

Sakaiah's eyes narrowed. "Apparently."

"I didn't intend to hurt you or anything," I assured her.

I offered her my hand to help her stand up. She ignored it and stood on her own, brushing dust off her clothes.

"Well, I was going to take you to town today, but now I'm not sure I should."

"Why not?" I asked.

"Because of what you just did! You looked evil, Twilight. I saw your Shadow. I didn't like it." Sakaiah sighed and motioned for us to leave. "Let's go see what Cobi's doing. He'll be out here soon to train, too."

"That I need to see."

Sakaiah glared. "Try not to hurt the poor fellow, will you?"

Oh, she was stirring it again. If she didn't want to see my Shadow and be offended by it, she could try not offending *me.* No. I was overreacting. It wasn't like I could voice my thoughts, anyway. Princess Sakaiah was fine, a nice girl; she just...

She's another threat, my Shadow warned.

My conscience objected to this. Once again, my natures were at war with each other. It didn't matter, though. I'd beat her at the duel, so I could shut myself up about feeling inferior for a while.

"Ah. There he is."

Sakaiah pointed out Cobi coming down the path with Il and Norva. She waved to him. He waved back, a blade hanging from a scabbard at his side.

"I'm not sure I'll get used to seeing him like that, but I'm definitely proud of him," I commented.

"You make him seem very incompetent," said Sakaiah.

"Not that. Just inexperienced."

And too afraid to use weapons before.

I expected a struggle when we entered the small training yard behind Cobi, and that was what we received. He asked to train with me first, holding his sword at the ready in anticipation of my magic. I went slowly at first in the hopes of acclimating him. He swung and missed. The first several orbs flew past his face.

"Not bad," I told him gently, though internally, I wished he would pay closer attention.

Maybe he couldn't, though. Was I being unfair in expecting swift improvement, even though it would probably be minimal?

Cobi batted away an orb that floated toward his eye, his face tense. He'd missed again, and he appeared to resent that.

"Keep going, Cobi," Norva encouraged him.

Il said, "Train your eyes on the magic and try to match your strike with the orb's arrival."

Sakaiah glared at him and looked back at Cobi.

Cobi re-positioned and asked me to go again. His tone was sharper this time, and so was the line of his jaw straining against the flesh.

I sent him one orb with no urgency. We watched it languidly drift Cobi's way, believing that this time, there was no way he could—

"Missed," he growled when the magic fizzled out behind him.

I sighed. "I know you're new to this, Cobs, but that one was purposely slow."

"He's learning, Twilight," the princess said. "If you're getting frustrated, why don't I take over?"

I resented her suggesting this, like she feared what I might do to my friend if he frustrated me "too much." I knew I wouldn't dream of hurting him over something so trivial, but if she'd seen darkness in my eyes and been genuinely concerned by my inner Shadow, I wouldn't resist her.

"Go ahead," I said, stepping away.

Sakaiah took my place and gently asked Cobi if he was ready to try again. He smiled and nodded, then took a swing at the first orb to come his way. Like last time—the last several times, rather—he missed.

"I like the determination," Sakaiah said. "Can you swing a little higher next time? Magic tends to float upward when it's moving alone."

"I can do that."

This time, Cobi tried Sakaiah's method. The orb dissolved upon contact with the blade, and Sakaiah clapped. "Wonderful. Look what happens when you keep swinging for the fences!"

Cobi beamed. "I took a stab, and I slayed my low expectations."

"My," Sakaiah said with a grin, "Cutting blades and wit? Sterling. It's about time someone pierced the monotony of this place. Well, you and this one." She smiled at me before looking back at Cobi. "Shall we go again?"

Cobi prepared again for a fresh round of orbs, but Sakaiah didn't have this in mind. A thin stream charged from her hand and met his blade as he'd thrown it up defensively.

"Good block! Now drive the blade forward to deflect my attack and send it back to me!" Sakaiah cried.

The sword jolted, returning the magic to the sender. Sakaiah let it dissipate over her, then fired a second time. Cobi caught this beam, too. Sakaiah let it ricochet when it met her. Cobi hadn't anticipated that.

Sakaiah paused and dropped her hands. "You're doing quite well, especially for a magicless person. Your future enemies will likely include magicians, though, so if you want to survive them, you'll have to anticipate changes in maneuvers and points of attack. Many magicians, like this one here," she continued, nodding at me, "Are nimble and fast. You must be ready for that."

"Thank you," Cobi replied. "I'll get better."

Sakaiah smiled warmly at him. "You're a beginner, my dear. Don't stress too much just yet. Would you like to go one more round? Maybe Twilight wants to join?"

"Sure."

The princess opened her palms back up and sent me a thought: *We're going to move around him this time and try to confuse him. He won't know which target to hit or avoid.*

Before commencing, Sakaiah had Cobi take up his shield. His face flushed when he tried, shakily, to raise it and hold it with the sword simultaneously.

Sakaiah frowned slightly. "Some physical training will benefit you."

Cobi reddened more. "I've *been* training."

"Ah. Well, more won't hurt. Balance those two as best you can. Hold your shield closer than the sword and ensure it's covering your torso. If you see a headshot coming, raise it to block that. You don't want a headshot."

Sir Korbin would agree with that.

Cobi did as Sakaiah instructed him, and we began our exercise. I took to his left while Sakaiah paced around his right. As expected, Cobi didn't know which of us to look at, but he faithfully kept his shield close. I attacked his flank. Sakaiah followed suit with her other one, and instead of deflecting one or both of us, Cobi got his ribs aglow with magic.

"Come on, Cobs. You could have dished it back out to one of us," I chided gently.

Sakaiah shook her head, giving Cobi's shoulder a squeeze. "Sorry, but she's wrong. You are doing wonderfully, Cobi." More quietly, she added, "Don't listen to naysaying."

"I'm not a naysayer," I protested. I realized it had come out more aggressively than I intended, so I corrected myself. "I mean, I'm only being honest. I'm not trying to be too hard on him, but I don't want him to die."

Sakaiah glared at me. "That is all good and well, but you need to give him time."

I felt like saying, "I am; I'm just trying to help him," but I held my tongue. Arguing wouldn't save the mainland. Unnecessary strife wouldn't defeat the beast in the Void or the beast in my father and his Shadow army.

So, maybe I was a naysayer. Maturity was letting the princess have that opinion of me. That was what I told myself to keep from saying things I'd sorely regret.

I tried not to dwell on the morning when afternoon rolled around. Princess Sakaiah was helping us, and no one could fault her for that. With optimism, she took me through the garden to a large open field behind it where sentries and soldiers of old trained.

"It's ideal for bolstering our army," she said. "In the last few centuries, we've limited our military since we haven't had much use for it. No one bothers us out here, and we have no hand in geopolitical affairs. Father has maintained a small but strong presence with law enforcers and highly trained sentries. We also have a reserve unit that trains monthly in the event of a conflict. This is where they come."

The broad field stretched to the edge of a jungle, and it was speckled with targets for shooting, magic, and swordsmanship. It certainly covered all the relevant combat bases. Lumens could practice magic, while Nons would use the targets to hone their marksman and swordsman skills. Cobi might have benefited from graduating to this field when he learned the basics with his own weapons.

"It's ideal," I replied. "I can easily see your army working out here. How many people do you think you could get if the decision goes through?"

"Oh, at least a few thousand. We might have several hundred more if we have eager women who can pass the fitness standards. We wouldn't need to draft people, either. The Bronze will gladly answer the service call if we place it."

I smiled. "You oversee a good nation, then, Princess."

She grimaced. "It's not quite my place to rule yet."

Puzzled, I asked what she meant.

Sakaiah shrugged. "Little point in hiding it. My parents, if you haven't already gathered, do not have much faith in my ability to rule. My father deems me foolish and immature. To prevent this land from collapsing under my hand, my parents asked me to sign an agreement that limits the extent of my power as a princess and reserves major decision-making for them—the original Prince and Princess. Only when I fulfill some arbitrary expectations will the agreement be terminated, restoring me to my full title and its privileges."

This could have explained her competitive streak and her desire to not be called by her title, or at least something that implied her royal status. I'd have been embarrassed to be in that position, too.

"I'm sorry to hear that," I told her. "If it's any consolation, I was forced to be a regal figure for the Sharavaks."

Sakaiah shook her head. "Terrible. I could never."

"Well, I did it, sadly. I'm of the opinion now that it's better to want to be something and not be it than be forced into acting as something you're not. I'm sure, though, that your parents will come around. You seem determined and confident."

Sakaiah grinned. "As do you. You came all the way out here to make a request of a foreign nation that doesn't associate with other nations. You have my respect for that."

"Thank you," I replied. "And you might not have gathered from my memories, but... I don't get along with my father, either. Then there's my mother. My grandfather, the Sharavak High Father, killed her when I was born."

Sakaiah's lips pressed together, and she glanced at me, her gaze burning with regret. "I'm sorry. I thought I saw something like that in your memories. And I'm sorry you don't get along with your father. I caught a glimpse of that, too."

I nodded, touching my starstone, which never left my neck. "It's okay. You get used to being alone after a while."

The princess looked away, folding her hands neatly on top of one another. "We will make things right. I believe your memories, and I believe it when you say our world is in danger. The Sharavaks usually fulfill their promises one way or another."

I laughed darkly. "Yeah. Father's monster in the Void—did you notice that when I showed you?"

Apparently, she hadn't—that memory hadn't made much sense to her—so I let her view it again. Her eyes glistened with fear when she'd seen it and taken it in.

"Despicable. Is this what we're up against?" Her tone spiked with anxiety.

"Most likely. I was supposed to be the one to summon it, but when I escaped, that didn't appear to change their plans. The Silver government and the Shadows are continuing their plot, it seems. Arkyaktaas is a key component for Myrkraas."

Sakaiah moaned and scrubbed her face with her hands. "Then it's worse than we thought. Your initial memories—the ones I understood—were only scratching the surface. Oh, gods. This isn't good."

Gods. Maybe she'd teach me about her religion at some point.

Sakaiah straightened up. "We won't be deterred by this. It's all the more reason to help your people. Helping your people will help the world."

I agreed. "Now you understand the burden on us. We don't have enough Akristuran Lumens to fight this thing and the army together, so we needed to seek another force to join us. Sakaiah, whatever differences exist between our cultures, I hope that you'll give us the help we need."

The princess placed her hand over her chest and said, "You have my honor that I will do what is in my power to convince my parents to help you. I will pass along this additional memory to them. Mother's never liked dark, devious things like that... that demon thing." She shuddered and moved away from the training field.

"Thank you," I called after her. "Again, I appreciate you trying. If you manage to save the world from certain doom, I hope your parents will see your value then."

Sakaiah turned, giving me a small smile. "And I hope your father sees yours and the errors of his ways. That would fix everything."

"It would," I agreed. "But I'm not holding my breath."

CHAPTER TWENTY

I T DID NOT DO to dwell on fears of the future. When I laid down that evening, heaviness nestled in me, and it followed me through the night. I disliked considering it, but it felt like a second presence had joined me when darkness fell. I was probably imagining things. After what Sakaiah and I had discussed, who wouldn't feel perturbed?

Sleep evaded me, so I rose even earlier than the previous morning and wandered outside my room. I didn't intend to poke into any off-limits spaces or investigate things that didn't concern me until I heard low chanting coming from the last door at the other end of the hall.

I stole quietly down the path, graceful now that I was "hunting" something. Sakaiah would have been pleased. The chanting was probably too low for normal ears, but I caught snatches of dedicated whispers through the far door.

The closer I crept, the more sure I was that the chanting was Sakaiah's. Maybe she was saying her morning prayers?

I decided to knock instead of stalking sounds.

"Is this the princess?" I called.

The chanting stopped. Moments later, the door opened, and a tired-looking Sakaiah greeted me.

"Good morning. Sorry if I've interrupted something," I said, bowing and darting a quick look over her shoulder to the room's interior.

The princess shrugged and bowed back. "Come in if you like. I've been worshiping."

"I see. Thank you for inviting me in."

Sakaiah sighed and stepped back so I could enter the sitting room. A rainbow assortment of different stones lined the windowsill. Sakaiah settled on her knees in front of them, gazing at them longingly as if musing over their power.

"Are these your...?" I paused so she could explain.

"My gods," Sakaiah said quietly.

Where she saw deities, I saw only pretty rocks. I sat beside her at the window and asked her which gems were responsible for what.

"The purple one," she explained, "Is said to contain a fraction of the moon's soul. It will grant peaceful sleep to those who pray to it."

"Interesting," I said. "Has it done that for you?"

Sakaiah smirked. "Not to my knowledge."

"Okay," I said. I pointed at a red gem. "And what about this one?"

Sighing, Sakaiah leaned back on her legs and answered, "That one is supposed to bear healing and wellness in response to prayers. I'm sure you'll ask, but I don't know if it has answered those prayers or not. I assume the gods are particular about which prayers they answer."

I nodded and picked up the one nearest me, a green gem. Sakaiah gasped and pried it from my hands.

"What are you doing?" She hissed. "You cannot touch them!"

"I'm sorry," I said quickly.

Sakaiah stared back at her collection. I stared with her and wondered how long she'd been trying to prise answers from them.

"I can tell," she said slowly, "That you're passing judgment on me for this. It is disrupting my ability to pray."

"I'm not," I assured her. "I've been part of a much worse religion, I promise. If you want me to go, though, I can, uh, leave you to it."

Sakaiah glared at me out of the corner of her eye. "You're an Akristuran now, right?"

I nodded.

"Mm. I don't like your type."

I chewed my lip and replied, "Respectfully, Sakaiah, I don't appreciate that, but you are entitled to your opinion."

Sakaiah chuckled. "That's quite right. What an opinion that is." Her mouth made an ugly shape, and I stood to go.

"Stop," she commanded.

I looked back at her. "Yes?"

She was beginning to anger me. It was better if I left, but her tension indicated she would rather hash it out with me.

"I just want to understand something," she said, "And pardon me if it comes out wrong, but I've had few opportunities to talk with Akristurans before... why do you think your god is the only one? What evidence do you have that only it exists and its foolish laws and rules are the only ones worth abiding by?"

Valid questions. I didn't feel knowledgeable enough to respond, aside from answering, "Personal experience." But I couldn't share my feelings with anyone. They lived inside me and only for me.

"I appreciate you asking. Honestly, I'm not far enough in my understanding to have the answers to those questions, but I know what I feel when I pray, what the texts say, and how I have grown since asking Akristura to cleanse me. When I pray, I..." I paused. "I sense that someone really is receiving my thoughts. They're listening, and they do care. I never felt that with Aadyalbaine."

Sakaiah's voice dripped with disbelief when she replied, "So, your beliefs can't withstand any prodding. Noted. You can go now."

That stung. I decided I'd ask Il and Norva if I couldn't answer the questions myself. They weren't awake, so I spent some time in my room reading through a condensed book of the Akristuran texts Sir Korbin gave me before I left. He'd said the tiny font strained his eyes, so I should have it.

Smiling at the memory, I read several pages when I came upon a startling sentence that said, "There is only One who is responsible for the planet, the skies, and all creatures inhabiting both. Though man and baine may claim other deities, some insisting that they themselves are gods, these are false; there is only One."

My heart jumped. The texts spoke of Akristura's unwavering deific status, but Sakaiah wasn't likely to believe this. Regardless, I had to show it to her.

"Sakaiah?" I said softly at the door in the hallway.

"I am praying," she snapped. "What do you need?"

"I wanted to answer your question," I replied. "May I?"

Sakaiah yanked the door open, smirking. "Go on."

"Well," I said, opening my book, "It says here in the Akristuran texts—"

"Get that out of my face." Sakaiah's eyes sharpened into swords, and she stepped away.

"I'm sorry?" It came out more as a question than a statement.

"I will not accept "answers" from a fairy tale," she hissed. "Leave me be. We'll train later after I've cleansed myself of this dark feeling that's come over me."

"What dark feeling?" I asked.

She shook her head. "Never mind. You won't understand. *I* don't understand." She patted her hair like it pained her and headed back to the windowsill.

"I want to," I said.

"Understand?"

I nodded. Sakaiah sighed and invited me back in.

"I'm sorry I threw you out earlier. If I overstep a boundary, you have my permission to defend yourself," she said.

I didn't respond to this. I'd been wanting to defend myself since yesterday.

Gently, I asked her to tell me what was wrong. When the question came, Sakaiah's lips trembled, and she silently swallowed back glimmering tears, closing her eyes against the morning sunshine.

"Since you arrived the other day, I've had this terrible sense of foreboding. I can't explain how or why, but it's even affecting my magic now. I've prayed. That has made it worse. When you dueled me yesterday, I became angry with you, and I don't think you noticed, but I was summoning dark magic at times."

I hadn't noticed. I assumed this was because I was too immersed in myself to care about anything around me.

"I didn't see," I admitted, "But I've struggled with my magic before, too. When I first used it, it was valdur, dark magic. But a little later, I discovered I could also heal. It confused me. As I progressed in the Sharavak lifestyle, I became disconnected from lumensa. It was harder and harder to use."

"Mm. Bronzians believe magic should only be used for benevolent and protective purposes by the few who possess it. It never occurred to us to use it for evil," Sakaiah said. "How did you eventually come back into possession of your lumensa, and what caused you to lose it in the first place?"

Trying not to picture the memories, I answered, "I used my magic the way any Sharavak does—to maim and kill. I took lives with it. I used my magic for tasks that required pain, punishment, and death." I lowered my eyes. "And I fulfilled them. That was what made the healing power go away."

Sakaiah moved off her knees and crossed her legs, gazing aimlessly at the floor. "I'm sorry. I've never used my magic like that before. I didn't know it could be deadened like that." I flinched. "You got it back, though."

"Yes. I begged that it would return, and in small bursts, it did. Then, when I decided to call out to Akristura, the power gradually strengthened. Dark magic was finally taking a back seat." I shrugged. "I still have a ways to go in training. I'll never be perfect at this or anything else, but..." I looked at her, hoping one day she'd understand. "I am better now, and I believe Akristura is the reason for that."

Sakaiah said nothing. I settled into silence with her. We sat like that for several minutes, enjoying a surprising mutual appreciation of the quiet. I hadn't experienced that with anyone but Solshek.

I hope you're okay, Sol, I thought. *Assuming Father let you live.* Eventually, when Sakaiah tired of the silence, she broke it.

"We should probably train. Do you want to?"

"Yes. If you find you're wrestling with dark magic, I can help you," I said.

Sakaiah smiled gratefully. "Thank you. I anticipate I'll need that help."

We took up our usual place in the garden and commenced practice. I admired both our agile bodies, how we sliced and glided through the air on nothing but nimble feet. Though I often had the upper hand, Sakaiah proved a formidable opponent with each bolt of magic she faithfully met and sent back to me. I grinned when one of my orbs zipped back my way, clipping the bottom of my ear on its passage.

"Princess Sakaiah, thief of hearing. But you know you're not supposed to aim for the head. Try going for more low-hanging fruit." I attacked her ankles, and she fell, giggling, on the stone.

"Are you good?" I asked through my own laughter.

I went to help her when she sprang back up and doused me. Lumensa flurried over my torso, its sparks decorating my face. I coughed and struck her again. As with the last several times, our magic met and did not easily budge. We enjoyed another shoving match. Sakaiah vowed she would win this time.

We pushed, locking eyes and goading each other on through the contact, but the confidence was quickly souring. In place of friendly pride seeped a disorienting darkness. It caused us to grind our magic harder until the pressure threw us back onto the stone.

Groaning, we asked if the other was okay while climbing to our feet. It was at this point that Karvo walked by, casting disapproving frowns at both of us.

"Good morning, Advisor Karvo," Sakaiah said loudly.

The beak-faced man dipped his head. "Good morning, Princess." He threw a glance my way. "Good morning, Evening."

"It's Twilight, sir," I replied evenly.

He apologized. "I thought it was that or Late Afternoon." He said it with no sense of a joke, then hurried off across the garden to the other side of the palace.

Sakaiah and I exchanged a look. We burst into laughter.

"Oh, I really dislike that man," she sighed. "But tell me… did you feel something strange come over you before he showed himself?"

"I did, actually. I sensed something off about him from the moment I met him," I confessed. "Is there a reason for this?"

Sakaiah shook her head. "I wouldn't know. I've felt it as long as I've known him, though. It's worsened in the last week."

I winced, hoping she didn't attribute this change to me.

She looked at me again, scouring my eyes for something she apparently didn't like. "It's there again," she whispered. "Your Shadow. Was it Karvo this time or something else?"

So, the darkness *had* manifested. I was sure the advisor had some part in it, but Twilight herself was plenty subject to her evil.

"I…"

Should I confess the truth? What if she had me tortured or killed for it? I searched Sakaiah's own eyes to seek her emotional state, as her heart rate had picked up slightly.

"Maybe my issue is mine alone," I admitted. "I'm still a Shadow, no matter how much training I do to… control myself. It's in my nature to fight. Certain environmental factors don't help." I nodded in the direction Karvo had gone.

Sakaiah loosed a breath. "That's not sterling. We need to look into this, Twilight." Her gaze brightened. "We can visit my friend, Gnapa. She's in town. I'll call for the carriage, and we can ask her what can be done with you."

She started back to the palace. I asked what her friend could do for me that I hadn't already tried, explaining that my improvement depended on Akristura. She dismissed this and had one of the palace carriages brought around in front.

"Have some faith in me," was all she said before ordering the driver to leave.

I wanted to trust her. The problem was I didn't have faith in people. I couldn't tell her that, and my curiosity compelled me to go with her, so we went.

I made mental notes of the sights passing by the carriage windows as we rode. How could it all be so green, so rich with life? So rich with things I never thought I'd see.

Everything about the Bronze, from its verdant vegetation to the noises of insects and the fluttering of brightly-colored birds, cried out, "Alive!" Mixed among the greenery were flowering trees drooping under their burden of blossoms.

"It's different, isn't it?" Sakaiah remarked at my side.

"Yes. The ocean was one surprise, but I love the colors in the jungle."

Pride echoed in Sakaiah's voice when she replied, "It is the most beautiful place on Aash, as I see it. I needn't visit the Caligin or the Silver to dampen my spirits; this is where true beauty lies."

I politely retorted, "The Caligin is plenty pretty, and so is the Silver."

Sakaiah shrugged. "It's your opinion."

And you have yours, I thought.

We moved through town and saw the liveliness of the Bronze in full swing. Women and children danced, beating belled instruments, while men sang together and downed their drinks. None of it had the oppressed atmosphere of Syndbur. It came across as genuine merry-making. All the heartbeats excited me, but the absence of heavy darkness and bald-faced evil prevented too much temptation.

After breaking into the lower sections of Valechka, we rounded onto a narrow side street along which a dozen or so small houses sat. When we reached the right one, Sakaiah called for the driver to stop.

"You may find my friend unconventional," she said, "But give her a try. Gnapa is a deeply spiritual woman, one of my good religious companions."

I frowned. "Spiritual" didn't always equate to "good." The Sharavaks were spiritual, after all.

Sakaiah knocked on the door, and a breathless older woman answered moments later. She beamed when she saw her visitor and cried, "Princess Seraphina! It is an honor. What can I do for you?" She bowed.

Sakaiah bowed back, wrapped an arm around me, and said, "This one needs a cleansing. Do you think you could help her?"

Gnapa took me in, her eyes widening almost imperceptibly. To me, though, little was imperceptible. "Why, Highness, I'd love nothing more than to help. Please come in." Her gaze continued to burn me after we'd entered her home.

Remove your shoes, Sakaiah thought.

I took them off and let Gnapa set them aside for me next to the front door. She straightened up and said, "Well! It's good to meet a friend of the Princess's. What sort of cleansing are we needing today, lovelies?"

Sakaiah explained that she needed the same one as me, a cleansing "for the spirit."

"Ours are both a bit jumpy if we're honest," she said.

Gnapa nodded quickly. "Okay. So, an anti-anxiety ritual, then. May I fumigate you?" She looked at me.

"Uh..."

"She'll be lighting candles in an enclosed space and letting you bask in the essential fragrances," Sakaiah said, grinning at my confusion. "Please excuse my friend, Gnapa. She's not yet accustomed to Bronzian ways."

Friend. I wondered if she meant that.

Gnapa chuckled. "Not to worry. I will also be praying over you, if I may."

Her saying this confirmed my concerns.

"Praying?"

"Yes," said Sakaiah, "To our gods. Yours doesn't seem to listen."

"That isn't true," I objected. "I'm sorry, Sakaiah, and I'm sorry to you, Gnapa, but... I'm not comfortable with this."

Gnapa's face fell. She looked to the princess for a rebuttal.

Sakaiah sighed. "You insist there are no other gods, yet you won't take the time to prove yourself incorrect? The more I pray to mine, the more I'm certain they listen, Twilight."

"I'm sure something is listening," I replied softly, "But what?"

Her eyes narrowed. "What are you suggesting?"

I shook my head. "I don't know. I'm of the belief that doing rituals like this"—I gestured to Gnapa—"invites things you don't want to mess with. I've read in my texts that baines impersonate deities, sometimes attracted to prayer directed at rocks and things—"

"Are you calling my gods "rocks," Twilight?" Sakaiah hissed.

"No, Princess, I'm just—"

"Unbelievable." Sakaiah sighed and bade Gnapa farewell. "Perhaps we'll see you at another time. If Twilight is uncomfortable, we'll leave it at that."

Gnapa's blue eyes went wild, and she gazed intently at me as if memorizing my features. I hoped she wasn't. After this unnerving journey, I wanted no one to look at me like I was a marvel of mankind.

Finally, her mouth pressed into a line, and she said, "Very well. Goodbye, Princess. Goodbye, Twilight." She performed the bow. I imitated it, and she continued staring until we left the house.

"You should have told me earlier about your reservations," Sakaiah grumbled.

"In fairness, I wasn't told what to expect," I answered.

"Are harmless things like that really against your religion?"

I nodded. "I don't believe they're harmless, but that is where our differences lie. I accept your differences, Sakaiah. All I ask is that you respect mine."

Sakaiah chuckled, shaking her head. "What would happen to you if you went through with it, though? Truly? What's the Sky Father going to do, rain death from above?"

Sickened, I said, "Please don't talk like that."

Shrugging, Sakaiah ordered the driver to take us back to the palace. I was glad about this. I wanted to spend the rest of the day away from the princess if I could.

I got my wish. Sakaiah left me alone, no doubt irritated about the Gnapa situation like I was. Evening came, and as Il, Norva, and Cobi were preparing for bed, I called them into my room to discuss the day's events.

"Shut the door, please," I told Cobi.

He closed it, and the three of them settled into the chairs around my empty fireplace to hear what I had to say.

"I'll share the memories first. Then we can talk," I said.

I projected the morning and afternoon to them and let them view what had taken place. Angry, Il withdrew first, his face blooming red.

"Royalty or not, the lass has no respect," he hissed. "What kind of young lady treats someone like that?"

"Il," said Norva gently, "Princess Sakaiah is not of our faith. We cannot expect her to respect or understand it." She patted his hand and looked at me to say, "Keep working with her, Twilight. Sakaiah is not "bad," if you know what I mean. She's young, she doesn't know what she believes, exactly, and as scary as it is to think…" She released a sigh. "It is possible she is being oppressed by baines."

The room fell silent. Il nodded slowly, mulling over the idea in his mind, whereas Cobi looked anywhere but at me. Fear was in the air—not enough to madden me—but enough to be concerning.

Norva said, "Don't give up on her, Twilight. None of us should." She looked pointedly at Il. "What we need right now is to strengthen our resolve because without that, what have we?"

Il sighed. "Anger. Anxiety. A burning desire to give that girl a tongue-thrashing."

"Il!" Norva hissed.

He shrugged. "You heard her tone, Norva, and you saw her face."

"That is aside the point." Norva clicked her tongue. "In other news, Cobi is improving with the sword. We're both very proud of him." She touched his shoulder, and he flashed her a guilty smile.

Guilty for what?

"What do *you* think of the memories?" I asked him.

He kept his eyes on the floor and mumbled, "They're interesting. Hopefully, she comes around."

His wooden tone frustrated me. I thanked the Akristurans for their encouragement, and Il thanked me for not giving Sakaiah any kind of thrashing, "Because that would be disastrous, as much as we'd all probably like to." Cobi uttered a tired "Good night" and passed out of my room with Il and Norva.

He forgot to close the door behind him, so I closed it myself. As soon as I did, a stifling darkness enshrouded me.

Unnatural darkness, not born from the mere absence of moonlight.

Baine.

I felt the creature's claws massage my throat as it seized me. A shadow of ripe stench, black and unforgiving, wiped away what little light passed through my curtains. Flailing, I tried to scream. The baine hissed a laugh into my ear as no sound came out of me.

"Myrkraas is coming, Myrk Maiden," its heavy voice dripped. *"You are too far gone to belong to the light, no matter how much you scheme against us and ours."*

I screamed Akristura's name in my mind, which the baine must have perceived. It growled at me and tossed me onto the floor. Before it could overcome me, I threw up my palms and urged lumensa to release. But when I saw the face of the entity in front of me, the lumensa sputtered and died.

The baine laughed again. Its every frigid breath was a mockery of my existence.

"Fear consumes you," it whispered. *"As it consumes others among you."*

The baine swept over me and perched on top of me, crushing my chest and filling my lungs with an arctic chill. It sat there on my sternum and grinned as it began to infuse my mind with disastrous thoughts.

Suddenly, I understood.

I was a killer. I had *eaten* my own kind.

There was no redemption for that.

Akristura's mercy had its limits. I was out of bounds.

I had no hope of comparison to a deity as pretentious and pure as Akristura. Even Sir Korbin had told me that.

So why bother?

I was depraved. Senseless. Murderous.

My carnality became me. Unlike anything Akristura could offer, the sins of my past completed me, and the shadows of eternal darkness *deserved* to oppress and brutally *slaughter* the wicked light and...

No. This is not the way.

"Akristura," I choked into the darkness.

The baine, which had begun to strangle me, snarled and whined.

Emboldened, I roared, *"Akristura, cast this thing away!"*

The baine whimpered like a wounded dog and whirled off, growling and hissing until it had disappeared into the walls. Gasping, I pulled myself off the floor and stumbled into my bed.

What had *that* been about? Was this the dark presence I'd felt last night, finally feeling bold enough to attack?

"I am being tested," I whispered, clutching at my throbbing heart. "Well," I said more loudly into the room, "That's fine. That means you fear me."

A growl echoed softly in the corner by the fireplace.

"Go ahead and growl at me," I challenged. "Akristura will not let you kill me, Void spawn. Leave!"

A shadow passed over the wall and vanished. I laid awake for a long while in prayer as I contemplated what had happened. What followed was a night besieged with nightmares.

CHAPTER TWENTY-ONE

T HE BAINE INCIDENT SEEMED to be the spark before the wildfire that plunged us into our first bout of chaos. No one was able to anticipate what came next.

I parted my sluggish eyelids to find several maids shouting around my bed and saw that it was barely dawn. Rubbing the exhaustion from my face, I asked what was wrong.

"A heavy rain fell during the night," one servant explained breathlessly. "It resulted in major flooding that has many of our people in the lower-elevation sections of town searching desperately for shelter. Princess Sakaiah has asked you to assist her in helping the people, miss."

Civilians potentially drowning in the streets! I couldn't stomach the thought.

"Take me to the princess," I said.

Sakaiah was fidgeting in the foyer when we descended, but when she looked at me, some of the gloom fell from her face.

"Thank goodness," she cried. "My parents have already sent out palace aid, but I want us to investigate things ourselves and do what we can. There's even flooding in here!" She jabbed a finger at the floor. "We may have to heal many people today, Twilight. Do you feel strong enough for that?"

"Yes," I replied. "I can probably handle a few dozen moderate injuries before I start to deplete."

Sakaiah's eyes darkened. "We may have more than a few dozen out there. But do what you can. Come on! We haven't time to waste."

The princess took my wrist and pulled me out to the waiting carriage. Bulging clouds of silver and shadow clashed in the heavens above us. As soon as we climbed into the carriage, we swept through the puddles and down the path leading to town.

As we descended into the lower sections, the danger became apparent. Floodwaters lapped against closed windows and took up residence inside most of the homes. Fountains, gorged with water, devoured the gardens and damaged the lower levels of each affected building, leaving many families stranded in the streets.

It was a cluster the likes of which I'd never seen before. The crowds in Syndbur had felt like managed chaos, but this was utter madness. Where had this sudden bout of rain come from?

"It fell within a matter of hours," Sakaiah explained. "Early this morning, the rains just... dumped. Everywhere. There's damage in the lower sections of the palace, too. It's bad."

Screams and wailing pierced the early morning air while a thin drizzle continued to thread down from the heavens. Children were sprinting toward their parents, weeping, and babies in their mothers' arms shrieked against the wetness invading their clothes.

Men were shouting at each other, shattering the Bronze peace and inspiring a few women to turn on one another. My head was beginning to throb between the roaring, caterwauling, hostility-heavy commotion and the forces of nature clamoring for destruction.

"Don't get overstimulated just yet," Sakaiah begged. "We must be strong for those in weakened positions."

I agreed, despite my anxiety, and we exited the carriage. When my shoes made contact with the road, a splash dampened my ankles and sent a chill through my legs. I gritted my teeth and let Sakaiah take the lead.

She was clad in a blue cloth tunic with a sun and star emblem stitched across the back of the collar, the symbol of the Bronze, and brown boots lightly caked in dust. That dust wouldn't survive for a moment in the weather.

We picked our way down into the throng, where Sakaiah pulled me onto the lip of a fountain with her to yell, "My people! Rest assured that the royal family knows your plight and sends its aid. There are already homes being pumped free of water and medics tending to the injured, and here, we are beginning a new round of healing. If anyone is wounded, my friend and I invite you to step forward now!"

At her call, numerous citizens began lining up around us. Sakaiah swiftly divided them into groups for her and me to take, and we started the healing process, tending to wounds as minor as scrapes to ruined bones and gashes.

Only hours ago, these same people had probably been laughing and merry-making. Now some of them were dying. I recognized some of the faces from our visit to town yesterday.

One little girl entrusted to me by her parents was terrified of me using my magic on her. She refused to come near. She was one of my last patients, as she was only minorly injured with a cut lip and a few small scratches on her knees, but she could not be healed until I became creative.

I remembered that the Sharavaks had made designs with their valdur back during the valdur display they had conducted for me and wondered if I could do the same with lumensa. I was poor with visual design, but I had to try if I was going to win the little girl's trust and heal her.

My first attempt was to sculpt a magic rose. It proved too intricate for me to cobble together out of thin air, so I reduced it to a simple flower design that I then sent floating into the little girl's hands. She giggled when the light magic reached her fingers. As she played with the flower, I caused a petal to break away from the assembly and trickle down to the child's knees, where I commanded it to soak into and repair the skin.

When the little girl saw what the magic had done, she gazed at the lumensa flower in her hands and stuffed it in her face. I laughed as the magic wiped away her tears and the bloody wound on her lip, restoring her to her uninjured self.

"That was clever, miss," the girl's mother commented appreciatively. "What is your name?

I beamed, reveling in the feeling of being useful. "I'm Twilight, ma'am."

The mother smiled and bowed. "And do you have a last name, Twilight?"

I bowed back and thought about it for a moment. I didn't want to be associated with my father anymore; my Shadow identity was behind me.

Gazing down at my gold-illuminated hands, I said, "Delvian. I am Twilight Delvian."

If I ever met with my mother again... no, I couldn't. She must never see me. I had to keep everyone around me safe, as I'd promised myself.

The people of Valechka, however, were far from safe. As the day progressed, the rains only worsened. Sakaiah, as I helped her lift pieces of wood away from the entrances to some of the citizens' homes, told me such intense weather was very unusual in the mild-mannered Bronze and that she had only heard stories from many years ago of such disasters before.

"Something is wrong. I'm sure of it now," she muttered. "It continues with this dreadful weather."

At a certain point, Sakaiah had to stop and recharge. Her magic had depleted.

"I feel awful," she moaned, scrubbing her face and leaning against the carriage. "Do you?"

"I'm tired, but I don't feel depleted yet," I said. "Do you want to go back and rest? Maybe we can trade places with Il and Norva."

Sakaiah nodded. "Good idea. We still have some people out here needing help." She dropped her hands and climbed into the carriage. "Take us back, please," she told the driver.

The driver stared grimly at the rain-slicked road before pulling away from the curb and urging the horse creatures up the hill. They plodded obediently through the storm until they'd delivered us back to the palace, where they began to spook from the thunderclaps.

"Let's eat," Sakaiah mumbled as she strode through a fresh curtain of rain into the palace. "Then I need a couple hours of sleep, at least."

"If it's still running empty by then, I can give you some of my magic," I offered.

She thanked me and asked a servant to bring us food and drink. "I'll crash in your room if you don't mind," she said. "That way, you can wake me if I oversleep."

We were at the staircase that led to the guest rooms when we ran into Cobi, Il, and Norva.

Startled, Sakaiah drew back from Il, moving closer to me. "Hello," she greeted curtly.

"Hello, Princess. How are you?" Il asked.

"Very tired," she muttered. "I'll be resting now."

Norva frowned and asked gently, "Do you need help in town? We've just gotten done helping free up the flooded spaces downstairs. We hear there are injuries down in the city?"

"There are," Sakaiah said, "And if you want to fill in for us while we rest, I'd appreciate that. I know my parents would, too."

"Okay." Norva took Il's hand. "Are you ready?"

"I am. Cobi?"

Cobi gazed longingly at us. "I'll stay with them until they go back out in case they need anything." He touched my arm. I thought he was going to help me up the stairs when he came around me and offered his support to Sakaiah instead.

"Thank you, dear," she moaned, leaning on his shoulder.

I took her other one, and we both shuffled up the steps until several servants came to our aid and took her from us.

"Oh, really," she snapped. "I don't need all this; I can walk. Thank you, though." She smiled at each of the servants, me, and Cobi, who blushed.

It felt wrong to be eating and resting when the entirety of Valechka was fighting a deadly storm, but there wasn't much to be done about that. I dropped onto my bed and felt that I, too, was worn thin. Neither of us could be expected to lend our magic when we had none left to give. It was better to sleep.

"Thanks for staying with us," I told Cobi. "Would you mind watching the time and ensuring we don't sleep more than two hours?"

He nodded. "Want me to go to my room?"

I chuckled. "Were you wanting to watch us sleep, Cobs? We're not that exciting."

His reddening cheeks gave way to awkward stammers before he backed out of my room and returned to his own. Sakaiah smiled in the half-light through the window.

"He's a good lad," she said.

"He is." I laughed at the memory of his scarlet face and rolled over onto my back. "I think I'm actually too tired to eat."

Sakaiah snorted. "I am, as well. I think I can sleep well enough knowing how many lives we impacted today. Thank you for being a part of that."

"My pleasure."

Silence settled over us, and I welcomed it. The longer I laid there, the deeper exhaustion soaked, as if it permeated my bones. Eventually, it gave way to unconsciousness. With no resistance whatsoever, I felt myself fading.

I wished I hadn't dropped off when I did, though. Dark things, things that had no distinguishable form, stalked through my sleep. I thrashed when they came too close, barely aware of my own consciousness and that I could affect things at all.

What I did know was my fear.

"It's time, Twilight."

"No," I whispered to the shadow entity in front of me.

Was that me looking at myself or a baine? Another Sharavak?

"Twilight... it's time."

Lightning cracked the foggy realm I wandered through, realizing my existence there. With a shiver, I looked at my hands and saw that they dripped crimson. My scars burned through it, igniting them and causing the liquid to sizzle. The scent of blood tickled my nose.

"It's time, Twilight. Time to wake up."

I startled, glaring at Cobi stooping over me. He backed away when he saw the look in my eyes and tried to defend himself, saying, "You told me to give you two hours. The princess is already awake." He nodded at Sakaiah waiting by the door.

"Are you okay?" She asked.

I nodded. "Let's go back and do what we can. I hope Il and Norva are okay."

I cleared the sleep from my throat and followed the princess downstairs to the foyer. Cobi came with. Servants opened the door for her, and she marched out to the carriage.

I stopped at the door and looked at Cobi, who halted behind me. "You should probably stay here," I said.

His eyes widened. "Why? I want to come with you and help if I can. They have traditional medics passing potions out down there."

I shook my head. "It's really better if you stay. I don't want you getting hurt."

Before he could speak, I followed Sakaiah and motioned for the servants to close the doors behind me. We crawled back into the carriage, and the horses reluctantly guided us through the continuing rains back to town.

"Let's finish this. I don't think two hours was enough for me," Sakaiah sighed when we got there.

We didn't talk much after this. We set out to find more people who required healing until we had reached everyone in our region, assuming Il and Norva still needed help.

Despite my joy at lending needy people my magic, my mood became increasingly foul as I pondered what this rain could mean. Erratic weather was one of the apparent "signs of the age," according to the Akristuran texts, a symptom of the second peak of mankind's wickedness. I hoped this didn't mean Father was on the verge of releasing Arkyaktaas.

"Excuse me, ma'am," one of my patients said before showing me their injury, "Why do you look the way you do? I've never seen someone like you before. Very interesting features."

Gazing back at the amber eyes drilling into mine, I answered, "I'm a person like everyone else. Can I see your wound, please?"

His energy edged on combative.

The man shook his head. "I don't mean to say you're not human. What would make you say that?"

My genes and my former religion, I wanted to reply. Instead, I said nothing and repeated my question.

The man smirked and withheld his arm. "I don't trust you. You look an awful lot like one of them Shadow things. What are you doing here in our city?"

I swallowed a harsh reply and said, "Sir, you don't need to worry about me. Now, do you want me to heal you or not?"

Healing was starting to not be the idea on my mind. If he kept antagonizing me...

Snorting, the man stood up and took several steps back to glare at me. "You're the worst kind of scum. Get out of Valechka. Get out of the Bronze, evil witch!"

Anger bubbled in me. I ground my palms against my thighs and hissed, "You have seconds to get away from me before—"

"Before what?" He laughed. "Before you skin me and eat me alive? Whatever, witch."

He took off. I watched him run and tried not to chase after him. How I would have liked to split his face open with my fists and give him a taste of what this "evil witch" was capable of.

"No," I moaned, forcing myself to turn from him. "Akristura..." I lifted my chin to the crying heavens and let their tears wash away my hunger.

I wandered back to the princess, feeling finally drained, and saw that she was wrapping up, too.

"We've done all we can for now," she said. "Your friends are in the carriage. My responders and some healers are cleaning up the rest of this. I don't know about you, but I'm truly beat now."

Sighing, she peeked into the carriage. As if the seating arrangement greatly affected her, she had me enter first, then slid in after me so I was sandwiched between her, Il, and Norva.

The Akristurans' eyes gleamed, and they clapped each other's hands.

"Good stuff," Il sighed, pulling Norva onto his shoulder.

"Sterling work, Twilight," said Sakaiah. "And to you two, as well." She nodded politely at them, but her eyes once again darkened at Il.

One day I might know what that was about.

It was early evening when we made it back to the palace. Prince and Princess Seraphina surprised us with their greetings in the throne room.

"Welcome back," the prince said. "We heard of your efforts in town."

"We are deeply pleased by and grateful for them," spoke his wife.

Each of us bowed back and thanked them for their acknowledgment.

"Fortunately, the situation in the lower floors of the palace has been resolved," the prince said, "And the rains seem to be slowing. Therefore, we would like to invite you all to dine with us tonight."

"We appreciate that very much, Your Highness," I said, giving an additional bow.

I heard the prince's smile when he said, "I see you have been practicing our greetings and expressions of thanks. That is good to see."

"Join us for supper in one hour," the princess told us, "And take this time to bathe and ready yourselves. Thank you again." She gave us a small curtsy, and we imitated it before returning to our rooms.

Sakaiah came with me, shuffling through the robes she'd placed on my dresser.

"This is the one you need tonight," she informed me, handing me one spun of plain bronze silk. "It's simple for a reason. We let the food be ostentatious for us at mealtime."

"Thank you."

I went to bathe and shower, not afraid to indulge a bit in the different soaps. As I scrubbed the grime off and soaked my curls, I reflected on the evening and considered it a success. If helping the citizens—minus that last one—hadn't buoyed my spirits, Sakaiah's parents personally thanking us and inviting us to dinner did the trick.

When I stepped out, I dried off and donned the appropriate undergarments for the robe. I then slid into the robe itself. Remembering Sakaiah's lesson, I slipped the sash cord through each of its loops and tied it neatly to the right. When I left the bathroom, I saw that Sakaiah had set out the necessary slippers, their straps shimmering gold. I stepped into them and went to the mirror to dry and lightly comb my hair.

Sakaiah asked to come in a few minutes later to do my makeup.

"Makeup is not required for any meal but supper," she explained, "Which is a pain since you then have to remove it before bed." She chuckled. "My own culture's rules confuse me sometimes."

"If it makes you feel any better, and really, it should... mine apparently thinks it's acceptable to be intimate with children," I said darkly.

Sakaiah's nose wrinkled. "We heard about that. It was reason number one-thousand and one that we decided to close our borders to you mainland lot."

"Not a bad idea."

Sakaiah sighed and applied gentle moisture creams to my skin, assuring me I wouldn't have to be nearly as elaborately decorated as her mother, "Who insists on being the most beautiful woman in the room."

She laughed and took some gold powder to my eyelids. With discomfort, I recalled that the last time I'd been "done up," Zemorah had been my decorator. I wondered how she was doing in prison or if she'd ever made up with her son... Father.

As Sakaiah worked, I shared memories of my grandmother with her and watched her gape in horror, then laugh. She blew air between her teeth and said, "In her natural state, she's not much of a looker, is she?"

I shook my head. "No. I felt bad for her. She always placed so much emphasis on youth and appearance. She even went so far as to use baby cells in her face creams."

Sakaiah paused mid-stroke. "Gods above. What a monster." Brows furrowed, she continued her work. "Life is sacred here. We value all of it. The Sharavaks don't seem to value any of it except themselves."

"Not even," I said, "Because the lower classes suffered and died, too."

Sakaiah scowled. "Not in this country. I wouldn't allow it. Do you ever think some of the better people in that society will change their ways and flee?"

I shrugged while she put the finishing touches on my eye makeup. "Maybe. Two of my "bottom class" friends wanted to escape, and I made sure they could. I hope they're okay now."

Sakaiah gave me a little hug. "I bet you were a fine ruler, despite your circumstances. The lesser Shadows probably loved you."

I looked down at my hands, wondering if this was true. "I don't want them to die the Forever Death," I whispered.

"Say again?"

"The Forever Death," I explained, "Is the eternity that awaits those who hate the Light. Some of the Shadows had a spark, some sense of life. But if they don't seek Akristura, then..."

"They die?" Sakaiah shook her head. "And where do they go?"

"To the Void," I croaked. "Forever."

Sakaiah set her brushes in the sink and began to clean them. "Interesting. Is this "Void" a physical place like it seemed to be from your memories, or does it only exist in your mind?"

"It's a real place. I physically went there through a portal. Shadows can pass through that portal and move about what at first looks like this pleasant little place, but then..."

I chuckled nervously. "Then it changes. Push the Dark One's buttons, and you'll see a whole new side to Toragaine. That's the official name for it."

"What is this Toragaine really like, then? I saw bits and pieces from your memory. It looked like fire and suffering, but shouldn't death be, well... simple non-existence?"

"That," I said, "Is something the Sharavaks believe, actually. They call it "nashk." Akristurans don't believe this. There is only Araveh and Toragaine, and everyone who dies immediately goes to..." I nibbled my lip, wondering if I hadn't missed something from the texts. Mother's sentence had to fit in there somewhere.

"To one of the two realms?" Sakaiah finished for me.

I nodded. "Right."

She came behind me and fluffed up my hair, admiring the curls before asking her last question.

"Where do you believe I would go if I were to die right now, Twilight?"

My heart picked up its pace. I met her gaze in the mirror, trying to delay the response by taking in my gold-eyed look. When I could take the silence no longer, I answered, "According to Akristuranism, Sakaiah, you would be going to the Void."

Sakaiah laughed. "Why? I'm not a bad person. I don't consider myself to be, anyway. Bronzians believe in reaping what you sow, so if you are good to many people, you will enjoy a happy afterlife in the clouds. Are you sure your "Light God" would truly send someone like me to the Void?"

I touched my collarbone, no longer wanting to look at her. "Yes, Princess. The former Sharavak High Father introduced a generational curse that has infected the entire human race, and this curse compels us to do evil. That is our natural desire."

"How strange." Sakaiah touched up her own hair before leaving the bathroom. "I don't like your beliefs or much at all about them," she said as we descended the guest hall steps into the throne room, "But you respect me, so I will respect you. Speaking of respect—eat delicately and quietly at the table tonight. Do not refuse anything put on your plate unless it presents major dietary complications. Eat everything you are given, and give thanks to the servants, the chefs, and my mother and father when you are done and you see that Father is done, too. He should raise his goblet to signal the meal's end. Excuse yourself at this point with a bow."

"Will do. Thank you."

She smiled and gestured for me to follow her into the dining hall.

I took careful steps inside, keeping my wonder at the size of the room under wraps. The hall was almost as big as the one in the Sharavak compound but much warmer and friendlier. Everything was painted in bronze and trimmed in gold. Several chandeliers occupied the ceilings and cast their inviting yellow light over a massive table spread with too many platters and dishes to count.

Sakaiah bowed to her parents when she entered, and I copied her, keeping my eyes to myself. Prince and Princess Seraphina nodded to us in turn.

"Welcome to the dining hall," said the prince. "You may take your seats."

I saw that everyone else was already sitting down. Cobi flashed Sakaiah and me a small smile before directing his gaze forward. Sakaiah patted the seat at the far end of the table opposite her parents so I would take it and assumed her own spot next to them, and with this, the prince made his official greeting to all of us.

"Welcome, honored guests, to supper. We are pleased to have you with us tonight after your devoted service to our people today. We have not experienced weather of this severity in many years. You, as guests, took it upon yourselves to aid our citizens in their hour of need, asking nothing in return. For this, you have our thanks."

Beaming, he raised a goblet so it winked in the chandelier light and took a drink.

Raise yours and drink, too, Sakaiah thought to the rest of us.

We followed suit, and the prince set his goblet down.

"Before we begin, I want to remind you all that we are still formulating our decision regarding our armed forces," the prince said, "So continue to be patient with us. We may utilize the entire month to consider this."

"We appreciate your consideration, Your Highness," I replied gratefully.

The prince nodded. "As you should. It is not an easy decision to make." He snapped his fingers. At this command, servants waiting in the room's shadows came forward to remove the lids from the platters and plates.

As they were stacking my plate, I broke one of Sakaiah's rules.

Meat. The servants wanted to place flesh on my plate.

A shiver inched its way up my spine and crept into the base of my neck as a slice of bird meat was slipped onto my dish. I watched it for a full minute as the sides were added around it, fresh vegetables and steamed rice with fish, grappling with the revulsion dancing in my throat.

The last time this had happened had been at the inn during our journey to Syndbur, but Il had thankfully noticed my discomfort and understood it, taking the meat for himself. Meat that was already dead sickened me, for some reason, like I couldn't bear the thought that something had died... unless I'd been the one to take its life.

According to Sakaiah, I had to accept what I received, but I couldn't eat this.

Not a human being.

"I... I wonder if I could receive another main course?" I asked timidly. "I do apologize. Meat just isn't to my liking these days."

Both Il and Norva glanced at me from down the table, concerned. One of them thought to me, *Do you suspect poison?*

No, I replied. *I wish it was that simple.*

"My lady, we have beef prepared if you would like to replace your fowl with that," offered one of the servants.

No! That was worse.

I shook my head gently and answered, "No, thank you, but I appreciate the offer. This will do."

I indicated my vegetables and rice and began to scoop some into my mouth when the prince cleared his throat and asked, "Is something the matter, Twilight? Is meat truly not your preference these days?"

There was a hint of mockery in his tone. I smiled at him across the way, still avoiding full eye contact, and replied, "Once it was, Highness. But the past lives behind me, and my former desires have died with it."

The prince nodded, mildly impressed, and nothing more was mentioned about my palate. I was curious to know when I would be able to look at a piece of meat and not grow squeamish, but I assumed it would require time. Hopefully, if that went away, my hunger for living flesh would go with it.

"It is intriguing, this weather," the prince commented as he took a bite of his food.

"Very," his wife muttered beside him.

"The timing, especially."

I felt the prince's gaze centering on me, and I cleared my throat before taking a sip of tea.

"I hope you aren't suggesting Twilight's presence, and that of her friends, is bad fortune, Father," Sakaiah replied quietly.

Silence draped the room. The prince finished what he was chewing and said, "I am not suggesting anything, daughter. I am merely stating facts. Try to recall the last major storm we've had here and tell me how many decades ago that was. Or was it centuries?"

Again, his gaze burned me.

I cleared my throat again, unsure what to say and unwilling to respond to his implications. I noticed that Princess Seraphina kept tossing glances my way as we ate, which told me she was nervous about something. Sakaiah saw it, too.

"It's not like she's the Fadain ascended, Mother," she said.

Princess Seraphina choked on her food and took a moment to compose herself.

"Do not mention that person in my presence," she hissed. She excused herself from the table and stalked out of the room.

Well... maybe we weren't doing as swimmingly with the royals as I'd thought.

"Please pardon my wife," said the prince. "She can be... touchy at times. But we thank you all for joining us tonight, especially you, Shadow." He raised his glass again, and I raised mine for another drink. Sakaiah gave me a knowing look when she noticed my empty plate.

"I very much appreciate your hospitality and this wonderful meal, Your Highness," I told him. "I also hope the servants and cooks know my gratitude. Thank you all." I rose from the table and bowed deeply.

The prince nodded. "Enjoy your evening, Twilight Mavericc. Sakaiah, I will speak with you later."

I shuffled quietly out of the hall, feeling I could finally breathe when I reached the guest room stairway. I released a breath and padded back to my room to contemplate what had happened. It appeared that the royals were giving me back-handed compliments. While they congratulated my work, they also implied that I was the reason it had to be done in the first place.

The princess joined me in my room a half hour later, distressed.

"Sorry I'm always dropping in on you. I don't want to be around my parents when I feel like this." She collapsed in one of the fireplace chairs and leaned her neck over the headrest.

"I'm sorry for something, too," I said carefully. "I don't want to say this, but I don't feel too wonderful, either. Did it seem like your parents were upset with me at supper? I got... not good impressions from them tonight."

Sakaiah moaned, placing her hands over her face. In my concern, I didn't realize how low her energy seemed. Exhaustion and fear emanated from her. I came and sat in the chair across from her.

"Are you okay, Sakaiah?" I asked gently.

She shook her head and groaned, "No."

My heart lurched. I hadn't seen her like this before.

"Do you want to tell me what's wrong? Maybe I can help you."

Sakaiah sat up straight and breathed a big sigh, propping her chin on her hand. "I saw a few people die today. My citizens." The familiar shimmer of tears touched her gaze. "I can't help but hold myself responsible."

"Oh, Sakaiah," I whispered, placing my hand on her free one. "Please don't say that. You did everything you could. I saw how eager you were to help them this morning before dawn had even fully arrived!"

Sakaiah laughed bitterly. "Maybe, but I'm sure my parents didn't think so. They probably could have responded more quickly and effectively." Sighing, she closed her eyes.

"Did your father tell you that?" I asked.

"No. I can just tell he believes that. He is happy you helped out, but he's not impressed I had to take a rest from healing. He seems to think magic is inexhaustible." Her mouth tightened, and she spat, "It's not."

I agreed. "So, if you know the reality and he doesn't, can you not at least be happy with yourself?"

Sakaiah bit back tears and whispered, "No, Twilight. Can't you see?" Her eyes opened, revealing their redness. "Nothing I do matters if it's not approved by my parents. But that is aside the point." She swept some of her tears away with a finger flick. "*I* feel bad, too. After all, what was this awful weather? Father is right; we've not seen something like this since... well, we don't even know when. And it killed people. *My* people."

I nodded slowly and digested this. "I am sorry you feel this way, Sakaiah. You have every right to be upset. But if I may say this, I was very impressed with how you handled things. Also, I understand the struggle of disapproving parents pretty well. I grew up with my father and stepmother. Neither of them seemed to like or care for me, so they saddled me with chores and screamed abuse at me. Some days, I didn't even get to shower."

Sakaiah scowled. "I'm sorry you went through that. Your parents sound a bit like mine: unwilling or unable to be pleased." She swept away a fresh dotting of tears. "I assume they treated you like you were incompetent, too? Even stupid, perhaps?"

"Yes," I said. "All the time."

"Mm. How unfortunate." Sakaiah's eyes lowered to the floor. "I think mine may be right about me, though."

"No, Sakaiah—"

"Yes!" She cried. "Regardless of the situations I find myself in, Twilight, I am always responsible for what goes wrong in this country because I am its ruler. As a ruler, any and every mishap—every tragedy—is my burden to bear. You are lucky to have escaped your position. I wouldn't wish leadership like this on anyone." She choked on a sob, and it twisted my heart.

I wanted to help her, but she might disapprove of my method.

"Sakaiah... would you be opposed to me lending you some of my magic?" I wanted to know.

She glanced at me, a puzzled look in her eyes. "What do you mean?"

I gingerly took both her hands in mine and said, "Let me show you."

Golden light trickled out of me into her skin, and I began to absorb her pain. The churning emotions, every dark curl of turmoil coiling around her heart, the spinning thoughts, and self-blame... I accepted it all as part of myself with the help of my lumensa. A quiet glow washed over us as her tears slowly stopped, and she raised her head to look at me.

"What was that?" She asked softly.

I shook my head. "Don't know."

I flinched at the new miserable thoughts clanging in my head and scraping against my heart. I offered the pain to Akristura. Though I would have rather dealt with it than leave it to Sakaiah, I wasn't strong enough to shoulder all her guilt alongside my own.

"The last time I did this, and also the first time," I explained, "Was with an old Sharavak friend of mine. She was a Zyvienkt, part of the lowest class of sorcerers, and her heart was better than most."

"What was her name?" Sakaiah asked.

"Mirivik."

The middle-aged woman had challenged me when no other Sharavak dared. I smiled at the memory. I wanted to be brave like that one day.

"Twilight, thank you," the princess said. "I do feel better. I don't know how, but whatever just happened has given me a new perspective."

"Oh?"

She nodded. "This was not my fault. I did what I could; if my parents do not see that, it is what it is. I've done what I can."

"Very good. Do not blame yourself for a perfectly appropriate reaction to a crisis and for being unable to do "more." After all, Sakaiah, who are you?"

She blinked. "What do you mean?"

"Who are you?" I repeated.

She smirked and answered, "Princess Sakaiah Seraphina of the Bronze Principalities."

I nodded. "Right. Which means?"

"Which means I am responsible for a lot, but not necessarily everything?"

We both laughed because, as a royal, the statement was true to an extent. Even I understood that. As the prior Myrk Maiden, it had been my responsibility to guide my people to victory against the light, and Father Sein would become fiercely angry with me at the slightest mistake.

I shared all this with Sakaiah, who listened in awe.

"The more details you unveil about your time with them, the more horrendous the whole situation becomes," she remarked, shaking her head in amazement. "You had no autonomy. The High Father controlled and abused you when you did not mold to his liking. How terrible."

"It was," I admitted. "In the beginning, I wanted no part of it. Every day waking up was a nightmare." Shivering, I continued, "But then, I began to... enjoy myself."

"Right. I remember feeling some of that from your memories. If you do not mind the question, how did you overcome yourself? Not only your desires but the guilt?"

"That, Princess," I said, "Treads into territory you may dislike, so I will let you decide if you want to hear it."

Sakaiah nodded. "Tell me."

I considered her for a moment. She would most likely not be receptive, but I told her anyway. Everything I'd been through was spilled, including my contacting Akristura, the Children, and the events in between. To my surprise, the princess did not interrupt me or try to divert the subject. Instead, her eyes registered concern and interest, like it mattered to her. Several hours later, she bid me a simple good night and thanked me for showing her a new application for lumensa.

She stood to leave. Cobi knocked on my door and peeked in when I asked him what he needed.

"Princess," he said with a bow. "I apologize if I'm interrupting something, and you may be too tired then, but..." He glanced nervously at the floor before meeting her eyes again. "Would you like to train with me tomorrow? I really appreciate your methods."

Sakaiah clapped her hands together and cried, "Of course! Thank you for asking. I hope to be replenished from this magic drought in the morning, but if not, I will gladly watch and support you."

"Thank you, Princess. That means a lot to me." He smiled warmly.

"Am I welcome to tag along?" I asked.

Cobi's eyes only briefly met mine before he uttered a half-hearted, "Sure." To the princess, he beamed and dipped his head before disappearing into the hallway.

"Such a gentleman!" Sakaiah exclaimed. "Ah, but I'm tired. I will see you tomorrow, Twilight. Thank you again for helping me today and for helping me right now. May the gods keep you."

I pondered what had just happened, trying not to focus on the sting Cobi had left me with. Once Sakaiah went, I stumbled to bed and said a last prayer before falling asleep, urging Akristura to continue working in the royals' hearts.

I'd felt something else when taking Sakaiah's pain. A connection stitching us closer together, emboldening the bonds of friendship. I hadn't experienced that since meeting Solshek. And the bond between Cobi and me...

I sighed, then turned on my mattress to go to sleep. My half-conscious mind detected something moving around me, and I knew, before I vanished into the waiting nightmares, that more baines were prowling for my downfall.

CHAPTER TWENTY-TWO

S CRATCHES AND MARKS COVERED my body the following morning. They zigzagged
all over, the deepest ones etched into my throat, and dark bags hung under my eyes.

The baine-infested nightmares had been plentiful and nothing short of terrifying.
Mother had even been in them, and flashes of Father, too, including another Shadow man
I wasn't sure I knew. Shivering, I informed Il and Norva about them after waking, and
they assessed it was because my new path posed a threat to the dark realm. Aadyalbaine
had not forgotten his former daughter.

No, I supposed he hadn't, and he likely never would as long as I lived.

The royals invited us to breakfast that morning, which took some of the edge off my
concerns.

The servants almost fed me more meat. When they realized their error, they swapped
out my dish with Cobi's. Instead of cow, I was given fish on toast... which, despite me
not having an aversion to fish flesh, wasn't the most appetizing combination. Regardless,
I plastered on a smile and ate, letting my joy at dining with the royal family obscure my
dietary reservations.

Sakaiah and Cobi went to train after this. I considered going with them until I remembered Cobi's strange reaction to me last night. I opted to train with Il and Norva instead,
so we met on the garden path where Sakaiah and I usually dueled. She and Cobi were
already training in the sideyard Cobi liked to use. I tossed a few glances their way and
decided I wouldn't focus on them or their laughter.

"You mad at Cobi for something?" Il asked slyly, looking their way.

"Nope. Just want to train," I replied, preparing my magic.

"Alright, then. Let's see what you've got, kid."

I attacked. Il met me and deflected my magic, but his was weaker than mine. I easily
overpowered him and threw him off balance.

"Not so rough," he grunted as he returned to his feet.

Norva chuckled. "She's doing as Korbin trained her to. How about we both take her on?"

The pair got a mischievous look in their eyes. Grinning, I took up position and invited them to strike. They didn't disappoint.

When both their magic came, I was able to push back without too much resistance. Still, the resistance I encountered made me stumble a little, so I had to plant my heels down and summon a small storm.

"Don't let her rain us out, Norva!" Il chuckled through gritted teeth.

Cobi and Sakaiah laughed in the distance. I let the storm snarl out of me. It raged toward Il and Norva, flashing purple, and rammed into their barriers.

Il was the first to fall. Norva tumbled after him when his supporting magic vanished.

Both of them had been visibly burned. I ran to them and quickly fixed their wounds with magic. Norva's eyes were wild with surprise, and Il's hardened in accusation.

"Were you not taught to control yourself?" He snapped.

Norva touched his shoulder with one hand and mine with the other. Her lips drooped when she asked me what was wrong.

"You had anger in your face, love," she whispered. "What's got you upset?"

More laughter came from the sideyard. I clenched my fists at my side and apologized but did not answer her question.

I shook my head and backed away from them. "I need to, uh, go for a walk. Clear my head. Sorry about this."

Hopefully, they wouldn't take that lightly. I really hadn't meant to hurt them.

Agitated, I meandered between the different garden paths and around hedges trimmed into decisive shapes. I was too foggy-headed to admire them, but I vaguely appreciated the artistry of the butterflies, suns, and clouds the leaves imitated.

As I walked, I wondered about Father. Usually, I thought about him when I was angry, pledging to myself that I, or someone, would make him pay for what he'd done and what he continued to do. This time, I pondered his well-being. How was he?

Maybe the valdur I'd just used had me feeling bruised and soft. Valdur didn't typically make me feel that way, though. Something stirred inside me. It was almost tangible... a desire to escape my magic and my fate. I'd experienced that before.

Was it my spirit talking to me? Had it been upset by the dark magic, and now it sought to convict me of my angry thoughts?

I sighed and enjoyed the aroma of the blossoms surrounding me. What a pleasant place for a post-freakout stroll. Smirking, I rounded the corner and found myself at the path's edge. The garden fence beyond was shadowed by the pressing jungle on the other side of it, and also...

Darkness brushed against me. My spirit recoiled at something ancient and oppressive outside the fence. I frowned and crept closer to investigate.

Voices trickled to my ears. A man's low tone rumbled a hundred paces ahead.

I inched forward another few paces myself when a hiss broke the sudden quiet, and it was then that the black-robed figures looked at me.

I gaped when I saw what had to be Advisor Karvo's mouth sneering at me from under the dark hood. Across from him stood someone taller than he was. I backed away, suddenly aware of how sickeningly sweet the flowers smelled, and sprinted back to the palace side of the garden.

Sakaiah and Cobi's training could wait. I had to tell her what I saw.

"Sakaiah!" I half-whispered and half-cried when I burst into the training yard. Both her and Cobi's eyes widened.

"Yes, Twilight?"

"I need to show you something," I said breathlessly.

I closed my eyes and poked around her mind to form a link. Once she accepted, I played the very fresh memory of the two figures, and Sakaiah gasped, pulling away.

"That was Karvo!" She hissed.

"I knew I wasn't seeing things! What could he be doing over there?" I asked.

Sakaiah groaned. "I don't know, but if it's Karvo, it can't be good." Her eyes narrowed when she looked out toward the garden's edge. "You didn't see the other person's face. How strange. How... unsettling."

"I'm sorry to be the bearer of bad news, but he also had a dark and bizarre energy around him," I told her. "Do you think that maybe he's..."

"His own brand of sorcerer? I don't know. He'd better hope he's not," Sakaiah growled.

"I don't know your rules here about practicing alternate spellcraft, assuming he's a non-magical, or what you would even do with him if he was a Lumen gone bad," I said, "But believe me when I say you don't want someone who dabbles in dark power in your court, Sakaiah."

Sakaiah grunted in agreement. "When I told you we Bronzians don't use magic for evil, I did not lie. We don't take dark magic lightly here. The Sharavaks are a plenty good reason to believe that there are evil spirits who work through it to accomplish destructive ends. If Karvo practices it in any capacity, I will have him executed."

She sighed deeply and headed back inside the palace without another word. Cobi and I followed her into the throne room, keeping out of sight as Sakaiah shared with her parents what I'd seen.

"Do you think, Father," she said in a hush, "That Karvo may be a threat to us?"

Prince Seraphina laughed. "Advisor Karvo has always been one of our best, Sakaiah. He has a bit of a questionable nature, but to imply he is evil? Worse, a dark magician? These things cannot be true."

"Why not?" Sakaiah demanded, her voice raising. "You saw Twilight's memories. Don't you want to know more about them?"

"How do we know the Shadow isn't manipulating things to take any perceived target off herself?" The prince asked.

"What target, Father? Do you suspect things about our guest?" Sakaiah hissed.

The prince noticed Cobi and me. He smirked and ordered us to come forward. Awkwardly, we left the corner of the room and stood before him.

"Whatever you saw," he said slowly, "You must never speak of again. You are not to be vigilantes inspecting the moral soundness of my court. Is this clear?"

Sakaiah spoke before we could. "Really, Father, you want to scold them for trying to help?" She snorted. "Tell me why you are fit to rule, and I am not."

"Enough!" Roared the prince. "You care too much about our guests' opinions to see past your own bias. As I recall, you have never liked Advisor Karvo. Why should I punish him for wearing what he likes on his off time and conversing with friends?" To us, he barked, "Return to your rooms. I'll have no nonsense from you while you are here."

"Yes, Your Highness," we said more quietly than we should have before shuffling up the guest hall staircase.

"What's going on?" Norva asked when we passed her.

"Come to my room; I'll show you," I muttered.

Il and Norva were as troubled by my memories as the princess. It was more than Karvo's inhuman face. The issue was the sheer evil of the energy around him, like he'd surrendered to it completely.

"I've never liked him," I admitted. "He mocked my bow the first time I saw him, and then he mocked my name. He's a lot like Silos, the Alash Vokar for the Sharavaks."

"Um, Twilight... what's an Alash Vokar? You're speaking Aadbaineos terms," Il said.

"Highest advisor. Sein's pet, essentially, and probably Father's now." I shrugged. "I don't know what's going on, but I don't think stumbling on him and his friend today was chance."

"No, probably not," said Norva. She smiled gently at me and held my hand. "Stay safe, Twilight. You may have more enemies here than you think."

I shook my head. "Apparently, in the prince, too. He just accused Cobi and me of doing vigilante work. Before that, he suggested to Sakaiah that I'm manipulating memories!" I threw my hands up and sat at the edge of my bed, taking a calming breath. "I can't blame him, though. I'm a Shadow. That title follows me around like... like my own shadow." I gestured to mine on the floor.

"Don't despair, love. Akristura knows your plight," Norva assured me.

He did, but did He plan to deliver me from it? Or—I glanced outside the window—was I supposed to be delivered to my enemies?

Sakaiah visited shortly after they left to apologize. "Don't listen to my father when he talks like that," she urged me. "He is angry at me for making my suggestions."

"I understand his reservations about me," I replied. "I'm a Shadow. Seems that will always color how people view me, but I can't blame him after what they've done to Valechka."

Sakaiah grimaced. "Right. Well, I'm going to go back out and train. Yesterday has me a bit perturbed by everything still. I will be privately investigating Karvo's affairs. The next time I see him go out, I'll send a servant to see what he does."

"Good idea. I'm sorry for any trouble I caused."

She dismissed this. "You did nothing wrong. If my intuition speaks truthfully, I am sure the advisor is not partaking in wholesome activities on his "off time." We can't assume anything yet, but I have him in my periphery."

I joined her outside for training. At a certain point during our session, she attacked with dark magic, and I had to calm her down. When I tried to help her, she burst into tears and put her magic away, insisting she didn't want to hurt me.

"You won't," I said, but she'd have none of it.

"Why don't you take the rest of the day to yourself?" She suggested through her tears. "I apologize for this and for yesterday, too. We aren't supposed to cry in front of others."

"It's okay," I said. "I don't mind. I'm not dignified company or anything."

Either she thought I was or didn't want me around anymore because she turned from me and went for her garden stroll. I prayed for her mental fortitude and protection, and then I sought out Il and Norva to train with them instead. I thought about inviting Cobi, but his lack of enthusiasm earlier jarred me again when I thought about it, so I decided against it. Trying not to be angry, I promised Il and Norva they wouldn't get hurt this time, and I'd be gentler with them.

"It's not gentleness that we need, Twilight," said Il. "It's lumensa we need to see. No dark magic."

"Right. Sorry again for earlier," I mumbled.

"Don't apologize," he chided. "You already did that. Just improve."

Another session of magical combat ensued.

I shouldn't have been surprised when the evening lent its torments. My war with dark magic—and the war against my body—seldom produced favorable results when I failed at it.

The dream dimension was a terror for me as soon as I trembled into its murky midst. In this place, beauty and longing were fulfilled, and the many hungry desires of mortal life were fed. But in this realm was also the slow-creeping darkness, populated by every ugly imagining and heinous action bloodying my past.

The evil waiting to greet me was my father. He had such a perfect face for a human being... only he was not human, and his unnatural beauty was maimed by a thousand hideous deeds.

Murder. Cannibalism. Blood-drinking. Magic.

No abundance of pleasing symmetry and pretty features could mask the ugliness of a twisted soul.

"Hello, Twilight."

His whisper was worse than a quiet call; it was a caress, every bit as sadistic and untrustworthy as the lips that birthed it. He grinned at me from a shroud of shadows, showing those teeth he used to slice apart his prey.

"Stay away," I ordered him, but Father only came closer.

"Come back to me, my young sorcerer," he hissed into my ear. "Reject your God of Nothing and return to your True Aaksa. Myrkraas is coming..."

"No! I don't care if it's coming!" I cried. "I am Akristura's now. Get *out* of my head!"

Father chuckled. How I hated that sound.

"I am your father, Twilight. Sein was your grandfather. Do you deny the power in your blood?"

I scowled. "I don't care about any of that."

Father leered. "Oh, but you do care. You care very much. The truth torments you and brings you a special kind of agony inside."

I spat at him, and he smiled, slowly sweeping the spittle off his cheek.

"You should have killed those Akristurans when you attacked them. That might have righted your mind." Father created the vague shape of a girl's face with his magic, admiring it before letting it dissipate. "But if you won't make Myrkraas happen, I suppose I will... with your mother at my side."

"What are you talking about?" I hissed.

He grinned. "Right. You wouldn't know. Well..." He projected a memory of something to me that chilled my veins.

The image of a human skeleton clothed in dirt and tattered fabric reached me. I recoiled from Father when I realized what it meant.

"You didn't," I whispered, quivering in horror.

"I did. Aaksa would not let me bring her back any other way."

My lips curled in disgust. I raised my hand to strike him, and he laughed.

"You won't damage me here."

"You're disgusting! Why would you do something so *twisted?*" I cried.

"Because," he growled, "I love her."

I vigorously shook my head. "You don't understand love, then. That's not love."

He smirked and inspected his too-long fingers before replying, "You can't understand. You're fifteen, soon to be sixteen. What would you know of it, Myrk Maiden?"

"I'm... almost sixteen?"

I didn't want to ignore anything Father had just told and shown me, but I was curious about my age. If my sixteenth birthday came and I couldn't tell my mother how sorry I was about it...

Sorry for what? I questioned myself. *Do you regret being born even still?*

"Yes," he answered. "Perhaps we'll even celebrate it together. You, the thief of life, and your mother, the giver."

"I didn't take her life," I countered, but the sting of his words drained some of the conviction from my tone.

"Right. Sein did. But it was your birth that rendered her vulnerable. You tore her body and weakened her to where she could not recover from Sein's attack. Thus, you are still to blame."

I laughed with no amusement and said, "And why was Mother there, Father, if not for you? Surely you blame *yourself* for her death?"

"Certainly," he answered coolly. "And now I am righting my wrongs. I do find her lack of hair interesting, though. I specifically charmed that to where it wouldn't fade."

He frowned, and I snapped, "You're a monster."

He replied with a composed and effortless smile, "And there are worse monsters to come."

"How? With your father's power you stole as he was dying?"

There it was again... a flinch. Father could conceal his twitches from humans but not from me.

Keeping his smile, he reached out and touched my hand before disappearing, swirling away in the fog. When I was certain the dream was over, my mother approached me from where he had been standing, a deep sorrow hanging from her face.

Her scarlet spirals lacked their usual bounce, and the luster in her gaze was gone. Aubri Delvian did not appear nineteen but something approaching ninety. Exhaustion, distress, and a ripening air of fear radiated from her.

"You used the dark magic again. It's been a while."

Moisture pricked my eyes at seeing her. Mother was the only part of valdur that I missed. Sometimes, I feared I missed it too much.

"I'm sorry, Mother. I didn't mean to—"

"Attack your friends," she said. "I know. It's okay." She smiled faintly, sorrow hanging from her lips. "But your father is not. He is too far gone."

I looked at the ground, chilled and unsure of what to say. Eventually, a question came to me.

"Is there anything to be done about Father at all? Can I save him, any part of him?"

Mother met my gaze and held it for one painful moment, measuring what she had to say and assessing the damage of the words once they were inflicted on me.

"No. There is no redemption for some. I'm afraid Damion has crossed the point of no return."

She erupted into tears, turning away from me so I wouldn't see them shed. The ones gathering in my own eyes escaped. We started sobbing together.

"I *felt my bones,*" she hissed, "when they were disturbed. When your father dragged them out of the earth and forced a spirit to inhabit them. A baine now lives in me, Twilight. Now you see why he cannot be saved. He has gone *too far.*"

Mother gripped my shoulders and pressed her forehead against mine. The tang of tears and terror washed over me when she commanded, "End him. For me. For you. For anyone you care about. *End him.*"

"You..." I stammered. "You hate him now, then? You don't pity him like you used to?"

Mother smiled absurdly. Dark madness crept into that smile, and she choked out a hoarse laugh.

"No. And neither should you."

I took her hand and pressed it to my heart, which throbbed with uncertainty and pain. I did not want to speak these following words, but for Mother... for her, I would. I loved her more than I loved him, I decided. Father had never loved me.

"I will deal with him," I said. "He has done the unthinkable, and it cannot persist. Damion will die soon, Mother."

She nodded quickly. "Yes. It's the only way. I need no further torment in this realm, knowing what comes after. The bastard... unearthing me like dung!"

Mother screamed. In that sound, a glint of light fractured my vision. The shrill pitch echoed into a distant past, so remote that I could see only blackness, but in that flash of light and the deafening static that followed was my answer.

Mother had not screamed like that since I was born. My existence, Father's existence, and Sein's curse stole the life from her lungs and the warmth from her bones. Father now

weaved those bones into a nauseating narrative of redemption for himself. When Aubri
had passed, so, too, had he. Resurrecting her would rectify that in his eyes.

But meddling with the dead only made him more of a target for the Akristurans and
me. Monsters were created, not born. Father had made his destiny. I would end that
destiny or die trying.

"I will fix this. I will make it right, Mother. Soon enough, my father will die," I vowed.
Mother nodded, satisfied. Her cruel smile widened.

"Then you have an assignment."

Several days passed without much event, but Sakaiah and I—everyone, really—sensed
a tension in the air. Dreams of my parents and attacks from baines didn't alleviate the
atmosphere.

During training one afternoon, Sakaiah informed me of the details regarding Advisor
Karvo.

"I've sent a servant to follow him several times in the past few days. He's only met with
this robed person once. Unfortunately, since they were outside the fence and not on palace
grounds, the servant didn't want to confront them, and I'm not ready to do that, either.
I don't want to sound a false alarm." She sighed, playing with a lumensa orb. "What we
know is this person he meets is tall, above the average male height here in the Bronze."

I stifled a shiver and asked her to go on.

"There isn't much to tell, sadly. It's a tall person with no visible face, and this time when
they met, they just... stared at each other."

"They didn't talk?" I asked.

"Apparently not."

"Strange. Unless they were using hursafar."

Sakaiah gnawed her lip in consideration. "Maybe, but why would they stand around
like that, acting all bizarre, and risk drawing attention to themselves? It's not like we don't
have sentries occasionally going down those paths."

I shrugged. "Your guess is as good as mine. I'm just throwing out suggestions. On an
unrelated note, I did want to ask... how is the decision coming along?"

"Oh, that." Sakaiah patted her hair and said, "I don't have answers on that right now."

"I see. I don't want to pry, but I am curious considering—"

"The world is ending, yes," Sakaiah snapped. "You've made that clear already."

I frowned. "I'm sorry, but did I do something wrong?"

Why so touchy about a simple question?

"Be patient, and you'll get your answers," Sakaiah said. "We don't—"

"Princess Sakaiah!"

One of her servants sprinted up to her and bowed quickly, exclaiming, "Highness,
please come inside at once! There has been an incident with the Bronze Bay."

Sakaiah narrowed her eyes. "What sort of incident?"

He bowed again and said, "Highness, it is an unexplainable thing, but thousands of fish in the bay have just turned up dead."

The princess's gaze darkened, and she thanked her servant, following him inside. In the throne room, shouting echoed across the walls.

"Tell me how thousands of local fish suddenly perish overnight. Is there poison involved? Did any of you even investigate the situation?"

"No, Highness, there does not appear to be a reason at present," a messenger told him with a trembling bow. "I apologize for the lack of information."

"And I apologize for allowing you lot to have a job," the prince muttered. "Dead fish..." He shook his head and roared, "Floods, dead food, what next?" He groaned and ordered Sakaiah and me to come forward.

"I will investigate this, Father," she offered.

"Do that, and report back to me when you're done." The prince's gaze lowered to me. "Take the Shadow with you. Perhaps she will have an idea as to the cause of this." I felt his burning eyes on my head.

"Father, must you insist on calling her that?" Sakaiah said gently.

He waved her off. "Go do your duty, Sakaiah. You want to be a ruler, so go. Rule your grieving, starving people, and when you return, bring a solution back with you."

An oily odor smacked us when we arrived at the docks. I had to cover my nose from the sensory overwhelm. Cobi, Il, and Norva had come with us to help Sakaiah assess the situation. When we arrived, dozens of citizens murmured their thanks to Sakaiah for visiting them, and several of them asked what she planned to do.

"This is a great loss, Highness," one fisherman spoke. "I haven't seen such a thing in my lifetime."

Sakaiah frowned as she looked over the waters. "There haven't been any shipping accidents that may have caused this?"

The fisherman shook his head.

I shuddered to see a graveyard of water, numerous gaping fish corpses bobbing on the surface. A light breeze blew a fresh wave of stench in our faces. Sakaiah wrinkled her nose and turned to address the people.

"If it is not poison and not oil, does anyone know what it might be?" She asked calmly. "Knowing this will enable me to help you."

Chatter broke out, and Il whispered, "It appears they died from unnatural causes... maybe even supernatural ones."

Sakaiah whirled on him. "You think this is the doing of your god?" She chuckled. "Don't scare my people with this nonsense. They are worried enough."

I looked at Cobi to see his reaction to her outburst. He briefly met my gaze and flicked his away, turning red. He reached out a trembling hand and touched her shoulder.

"Sakaiah... do you think you might be able to consider it?" He asked softly.

She smirked and glared at me. "What do you think? Is this the Sky Father? Is he to blame?" She laughed and looked back at her people. "So, we cannot use fish for our economy or consumption at the moment. What do you all feel is an appropriate reaction to this?"

Puzzled, a citizen said, "You're asking us, Your Highness?"

She nodded. "I am. I care for your well-being and want your input to know how to make this right."

"Well, we... we'll need to clean up the bay and rid it of the dead fish," he mumbled, "And perhaps you could pay us for that so we have some money to line our pockets while we wait for the area to recover?"

"It won't recover quickly," another fisherman grumbled. "The whole bay has just died. You see all that?" He jabbed a twisted finger toward the corpses. "That's most of the bay, if not all of it."

Sakaiah's face pinched. "I am sorry this happened. Many of you, I can imagine, are out of work because of this. I have not heard that things are like this on the other side of the island?"

The lead fisherman shook his head. "Not yet. Just here, where we catch the bulk of 'em."

"Okay." Sakaiah, struggling not to look deeply unsettled, said, "Then I will personally pay you all to clean up this bay. When you finish that, I will pay your way to the other fishing zones to continue work there. Those who want to remain behind may choose other work. To recover from this fish loss, we ought to increase our gardening and grove growing here."

"How? The floods washed away the soil and many of our gardens," a woman at the crowd's edge complained.

Sakaiah's expression was approaching a look of pain. "Try to regrow things when and where you can. Take up work in the mines. And..." Her eyes lighted with a sudden realization. "Make weapons. My people! Make weapons. Go to the mines. Mine all you can find! Take up smelting and smithing and armor-making. We may need these things soon."

This statement brought about further murmuring in the crowd. Several citizens asked if the Bronze was preparing for war, to which Sakaiah responded with a cryptic, "I do not know."

"Regardless, we need your craft and expertise," she told them. "So, go, and do as I have commanded; subdue the mines and make your weapons."

"Who will be buying these things?" Someone asked.

Sakaiah smiled. "Perhaps you soon, or your neighbor, son, or friend. But for now... the Bronze royal army and the Seraphina family will take your business."

The chatter reached a high volume, and Sakaiah passed quickly through the crowd back to the carriage. Her smile was somewhat smug as she climbed in and ordered the driver to take us back.

"This solution I've come up with," she explained, "May force Father's hand. If we've to wage war with the Sharavaks, we will need weapons and armor, a great many of both." She chuckled, and Cobi looked at her with nothing short of pure admiration.

Or was it adoration?

"Still..." She sighed and drummed her fingers against the carriage window. "I don't like the feeling I've been having lately. I also don't like that this tragedy is coming so close on the heels of the last one. The flood."

I could tell she took these events personally and that they affected her faith in her leadership. I made sure to thank her for her efforts to help her people and us in the process by making this strategic move.

"Hopefully, your parents won't be too angry about it," I said. "I don't get the impression they care much for me as it is."

She snorted. "Father can have suspicions as long as you don't do anything. I won't let him do anything to you. You'd have to attack me or something to convince him to drop his consideration."

"That's good. I'm glad we have an ally in you. Thank you for that."

Sakaiah gave me a quick hug. "Thank you for visiting us. Not everything that's happened since you came is good, but it's certainly not been dull." She laughed and went off to her room, leaving me feeling grateful for the way even terrible events turned out somewhat okay.

But still, a darkness that seemed to be measuring the precise point of attack hovered over things. I prayed whatever it did when it inevitably descended would not dismantle everything we were working for.

CHAPTER TWENTY-THREE

I DIDN'T SEE SAKAIAH nearly the entire next day. Everyone assumed she was tending to royal duties, so we trained alone. I thought more about Mother's request to kill Father, disturbed by the likelihood that I probably *would* have to end him.

Could I be blamed for that, though, when he'd made it abundantly clear there was no good in him anymore? Still, Mother's statement that he was "too far gone" frightened me. Was she right?

If she thought Father was too far gone, what did she think about me? I would have considered myself the same.

Restless, I went back to my room when I heard more chanting coming from down the hall.

Sakaiah. She didn't sound happy.

I should check on her, I thought, *But...*

But what? If the princess needed more of my magic or even just someone to listen to her, I shouldn't have withheld that.

"Princess?" I whispered, giving a gentle knock on the door.

No answer. I frowned as her voice had stopped. I sensed something in the void of sound. The darkness again...

"Paranoid," I muttered to myself.

I started to walk away, deciding if she wanted to be alone, I ought to honor that desire. Besides, I didn't like the energy I was feeling.

It seemed...

What did it seem like?

Confirmation.

But of what?

Shaking my head, I took a step back down the hall when from inside the room, Sakaiah called, "Come in."

I stifled the sense of wrongness in the air and turned the handle, but it wouldn't open.

"The door's locked, Sakaiah."

Several seconds passed with no answer. The longer the silence stretched, the more I was certain my spirit wasn't misleading me. Something—I didn't know what, but *something*—was wrong.

I went to leave again when the locks squeaked out of place, and the door slowly swung open. Sakaiah stood beyond the threshold, but it didn't look like her. People spoke of lifeless bodies and their little resemblance to their living counterparts. I felt that looking at her then... especially her eyes in their clouded, darkened state.

"Is everything okay?" I asked tentatively.

She smiled faintly, but the expression didn't reach her hollow eyes. "Come in," she said, stepping aside.

I entered and suppressed a chill at the frigid air. "How did it get so cold in here?"

I almost knocked her crystals over when I took another step forward. I gasped and drew back before I hit them. She'd arranged them everywhere... in a circular shape that she resumed sitting inside.

"You've been praying, I see."

Sakaiah nodded, but the motion struck me as odd. Why did she move like that, so rigidly?

I touched her shoulder. "Sakaiah... are you sure you're okay?"

More silence. Sakaiah stared straight ahead at the ground and did not move. She seemed to be holding her breath as if in preparation for something, whatever that something was.

"I know the past few days have been hard for you," I said softly, "But you've handled it wonderfully. In fact, you make me realize that even if I'd stayed with the Shadows, I'd have been a terrible ruler." I smiled and nestled beside her inside the circle, but she still did not move. "Sakaiah—"

She shoved me over and leaped to her feet, glaring hatred at me.

"You brought a curse upon us all when you came here," she breathed. She took a step toward me, and I rose from the ground, uncertainty fluttering in my chest. "Agent of darkness. That is what you are. You intend to kill us all."

She unleashed magic. In the blink of time required for the power to issue forth, I noticed, with a chill, that it was not golden in color. Sakaiah had summoned dark magic. A shiver gripped my vertebrae at her words.

A proclamation of doom. The darkness hovering over her was so unnatural...

"But I will kill you first."

Baine. One of the Dark One's children had stolen inside her.

I raised my hands as if in surrender, and Sakaiah gazed at them with predatory interest. Her lips curled into a feral smile, and she nodded slowly.

"Die a coward and a traitor to your new path. How typical."

The magic came quickly. I discharged lumensa in response and nearly fainted with relief when the dark power ricocheted, but Sakaiah was not deterred. Rather, the thing inside her was not.

She maintained her feverish grin as she threw several more orbs my way. I deflected two of them, but the third caught me in the chest. I gasped and toppled back into the windowsill, keeping my defenses intact.

Before launching my own offensive, I felt a familiar tightening about my neck. No... Sein had choked me, Father could do the same, but not—I squirmed for air—not... Sakaiah...

She was raising me off the ground, the baine and her natural abundance of magic working hand-in-hand to eliminate me. I was allowed just enough oxygen to maintain my feeble grip on reality, but I couldn't move my arms... couldn't conjure my magic...

Akri... stura...

Sakaiah bared her teeth and slapped me with invisible magic using the hand that did not restrain me.

"Silence your thoughts before I silence them for you!" The baine demanded from Sakaiah's lips.

The tightening worsened.

Panic was flooding in, and fear.

Finality.

"Twilight? The Prince—"

A gasp. One of the servants had found us.

"Highness!"

Sakaiah used her free hand to blast the servant out the door and into the hallway wall. The woman crumpled. Shouting ensued somewhere in the distance. Sakaiah turned back to me, and I would have wept at the darkness bleeding from her eyes, casting shadows over her face.

I had looked that way once.

Consumed.

Akristura!

"Hey!"

The princess whirled again, this time confronted with...

No.

Cobi.

What could he do? He was only human, too frail for this manner of combat. He wasn't enough!

The baine seemed to understand this, for it latched onto its opportunity to torment my friend while maintaining its hold on me.

"Turn back, mortal," it purred in Sakaiah's voice. *"You're not what you think you've become. You are the same as you have always been, and your ability to play with toys does not impress anyone. Go."*

The words uttered from a dark being's spirit were heavier than if they were spoken from a person, for the baines knew things about us that even we were not completely aware of. They stalked us day and night, ever watchful of our habits and fears.

Cobi looked to be succumbing. I struggled, and Sakaiah's hand only grew firmer.

"No," Cobi replied. He drew out his sword from its sheath, trembling but certain. "Don't make me do this, Princess. I know you're in there."

"This is my body," the baine snapped back. *"But if you destroy it, I will find another. It is not so simple for the princess. Will you damn her trying to get to me?"*

"I won't," Cobi answered. "I'll be sure to damn you, though."

Sakaiah lashed out. Cobi hastily deflected the strike with his magic-resistant sword as he had done many times in his training sessions. The princess fired again. Again, the metal proved faithful.

"By the authority of Akristura," Cobi began, "I..."

Sakaiah roared and sent a frenzy of dark magic at him.

Cobi staggered but kept his ground.

"Cast..."

The princess became more aggressive. Cobi was struggling to stay on his feet, but the training sessions—he had practiced for a moment exactly like this!

"You..."

The last barrage was too much. He lost his footing, and the magic made its mark.

"Out."

The sigh slipped out before he collapsed. Sakaiah fell next. I was the final body to drop as the princess's magic lost its power. Blinking away the pain, I sprinted to Cobi's side.

"Are you good?" I asked him.

He nodded and winced when his hand passed over his arm where the magic had embedded. A light stream of blood dribbled out.

"I can fix that," I assured him. "Here."

He nodded, and I set to work drawing out my lumensa. No doubt the princess would need it, too, after her inhabitation.

"Thanks," he said when the healing was done.

"Thank *you*," I replied. "You were incredible with that sword. And Korbin taught you how to cast out baines, too?"

"Yes. He emphasized that it should never be used unless it absolutely needed to be, but..." He glanced guiltily at Sakaiah. "I think this was one of those instances."

I agreed. "Let's hope she accepts Akristura because if not, you know what happens. Anyway, it looks like your training is paying off."

"Yes," he muttered. "Training I've done with her."

He nodded at her unconscious form. I hugged him fiercely and thanked him again, marveling at the firmness of his muscles.

"You've been doing well." I poked his arm. "Wow. I'm... sorry I ever doubted you."

He smiled gently. I moved to help Sakaiah when another servant entered the room... only it wasn't a servant. It was Advisor Karvo, his dark eyes and sneering lips contorted into a scowl.

He looked at me and growled, "What have you done, Twilight Mavericc?"

"It's not what it looks like!" I snapped. "So please don't tell anyone that it is."

Karvo smirked. "I heard the commotion, and I see you crouching over the princess's unconscious body. Don't try to tell me it's not what it looks like."

He whirled off, and Cobi ran to stop him. Karvo barked at him to stay back.

"No," I moaned. "He's going to tell her parents!" I shook my head and touched Sakaiah's neck.

A steady pulse. She would survive, but her soul was another story.

The prince was furious.

My self-defense from Sakaiah's attacks was perceived as an attempt on her life, and Sakaiah had no memory of the incident. The baine had wiped her before fleeing. It was my word against her father's.

Cobi tried to interject but was thoroughly silenced by the prince's vicious hollering when he opened his mouth.

"I do not want to hear from the murdering sorcerer's accomplice!"

Murdering sorcerer. There it was, what he and his wife truly thought of me.

I was far too angry and frightened to pray. Akristura was not with me. How could He be with as much of a disaster as this was?

First, it was the flood. Then, the Bronze Bay. And now the princess was injured. All signs pointed to me, the wielder of dark magic.

The filthy Shadow.

It didn't help that no one in the household believed in Akristura, that they wouldn't consider their seeming reluctance to help us as an affront to Him. Il had been onto something about the bay incident, calling it a supernatural event. It wasn't wrong to assume that maybe the flood was a similar situation. And Sakaiah with her baine...

"It appears I will have to hang you," the Prince decided. "You certainly aren't guests in this home anymore. You are prisoners, and you remain as such until I have you all executed. Do you have anything to say for yourself, Shadow? How about your friends?"

How? Why? Why now? Why, Akristura? I thought frantically.

A new idea emerged from the black emotions roiling in my mind; *You are not dead yet.*

Before I could speak, Sakaiah, who stood at his side, intervened.

"Father, no," she pleaded. "I—"

"This is not the time!" The prince snarled. "This *witch* tried to kill you! We should have never let her come here, especially not on your foolish whim! You *can't* read people as you claim, Sakaiah—you are a girl like all others who does not know her place, thinking she is greater than she is. You are a *fool.*"

Sakaiah was seething. I could feel it in her energy, pulsing from her spirit in a wrath that ached to unleash.

"I may not know what took place when Twilight used her magic against me, Father," she began slowly, "But I do know that whatever she was doing was, in fact, in self-defense. One of the servants can attest to this, too. Something came over me, something I can't fully explain, and the rest is blank in my mind. I woke to Twilight healing me. Tell me, Father; why would she do this if she had wanted to kill me?"

The prince snorted. "For appearance's sake, of course. I love you, daughter, but you are frightfully dim and tragically unaware. Get out of my sight, and try not to die on your way."

"No!" Sakaiah screamed. "I won't let you kill her! She is my only friend in these walls. Try to end her and see what happens."

"Insubordination! I have had enough of it from you, child. Sentries, take all these damnable people away from me, down to where they belong. The next time I see them, I want them dangling from a rope."

"Your Highness, please—" I cried when the sentries gripped me and began to steer me past the throne room.

Death, was that what this was all coming to?

The prince dismissed me, and the sentries shoved us forward, immune to our protests. They marched us past the dining hall and down two stone staircases into a kind of place I was too familiar with. A dungeon where hope died and prisoners waited for their own deaths.

"Now, wait a minute," Il cried when he and Norva were thrown into a separate cell from Cobi and me. "We weren't part of this, and I know Twilight wouldn't have done any of the things she's been accused of, either!"

"You are accomplices," the sentry grunted, "So you are set for execution, too."

Il gripped the bars and demanded more answers, but Norva pulled him back. She smiled sadly at me in my cell opposite theirs. I hugged Cobi and loosed a shallow sigh as my stomach and chest were too tense to release a deep one.

"This isn't good," I muttered. "Seems like Akristura might have just handed us over to the enemy."

"Don't say that," Norva chided. "Did you try to show your memories to anyone? I know the prince didn't give you much chance to explain yourself."

I shook my head. "It wouldn't have mattered. He barely believes in memories as it is, I think, and Sakaiah..." I rested my head against the cell door. "She doesn't remember what happened herself. It's not like my memories would jog hers if the baine cleaned them out."

"Mm. This is tough. I'm so sorry you were accused of that, Twilight," Norva said quietly.

I shrugged. "I deserve it."

"No, you don't. I'll be praying for us all," she said. "I suggest we wait and see what the royals want to do with us. I believe Princess Sakaiah will come to our defense."

I smiled, toying with a lock of hair. "Probably."

But until we received our official sentences—or our deaths—we had to wait. The guards preferred this waiting in silence, so sometimes we communicated via hursafar. Norva urged everyone to remain hopeful, but as the second day in the cell dragged on, I wondered what our fates would be.

On the one hand, we hadn't been executed yet. Living to a second day in our cells meant the royals must have received some pushback. I only hoped Sakaiah cared about us as much as she let on.

On the other, the prince and princess might have organized something showy and public for our executions. I grimaced and shuddered in my cell, not willing to believe I could be summoned to death at any moment.

Sir Korbin's words came to mind as I sat in the humid funk of the cell, replaying my life choices and memories. What had he said? Something about thinking of Araveh if I ever found myself dying or about to die.

How I wished I could see him then. Him, in his strength and wisdom, and my little siblings. I tried not to cry, counting all the kisses I'd given Josha during my time at the Akrisruran commune. Had a dozen a day been enough? Maybe I should have been more generous. And Aullie... had I taught her well, set her on the path to success?

Then there was Susenne. A throat lump rose while I thought of her, wondering if she was okay. Did she feel safe? Was she training hard and controlling her appetites? And did she know how much I really did love her?

Cobi curled an arm around me and pulled me into him to comfort me. I let him, too weak and limp-hearted to care. In fact, I craved his warmth because it was his, and it was different from the seeping heat that oppressed the air around us.

"It's okay," he tried to assure me, but it was not.

None of this was okay.

"I hope you're not doubting Akristura too much, love," Norva whispered across the way.

I didn't answer. I was, and no one needed to know that.

Things did not improve from there. That evening, we got a visit from one of the sentries, who had come to inform me that Princess Seraphina had fallen "inexplicably ill."

"I wonder why?" Il quipped in the corner.

Norva smacked him, and she shook his head.

"Prince Seraphina has requested your presence," the sentry informed me. "I will take you to him."

I looked at Cobi, then Il and Norva. Norva flashed me a hopeful smile, but I didn't feel hopeful.

Was this where the prince gave me a personal execution?

Trembling, I let the sentry escort me out of my cell and up the stairs to the palace's main level. I was pushed onto my knees in front of the prince in the throne room. If his gaze used to burn me, it threatened to vaporize me then.

"My wife," he growled slowly, "Is sick. No one knows why this is. Do you care to explain, Shadow?"

I raised my head to him, keeping my eyes down, and answered, "No, Your Highness."

"Mm." He chuckled darkly. "Seems there are many things you claim not to know. Yes, you were right to think I was indirectly accusing you of what has been happening in my country lately. Why, I'd never seen such a powerful storm before you came here."

"I am sorry for the perception you have about that, Highness. You know, I hope, that I cannot control the weather."

The prince shrugged. "Do I?" He sighed. "Then we have the Bronze Bay. A curious event. Very unfortunate for our economy and food supply, but I'm sure that was the point, wasn't it?" His tone dipped into a sarcastic bite.

I shook my head. "Respectfully, Highness—"

"Spare me the "respect" act!" He snapped. "You Shadows and your gilded tongues. You Shadows and the way you destroy everyone and everything around you... including my wife." He clenched his fists so hard his knuckles popped. "However, your healing capabilities are undeniable. I will ensure that you undo the evil you inflicted on my wife. Come, monster."

The sentry behind me nudged me forward. The prince dismissed him and headed me out of the throne room himself with a satisfied smile.

"Whether you heal her or not hardly matters, as you will be punished regardless. It has been years since I witnessed a good execution."

"I hope I prove a worthy attraction," I replied quietly.

The prince chuckled as the sound of his robes swishing on stone echoed behind me.

"I see why Sakaiah likes you. She can't help but find a kindred spirit in your fierce tongue, which you seem to keep well under wraps. Fortunately, the rest of us do not have to suffer with it once it hangs limply in your mouth, much like your broken neck. Take these stairs here, and don't think about running—feel that nice blade on your back?"

A sudden sharpness pressed between my shoulders. "It will start to run warm if you get any ideas. Now, move."

I grimaced and made my way up the stairs at as brisk of a pace as I dared. The last thing I needed was a dagger lodged into my spinal column.

"Walk straight until you reach the end of the hallway, then turn left into the last room," the Prince ordered once we reached the top of the stairs.

The prince and princess's hall was much warmer and more decorative than the guest hall downstairs, but the atmosphere was the same. Everything about the Bronze palace was warm and relatively comfortable. The same could not be said of its inhabitants.

When we entered the royal quarters, I wanted to be taken aback by their many paintings and the overall splendor, but the dagger at my back reminded me I was not visiting on pleasant terms. Further darkness seeped into my heart at seeing the elder princess, silent and sallow, resting in her bed.

Had Akristura really done this to her? Or was it another sorcerer in the Bronze court? Perhaps, I thought, grinding my teeth, it was Karvo.

Several servants fussed over the fallen princess, but her husband had them all stand back. He nudged me forward and demanded that I break the curse I placed on her, but of course, I'd never planted one in the first place. I tried to explain this, but he waved me off.

"I'll prolong the hanging process every second you waste arguing with me about your guilt," he threatened. "You deceive no one with your potent lies, Dark One. Heal my wife now, and shut your mouth."

Dark One. That was Aadyalbaine's name, not mine.

Desperate, I began to pray. I worked to coax the lumensa from my body, feeling hopeful at the sight of it when it appeared, but a knock at the door startled me.

Something was amiss in the air. I didn't feel quite right.

My heart started to race without explanation, and the prince asked what he had been interrupted for.

"You have visitors, Highness," the servant informed him.

"Ah. Thank you for letting me know. I will be down immediately."

The servant bowed and departed, and the prince followed after him. As soon as he left after tasking the servants to watch me closely, the dread that was born in me blossomed further.

Something was very wrong.

Sakaiah appeared in the doorway minutes later.

"You," she said to the servants, "Do not breathe a word. I command it. And you..." She looked at me. "Come. We need to go now."

"What's going on?" I asked. "Something's wrong; I can—"

"Feel it, yes," Sakaiah interrupted. "I felt it, as well, and damn if I wasn't right. The Shadows are here."

The blood surging in my chest dropped to my feet.

"Here?" I whispered. "For me?"

So Father had found me after all. I supposed it shouldn't have been difficult to figure out where I was going, assuming he hadn't known my exact location in the first place. But why were they showing up now?

There were tears in Sakaiah's eyes when she nodded at me.

"Let's go. We're grabbing your friends downstairs and getting out of here."

She took my arm and guided me out of the room, ordering me to move down the stairs as quietly as possible. We made a swift exit toward the back of the palace. As we moved, I heard a familiar voice and immediately halted, pressing myself against the wall.

"What are you doing?" The princess mouthed to me.

I held up my hand. I needed to hear this.

"The Fadain will not be pleased if she is harmed. We trust the fugitive has been properly preserved since you sent your letter?"

Letter?

And the voice asking for me was...

"Solshek, wasn't that it?" The prince murmured. "I have your fugitive upstairs. I will send one of my sentries now to go and retrieve her. Please wait a moment."

Footsteps were heading in the direction of the royal quarters. Sakaiah motioned for me to keep following her as we maneuvered through the banquet hall. On the way, she sent warning looks to each of the servants and guards monitoring the room.

"I'm going to get your friends and you out of this palace," she said.

"But the plans... and where will we stay?" I fretted.

Akristura, how could this be what You want for us?

"I have it covered," the princess assured me. "I know someone out in town who will not reveal you, someone you've already met, in fact, and you will live with them while I sort through the rest of this mess. Once I get you there, I will explain what's going on."

I could only assume this meant Gnapa.

By Sakaiah's expression, she had been hiding something throughout this entire situation, and I had a feeling I wasn't going to like whatever she was going to tell me. We reached the dungeon and found the cells containing Cobi, Il, and Norva.

"Thank Akristura, you *are* on the right side," Il said to the princess.

"After losing a lot of people and things I care about," Sakaiah muttered. "We're going to get you out of here, and then we're taking that exit there," she said, indicating a door at the end of the wall of cells. "I hope you're ready for some exercise because this run has no stops until the final destination."

"What about the guards and servants?" Il asked. "You do not have ultimate authority here; will they not report you to the prince?"

Sakaiah shook her head. "I cannot confirm what they will do, but I know that the servants here like me, so they will be more inclined to tell... incomplete truths to cover me. Enough chatter, though. We need to move."

Sakaiah had already taken the keys from the key rack and jammed them into each of the separate locks, freeing my friends. She smiled at everyone and said, "That's that. Let's hope we don't run into any trouble out-of-doors now."

Maybe it was her words that condemned us. The moment we stepped outside into the fading sunlight, we were confronted with trouble. Someone I'd hoped to never see again stood before us.

"Hi, there, Twilight!" Greeted my Shadow grandmother.

Zemorah.

How had she gotten to the Bronze?

The sultry woman had been something of a friend to me during my days in the compound, teaching me about reading, math, and various things related to manners and etiquette. Still, she had also never liked me, despite her sugary claims.

For one thing, she was indwelt by a baine. The parasitic creature feasted on her ample ego and fueled her lust for attention and men, but Zemorah also viewed me as a rival. There could be no reconciliation between us, especially then as she was preparing to smite us all with dark magic, her red lips curled back in a cutting grin.

"Like my new hair? Your father restored me after imprisoning me and making me ugly, wasn't that sweet of him? He even had these tresses harvested just for me."

Zemorah swept a ring-bedecked hand through her wavy blonde wig, a change from her former straight black bob with the bangs that used to frame her face.

Her outfit was as outrageous as usual. She had gone from suffocatingly tight, armor-clad black leather bodysuits to red ones that exposed her navel and spilled out enough of her chest to make anyone's head spin. Even in a fighting position, she could strike a pose, dramatic as ever.

I smirked. "Hello, Grandmother. You're looking mighty fresh. Though that bright red lipstick makes your thin little lips look a bit old. Maybe tone it down a little?"

Zemorah huffed. "No fashion sense, as always. As long as my friend is inside me, I won't have to worry about aging so much. But you do. You'll still age slower than the rest of these fools, but you revoked Aaksa's blessings. We're about to see where that got you."

She blasted me with her valdur, to which Sakaiah responded with a swift barrier of lumensa. Zemorah pushed against it, but Sakaiah held firm. She even started laughing at Zemorah's angry expression.

"You're no assassin," the princess said lazily. "I don't know who sent you down here to guard this door, but they're terribly incompetent, letting a sentient mannequin think she can play the part of a killer."

It was this statement that changed the game.

Zemorah snarled and her slanted black eyes, eyes that once made her beautiful, darkened further. There was no loveliness in her now, only the shadow of a monster lashing out from her soul.

Defending herself with magic in one hand, Zemorah withdrew a long black blade from a sheathe on her back and hissed, *"From the Void, you came, and to the Void, you shall return."*

I recognized the blade as stygionyx. The dark stone possessed magical properties valdur wielders could draw on.

Zemorah lunged forward, slicing the sword toward me. I hastily threw her off with my lumensa, Sakaiah helping, but my grandmother was as youthful internally as she was on the outside, for she regained her footing too quickly to be staggered by a new attack.

Ducking as our light magic sailed over her head, Zemorah laughed, the sound rich with baine influence. She swept forward again to stab me. At the same time that she advanced, she used her magic hand to shoot Sakaiah in the ribs. The princess gasped and fell back. The Akristurans moved in to intervene.

"That's enough for you," Norva told Sakaiah. "You don't need to prove yourself anymore, Princess."

"Keep the Non safe!" Il ordered Sakaiah as he gestured to Cobi.

He moved away after granting her a quick bout of healing magic and came to my defense with Norva. Zemorah backed up, clearly intimidated by the three of us going against her. It looked to be a victory.

Until she vanished into the growing evening darkness.

"What?" Norva cried.

"Show yourself, Shadow!" Il yelled. "Fight with some dignity!"

Not a beat later, Zemorah materialized, shrouded in black magic, at Il's side and whispered, *"Or I can take your dignity from you."*

She giggled, and a sudden crunching sound broke the air. Il dropped to the earth with his neck at an unhealthy angle, shattered beyond repair.

Zemorah had just murdered him. A friend.

"Damn you!" I roared at her, feeling my palms beginning to sear from a familiar burn.

"Watch your magic!" Norva cried.

The golden flames were shifting to violet. No! Why did this always happen to me?

Lumensa, destroy this woman, I ordered my magic.

I blasted Zemorah in the side with it while she ran from us, apparently tired of the killing game after scoring one success. How I hated her!

"Il," I wept, kneeling at his side.

I hadn't known him for long, but his death was deeply unsettling. It felt like the culmination of a series of tragedies and negative events.

"Akristura!" I wailed. *"Have You forsaken us?"*

"Twilight, please, now is not the time," Norva whispered.

There were tears in her eyes and voice as she said it, but she was right. We had to keep moving. We took one long look at Il and made to leave when Norva tripped and fell on her face. She yelled as something started to drag her away from us.

"Zemorah!" I snarled.

Norva gasped when invisible punches landed on her face, torso, and finally, in her intimate area, laughter echoing around us. I didn't have time to hit Zemorah myself; she fled as quickly as she'd placed the blows.

Next, it was on to Cobi.

Sakaiah tried to aim her magic at Zemorah but received a face full of valdur. The princess howled and tumbled across the ground, barely preventing a death wound with her barrier that allowed only some of the dark power to filter through. Now, though, Cobi was at Zemorah's mercy—unless I could kill the harlot myself.

Flashes of her appeared in moments of violence. She had Cobi on his stomach in the dirt while she stripped him of his weapons, and when I went to knock her off of him, she blasted my feet and knocked me down.

Norva was climbing up when Zemorah zapped her back down again, too, and Sakaiah had blood flooding down her eyes, unable to see.

"Pretty toys for a pretty boy," Zemorah cooed, pointing the barrel of Cobi's gun at the back of his head. *"One little oopsy and nobody's magic will be bringing you back. Won't your brain matter make for a nice painting here to remember me by, zyz?"*

"Don't!" I screamed from the dirt.

I projected my lumensa at her from the ground, but Zemorah just waved it off. When I moved to rise, she snapped, *"Take a single step and watch me blow him away, Myrk Maiden. Or should we call you the Religious Adulterer?"*

The baine in Zemorah laughed, and she shoved the gun barrel against Cobi's head.

Why? Why!

"Zemorah..."

I can't do this. I won't. What about what I was supposed to do? The plans for my life? Why, Akristura?

But if you don't, Cobi will die. Your friend. She already killed Il! You would risk your good friend's life, too?

"What do you want from me?"

The question sighed out of me, empty, defeated.

Zemorah turned, grinning, and answered, *"It is not what I want; it is what the Fadain wants. He desires you back among His people."*

Oh, hell, I thought miserably. My heart sunk a little deeper in my chest while I considered.

Cobi's life or my soul? Cobi was already claimed by Akristura, but if I was taken back to the Sharavaks...

You'll be destroyed. Everything you worked for, and all you strove to become, will be undone.

"I... just..."

You can't do this! Cobi at least has something to look forward to when he dies! What will become of you if they take you back? You'll become Aubri.

Oh, the fear, the stinging reluctance at the very thought of returning to that dark pit of misery, that nightmarish realm of demons and dark, unnatural powers...

"Take me," I moaned.

Wrong decision, bad decision, should have saved yourself, my mind crowed.

It's better me than him, I snapped back. *Better that my friend lives than I do. Akristura wants it this way. He wants me dead.*

"Good," Zemorah purred. *"We will go back to the rest of the party now."*

That low feeling slithered in my guts again. The loss. Despair. A grip of fear.

I had just swapped my life for Cobi's. I had offered myself to this exchange.

Akristura, You surely want me dead, I thought as I climbed slowly to my feet.

It required every effort to drag myself to a standing position. Nothing seemed right anymore.

I was going back to the Shadows. I was—

"Uh!"

Zemorah suddenly buckled under Cobi. He had managed to swing himself onto his side, throwing her off, and in one swift movement, he had *her* pinned against the earth. Cobi pried his gun from her hands and pointed it at her head while he stole his sword back from her.

"Don't make me pull this trigger," he warned.

Zemorah coughed a laugh into the dirt.

"You're no killer."

"Not yet," Cobi replied bleakly. "Don't be my first."

That statement sent a chill through me, and for one brief moment, I regretted knowing him. He'd inevitably have to kill in the coming battle, war, or whatever Myrkraas would bring, but I wasn't ready for it at that moment. I couldn't prepare myself for the vision of *him*—Cobi—sending my grandmother to the Void.

"Knock her unconscious and let's go," I begged him.

Cobi raised an eyebrow at me. "You don't want her dead?"

If you keep saying things like that, I thought, *Then I'm going to wish our friendship was dead. Moreover, that it never was.*

"Who even are you?" I whispered, chilled.

Cobi's eyes narrowed. Norva crawled over to the princess and began to heal her wounds. Zemorah thrashed beneath Cobi, and his next move seemed to pain him. He whacked her on the back of the head with the hilt of his sword. Zemorah fell quiet.

"Let's go!" Norva cried. "The princess is better now. That dark magic did a number on her, but we're ready. Take us to the safe house, Highness."

Sakaiah nodded and got to her feet. "We take the back alley," she ordered. "Go straight.

Chapter Twenty-Four

MORE TROUBLE WAS WAITING for us ahead.

Zemorah hadn't been the only Shadow tasked with guarding the back exit. Three more were positioned for us up around the corner. Sakaiah engaged first. Her feral cries stirred my primal rage, which manifested as lumensa that was just shy of bleeding purple. I went to hurl my magic at the nearest opponent, the leanest of the trio, when I recognized the face.

Solshek. He *was* alive. I hadn't misheard the prince.

When he saw me, he turned on his fellow Shadows. The fight finished quickly with my friend as the victor.

Sakaiah raised her fists to smite him when I yelled, "No! He's on our side!"

Sakaiah shot me a puzzled glance. "He's a Shadow," she stated flatly.

"Yes, but he's not a *bad* Shadow," I explained.

"Like you?" She asked.

There was no sarcasm in her tone. The princess of the Bronze honestly did believe I was who I said I was.

Touched, I nodded.

Solshek let his hands down and bowed to Sakaiah. "Your Highness, it is good to meet you. Alive." Sadness colored his gaze.

Sakaiah chuckled. "And in one piece. If you're really who Twilight says you are, you must come with us. Come on!"

"Where are we going?" Solshek asked as the princess steered us all onto the beginning of the back road that wound through the city.

"Somewhere safer than here, I hope," Sakaiah replied. "Come on, you lot. Steady pace, now!"

The princess led the charge, ever the energetic one. We sprinted past dozens of homes, a weaving together of affluent and impoverished places, with no segregation separating the realms of rich and poor.

Several citizens who recognized us waved to Sakaiah, who ordered them to stay quiet until we moved to another small alley. Here, Sakaiah pulled the hood of her simple gray robes over her face and told the rest of us to keep our heads down.

"Don't be obvious about it, though," she added. "Cobi!"

"What?"

"You're the reason why I said what I just said!"

Cobi raised his chin a little higher, and we continued on our trek across the various side streets, pausing and hiding behind bulky objects whenever a carriage rattled by. No doubt the palace's forces were searching everywhere for us. At one point, though, a carriage came down one of our roads, and it appeared we had been caught.

Akristura, must everything go wrong? I wondered bitterly.

By turning our backs and feigning interest in rifling through the boxes of rubbish around us, we got away without the carriage stopping us. Small mercies were everything.

"Come on, we're nearly there," the princess said. "Let's get a move on."

A few more minutes passed, and we arrived at Gnapa's house, rattled but unscathed.

"This lady is one of my friends," Sakaiah explained. "Twilight's met her before. I believe she will take care of you if I ask her to."

I didn't want to say it, but in my mind, I fretted over how relatively easy everything had just gone. Solshek, alive and at my side? The rest of us, alive and not executed? I frowned and wondered if this wasn't all part of a bigger scheme I wasn't aware of. Zemorah's presence—any Shadows in the Bronze, really—was far from ideal.

Princess Sakaiah definitely owed us answers for some of this.

"Princess Seraphina!" Gnapa cried, stepping out of her house, "How good to see you again!" She looked over at the rest of us. "Or else not good?"

Sakaiah explained the situation. We watched the woman's eyes stretch wider and wider.

"They're in trouble with your court? Gods," she breathed. "I will take them, Highness, and I wouldn't do this for anyone else. I do fear what may happen if the court searches all our houses and they find your friends, though."

"I understand. I cannot ask you to endanger yourself, but if you keep my fugitives well hidden, no problems should arise. All of them are capable of defending themselves and you if something does happen, and they will make for polite guests. It has been an honor having them in my home."

Sakaiah looked at us and smiled.

"Thank you, Twilight, for bringing certain realizations to mind and being my first genuine friend in that palace who wasn't one of my servants. On my honor, I will again make a vow to do all I can to protect you from your grandmother, who my servants will kill or die trying, and my government. I will also continue to pressure my parents to help your people on the mainland. I sense it now, stronger than ever... something is brewing in the world. A bad storm."

I nodded. "Thank you, Sakaiah. I appreciate your efforts, especially if Zemorah is gone. But... what are we to do in the meantime?"

Sakaiah contemplated for a moment. Finally, she answered, "Stay here, and give me a few days at least, please. I need your patience. My parents..." She trailed off, appearing embarrassed by something.

"What did they do?" I prompted.

"Damn that I've been crying so much," Sakaiah hissed, wiping moisture from her eyes.

Gnapa took Sakaiah's hands and guided her to a bench where she had the princess sit down. Sakaiah patted the empty space beside her, and we all perched ourselves next to her to hear her story.

"Twilight, my parents never intended to help you. Not unless they considered serious value to be in it, because a long time ago..."

She bit back more tears, and I wrapped my arm around her to console her.

"A long time ago, centuries before my time when the Sharavaks were first rising to power, one of the former Bronze princes received a visit from your former superior, Father Sein. The bastard had words for our people. He needed allies."

There it was again. That chill unfurling in my stomach.

Why was it that Sein was responsible for nearly everything wrong in life?

As the origin of mankind's condemnation from Akristura, he had doomed us all to Toragaine, then he had manufactured the Devastation, corrupted the Silver government, and apparently... no, it was too terrible to think. I would let Sakaiah confirm those suspicions.

Please, no.

"I want to show you the memory," she said. "It isn't my own. It has been passed down to every generation since it took place. I am sure some of it is rather distorted, and not every detail is concrete, but..."

She took my hand, and I sensed her wanting to establish a hursafar link. I accepted, and the memory faded into my mind.

It centered on a dinner between two men in what appeared to be the Bronze palace dining hall. The person we were experiencing the memory through pulsed faintly with nervous energy, while the man across from him was unreadable.

I knew that face. Though it was considerably younger—probably by a thousand or so years—it was unmistakable. This was Sein, and by the opened scroll in front of him, he was not visiting the Bronze on friendly terms.

He began to read the contents of the scroll.

"On this second day of Forthfire, in the year 1,612, I, Sein Leidyen of the Sharavaks, request a peace pact with the Bronze Principalities interminably."

It just gets worse and worse, I thought coldly.

Sein went on to explain that the Bronze was forbidden from attacking the Sharavaks or harboring any of their fugitives. If they did, the Sharavaks "were within their full right" to declare war on the Bronze. This confrontation would be devastating for the isolated, anti-war nation.

I observed the memory in quiet amazement at Sein in action. Young, or at least younger, and dangerously confident. His tone was unwavering, and no weakness was perceivable in his eyes or body language. His very aura was silent but solid. This version of Sein was the one who had stricken fear in human hearts.

As the memory came to a close, I watched the owner of it slowly scribble his signature across Sein's peace pact. We felt Sein's smile burning into our backs. While we wrote it, we thought of our children and how we were doing this for them. For as the Shadow man had said...

"You will not survive if you decline this deal."

The memory crumbled into nothing, and the princess withdrew from my mind. We shared a dark look.

"According to that pact, we were not allowed to keep you around, Twilight. You are their fugitive. But my parents and I were not averse to the idea of altering our alliances when you showed up."

She smiled faintly. "Before things started going wrong, they were very curious why a former Sharavak was working for the "light." I was able to convince them to let you stay for a while so they could observe you and decide whether or not they wanted to reject the Sharavak pact and embrace the Akristurans instead. After all, with Sein dead, they believed there might be hope for taking back their power. While we are not fond of your religion, we are even less fond of the Shadows, and we have longed to end the forced alliance for years. I thought that maybe my parents could be the first generation to do so after the tragedy several decades after the pact's institution."

I digested this information with nothing short of horror, then asked, "And what did they do to your people when that tragedy occurred? I assume someone revolted?"

The princess nodded. "Yes, Prince and Princess Dokor. We have a statue of the princess outside the palace, in that fountain. They waited until the Sharavak ambassadors, who ensured our integrity with the pact, made their yearly visit to tell them off. They wanted no part in the pact. The ambassadors did not take this kindly."

She shuddered. "They slaughtered the royals and almost killed the children, but the sentries fended them off before that happened. The ambassadors then went out into town and set fire to the villages. They took people from every background, of every age, as their... their food source... and burned the rest alive that night in sacrifice to their god."

Sakaiah's lips tightened, and her eyes narrowed as she imagined the gruesome imagery.

So, *this* was the incident Sir Korbin had told me about.

I shuddered. "So you and your parents, by Sharavak law, are not allowed to associate with me," I said. "But they were willing to before things started going awry because they thought I might be the confirmation that the light was better than the dark and that they could escape the pact."

"Yes," Sakaiah answered softly. "And I tried to make them see this. I told them about the strength in you, something that was worth hoping for, and that you might be the answer to the end of our enslavement to those monsters. They agreed to let you stay with us.

"When you "attacked" me, though, Father had had enough of the sudden disasters and tragedies. He delivered a message to the Sharavaks informing them of your whereabouts and was promised rewards in return. So they came, and here we are now."

A sting prodded from the cold inside me.

Sakaiah *had* been hiding things from me, from all of us. It explained her reluctance to answer my questions about the army.

The Bronze royals were as much slaves to the Shadows as the Silver. The corruption was rampant. Was there anything my diabolical grandfather had *not* touched?

"So now you're going to keep trying to convince them to train that army?" I asked. "Won't your father continue looking for me, maybe try to kill my friends? Turn me over again?"

Sakaiah grabbed my hand. "I won't let that happen," she promised. She let go and stood up to leave.

Solshek shook his head. "I wasn't aware of any of this," he said. "The new Fadain sent me here with the others. He wanted to punish me for reasons Twilight knows best, so we were supposed to take her back with us, but I had a feeling it wouldn't go according to plan." He smiled and bowed. "I am grateful to be here and that you are not part of the corruption, Your Highness."

Sakaiah smirked. "Glad you're not on the wrong side yourself. And for your knowledge, I hate bowing unless it's the reciprocal kind we do to each other here in the Bronze. Drop the manners when you're around me. I'm not much of a lady."

Cobi replied, "No, you're *the* lady. The lady of the land, and I'm sure your parents will see that someday. When will you be back with news for us?"

"I do not know," Sakaiah confessed. "But stay here, and stay safe. Practice your respective training if you can." To Gnapa, she added, "Please take good care of them for me. Here is some gold for your trouble."

The princess produced a heavy sack of coins from her robes, but Gnapa refused them.

"To serve you, my friend and princess, is all the payment I require," she stated.

Sakaiah snorted. "Gnapa, dear, we have known each other for a long time, but I have never asked something like this of anyone. I insist you take the gold."

"But I insist on refusing it, Highness," Gnapa replied politely.

Sighing, Sakaiah handed the gold to Norva. "Make sure she uses this for your meals or something of the sort," she told her. "It is easy to spend gold. She will find a use for it. Also, I am sorry for the loss of your friend. I will ensure he is buried and mourned, and I am sorry I can't do much more for you right now."

She dipped her head to us and bid us goodbye. The heaviness that had developed in me only intensified at watching her go.

"Wait!" Cobi called.

She looked back at him. "Yes, Cobi?"

He straightened his shirt and said, "I'd like to give you a hug before you go."

Sakaiah cracked a grin and pulled him into one, squeezing him so tightly he had to poke his head up and beg for air.

I chose to look away and find Solshek's gaze instead. I'd missed those eyes more than I would probably ever miss anyone's... minus my siblings.

I am sorry, Twilight. For everything, Sakaiah thought to me with one last look over her shoulder.

Those amber eyes, bright with sincerity and understanding, rippled with pain. She had every right to be angry with me for her sick mother, damaged economy, and devastated citizens, but it was she who offered the apology.

What, in all honesty, had I really given her? Apparently, Akristura's judgment.

To her, I thought, *So am I.*

And she was gone.

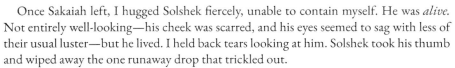

Once Sakaiah left, I hugged Solshek fiercely, unable to contain myself. He was *alive*. Not entirely well-looking—his cheek was scarred, and his eyes seemed to sag with less of their usual luster—but he lived. I held back tears looking at him. Solshek took his thumb and wiped away the one runaway drop that trickled out.

"I'm happy to see you, too," he whispered.

"We have to talk later," I sniffled, "But right now, I'll introduce you to everyone, and… and we'll get settled in here. Yeah." I smiled through another wave of tears and turned to Cobi, Norva, and Gnapa. "This," I said, "Is Solshek. He's a former Shadow, but he was never aligned with them. He actually worships Akristura, and…" I looked at him, melting at the beautiful truth that he still breathed. "He's my best friend."

What blush he could muster touched his cheeks, and he nodded, smiling at the ground. "Thank you, Twilight. I'm glad you think that, and I can say the same about you."

Cobi's eyes narrowed. I grabbed his hand and brought him to Solshek to introduce the two.

"I know who you are," Cobi said flatly.

Why are you acting like this to the person who helped save our lives? I thought to him.

He met my gaze briefly and looked away. "Thanks for getting us out of the compound."

"Not just the compound," I corrected him, "But your holding cell, too. We wouldn't have escaped without him. And then, when Father attacked…" I looked to Solshek to fill in the rest of the history.

"I'll explain later," he said quietly. "I thank you, ma'am, for taking us in." He dipped his head to Gnapa, who smiled in turn.

"It's my pleasure to help the princess and her friends," she replied.

"And who might you be?" He asked Norva.

Norva's eyes glistened with her own unspent tears. No doubt she would grieve the loss of Il for a long time, as all of us would. He and Norva had done their own rescuing for us when we'd escaped the Sharavaks' dwelling. They had been the ones to bring us across the Caligin and into the Silver and eventually to my new life.

"I'm so sorry, Norva," I said softly. "I miss him, too."

"And me," Cobi said dolefully. "He was a great mentor."

"And a great friend to me," Norva whispered. She swallowed the tears in her throat and whispered, "We were going to get married. We had the date set, and Korbin was going to minister the ceremony." She turned from us and collapsed on the bench Sakaiah had been sitting on to cry. "Please just give me some time to process this," she choked. "I'm sorry."

Gnapa frowned. "Oh, you dear girl… come along. I'll get you situated in your room. The rest of you can follow if you'd like," she said.

"That's Norva," I told Solshek. "She helped us escape from the compound while you were, you know—"

"Tending to the Aakira Fadain, yes."

I grimaced. "I hate to think what punishments he had for you, keeping you alive."

His own mouth tightened. "We'll discuss that soon. Truth be told, I feel uneasy that our party was so easily defeated and that I'm even here with you. But..." He gripped my hand, looking into my eyes. "I'm certainly not complaining."

Gnapa got us set up with our rooms after getting Norva settled in. We'd be sharing a bedroom. Solshek and Cobi were given their own place, and between the use of cots and blanket assemblies on the floor, we each had somewhere to rest our heads.

With Gnapa's cooking skills, we would not go hungry anytime soon. That night, after helping her prepare a meal and sitting down to dinner with everyone, I felt my first stirring of gratitude in a while.

I could have been dead or worse instead of at that table with my three friends under Gnapa's kitchen ceiling decorated with pleasant drawings of stars and constellations.

Il had not survived, but I was confident I'd see him again someday. Solshek... at least he was with me. He was alive and by my side, no longer imprisoned with the people he despised and who despised him.

After dinner, we were finally able to talk privately.

"I'm sorry for everything I said to you before," I gushed, trying not to sob. "In the compound, when I was, you know..."

"Under the influence," Solshek finished for me.

He embraced me, and we stood together for a full minute, once again enjoying the physical evidence that the other was alive.

"What happened during everything?" I asked. "How did you get left behind? And what is that scar on your cheek?"

Solshek smiled gently, sliding his dark, unruly hair out of his face with one hand. His countenance was kind. I had not forgotten that. What I had forgotten was the simple beauty of his features, how his blush-brightened cheeks confirmed that his existence was more human than mine. This, and the warmth and intelligence that exuded from his deep brown eyes.

Depthless. As his mind, so was his gaze.

"Korbin had to, Twilight," he answered softly. "Leave me, that is. Here. Let me show you..."

He closed his eyes, and his mind knocked on the door of my own. He wanted to share his memories of the incident via hursafar. Sizzling sparked in my head the moment we connected, and I winced. Hursafar was seldom simple with Solshek. Then again, few things ever were.

Once his inner realm paired with mine, Solshek's memories began to play in my head. They picked up immediately after I had fled the compound with my family through the infirmary's hidden door.

Hazy images of Father and Sir Korbin materialized. Light and darkness flashed across the screen of memories, depicting a wounded Sir Korbin struggling to dominate Father's valdur with his lumensa. Father's movements were effortless, slick with grace. So, too, was the steady stream of black magic gushing from his palms and directly into his opponent's chest.

Sir Korbin gasped and fell back against the infirmary wall. Father then turned Solshek's way. A new duel ensued.

I clamped down on my tongue at Solshek's pain from the blast wounds. Father relished it as he was beginning to steal the life from Solshek, and Solshek struggled to fight back.

He yelled when his lumensa stream finally flickered out, and Father's valdur, always projected from a stable hand, pushed into Solshek's torso. Solshek collapsed on the stone. Sir Korbin was rising behind Father, who quickly snapped back to his stronger opponent to put him down.

Sir Korbin chucked one desperate orb at Father. It met its mark. Father was knocked aside, allowing Korbin to rush to Solshek and heal him. Solshek attempted to give some of his healing power back, but Father was back on his feet, his eyes glittering with promises of demise for both Akristuran men.

"Go," whispered Solshek from the floor. "You can't heal me in time. The others—"

Sir Korbin fended off a quick attack, trying to heal Solshek some more, but Solshek wailed, "Go! Take care of them!"

Korbin's kind face drooped with despair as he realized he could not save both of them. If he, the leader of the Akristurans, perished, so would Solshek. So might many more Akristurans, even my family and I, who were escaping then.

I could see it in his eyes... Korbin's mission failing would entail the failure of many others.

He fought my father for a few more quick rounds. After exhausting his power reserves, he attempted one last time to take Solshek with him, but Father was recovering again. Sir Korbin had little magic left to give.

He fled. Solshek was left behind. And my Father...

Panting, he dragged himself from the ground and ripped at Solshek's collar, pulling him to his feet. He laughed at the fear that surely sprawled across my friend's face and took his index finger to Solshek's cheek. *Slice* went the nail as it slashed through the skin.

"My daughter," he hissed, "Is gone. But you, little defector, are not. No one will save you now."

Solshek fought for air as Father's fingers clamped around his throat. He managed a weak, "I won't die," which made my father smile.

"Is that right? We will put this theory to application. You belong to me now, Zyvienkt scum. I see why Sein despised you, but he did not utilize you properly. I will give you a purpose."

Father released his hold on Solshek, and my friend tumbled onto the stone.

"You will find Twilight when I send a hunting party to procure her in time. You will then bring her back to me. After you have done this, you shall kill her as punishment for your double life. Really, for the fact that you exist at all. Fodder has no place among my ranks."

Solshek shuddered at these words, but Father was not finished.

"If you fail to return the fruit of my loins to me, then I will torture you until you reject your foolish deity, and after that, I will kill you. Your saas is going to taste nice; an Akristuran's residue is always savory stuff. Don't disappoint me, Zyvienkt."

Solshek retracted his thoughts. He looked at me, his gaze sagging with heavy emotions.

"I guess Father never anticipated the Bronze being on my side," I said. "If he had, he might not have sent you here to catch me. He thought he would have his reliable forced allies to lean on if I escaped, but... here we are."

Saying this felt wrong. Was Father that incompetent to think Solshek couldn't have escaped?

Doubtful.

Solshek looked uncomfortable at the suggestion, too.

"Here we are," he echoed quietly. "I hope you don't hold anything against Korbin, Twilight. He did his best."

"I know." I sighed. "I really miss him right now. Korbin would be able to make all this feel less horrifying. But the world seems to be in terrible danger, Sol, and I can't shake the fact that I'm... too deranged to handle it. Too evil and monstrous to make a difference."

If I was more like Solshek, life would be better for me, but I wasn't. I wasn't as bright as he was, and I wasn't as strong. Solshek was also three years older than me. He wasn't a kid anymore, so he had a better grip on things.

"Maybe you are a little out there," he replied gently. "A little monstrous. But that isn't entirely a bad thing. It is what you make of it."

I laughed. "You tried to sell me this back at the lake when I was lamenting feeling like I was weird, remember that? By the way, you never said what was so great about being that."

Solshek nodded. "True. I had other things on my mind that night, but I'll tell you now if you'd like."

"Please do."

Solshek had me sit on the sofa, where he began to explain his personal experiences with the benefits of being strange, even "deranged." He used his poetry as an example.

"You may think everyone is born an artist," he said, "But that isn't entirely true."

"I don't agree," I objected. "Everyone can be creative. Anyone can make art."

Solshek smiled at my spirited outburst and replied, "That is true. To an extent. Not everyone is equal in every way, though. Consider your magic; is everyone just as powerful as you are, or are there varying degrees of ability?"

"There are varying degrees," I answered. "Most don't have any at all."

"That's correct," said Solshek. "Like me. I have less than average magical ability, being more of an alchemist than a direct healer. I like my potions. If I wanted to manufacture my strength over many years of saas-consumption, I might be able to, but I'd rather not damn myself like Sein. However, when it comes to writing..."

He withdrew a worn pocket notebook from his robes and cracked open the front cover. Neat letters curled across the tiny pages.

"I am probably more talented than the average person."

He looked horrified for a moment, as though he'd made some gruesome confession, and quickly said, "Which I don't say to boast, of course. Please don't misinterpret me."

I waved him off. "You're stating a fact, Sol. You're very good at your craft. But what does this all have to do with being an outcast weirdo monster thing?"

Solshek laughed. "An interesting choice of words. It has many things to do with being such a thing, Twilight. You and I are strange entities, tossed into this world to serve as the garnish on the bittersweet dessert of life..."

He trailed off, and I had to prompt him to answer my question to bring him back to reality. Well, a reality that wasn't like the one in his head.

After a moment's contemplation, he said, "What I mean to say in my many words that I can never seem to condense is that we are all given specific strengths in life. In addition to these, we have flaws. If you are gifted with magic and inborn genetic abilities, and I am good at writing where others might not be, then being strange—even monster-like or "deranged"— may be our unique strengths, as long as you don't let your desires consume you."

I grimaced. He shrugged.

"Stronger feelings and senses can be dangerous. You have bainic blood, and I imagine this has been challenging for you to control. Just keep in mind that people who know you... who know your weaknesses... may exploit that, so be careful. Despite what you've been through, you seem to have retained your child-like strength, sense of wonder, and even a smidgen of purity. I am similar. I never let the Shadows completely break me."

He swallowed and nodded to himself. A tear hovered in the far corner of my eye, listening to him describe us, especially his mention of my lingering purity. Whatever purity I had was not mine. I couldn't claim it... but he was right. I still felt it sometimes in my optimism and my desire to change.

I touched his shoulder, unsure what words would be adequate for him and the feelings he'd brought upon me. How were we the same but so different?

"Thank you," I said.

Solshek flicked his eyes my way. I would never adjust to their captivating power and the way they peeled away every veil from my genuine self.

"For?"

I smiled and averted my eyes, heat creeping into my cheeks. "For caring when no one else would. I may have been the Aaquaena, but I never felt like I had many true friends in that compound. You were the exception."

Solshek nodded. "I saw something in you that refused to die. I wanted to keep that deathlessness alive. Even in your worst moments, your spark never extinguished, but I did fear for you. I prayed. I asked Akristura to spare you constantly."

Touched, I was about to blabber some useless response that could never fully explain how I felt about that when Cobi stepped into the room and looked over at us. His eyes darkened.

"You should probably get some rest, Twi," he said quietly. "It's been a long day."

Solshek nodded at me. "It's true. Tomorrow, you and I should talk more. Sleep well."

"Sleep well, both of you," I said to them.

Cobi's eyes grazed over Solshek and didn't leave him until he'd vacated the room. If Solshek noticed this, he gave no indication. To me, Cobi gave a faint smile and a nod before heading off to bed himself, a shadow never leaving his face.

Chapter Twenty-Five

MORNING CAME. I WOKE to Norva weeping softly in our bed, and when she noticed I was awake, she stilled. I wouldn't bother her. What could I even say to ease her pain?

Gnapa greeted me downstairs. She'd already cooked breakfast, and Cobi and Solshek were awake. They each ate quietly at opposite ends of the table, brightening when I entered the room.

"Good morning," Solshek said gently. He smiled behind his tea.

"Morning, Twilight," Cobi followed, flicking dark eyes my way.

What was *his* problem?

"Now, Twilight," said Gnapa, pulling out a chair for me and setting a plate of bread and fruit on a constellation-themed placemat, "I was just explaining to the boys the simple rules I have here. First, I strongly suggest you all stay on the property and don't wander around outside. I do not want to get in trouble with the Bronze government for keeping you here, and I don't think you want that for yourselves, either."

I nodded. "Fair enough. Is there anything else?"

She smiled lightly. "Just one other thing: I have a greenhouse where I grow herbs and other medicinal plants. I'm very fond of it, so I have to ask that none of you enter it or go anywhere near it. Is that okay?"

"Medicinal plants?" Solshek perked up at this.

Gnapa nodded.

"Would I be able to use any of them, by chance?" He asked.

Gnapa shifted uncomfortably at this and shrugged. "I would prefer to get you your own. We can talk about that more later, but are we all okay with the rules?"

"Of course," we mumbled in unison through our full mouths.

She clasped her hands in front of her. "Wonderful. Thank you, dears. If you want to train, feel free to use the backyard." She pointed to her back door. "It's sufficiently shielded by trees, so you'll have privacy. I also ask, for your safety, that you don't use guns while here—they make a lot of noise and could draw attention to us. This house is usually very quiet, so I don't want to raise any alarms."

Cobi sipped his water and said, "Smart. I'll limit it to swords, then."

"I appreciate it. I'm only trying to keep you safe."

"And we appreciate you," I told her. "Thanks for breakfast. It's good. Don't tell Sakaiah, but it's a lot better than fish toast."

Cobi chuckled, and Gnapa pinkened. I remembered the Bronze Bay incident and quickly stopped laughing.

"Sorry," I said quietly.

Gnapa brightened again. "No worries, lovely. Do you know what that was about, though? Why does the princess want us forging weapons? Everyone is confused by that."

I swallowed a bite of toast and replied, "I'll let Sakaiah explain that in time. All I can say is that things might be happening in this world soon."

Gnapa nodded. "So secretive. Well, I don't have many responsibilities, so I don't feel as much need to press you about it, but... I hope we'll be okay. Do you think we will be?"

I paused, considering. "I really don't know," was all I could say.

Gnapa accepted this. "Thanks for your honesty. I'm glad you like my breakfast, and I hope you'll enjoy your stay."

"With your hospitality," Solshek replied, "We are sure we will."

He looked at me and thought, *I have some things to discuss with you if you'd like to do that after eating.*

I nodded. *Sounds good.*

It would be beneficial to talk with him after everything that might have happened since I left the Shadows. Father unearthing Mother... did he know about that? Solshek would hate to know it, as he had loved Aubri as a child. I envied him for this. He'd known her more than I ever would, even though I could communicate with her in maktas.

Maktas, which I'm not sure exists, I thought with a frown, remembering my conversation with Sakaiah in the bathroom. But it had to because Mother was there.

"You want to go outside? We'll keep our voices down, of course," Solshek said, interrupting my thoughts.

I swallowed the last bite of fruit and nodded.

We retreated to the garden, which was as private as Gnapa had said. I sat with Solshek in the shade of a massive tree. Gnapa had her hands full with plants between the backyard and the greenhouse.

"There's no lake view," Solshek commented, "But it will do."

We shared a look and remembered our first time sitting together before the star-illuminated water on the Sharavak grounds. Our one place of peace in a home of horrors.

"I like trees," I offered. "Even after having slept in one."

Solshek chuckled. "Yes, I remember you telling me that." His amused expression withered when he looked at me. "I'm sorry to deliver unfortunate information, but it needs to be said. Since you've been gone, your father has made significant proclamations about Myrkraas and his intentions for that. He finally revealed to everyone what he plans to do."

"He wants to unleash the monster in the Void," I said. "I know this because I was shown it toward the end of my time there. Aadyalbaine said I was to control it."

Solshek grimaced. "I'm sorry to hear that. You're correct, though, and that monster was the topic of his latest assembly before I was sent here." He shuddered. "He says that the original plan was to summon the beast in about a year, but it's actually been lessened now. He coordinated with Aadyalbaine, and it's apparently going to happen sooner."

"What?" I whispered. "But how? He has to be using Sein's energy from when he died. There's no other way."

Solshek looked at me quizzically. "You think he stole the Fadain's saas?"

I flinched at the terminology. "It's very possible. I didn't see him visibly steal it, but that doesn't mean it didn't happen. He killed Sein, Sol. I was there."

Solshek gaped slightly, then slowly nodded. "Ah. So he was finally murdered by his superior subordinate." He shook his head. "What a pity."

"What do you mean?"

"I mean," he said, "That Sein probably could have been anything he wanted, yet he chose to be a pawn of Aadyalbaine. That's tragic. How did he die, exactly?"

Gripping my collarbone, I forced myself to retrieve the memory and shared it with Solshek. I included the part where Father and I discovered our dark lineage, and Sein had taunted us about it. I remembered the look in his eyes... hollowness, malice, and defeat simultaneously, a dizzying emotional concoction.

Solshek's warm eyes softened further when the memory ended. He looked at me and said, "I'm very sorry you found this out in such a way, Twilight. What a horrific thing to learn."

"Yeah." I chuckled and pulled at tufts of grass beneath me. "Sein's my grandfather, Zemorah's my grandmother, my father is my father, and my mother is dead. Then there's me. I don't know who or what I'm becoming, but I won't be able to live with myself if it's not someone better than Shadow Twilight."

Solshek took my hand and squeezed it. "You have Akristura's spirit now."

I looked at him. "How did you know?"

He smiled. "I can tell. I feel it."

I laughed at the absurd accuracy of his intuition. "You're right."

Solshek beamed. "What caused you to turn to Him?"

I hesitated, trying to fully remember the feelings that had compelled me to reach out to the divine. "It was several things, I guess. I felt so guilty about my heritage and my deeds with the Shadows. It was the ugliest feeling. I... couldn't stand it anymore." I laughed quietly. "Myself. That was what I couldn't stand." I traced my palms.

Smiling, Solshek loosed a breath. "How wonderful that you reached out. He listened. I knew He wouldn't refuse my prayers. I sense He has a grand plan for your future, Twilight."

"Doesn't He for everyone, though?" I asked.

"Yes. But it's different for you. You're the old Shadow queen. And on that note..."

"Father and Myrkraas," I sighed.

"The issue," he explained, "Is that there's not much we can do to stop this. It's something I needed to pass along to you, though. It's all the more reason to hope the royal family will help us."

"Right," I said, "With their army. I'm here to enlist their help so we can merge the Bronze Lumens with the Akristurans in the Silver. Does Father know that?"

Solshek sighed. "I don't know, actually. It seems he knew you were here because you used valdur?"

"Ugh. I should have known."

"This pact breaking complicates things," he said. "That's both good and bad because if they do make a decision in your favor? The Shadows will probably retaliate. But they might take a while to do that if they're preoccupied with Myrkraas on the mainland, which it seems they are."

"What do you think happened to the Shadows you came with?" I asked. "Did any of them survive?"

Solshek shook his head. "The ones you saw were all there were, and I... killed them." His eyes dropped, and I sensed a darkening in his spirit.

I touched his hand. "Didn't you say back at the compound that you'd never taken a life before?"

Solshek nodded. Tears amassed in his eyes.

"Oh, Sol," I said softly, leaning into him. "You did what you had to do. We're different, you and me. I killed people for sport. That's not what you did."

His eyes continued to stream. "I don't find that it matters," he whispered. "I still took lives. Shadow or not—in self-defense or not—I've taken them away. I've sent them to the Void... and they will never truly live again."

The weight of this fact pressed on us both for a moment, causing us to lean into each other for support. For warmth and a sense of solace.

"I understand," I finally spoke when the appropriate amount of silence passed. "And I still don't blame you because they were going to kill us. And Sol, you know we'll have to take many more lives soon?"

He groaned quietly. "Yes. I'm not looking forward to it. It feels like something shredded in here, something cracked." He touched his sternum.

"I feel that every day to some degree," I replied, looking at the ground. "And I probably always will. And Sol... I'm worried, too. I'm panicking. I don't tell people that because I'm holding out, but it's difficult to wait for fate to move."

He agreed but straightened up with a weak smile and said, "I know our current circumstances look daunting, Twilight, but I have stared your father in the face and survived. Akristura delivered me from that, from a place I had loathed for years. You were my sign that it was time to go. Here I am. Here you are, too. Damion hasn't killed us yet."

I laughed darkly. "Give him time."

"Hey."

Cobi had come out to join us, his sword in hand.

"Hey, yourself. Ready to train?" I asked.

He nodded. I resented the glum look on his face because I suspected it didn't have to do with Il but something else—something not noble.

"Am I good enough to train with you now?" I teased, half-joking.

His brow furrowed. "What?"

I waved him off. "Never mind. It's not important."

He shrugged, and we moved to the center of the backyard. It wasn't large, but neither was it small, so it would enable us to train effectively.

Cobi stood across from me, and I threw my first orb at him. He dodged it. When I threw the next one, he performed a twist, throwing his blade against the magic and knocking it back to me. I dispelled it and brought out the streams next.

He kept his blade faithfully in front of him until I strengthened the magic. With this, he started to fall back. I blasted him, sending him to his feet.

"Well," I said worriedly, "You're definitely going to need your shield if you want to survive, but your moves are impressive, and so is your deflection technique."

"Say," Solshek spoke from the side, "Mind if I join?"

Cobi darted an irked look at him. "Twilight and I are fine, thanks."

"Cobi, come on. Let Solshek help you. He might save your hind end one day, you know."

This statement further darkened his eyes. "I'd rather fight him one-on-one, actually. Let's go, me and you," he said to Solshek.

Solshek shrugged and positioned himself in front of Cobi with his magic out. He quickly fashioned it into a sword, but it was a feeble one. Cobi commenced the attack, slashing at Solshek, only to be met with the lumensa blade that drove him back.

"Good parry," Cobi grunted before diving back in.

Again, Solshek fended him off. Cobi was starting to look agitated. He threw all his weight forward on his third strike, but Solshek stepped out of his way. Cobi ended up sprawled on the grass.

"Not bad," Solshek commented. He extended his hand to Cobi.

Cobi ignored it and climbed to his feet, speckled in dirt. "Another round," he muttered.

"Okay," Solshek agreed.

I was starting to realize what was going on. The second wave of movements confirmed my suspicion when Solshek, who hadn't dodged quickly enough, was sliced in the hip by Cobi's sword.

He gasped and fell back as the blood surged forth. There was a slight stain on Cobi's blade as he watched Solshek fall.

"Won't you be more careful?" I snapped at him. "If magic wasn't a concept, that would have been a disabling injury."

Scowling, I healed Solshek's wound and helped him back to his feet. When we turned, Cobi was gone.

"What is wrong with him?" I wondered aloud. "This isn't like him." I gestured to where Solshek's injury had been.

He frowned. "I think it's safe to say your friend may be suffering the effects of current events as much as you or me. The baines are on the prowl. They're everywhere, and they weigh on all of us."

I sighed. "You're not wrong. They've attacked me in my sleep several times already."

Solshek frowned. "That's not good. Ask for protection, Twilight, so they can't do that anymore. Anyway, I'd like to train with you, too, but I am also considering getting back into alchemy. If I had some herbs and plants and a nice big pot, I could cook up some useful things. Unfortunately, Gnapa doesn't seem to want me using hers."

He glanced at the greenhouse.

"Her plants are important to her, I guess. Maybe she can pick some up for you," I suggested.

We asked Gnapa, and she liked this idea.

"I will gladly purchase some for you in town," she assured Solshek.

This was fine with him, but his own dark expression appeared on his face when he looked at her.

We took the next day to work on our respective training. Solshek received his equipment and ingredients, and with sprinkles of magic, he diligently simmered them into potions.

"I've got a few poisons here," he informed me, "And some restorative potions. Now, potions will never heal you like lumensa—not even the most potent ones can repair wounds and some sicknesses—but they will strengthen you. Take a few."

He slipped me a couple small vials and told me to stash them in my clothes in case I needed them. He offered some to Cobi, too, but he refused them.

"I'm sure Twilight will heal me if I get hurt," he snapped when Solshek insisted.

"Hey!" I hissed. "I'm not always going to be able to protect you, pal. Get off your high horse and take the potion. What's wrong with you lately?"

Shouldn't have said that. Too abrasive.

Cobi scowled and took a hard swing at the makeshift target he'd set up for himself. He'd been attacking it wildly for the past ten minutes without pause. This time, he cut a large chunk off the target and scattered its pieces across the lawn.

Solshek frowned, and I gaped at this violent display.

Fuming, I turned and headed to my bedroom to cool down. It wasn't right that Cobi, my sunshine friend, acted so stormy. That wasn't him, and it wasn't becoming in the least.

I stumbled upon Norva. She sat quietly at the edge of our bed, sniffling and dabbing at reddened eyes. She looked up at me and forced a smile.

"Hi," I said. "Uh... how are you? Considering, you know, everything?"

She smeared the tears away and answered, "Not much better, but I've been praying. I know Il is in Araveh now." This thought caused her to smile.

"That's right." I sat down beside her and gave her hand an awkward pat. "I'm not too great at comforting people. My magic is better at that than I am. If you want some—"

"No." Norva shook her head, gazing at the floor. "I want to sting. I want to ache and remember him because he deserves that. I will never find another man like Il."

"Don't say that," I started to say, but she cut me off.

"I mean that. I will die before I find another man like him. He was the one. Akristura... He chose to take him from me, but that's okay. He died valiantly like I always knew he would." She smiled through her tears and looked at me. "I'm sorry. I've been neglecting you and the boys. How are you all?"

I blew out air and said, "Not great, honestly. Cobi's been doing this..."

I shared the memories.

"Mm." Norva nodded to herself. "He's definitely upset by something. Do you have any idea what that might be?"

"No. Do you?"

"Yes, actually," she said. "Remember when you attacked Il and me during training?"

I blushed, though my cheeks weren't capable of bearing the glow. "Yes."

"What were you thinking about when that happened? Were there any environmental factors, perhaps?"

I paused and reflected on it. There had been, but...

Norva smiled faintly. "You likely recall what those were. Do you think Cobi might be jealous of you and Solshek now?"

"I was never jealous," I answered quickly, "And neither is he."

She chuckled. "If that's what you have to tell yourself. But do think about it, and try not to favor either of them, love. Those boys both adore you. Unfortunately, you cannot choose both of them, and I personally don't think you should pick either right now. There's too much going on, and you are too young."

I shrugged. "I like them—and I feel something for both of them—but now's not the time or place for romance. I don't know if I'll ever actually be ready for that."

She patted my shoulder. "That's perfectly fine. If this is true, then treat them both fairly. If you care for them, you won't favor one over the other, and you'll be careful to spend time with them as they both need. I am sorry Cobi is acting rather... childish, though."

I laughed. "He's a work in progress."

Norva ran her hand down my hair. "So are you, sweetie. So is everyone."

Feeling guilty, I sought Cobi out and asked to talk with him. He followed me cautiously into the hall, where I said my piece.

"You don't need me or anyone to tell you things are bad right now. I want you to know that I, you know, care about you, and you are always welcome to talk with me if you need to. Even if you don't need it, and you just want to—"

He hugged me and drowned out the rest of what I was going to say. When we pulled apart, tears glistened in his eyes.

"I watched someone die the other day," he whispered. "It was so sudden. Il never deserved that. Then, when I attacked that woman, it felt *right*. For one second. Afterward... wrong. Yet she's far from the last I'll have to do that to, or even worse. Twilight, I'm sorry, but... I'm not ready for this war. This "Dark Hour" thing. Does that make me less of a man?"

Less of a man? Am I less of a child of Akristura if I admit I'm just as afraid as he is?

I shook my head. "Not at all. No one wants this war, Cobi, including me."

Especially me.

He nodded slowly and looked down at his blade. In his gaze was a weary reluctance yet a dancing pride that he was bonded to this weapon and could wield it effectively. In knowing this, he also understood the weight of such abilities.

It was powerful to take a life. With power, however, was an unavoidable degree of regret if it had to be used for destructive means.

"I don't consider myself a pacifist," I told him, "But neither am I jumping for joy at the idea of killing people. To think of the potential casualties on our own side is even worse. Akristura is with us, though, Cobi. Do you still believe that?"

He looked at me and asked, "Do *you?*"

The part of me hardened by the baines hissing at my spirit immediately screamed against this, but my reasonable self whispered its affirmation.

"Yes," I answered. "I do. It's the only thing we have left at this point."

Cobi nodded. "Then we keep training and preparing. We can't avoid the future, but we can shape it into what we want it to be. What Akristura wants it to be, that is."

The question was, what did Akristura want our futures to be?

CHAPTER TWENTY-SIX

I SMELLED THE SCENT when we were outside eating with Gnapa's favorite star-themed plates. I found her preoccupation with the sky amusing, as it reminded me of my obsession with the "Hour of Twilight."

I definitely wasn't fond of the smell, though. It smacked me as it wafted around the house, but the boys couldn't smell it.

"I remember this smell," I whispered to them, setting down my dish and breathing in.

It wasn't like the bitter scent of whatever plants grew in Norva's greenhouse. Those scents were familiar, though I couldn't place the memory of where I'd first smelled them.

The sweetness was familiar, too, and unlike the plants, it bothered me wondering what, exactly, it reminded me of—Marcia, maybe—so I decided to investigate. I turned the knob on the back door and started inside when a clatter spooked me. I groaned. Gnapa had been cleaning; she'd placed one of her living room drawers in front of the door, causing a small vase to crash.

I stooped to collect the pieces when Gnapa stepped through the front door, smiling. Her grin fell when she saw the shattered vase, but she quickly recovered and helped me pick it up.

"No harm done," she assured me. "Are you done out there?"

"Yes, and actually, I'm thinking of going for a walk. Do you, uh, have any clothes to help hide me?"

Gnapa frowned. "That's really not a good idea, Twilight. Remember what I told you a few days ago?"

I nodded. "It's dangerous out there, I know, but Gnapa—"

"I want to come with her."

Solshek entered the back door behind me. He smiled politely at Gnapa.

"I think she wants to look into something important. Could you help us? We won't be gone long."

He sensed my intuition, knowing I was concerned by the smell. I didn't know why, exactly, but it was worth looking into. My Shadow senses rarely misled me.

Gnapa sighed and told us to give her a minute.

"Tell me what you're thinking," Solshek said in a hush while she went upstairs.

I sniffed again, but the lunch scents inside partially obscured the sweetness.

"I don't know," I admitted, "But the scent I've got reminds me of something. I have to look into it."

Solshek's lips tightened. "Zemorah?"

I gaped at him. "Actually... yeah. I think you hit on it."

He nodded. "We'll see if I can pick up on it out there. I used to help her make some of her perfumes, so if I recognize it, we'll know she's here and is looking for us."

"I hope not," I whispered. "She's awfully close."

"All the more reason to determine if it's her."

Gnapa came back down with two hooded bronze-silk robes for both of us.

"You might stick out a little with these, but if you've mastered the Bronze way of walking, you should blend sufficiently," she said sternly.

Solshek looked at me. I smiled awkwardly.

"I can do the walk. I don't think you can, though."

"No. I haven't been here long enough."

Gnapa sighed. "You don't want to be out there too long, anyway. But what are you going out for?" Her heart stuttered with anxiety, and heat filled her cheeks.

"Don't worry, ma'am," I told her. "We just want to look into something. And if we do get caught, maybe Princess Sakaiah would get us pardoned?"

Gnapa shook her head. "Don't count on that, lovely. Be safe instead." She glared at Solshek. "Take care of her, young man."

Solshek dipped his head. We donned our robes, drew up our hoods, and stepped out into the afternoon sunlight.

What are the odds we get caught? I thought to him.

High only if we linger, draw attention to ourselves, or pass by many guards, Solshek answered. *Let's try to do none of those things and simply follow your scent trail.*

I strode forward and stole swiftly down the street with my nose as my guide. The flowery aroma intensified as we crept further from Gnapa's house. We reached a bend in the road that spilled out onto the main street, and I indicated we should take a left.

It's up a little ways from here, I thought. *It's getting stronger.*

Solshek nodded, trailing slightly behind me to my right. His energy had picked up. No doubt he worried for our safety should we encounter any guards—or worse, Shadowy grandmothers.

After passing several blocks, we reached Valechka's main plaza. It buzzed and thumped with heartbeats and activity that momentarily distracted me. I blinked and kept walking, carefully sipping in more of the scent. It had notably strengthened since Gnapa's.

I'm starting to smell it now, Solshek thought. *Somewhere along these storefronts.*

I agreed. What he detected faintly, I was almost suffocating on. Frowning, I paused and analyzed the different stores, wondering which it could be. Did I dare enter some of them to find out?

As if to answer my silent question, a blue-robed figure stalked out of the store a few buildings down from us. Immediately, my spirit throbbed. Their energy bloomed with a heavy darkness nearly as cloying as the perfume.

That person, Solshek thought, *Has awful energy. It's off-the-charts bad.*

I agreed. *It reminds me of someone.*

I had my suspicions, but I wanted to confirm them.

Solshek thought, *Wait here.*

He took off after the figure before I could stop him, leaving me standing anxiously back. Solshek stopped the person and said something to them, but he was quickly dismissed. He hurried back to me, adjusting his hood.

He relayed the person's face in my mind. I gasped quietly.

That's one of the Bronze Palace's court advisors, Karvo! I saw him once talking to a tall robed figure at the edge of the palace garden. He's had a dark energy from the start.

Solshek stared at the store Karvo had come out of.

Do you think his tall friend was Zemorah? Because I recognize that scent. I think she's in there. He nodded at the clothing business.

I ground my teeth, feeling a growl burn in my throat.

It makes sense. She must have been using him for information about us! Father did know where I was going when he saw into my mind, and he must have sent Zemorah here to find me and watch me. I glared at Karvo's retreating back and tried not to toss myself at him in rage.

Careful, Twilight, Solshek thought gently. *You're shaking.*

He took my hand and pulled me back through the crowd before I did something I'd regret.

Or else not regret.

We shuffled quietly to Gnapa's house, keeping out of sight.

Before we go in there, Solshek thought, *I think we ought to keep this information to ourselves for now. Let's avoid getting Gnapa entangled in this situation.*

You're right. I don't want to scare her.

Solshek frowned. Shadows haunted his eyes, and he opened the door for me to go inside.

"You poor things," Gnapa cried, hugging us. She had been waiting for us. "I hope you found what you were looking for."

Solshek gazed at her and nodded. "Something close enough. Thank you for the robes, ma'am." He shouldered out of his, and Gnapa took it with nervous fingers.

She threw us a worried glance and headed back up the steps to put them away. Solshek stroked a spot of star-themed wallpaper and gazed after her as she went.

Solshek and I agreed there wasn't much to be done about Zemorah for the time being. We couldn't conduct our "vigilante work," as the Prince termed it, when he and his government were presumably still searching for us. I felt restless trapped in that house. Gnapa's spiritual rituals concerned me sometimes because I knew she invited dark things into her heart when she did them.

Sometimes, she'd disappear to her greenhouse for hours doing no one knew what. I pitied her because when she returned from these little escapes, she seemed drained and disturbed, with redness in her eyes.

As if she didn't want me to worry, she'd smile as reassuringly as she could and then crash in her bedroom. Solshek seemed to worry more about her behavior than the rest of us.

"She's been consorting with baines for years and doesn't even know it," he sighed, looking over her gem collection.

"That she has," I agreed. "She's very sweet, though."

Solshek's dreamy expression hardened, and he checked the time. "She's been out in that greenhouse for an hour now, and she probably has another hour or two in there. Could you watch the door, please?"

Puzzled, I asked why.

"I'll tell you in a bit," he promised, slipping away up the stairs.

Frowning, I assumed the post of the back door sentry. I smiled when I saw that Cobi had fallen asleep under the big tree, his sword beside him. He looked pure in slumber's stillness. How I hoped he'd remain that way, his attitude issues aside.

Solshek stole back down the stairs a few minutes later. His heaviness was almost tangible.

"Look at this." He closed his eyes and communicated a fresh memory.

"Gnapa's bedroom?" I asked. "What were you—"

The magazines flashed in front of me.

She'd subscribed to a monthly issue of *The Enlightened Society,* which featured familiar hand gestures and symbols Sir Korbin had warned me about in Syndbur. To me, the covers with the Salutation and Enduring Fate gestures meant something, but the uneducated eye saw this merely as a fun magazine for home life and gardening. The insides, though, were more complex. It had all been written in a coded language.

I withdrew and sighed. "You know about these people, too?"

Solshek nodded. "The compound library had plenty of books documenting non-magical religions and how the Sharavaks influenced each. The Enlightened Society is just another name for—

"The Brethren of Myrk." I shook my head. "So, Gnapa's very spiritual. This doesn't necessarily mean anything. Sir Korbin showed me these hand gestures in town, and he said that the people who use them are either deeply religious or ignorant. Don't you think Gnapa's a little too flighty to take this stuff seriously?"

"Perhaps. But what if she's not? And what if her flightiness has a cause?" He nodded at the greenhouse. "Those plants of hers? They're medicinal, all right. They're drug plants. I would know because Sein had me collect them for him sometimes. Drugs and bainic rituals don't mix well."

These were valid concerns, and they explained Gnapa's frequently glazed eyes. However, we had bigger issues at the moment—like the strong possibility that Zemorah was working with and through a Bronze Palace advisor to achieve... something. I told Solshek this.

"You're right," he said. "It is something to consider, though. The worst part is what will happen to Gnapa if she continues down this path. She may find her spiritual games and substance use fun for now, but if she were to meet with those "Society" people, I fear she'd be devoured alive."

"Probably literally," I muttered. "But are you really that concerned?"

His eyes shifted to her drinking bottle on the counter. He patted something in his pocket, slipping it out when he reached the bottle, and I gasped.

"You wouldn't!"

He looked at me before uncorking the vial in his hand and tipping a few drops of it into her bottle. Satisfied, he closed it back up and stashed the vial again.

"Not nearly enough to kill her," he promised. "Just enough to make her sleepy and induce fatigue."

"You're horrible," I whispered. "You better have a real good reason for poisoning our host, Solshek."

Despite the firmness in his earlier expression, he softened under my words.

"I'm sorry. I don't want to harm an innocent person, but my intuition has been telling me she is "weird" from the start—and not in a good way. She might even be a drug dealer."

"Okay," I hissed, "Sure, that's not good, but she hasn't done anything to *us*. And what compelled you to rifle through her *room?*"

He checked behind him before answering, "My intuition doesn't mislead me, and I heard her doing some strange rituals in their—"

"She's always doing strange rituals!" I interrupted. "What made these ones special enough to snoop, Sol?"

"Do you want the memory?"

Of course I did.

"And I did not rifle through her belongings; the magazines were sitting on her desk."

Solshek sighed and let me listen to his recollection of what seemed to be Gnapa chanting and holding a conversation... with another low voice in her room.

"She didn't have any friends over?" I whispered.

"No. She was alone, as far as I know. I didn't see anyone come into the house, anyway."

I frowned. "I see. The conversation didn't sound happy." I looked over at her drink bottle. "Maybe you're onto something."

I went to bed that night, perturbed by the day's scents, sights, and conversations. If Zemorah was prowling about and this royal persecution situation was resolved, I'd find her. She couldn't hide from the Aaquaena's senses.

As I was drifting off, I heard a soft laugh in my ear.

Somewhere in my half-conscious mind, perched between the physical realm and the mental one that intersected with the supernatural dimension, was a baine tormentor. Its dark eyes watched me with savage pleasure before it reached for my neck and began to squeeze.

"Smile."

The creature's hand shifted to my mouth while the other continued to choke me. It jerked back my lips, exposing my teeth before bending into the space to...

No.

Arctic air swept into my lungs as the thing pressed its face against mine and breathed into me. As soon as its frigid stench made contact, the memories resurfaced like scars un-pieced.

Sein. Father. Magic.

Aaksa.

Killing. The thrill of it, so sick and deluded, so deliciously unholy!

No!

"Yes."

No! I wailed. *Akristura!*

The baine roared, and I woke in the same instant, weeping.

Norva clutched my hand. "What happened?"

I pointed in front of me as if the entity still lingered. It probably did.

She nodded, her eyes narrowing as she looked about the room, and she prayed with me for protection.

"They know what you're trying to do," she whispered, "And they've elected to destroy you for that. Don't let them haunt you, love."

I tasted better sleep after this. No baines seeped through the unconscious realm. No Father or Mother appeared to me to make their demands and requests.

But I still woke to the feeling of immense discomfort when morning came.

"I hope you have all been busy."

Princess Sakaiah entered the house at dawn, followed by Gnapa. She whipped back her hood with cheer on her face, but there was a coldness in her spirit.

"Sakaiah!" I exclaimed, sprinting to the front door to greet her. "We've missed you. How are you? How is the situation?"

Sakaiah smiled gently and said, "The situation has been settled. As a result, so has some of my mood. After much convincing, my father has decided to gather together forces for a potential war on the mainland."

Everyone in the room cheered at this, and the princess continued.

"Additionally, he no longer seeks to execute you. I recovered some of my memories of our incident, Twilight," she said, looking at me, "And after enough discussion and consideration, he has asked that you return to the palace tomorrow morning."

"Wow. That's a pleasant turn of events," I replied.

She nodded. "It's sterling. What isn't sterling, though, is my mother's condition. All the healers in the land have tried to restore her, but her ailment only worsens. We... are going to try one last method tonight to see if it works. A cleansing ritual for the whole palace. I didn't think you would want to be around for that, so I will bring you back tomorrow."

"I'm sorry to hear this," I said softly. "I can try again to heal her if you would like."

Sakaiah's amber eyes flashed. "Yes, please. We need as much help as we can muster. I appreciate that, Twilight."

She hugged me briefly, then grinned when she saw Cobi. "Come here," she chuckled, and he threw his arms around her.

"I'm happy you're okay, but I'm sorry about your mom," he told her.

She sighed. "We all are. I don't know what's wrong." She looked elsewhere for a moment to gather her bearings. "The Shadows that came with you—" she pointed to Solshek—"Are dead. I am concerned that the ones who sent them will wonder why they haven't come back, though. Father mentioned this, too. Even if we don't need to prepare our forces to help *you* lot, we will need to be ready for whatever punitive action comes from the Sharavaks for our rebellion against the pact and their missing lackeys."

"Well," I said glumly, "You may experience that sooner than you think. Solshek?"

He cleared his throat. "A giant monster is scheduled to erupt from the supernatural realm soon, Your Highness. The Sharavak High Father originally planned to unleash it in a year, but he informed us during an assembly that that timeline has been moved up. We're looking at just months to prepare for conflict."

Sakaiah blew air out of her mouth and huffed a dark laugh. "Thank you for that."

"I'm sorry," he replied.

She shook her head. "I feel much better now about convincing Father than before. As soon as I go back, I am appointing generals and beginning the selection process for recruits." Her gaze glimmered with resolution.

"Good idea," I said. "I do want to ask, though... have you found my grandmother?"

Solshek and I shared a knowing look.

"We haven't. I know I said we would find her, but we haven't," she answered softly. "I'm sorry. We've been scouring for her, too, especially around the palace and in that part of town. You haven't had any indication of her, right?"

Solshek glared at me out of the corner of his eye. Irritated, I almost spoke anyway, but the warning in his eyes compelled me not to.

Stifled, I answered, "No."

Sakaiah nodded. "Okay. Well... I will see you tomorrow. Thank you for doing this, Gnapa."

Gnapa bowed deeply, and Sakaiah shook her head.

"Have you been using my gold?" She wanted to know.

Gnapa grinned and pointed to a collection of plates and bowls painted with constellations.

Sakaiah laughed. "You and your love of space. Goodbye, everyone. Stay safe for one more day, please."

We thanked her and bid her farewell until tomorrow. She headed out, leaving what felt like a void in her absence.

Gnapa sighed and collapsed on the living room sofa. "Solshek, Cobi," she moaned. "Could I trouble you with weeding my garden today, the part outside the greenhouse? I feel a bit unwell."

Solshek shot a guilty look my way.

"Of course," he said.

Cobi had been trying to avoid Solshek as much as he could the past few days. He didn't look happy to know he'd be working with him now, but he didn't object.

"Are you sure you're okay with us being in your garden, though?" He asked.

"Oh." She waved off his concern. "I don't mind right now. I can't be choosy when I feel like this." She squirmed on the sofa, dropping her forehead in her hands as she leaned into the cushions.

You've poisoned a good person, I thought angrily to Solshek. *Look at her suffering!*

The same expression that had come over him outside during our conversation about murder touched him then. He flicked nervous eyes away from the groaning Gnapa and offered to go outside. Cobi followed him, leaving her and me alone.

"Lovely?" She said softly.

I sat beside her on the sofa, and she took my hand.

"Yes, ma'am?"

She smiled faintly, her dull eyes flickering. "I have a small favor to ask of you, too, if you'd be so kind. It's not necessary, but I would appreciate it."

"Of course," I said quickly. "What do you need?"

She chuckled. "Truthfully, I don't *need* what I'm about to ask for, but... well, I've not been in the best mood lately." She sighed. "I sense darkness around me. I don't know where from or why, but it's been weighing on me. Perhaps this explains why I feel so sick." She reached for her drink bottle to take a sip when I plucked it out of her hands.

Her eyebrows raised, and I quickly explained that I wanted to fill it up for her and freshen it. Solshek might have poisoned that morning's batch of it, too.

"Thanks, lovely," she said quietly. "You're very kind."

How wrong you are, I thought sadly.

It would be better if someone like Gnapa didn't know my past. The truth would likely break her.

As I washed out and filled her cup, I prayed Akristura would guide her away from seeking answers from stones and gems. Like many non-magicals, it seemed, she sought divinity in the wrong things, things that stole rather than gave. Things that were, I thought worriedly after handing her her new bottle, conduits for baines.

She swallowed several large gulps of water and exhaled contentedly. "Thank you. There is nothing like heaven's blessed water." She smiled, but her red eyes crinkled with pain. "I was wondering if you might pick up something for me in town now that you can go out."

"Sure."

She fished some gold from her pockets and dropped it into my hands. "There's this lovely star-patterned dress at one of my favorite stores along the main road. It's by the plaza; you'll see it in the store window. If you could get that for me before someone else snatches it up, I'd love that. And get something nice for yourself, too. You might be surprised by something pretty there."

I accepted the money and her request. I made sure to fill the water skin Il had given me what felt like so long ago with several of Solshek's potions. Once filled, I cast one last glance out the back door at the boys on their hands and knees weeding together and left.

I stepped out into the welcoming ocean of sunlight splashing over the city and made my way to the plaza, keeping an eye out for clothing stores. I followed the same general path I had the previous day when sniffing out the strange perfume.

I will enjoy this lovely day, I told myself. *And I won't get accosted by Shadows.*

On my journey as an undisguised passerby, I encountered groups of Bronze citizens who noticed me and expressed delighted surprise. They'd recognized me from my healing work with the princess.

Several of them requested that I heal their injured relatives. I could not refuse them, of course. My first afternoon back in the outside world was as productive as it was relaxing.

"Do you wield the power of the gems?" One woman asked. "There is light inside you that does not come only from magic. What is the source?"

I thanked her and said, "I would have to credit that to the Light God, ma'am. We call Him Akristura."

Not everyone was receptive to my message, but they all listened politely.

As I walked, I kept my eyes out for the store Karvo had come out of. It had been on the main road where I found myself then. I paused to take in the scents. Maybe I'd smell the perfume again. If I did...

You can't be hunting and attacking people right now, I scolded myself. *Besides, there's still no proof of anything.*

I chuckled darkly to myself.

Yet.

It was then that I saw the starry dress. A mannequin posed in the form-fitting fabric behind the glass of one of the storefronts, as Gnapa had said. My breath caught, realizing that this was the clothing store Karvo had come out of and the place where the scent trail ended. Coincidence?

My animal senses prodded me to investigate.

Enter the store, they whispered, *And discover. Hunt, if you must.*

My tongue poked my teeth. Hunting sounded fun.

I'd have to enter it, anyway. Gnapa wanted this dress. I smiled coldly to myself and vowed I'd deliver.

Once I crossed the store threshold, I sensed body heat, but I didn't smell the incriminating perfume. I kept my footsteps light, and my ears pricked for any sounds.

Whoever owned the business appreciated gaudy things. How... familiar.

That was most Bronze people, I realized, but the sheer amount of multi-colored clothing burned my eyes. Seeing no shopkeeper, I moved toward a staircase in the back of the store when I stepped on a creaky floorboard and gave my presence away. In response, an older female voice called, "Welcome! I'm up here! Come visit if you have any questions."

Oh, I will, I thought, sliding a gentle foot onto the first step.

I tensed and readied my hands with magic. If I ended up attacking someone who was not who I thought they might be, I would run and explain myself later.

The staircase led into a loft-like room where a large window threw light across an arrangement of supply-strewn tables. Near the stairs was a full set of mirrors and a vanity lined with products. I didn't see the store's owner, but I could feel the body heat intensify and hear a faint pulse.

She was behind the closet door across from me.

I moved forward, magic burning, and gingerly touched the handle. I turned it and raised one hand high. The door opened before I could pull it toward me, and I paused and blinked at the figure standing there with fabric draped over their shoulder.

Bright green eyes. Red hair. And a blade flashing into my flank.

Blood exploded from my torso. The blade had sliced a clean path along my ribs, and the pain and surprise rendered me temporarily immobile. I recognized the woman despite her first-glance appearance. Hot pink fabric clung to all her curving parts in a dress that ended just above her unnaturally pale mid-thighs. She beamed, sliding a crimson curl out of her eye.

"Hi, again, Twilight."

Her lightly accented voice filled me with rage.

Zemorah shoved me against the wall and bound my hands together at an angle so I couldn't burn the tethers off with magic. She then gripped my hair and dragged me to the large mirror where rows of makeup and styled wigs waited.

"Sit down," she ordered, shoving me into a chair, "And don't speak. Grandma wants some quality time with her grandchild."

Zemorah seized the knife handle in my side and robbed it from its hole. More scarlet stains scattered on the floor, but Zemorah was preoccupied with another scarlet item on hand... and then *in* her hands.

I gaped again at her true form, which wasn't as glamorous as she liked to portray. Zemorah hadn't much of her own hair to work with. It was why she wore wigs. And the red one she had—

"Yes," she said smugly, turning the wig over in her hands before setting it on the vanity and placing the blonde one she'd worn before on her head. Next, she popped out her green contacts, revealing her soulless black eyes beneath. "Quality time." She patted my cheek and began to busy herself with heating a hair iron and inspecting the makeup on the counters.

"What... are you doing?" I hissed through my stinging wound.

She chuckled. "What are *you* doing? That's the better question, Aaquaena."

I flinched. She noticed and ruffled my hair.

"No time to be proud; you're in Grandma's care now."

I choked out a laugh. Zemorah ignored me and gestured to her spread of creams, powders, and colored contacts assembled in front of me. She told me to pick an eyeshadow I liked best.

"They say your makeup choices reveal your character."

"So, yours is flashy and substanceless?" I coughed.

Zemorah ignored me. "I wonder how much like your mother you really are. She was a bit frumpy." Zemorah tapped the chain of my starstone necklace. "Court manners and all that." She shrugged, opening the neckline of her dress to inspect her chest. "Some of us are also royalty and don't adhere to all the outdated customs."

I snorted. "Like what? Decency?"

Zemorah grinned, her dark eyes lighting. "Sure."

She gently pushed the wig to the side, giving me a better view of her makeup. None of it was to my liking. Everything was in shades of neon, glitter, and anything but subtle hues or quiet matte colors. I seethed. Zemorah and her opulence.

"What's wrong?" She asked, faking a pout. "Don't like my selection? I guess *your* personality can be summed up as "unforgivable bore," hmm?" She laughed. "While you settle on something, I've been tasked with delivering a message to you, Aaquaena. Your father—my son—is displeased with your conduct as the Shadow Queen."

"My bad," I grunted. "I stopped feeling good about my *conduct* after the first dozen people I killed."

Zemorah smirked. "What you feel and what you are destined to do don't always intertwine, dear."

"Really? You're the one who cheated on the High Father," I snapped. "You act on every whim." I coughed again and felt more blood ooze. Zemorah wet a cloth and pressed it to my side.

She cupped my chin, bending into my neck and sniffing the pulse there. "Not every whim," she growled softly. She let go and continued to explain, "Part of the reason I'm here right now is that Damion wanted me to make it up to him for the little lie Sein and I maintained until recently."

"Some small lie to hide someone's heritage." I grimaced. "And Father continued that lie with me."

He'd never told me who my actual mother was until he was bringing me to the Sharavak compound. He hadn't told me *anything* about who and what I truly was.

Zemorah unveiled another terrifying reality that, in light of recent events, almost didn't strike as surprising.

"Guess who sold you out to me, Aaquaena?" She laughed and clapped her hands. "Yes, guess!"

"I..."

No. She can't have. She's not the monster Solshek feared she was, and she wouldn't have done that to us even if she was just ignorant, I thought desperately.

"That's right. You already know, on some level." Zemorah nodded arrogantly. "Gnapa, your sweet little homely host. Only she's not so sweet. She's been praying baines over you since she first laid eyes on you when the foolish princess brought you to her dwelling." She grinned. "Nice, hmm? She almost ditched her religion when she saw me. Said I was the most beautiful person she'd ever seen and that I deserved worship."

I choked on saliva and slumped back in my chair, a twisted feeling toying with my insides.

Akristura, no. Not Gnapa.

So, Solshek had been onto something after all. The magazines. The rituals. The drug plants, the baine attacks, and how she stared at me like I was a wonderful, frightening thing... all of it had led to this. She'd baited me into this shop for a "dress," and if I hadn't smelled the perfume and followed its trail beforehand... well, I'd still be in this situation because Zemorah's disguise had caught me off guard.

The worst part of this was that Gnapa and Zemorah were *friends.*

I hated thinking about what was happening to my own friends at that moment.

"Return to us, Twilight," Zemorah said softly, her gloating smile fading. "Your father will accept you. You'll be showered with glory and praise, and everyone will love you." She caressed my cheek, and I shivered.

Once, I'd been desperate for people to love me. Everyone seemed to hate me before, but the Sharavaks had given me purpose. I wasn't with them anymore, though. I could never belong to them again.

"If you don't submit now, there will be pain and loss later," Zemorah assured me.

A chill danced through me. I *did* feel assured of that.

But there would be pain and loss much sooner if I didn't figure out how to get out of there.

Zemorah began to take foundation to my face, smearing it on as thickly as she'd done in the compound. She then took black eyeshadow to my lids. I realized what she was doing as she packed it on.

Emotional manipulation. She'd reminded me of my mother to make me sore. Then, she'd tried to break my faith in people by revealing Gnapa's betrayal. Next, she'd appealed to my innate loneliness by promising that "everyone" would love me if I'd only return to the Shadows. Now, she was decorating me exactly as she had in the compound before I'd been presented to my people during an assembly. I assumed that the hot iron on the counter would be used to straighten my curls soon.

Zemorah took my silence as contemplation. She admired the red wig on the counter, smiling as she worked on me. She picked up the iron and brought it to my head, as I suspected.

"Remember when we did this before?" She gently placed a coil between the clamps.

"Yes. Why are you doing it now?"

She dragged the iron down, flattening the curls. "To remind you of your destiny that you threw away for lesser things. Lesser gods."

While she straightened, I thought of ways to undo my binds. I'd have to cut them somehow, but I'd only be able to do that after disabling her. Afterward, I would chug Solshek's potion and hightail it back to Gnapa's. I studied Zemorah's slow and surprisingly thoughtful motions with the iron and wondered if she'd make me angry enough to break them myself.

In her true fashion, she didn't disappoint.

While heating another group of strands, she nodded over at the red wig on the counter. "Interesting thing about that..."

"What?" I asked.

Zemorah smirked. "It's actually not a wig at all. You'll recall my first hairpiece, the one that so closely resembled what my hair used to look like."

Don't say any more, I thought. *Or do. This may be what I need to hear.*

The creeping cold came. Damn if I wasn't always right in my private mind, the one I didn't allow to speak up.

"Yes," Zemorah said. "A scalp job. I don't settle for synthetic. Damion didn't like that when he dug her up, so here I am, serving my sentence."

She grinned at me in the mirror, and I could have melted through the chair and fallen through the floor. Truths like these were too terrible to accept, yet there was Zemorah, her leering white smile biting into my denial and shredding it to tatters.

"I took it from her after death. I didn't want something so beautiful wasted, and my son, well, he didn't like that very much. Mumsy can't blame him, the poor thing."

I didn't think. If Sir Korbin had seen me, he would have locked me inside for weeks. Maybe he would have put me down.

Better that he wasn't around to watch what happened next.

"Horrible witch!" I screamed.

My binds snapped with inhuman anger. She'd done it; she'd set me off.

I sprang for the straightening iron and clamped it down on Zemorah's hand, using my other hand to shove her away. She toppled into the table behind her, giving me ample opportunity to end this.

Kill! Kill! My chaotic magic ordered.

I will, I'll slaughter you, I thought to Zemorah.

I threw myself on top of her to finish what she'd started.

Zemorah latched onto my hair and wrapped a set of strands around my throat. She tugged, and I dropped to the floor with her. She pinned me down and kept yanking at the hair, constricting my throat until my vision was filled with dark patches, and I drove my knees into her face.

She responded by whipping out a makeup palette and blowing eyeshadow dust into my eyes. I gasped and blinked madly at the invasion when a sharp sting sank into my arm. The monster had stabbed me again, this time with the pointed end of a makeup brush.

I growled and lunged at her neck.

"You wanna scalp my mother?" I snarled. "You want to steal from a dead woman? *My mother?*"

The old Twilight, and not the healing one, was taking over. Like Zemorah and Xanactyzaas, I, too, had my dark friend. I surrendered to it, gripping my grandmother's neck and wrestling her against the vanity.

I ignored the searing pain in my side. Shadow Twilight had other abilities her calm counterpart lacked, so the only thing on her mind was *inflicting* pain—not feeling it. And inflict it, she did.

Zemorah was growing stronger beneath me, and her eyes, in the glimpses I caught of them, had gone fully dark. Her baine inhabitant was rousing.

My head slammed on the counter.

"I scalp who I please, Aaquaena," Zemorah hissed. *"And I could use your mother's locks in a nice shade of black."*

I spat in her face and clutched at the blonde scalp job on her head. She howled and lashed out with her nails. Forcing myself off the counter, I spun her around, ignoring her claws pressing into my collarbone, and thrust her face-first into the mirror.

Glass punctured the air and sprayed around me. Zemorah wasn't going to recover from those wounds, and I realized I didn't want to end her. Her ruined face was punishment enough.

I fled from the scene, snatching up the water skin as I ran. I tripped over numerous articles of clothing on my way out of the store, and I sprinted into the street. I took a hearty swig of Solshek's potion and stumbled onward.

I had to get back to my friends—assuming there was anything to get back to.

CHAPTER TWENTY-SEVEN

BLOOD AND FLASHES OF pain accompanied my every step. Still, I pressed on. Solshek's alchemist magic would sustain me.

My friends were home at Gnapa's mercy. I loathed thinking what she might have done with them while she'd had me delivered, like a little present, to Zemorah. Scowling, I burst into the house with my lumensa lit.

The first thing I noticed was Solshek on the floor.

"Twilight," he groaned. Blood pooled around him.

"Sol!" I dropped to his side and worked quickly to heal his chest wound.

"She stabbed me," he wheezed. "With a knife she put my poison on." He shivered in my arms. "She used my other poisons to subdue the others."

"Where did she take them?"

"The backyard."

I nodded and finished healing him. He tried to heal me, too, but his lumensa was too weak to change much.

"I drank some of your potions," I said. "I'm going to go get everyone. You should stay here, though; you're fixed, but you've lost a lot of blood, and there's poison in your system."

"I can't let you go alone," he croaked.

He staggered and tripped into the sofa.

"You need to," I told him sternly before entering the backyard. I looked around briefly before heading for the most obvious place—the greenhouse.

"Greenhouse," I whispered, "Or slaughterhouse, Gnapa?"

I hissed between my teeth and slammed through the door. As soon as I entered, the bitter plant scents smacked me, and I remembered where I'd smelled them: in the back parking lot of Syndbur's Better Version Beauty. It was the least of my problems, though, considering the sinister presence in the space and the smell of Gnapa's ritual spices. A dark door waited at the back of the greenhouse.

I staggered through it and down a set of stone steps underground. Darkness accented with flickers of light waited inside, and a heavy incense swarmed my face. A woman's chanting halted. Further in, the dark female shape it belonged to turned my way.

"No!" She snarled.

I sent Gnapa to the ground with magic, careful to use the right kind, and glanced around for any accomplices. Unless they were Shadows and could become the darkness, none were present.

"What on Aash?" I whispered when I saw my friends.

Both of them had been gagged and bound inside an arrangement of candles.

Why not Solshek, too?

I stooped down and started unbinding them. Norva yelled through her gag. A swift knock to the head had me on the floor where several candles scattered, their flames lighting my clothes.

"You'll make a fine sacrifice to the Star Gods!" Gnapa laughed.

She struck me in the back with a staff when I tried to rise. I returned the favor with lumensa. Gnapa screamed and flailed backward, giving me time to stand and apprehend her. I pounced on her, small but blooded with adrenaline, and contemplated.

"The Star Gods?" I snorted. "You couldn't sacrifice them to a real deity?"

Gnapa spat on me. I considered, for one dark moment, bashing her in the face with her staff.

Don't kill her, Norva thought desperately.

It would be so nice, though. She was about to murder my friends; why couldn't I return the favor? Plunge my teeth inside her and shred down. Gulp her fluids. Make a mess of her until she was nothing more than a mural on the wall...

"Twilight!" Norva grunted through her gag.

I settled for knocking her out cold with a hit to the head. I dropped the staff after the first strike, wishing I could do more.

After this, I found some thick cord in a storage closet that she'd used to tie up Cobi and Norva and bound her hand and foot. I moved her aside and untied my friends. Both of them hugged me fiercely once free.

"You just can't trust anyone these days," Norva sighed when we returned to the house.

Gnapa had been thoroughly tied, and then we'd blocked up the greenhouse "inner chamber" door with bags of soil and cement blocks so we could convene and decide what to do next. After that, we planned to take turns watching her to ensure she didn't escape.

No one was particularly pleased to learn that Zemorah was still alive and well. Norva, however, was grateful that I hadn't taken her life in malice.

"Keeping your composure in moments like that isn't easy," she said while she healed my wound in full. "You obeyed your conscience. Akristura bless you for that."

Shadow Twilight had warred for Zemorah's blood spillage; a few weeks ago, that version of me would have prevailed. Maybe I was progressing after all.

"I think we're all happy about that, at least," said Solshek. He smiled warmly. "We may be in serious danger now, with her prowling out there, but this is a triumphant moment of growth for you. Not everything—or everyone—has to end in violence."

I thanked them, but the issue of a rampant Shadow female remained. Gnapa, too. We all agreed that it was best to watch Gnapa until Sakaiah came the next morning. We'd tell her everything then, and she could decide what to do with her murderous friend.

"The stars give signs," I muttered, glancing at the wallpaper, dishes, and placemats containing celestial bodies.

"Speaking of signs, maybe we ought to investigate her room more and determine why she did this," suggested Solshek. "There had to be a reason Zemorah found and enlisted Gnapa."

We looked through her bedroom items, searching in drawers through bags of powder, under papers on her desk, and then in her "Enlightened Society" magazines... which is where Solshek found the note.

"I'm glad to have found you. You have likened my people to gods. In a way, we are. If you want to please your gods and us, send me the rogue girl, Twilight. Kill her friends if you want as a sacrifice to your gods, but leave the Solshek kid untouched."

He paused and shook his head, tapping his front. "So much for not being touched."

He continued. *"You'll be richly rewarded for this. I will personally secure a spot for you in the Brethren of Myrk, who encourage all kinds of beliefs, and fund your international travel. I will visit you from time to time for updates and discussion."*

"Well, we don't know how they got in contact, but—" I started to say.

"Actually," Solshek said, "We do." He held up another opened letter from Zemorah.

"I hear you've been striking deals with Advisor Karvo for quite some time. I've got a deal for you. How about you meet me at Eccentric Attire at sundown? Feel free to walk in; you won't have to worry about the shopkeeper stopping you," he read.

"There it is. Karvo was meeting with Zemorah this whole time, and he apparently already knew Gnapa. Probably because of the drugs." I pointed to the powders she'd created from the plants in her greenhouse. "Zemorah must have delivered the letter after we were sent here so we'd be captured." I shook my head.

"I wonder how much the princess knows," Cobi muttered.

"Hopefully, she wasn't conspiring right along with them," said Solshek, "Though I don't feel that she is. Maybe that voice I heard one night in this room was Zemorah."

My blood chilled. "You might be right. Goodness. She was in the same house among us the entire time."

Everyone paused to think about this. Solshek offered to guard the house's front door for a few hours and alternate with me in case Zemorah showed up. Norva headed out to watch Gnapa with Cobi.

"This is wild," I said. "Zemorah plots with the Bronze's advisor. Our drug-peddling spirituality host sells us out to her for a spot in the mainland's secret society. The Bronze has a pact with the Shadows. And Sakaiah was apparently too blind to see most of this." I sighed. "At least Prince Seraphina has finally seen the light. I don't think Zemorah's done, though."

Solshek agreed. "She'll be back." He squeezed my shoulder. "And we'll be ready."

Norva burst through the back door, Cobi panting behind her.

"Gnapa's dead," she gasped.

"What?"

She nodded. "She had these scratches and marks all over her throat, and her face was purple. She looks to have been strangled."

Solshek and I shared another horrified look. He blew air between his teeth and said, "It must have been a baine."

"A baine?" I whispered. "It physically killed her?"

"Yes. They can do that to their hosts if they're far enough down a dark path. Some of them commit homicide, and others compel their hosts to take their own lives. It's happened to a few Sharavaks before."

I blinked. "Wow. What an awful day this has been." I dropped onto the living room sofa, drained. Norva, Cobi, and Solshek gathered around me.

Norva gripped my hand, her blue gaze fierce but soft. "Don't become cynical. It's looking bad right now, girl, but we'll survive this. At least baines can't kill *us.*"

I thought of Sakaiah, grimacing. "They can through their hosts."

Norva agreed and led us all in prayer. The best we could do with every tortuous thought and damaging emotion was to offer it to a higher power. It was too much for us.

Sakaiah fumed when we showed her the memories and Gnapa's body the following morning.

"I cannot believe it."

She clenched her fists until veins rose along her arms, and her nostrils opened large enough to resemble portals. "Gnapa, of all people." She laughed bitterly. "Perhaps Mother and Father are right to keep me from the throne. How could I effectively rule when my closest friends are monsters? I don't even know what to say... when my parents hear, they will give me hell for befriending the commoners."

Her eyes flicked down, and her fists released. She sighed and invited us into the carriage. We returned to the palace, and as we went, she explained that the gem cleansing ritual had been "an inconsequential disaster."

"I still need your help, Twilight," she said humbly. "I know my father would appreciate it. We've officially exhausted our resources."

"I'll tend to her as soon as we get settled back in," I promised.

"While you do that, I will be raiding Advisor Karvo's room," she said bitterly.

Sentries helped Cobi and Norva back into their rooms, while Solshek opted to come with me to help Princess Seraphina. We had to pass through the throne room to reach the royal quarters. The prince was there. He looked tired, slumped on his throne, like the weight of his lofty seat dragged him down.

"Evening," he grunted.

"Morning, Father," Sakaiah corrected.

He dismissed her. "All the same in the end."

Sakaiah shared a concerned look with me before explaining our situation and what had taken place—minus the Karvo part.

"So, your consorting with the people led to disaster and betrayal?" He snorted, shaking his head. "Sakaiah does what Sakaiah wants. Sakaiah sneaks her then-fugitive friends off to un-safe-houses," he mocked.

"Father—"

"No." He raised his hand. "I don't have the energy for your excuses, daughter." He glared down at me. "Welcome back, sorcerer." He cast amused eyes at Solshek. "I presume you're on your way to heal my wife?" He scowled. "If she dies in your hands, I could not have prevented her death apart from your interference anyway, so I suppose it does not matter. Fortunately, I think you were wise to warn us about the Shadows. Our army commenced recruitment training because we've elected to break off from the pact."

I bowed. "Thank you, Your Highness."

He waved me off. "Don't thank me. I did not want this, but I suspect you're right; the Shadows must be stopped. If we must battle them on the mainland to prevent them from destroying the world with this monster of theirs, then it is worth our army and our efforts." To Sakaiah, he said, "I hope you're ready to lead this army into battle if something happens to us."

Sakaiah gaped at him. "And what should happen to you, Father? You know I'd never allow harm to befall you."

He smirked. "You said that about your mother. Now she dies from the inside."

"That's different," Sakaiah objected softly.

"Hardly. If..." He winced like these next words would hurt him. "If her ailment *is* spiritual, then I am not safe, either. No one here is. Perhaps the rogue Shadow will use her magical religious powers to undo this curse." He sighed deeply and dismissed us.

"I see he still doesn't care much for me," I whispered, following Sakaiah's lead.

She didn't answer. Her father's earlier comment seemed to have darkened her mood.

"I believe your mother has a baine inside her," I said as we walked.

Sakaiah's brow raised. "Do they frequently inhabit people?"

Screams bled through the Seraphinas' door just as Sakaiah touched the handle. We each glanced at each other, the answer unspoken, and she slowly opened the door to peer in at the princess. The wails grew louder.

Sakaiah gasped and slammed the it when a thud knocked against it.

"She's throwing her shoes!"

I shouldered past her and started to open the door with Solshek, but she drew me back.

"You want one of those eight-inch heels buried in your eye socket?" She hissed.

I looked at my scarred palms. "I've felt worse pain."

"Twilight—"

I ignored her and stepped into the space, immediately regretting what I saw. Princess Seraphina was in much worse shape than Sakaiah, but then Sakaiah hadn't been left to rot with her condition. The princess wasn't lying down; instead, she looked like she'd been strewn across her bedsheets, then tangled up in them to the point that she'd imprisoned herself in the cloth.

All except her hands.

I ducked when a second shoe with eye-impaling heels was dashed across the room, then again as it was followed by a lamp, a candy dish, and a pair of stockings.

"Easy, Highness!" I cried, dodging a fork.

The utensil rammed into the wall with a twang. By the inhumanity in the princess's eyes, she was only getting started.

"Get away," she snarled in a voice that was not her own. Her fierce eyes flicked to Solshek.

"How do you want to do this?" He asked me. "If we cast it out—"

"It'll just come back." I sighed. "But we can't leave her like this. She wouldn't even listen to reason in this state. No... we have to tell it to leave."

The princess screamed and dropped onto the ground behind her bed. I slowly came around the corner to find her huddling and shaking as she held herself.

"No wonder you're sick," I said softly, noting the blankness of her skin.

Her baine drained her of color, of vitality. Her skin was still umber. However, with the attachment feeding on her life force, it was paler than it should have been.

"You deserve nothing," she rasped. "Nothing but damnation and death."

"Actually, you're right," I said. "After all, I was born evil."

The princess laughed. "You weren't born evil. You are evil because you reject Aaksa!"

"If you weren't evil, and if I wasn't," I said, "Then you wouldn't be inhabited by a baine, and I wouldn't have been crawling with them, either. You attract what you are—"

The princess leaped at me from behind the bed.

Solshek threw himself between us and was thrown to the ground. The princess's strong fingers closed around his neck. Inches from his face hung a salivating countenance where supernatural horrors leered at him through their chosen flesh. I shoved her off of him, and she began to spasm violently.

I dropped and laid my hands on her chest while Solshek held her down. She dug in with her nails, snarling and growling.

"By the authority of Akristura," I chanted, "I command you to leave!"

The princess raked her nails over my arm, then went limp beneath me. I mopped the sweat off my brow with the back of my hand and stood from her on trembling legs. Solshek caught me before I fell.

"Are you okay?" He inquired gently.

He held me and pulled me away from Princess Seraphina's unconscious form. I clutched him, suddenly terrified by what we'd done. It would come back. It'd return with a hideous vengeance.

Solshek let me drop my head against his chest.

"I wouldn't have let her harm you, Twilight," he whispered.

Araveh above, his voice was soothing. I wished he'd been around to comfort me every time something horrible happened.

Tears touched my eyes. "I'm more worried about her than me."

He nodded and stroked my hair. "A valid concern. We'll look out for her. As long as Akristura lets me live, Twilight, I will be here to help you."

The moisture spilled, and I half wept, half laughed, "I hope that's forever."

He smiled. "It will be, even if it's not here."

Sakaiah walked in on us then, and her eyes immediately went to her mother. She fell at her side, touching her pulse and squeezing her hand before looking back at us.

"Is she okay?" She cried. "Will she be better? Did you make her better?"

I stroked my collar and whispered, "Only for now. But it'll be back, Sakaiah, and so much worse..."

She frowned and called for attendants to transfer her mother to the infirmary.

"Whatever the case, her aura is much cleaner now. Bless you, Twilight. You have the palace's thanks."

At least there was that. But how many times would I have to do this before they woke up?

"I hope my mother truly is better this time."

Sakaiah led me back through the throne room and to my room in the guest quarters. She looked more than sad; she quivered with unspent angry energy.

"What's wrong?" I asked. "Karvo?"

She nodded, her eyes narrowing into rage-filled slits. "Check this out..."

Memories of her and several servants rifling through the advisor's belongings appeared. Nothing incriminating had been found in any of his papers, drawers, or in his personal closet. Then Sakaiah got the idea to check under the bed.

There, tacked to its frame, was a small leather notebook containing rambling notes about a portal of some sort in the Inahi forest. The spot had been erased and re-drawn several times, eventually placing the portal mark deep within a forest.

Sakaiah withdrew, scowling, and said, "Inahi is our second largest city here in the Bronze. Just this morning, before I came to get you, Karvo took filed leisure time there. The palace requires that all court members log their intended destinations and purposes for visiting them before they leave. Know what he said? "Visiting friends." What friends? No one knows. But I think you and I know."

I nodded. "Zemorah. And what's this about a portal in the forest there? Do you know anything about that?"

She shook her head. "We've always known that Inahi has a bit of a disturbed forest. Evil spirits are said to plague it there, driving wanderers to madness and murder. Even self-murder." She sighed. "I don't know what this portal nonsense is about, but I'm inclined to believe anything at this point if it involves the Shadows. And I think, since your grandmother failed to capture you yesterday, that she may have other ideas in mind..."

"Like opening portals?" I bit my lip. "You're sure there's no such thing in this forest?"

Sakaiah shrugged. "We've never had much reason to look into a thing like that. The locals don't speak of portals, just evil that permeates the wood. And since it provides no relevant resources—most of the trees have useless wood, and the nutrient density in the soil is very poor—we've simply left it alone. The locals have, too."

"I see. Well, then... if Karvo has gone to this place, what are we going to do?"

Sakaiah grinned. "I think you know, my friend. I'd be packing a little bag if I were you."

CHAPTER TWENTY-EIGHT

W E LEFT FOR INAHI at dawn.

Sakaiah's father disapproved of her visiting and investigating Karvo, but after she showed him the memories and the notebook in his room, he let her go. Sakaiah looked bothered when she told us.

"He seemed so defeated, even with Mother on the mend," she said quietly, gazing out over the water as we took a ferry to the city. "I think the army and the Shadows, all of it, really, has been taxing for him."

I could relate to that. I'd nearly been killed and kidnapped twice in less than a month, never mind the flood, Bronze Bay incident, Sakaiah's bainic moment, and everything in between. The emotional turmoil alone was enough to weaken me.

Cobi and Norva stayed behind at the palace while Solshek, Sakaiah, two sentries, and I took to the city. When we arrived a couple hours later, I noticed immediately that it had a distinctly different atmosphere from Valechka.

More like Syndbur, the bustling metropolis stabbed at the sky, sprawling landscapes of pavement and housing complexes replacing the gentle greenery of the capital. A few vehicles were on the roads, but far more carriages were in effect. It was a puzzling embrace between the sophisticated modern era and a simpler, more rural setting, like the Caligin meeting the Silver.

"Welcome to Inahi," the princess stated as we left the docks. "The second most populous city in the Bronze caught somewhere between the Second Era and the Third."

"Why does the Second Era still linger when all these other modern conveniences exist here?" Solshek wondered.

Sakaiah chuckled. "Because we are the Bronze. We don't usually make much sense."

The Eventide Forest, as it was called, laid beyond the glittering foreground of Inahi on the first portion of raised earth jerking up from the flat, paved cityscape, foreboding even from a distance. The dark mass of trees looked impenetrable. After hiring a carriage to deliver us to the agricultural district, we watched the forest creep closer, ensconced in a matted mess of bushes and crowned in thorns.

"It's beautiful if not a wee bit frightening," Solshek commented.

"Just wait until we find what's inside," Sakaiah muttered. "Assuming we do find it."

Our sentry company tried to maintain even expressions as we swept by fields of crops dotted with scattered laborers. Sakaiah paid the carriage driver a generous sum once we arrived at the outskirts of a tiny village, and we were on our own, at the mercy of whatever information they could provide us.

"Excuse me," Sakaiah called to one of the men working the land.

He glanced up, brows furrowed, and asked, "How may I help you? I am busy at the moment."

"So are we," Sakaiah responded. "Are you too busy for the princess of the Bronze?"

The laborer was still for a moment, narrowing his eyes in scrutiny at Sakaiah. His face illuminated, and he cried, "My, it *is* you, Highness! Please forgive my rudeness." He bowed deeply, and Sakaiah quickly said before he could further embarrass her, "We only need a few answers to some questions. We hope you or someone you know may have them. It is an urgent matter."

"Of course, Highness," the man replied. "What would you like to know?"

After presenting our problem, the laborer physically paled and shook his head.

"You ask about the *forest?* Highness, what would you like to know?"

"Do you know where inside the forest this might be?" She asked, presenting the drawn map.

The man looked at the drawing, then at her with nothing short of desperation, and said, "The forest's heart, Highness? Oh, no... if I tell you what I know, you must not go in there, Highness! You mustn't!"

"Why?"

"Because," the laborer said, dropping his voice into a whisper, "It will destroy you. The forest's heart is the most cursed, Highness! All you have heard is true; do not sacrifice yourself to test the rumors. I tell you, they are true!"

Sakaiah dismissed his fears. "My friends and I came prepared. Tell us where this "most-cursed" place is, friend. We need to know."

"Highness," the man moaned, on the verge of weeping.

"Don't be afraid for us," I intervened. "See this?" I displayed a palmful of lumensa for him. The man's eyes danced. "This will protect us, this and the One who gives it to us."

He smiled, and a tear slipped from his tired eyes.

"A happy sight," he breathed. "The three of you may be able to protect yourselves, but no one without magic will survive what lurks in that darkness." He glanced nervously at the sentries. "It is unlike anything you know."

Try me, I thought.

"It's okay," I assured him. "We'll do our best to stay safe. Now we just need you to tell us where this place is."

"That tree does *not* look like a dead man."

Thirty minutes into the Eventide Forest hike had us struggling to identify all the markers the laborer had noted for us to look out for, one of which was a small tree that was supposed to resemble a deceased person.

"Yes, it does," I argued with Sakaiah. "I bet Solshek thinks so. See the branches that look like arms folded over a chest?"

Solshek nodded. "She's onto something, Highness."

"For the last time," the princess sighed, "It's *Sakaiah.*"

"My apologies," Solshek said. "Perhaps if you carried yourself with less dignity, I would think less of you." He winked, and Sakaiah raised an eyebrow.

"You think I carry myself like that?" She asked. "My parents don't, and I'm starting to think they never will."

The sentries exchanged worried looks.

I shook my head. "They don't see you, then. You do the best you can, and it's a very good job, especially considering everything we've been through. Also, why am I not surprised Karvo would choose to visit the "most cursed" place in the forest?"

Sakaiah snorted. "The only surprise is how I haven't gotten my hands on him yet."

Silence followed that statement. There was a chill in the forest due partly to its ample shade but also to something else; an intangible existence that could not be defined as wind or weather.

"I think we're getting closer," I said softly twenty minutes later.

Our surroundings had progressively darkened. What had been an inspiring jungle minutes ago, spotted with flowers and the occasional intrepid butterfly, was devolving into barren tangles of shadowy confusion. Even the scent was different, heavier, sweeter with decay.

"We've only followed three of the six markers if the ones we've followed are even correct," Sakaiah grumbled. "We're hardly close."

"The other markers might be near each other," Solshek pointed out.

Sakaiah hissed between her teeth. "And what if they're not?" She snapped. "We've been trekking through this miserable place for an hour now, and we've found nothing!"

Solshek and I looked at each other, then at the sentries. They, too, were beginning to grow irritable, but they kept quiet.

"Sakaiah," I started to say when my foot caught on a root, and I went tumbling into the undergrowth.

Sharp pains erupted everywhere on my body from the thorns and pointed twigs stabbing into my skin. Solshek pulled me out of the vegetation and had me sit on a rotted log to heal my cuts.

She's feeling the influence worse than we are, he thought to me while he soothed away my scrapes. *So are the sentries.*

"I can't even smell anything out here other than rot," I muttered. "Feels like my nose will never recover. I'm hoping if I get a whiff of one of these fools—"

"Gah!"

The princess had her head clamped between her fists. Solshek and I watched her for a moment to see what she would do next. One of the sentries rushed to her side to comfort her, but she settled down as quickly as the episode started and fired an angry glance my way.

"Are we going anytime today?" She demanded.

"Just a moment," Solshek muttered. Looking concerned, he ministered to my remaining cuts, and we cautiously resumed our walk.

I was starting to wear down under the effects of whatever was around us, too, but we had to soldier through it. It could only mean we were growing closer to Karvo and, presumably, Zemorah.

This might be a situation where activating our lumensa barriers is in good order, Solshek thought.

You think they can protect us? I asked.

He nodded. *If there are any physical dangers or dark things around, it can help ward those things off. Lumensa can protect from magic, baines, physical attacks, heat, cold, and whatever else is necessary to protect the wielder. Remember, it has your best interest at heart.* He smiled gently and activated his own trembling shield.

It immediately sliced a swathe out of the darkness pressing around us. Sakaiah groaned, and before I had my magic out, she was lapsing into another series of gasping and head pains, which had her doubled over this time.

"It's near," she choked out. Spittle dribbled from her mouth. "And so are they. Go without me."

"What?" I cried. "We can't leave you, Sakaiah! Let us heal you of whatever has you like this, and we'll go on ahead."

"No," the princess spluttered. "You... don't understand... I can't stop your grandmother or whatever else is here. You're the only ones."

She hit the ground a heartbeat later.

"Sakaiah!" I screamed.

Her sentries stooped to her aid and diligently checked her pulse. They nodded at me to indicate that she was alive. I didn't care. She was suffering, maybe dying, and—

"Don't!" Sokshek hissed, restraining me from her.

"What are you *doing?* Let go!" I yelled.

Solshek slipped his hand over my mouth and whispered, "Mind the noise you're making! You can see we're close to the heart; look at the princess and her guards! Let's not trumpet our arrival to everything evil in this wood, like your grandmother and her assistant. Sakaiah will be fine."

I pried Solshek's hand away and pushed him. "How dare you hold me back like an animal," I snarled. "I think she's dying! How do you know she isn't?"

"Would you just listen to me, Twilight?" Solshek snapped. *"Listen* for once! Sakaiah is being affected because she does not belong to Akristura, and we do. Same with them." He gestured to the sentries. "That is why we're not dropping like she did. Do you want *us* to go mad, though? Is that what you want?"

I laughed. "I'm already mad. I'm damn near a *maniac,* you fool."

The black rage was rising and churning in a maelstrom of unspeakable wickedness. Every influence around me lent itself to my thirst for destruction. It was more kindling on this already healthy fire, but not healthy because it was *sick,* so sick.

Twilight, come back to Me...

Akristura? The distant light?

"Twilight, come back to me."

Solshek.

I shook my head and thought again of annihilation, but he took my hands before I could use them against him and—

"Here."

Lumensa trailed into my wrists, and a warmth crept over my frigid flesh. The dark thoughts were retreating. Solshek closed his eyes and continued to drain my fear and anger from me, taking it into himself as I had done with Mirivik and Sakaiah.

"I can only do so much," he told me when he finished. "You know where you must direct these thoughts in the end."

Nodding, I let him tend to Sakaiah.

"Stay with her," he ordered the sentries. "Not that you were coming with us to begin with. Stay safe."

I distrusted the many emotions passing over their faces and prayed they wouldn't hurt the princess. If they did...

"Come," Solshek called.

I let him take the lead as we pressed on and closed in on the core of the evil essence. I was detecting new scents. Human ones, the bite of blood, and...

"Her perfume," I whispered, chilled. "It's up there, inside that little cave."

I nodded to a small, otherwise unassuming-looking dark mouth yawning from the shadows. The princess would have to stay behind, as she'd said. She was of little use to us in her current state.

"Yes," he whispered. "She's in there." His heart fluttered. "Put up your barrier, Twilight."

As soon as I activated it, I worried about how much we would be depleted after this errand. We needed to have enough magic to fight Zemorah, and her friend, who was doing Akristura only knew what inside that black cavern.

This time, I'll kill you, Grandmother.

I squeezed my fists and dropped to a crouch as we neared the cave.

The opening was like the mouth of the Void beast if it were to part; depthless, dark beyond comprehension, and silently deadly. A waiting trap ready to consume its victims. Solshek followed closely behind me.

I knew we were in for trouble when we stepped inside.

The blood smell grew overpowering, combined with scents of decay and mildew to make for a foul combination. Zemorah's favorite perfume spotted the air, too, and so did that other human scent. I gasped internally when I remembered the scent—it was the seed of "human intimacy," as Sir Korbin had called it when he'd led us to it that day in Syndbur.

If only the Akristuran cleric could see me then.

I didn't like to think of what we'd find inside this cave, but the only sound was a rushing noise deeper in. Everything else was still.

I'm really not liking this, Solshek thought. *Not even the Sharavak compound feels this oppressive. Do you think this could actually be...?*

Don't finish that thought, I warned. *Let's not jump to conclusions.*

What else were they doing, though? What sort of ritualistic nonsense were they up to?

Probably just summoning more baines to torment us, I thought nervously, *Especially now that the Bronze has broken the pact.*

How I wished that had been the true answer.

When I saw the swirl of colors and darkness further in—and a fallen body resting in front of it—I knew it wasn't that simple.

"Araveh above," I breathed, sliding cautiously to the end of the sloping tunnel and stopping at the body.

Pale fluid spattered the basin behind it, and around it seeped a slow-cooling scarlet. The pinched face on the body was smothered in dark red lipstick. Below, in the neck, a hole had been bitten. The tooth marks were human enough, but the longer gouges were distinctly Sharavak imprints.

Solshek blanched at the sight. "It seems she... she..."

"Killed him while having fun with him," I whispered, shuddering at his ruined neck.

"He was the sacrifice," Solshek said softly, "To open *this*. A *portal*. A portal in the Bronze Principalities. Sein must have—"

A tugging sensation dragged us into the throbbing colors.

"No!" I cried, grasping for the real world, but the portal only continued to devour us.

"Twilight!" Solshek shouted.

We could not stop it from consuming us.

We landed in fire.

That was what it felt like when we descended into a realm that resembled nothing of the Void I had been shown—before it had devolved, anyway.

For several beats, everything was intense.

The heat, the searing colors, the black vapors belching from vents in the superheated ground, and the screams. This was, indeed, the dwelling of the damned.

Across the way, in the various furnaces and fire pits throwing forth their agonizing orange glow, were the everlasting dead themselves. Tortured with molten rock forced down their throats and in their eyes, with strange, segmented insects writhing under their melted flesh, every person was alone in anguish.

Baines oversaw their suffering. Their gnarled and ruined fingers stoked the flames and fed the prisoners their steady diet of burning rock while Solshek and I looked on in desperate horror with our lumensa shields barely holding. We both wanted to comment on what we were witnessing, but the fear was too immense to allow for words.

That would have been my fate.

Choking on fire. Bleeding worms from my eyes. Stabbed and branded over and over again by sadistic creatures that knew nothing of mercy or light.

This was Toragaine.

The cursing was ear-piercing and heart-shattering, but where were the monsters? Did I want to know? And what about the giant monster... the Void beast?

I was distracted by one of the human inhabitants. This individual was isolated from the rest and tortured the most harshly as multiple baines surrounded him, laughing while they clobbered him with torches, pokers, and clubs. I knew that broad frame...

Frowning, I squinted through the smoke and heat to see him better. I swallowed hard when I heard his screams rising above the others. It was Father Sein.

"Look," I called to Solshek, nodding in Sein's direction.

Solshek's face darkened when he beheld his old tormentor, a blend of emotions born on his face. I didn't miss the sorrow there. Even a touch of regret.

Sein's cries hit me harder than the others. Of course, I was familiar with Sein and not the other prisoners, but I had probably known the man more than most. The former Fadain had harbored many secrets through his over two-thousand years on the planet.

When he'd passed, he had been given no mercy by his Aaksa or the Dark One's baines. I shivered, remembering how they had devoured him, lapping up the lingering residue of his spirit as his face dropped away and his final wail, the last one to be birthed from his living mouth, ushered out.

Pity gripped me then. In the realm of misery, it was the clearest emotion of my own that I could feel.

It appeared he was in the center of the burning lake. That, according to my memory, was where Arkyaktaas rested.

We need to get out of here, I thought to Solshek. *We should—*

"*Myrk Maiden.*"

A massive baine swooped in front of us, bearing a sword that looked to be composed of worms in its left hand. The worms held their blade shape by way of magic, gnashing their fangs and struggling against each other in formation, prepared to devour more meat.

"*Your curiosity will now kill you. My children are hungry,*" the baine laughed.

Its eyes were endless sockets, out of which more worms crawled. When it grinned at us, the creatures wriggled between its teeth and dropped from its tongue. They started squirming toward us.

We blasted them away, and the baine swung.

My barrier, weakened since we arrived, trembled upon impact. I prayed for it not to disintegrate, and it held, but barely. With another hit, it would be gone. The disastrous heat around us would kill me instantaneously, assuming something else didn't first.

The shield was not allowed to fail.

Solshek moved forward and slashed at the baine with a lumensa blade, sending it staggering back. It began to spar with him with its worm sword. Every time the blades met, a few of the things dropped from their assembly and came after me.

I didn't have time to worry about the worms, though. Another baine landed behind me. This one had a torch in its hand. It jabbed the burning end at my shield and taunted me, growling, *"One strike and your god will have proven He's forsaken you. Let us dance, sorcerer."*

We danced.

When the monster swung, I sidestepped, practicing what I'd learned with Korbin and Cobi sparring and deftly evading death. I managed to snatch up some of the worms with magic and shove them into the baine's face, but I noticed too late that it was fighting me into a corner—of lava.

I fell. Solshek shouted nearby, but his voice was distant compared to the roaring in my ears. The heat was increasing. I was collapsing.

It's over.

Only it wasn't. My magic *held—*

"Twilight!"

I rose on quivering legs atop a churning lake of fire. I was not *in* it, but on it, my feet safely inside the light surrounding my body. Snarling, the baine that had backed me into it hissed, *"Impossible. You will die today, I promise you."*

Glancing quickly at my feet, I laughed and looked back at the entity.

"Make your promises, devil. We all know the only language you speak is lies."

The baine roared and sailed at me from the rock ledge it had pushed me. Unfurling its weathered wings, it glided onto the lava and took a swing at my head with its torch. I ducked and fired lumensa at its torso. The baine took the hit and went spiraling into the lava with a screech.

I should have been like that baine, but I was alive.

And the monster of the Void was...

Directly beneath me.

I'd never forget it. It was spindly-legged like a spider with a gruesome, too-long tube for a neck, six crests rising from its contorted face, and three spine-encrusted, flesh-fanned tails... sentient chaos. I despised its empty black eyes and insect-like mouthparts.

I started to run when a body slammed down on top of me. Solshek had been pushed in, too.

"We have to get out of this!" I screamed.

A black curtain descended upon us, bringing a stifling cold in its wake. Solshek gaped at the sudden shroud and yelled at me to turn around. Peering at us from the dark wall was a vaguely human face. Rotting teeth bared at me in a mocking grin, and I knew this entity was much more vicious than anything we'd yet faced.

Aadyalbaine. He had come to kill us.

Akristura, I began to pray, but the Dark One's vast, arctic presence withered my warm thoughts to bitter bits.

That smile.

My grandfather had grinned like that once, but his madness was a crumbling imitation when faced with its unyielding source.

No man or creature in existence held a purple candle to the Myrk God.

"What are you doing?" Aadyalbaine asked, his thick voice rocking through my core. *"Those you seek have already fulfilled their purpose. Myrkraas was your purpose, and it can be so again."*

I opened my mouth to answer but found that my tongue was dry and useless behind my even more parched lips. Aadyalbaine's atmosphere shoved at my light barrier, pressing on the confines of my mind.

Unadulterated hatred. Contempt for all life.

And it can be yours.

"No," I whispered soundlessly.

Not again.

Anything I tried to speak was sucked away into the void that was the Dark One. If I stood before him for much longer, I was going to—

"Run, Twilight," Solshek croaked nearby.

Aadyalbaine glared at Solshek. *"Kill the Myrk Maiden, boy, and claim her power. You are nothing now... but this can be remedied."* The dark wall sidled up next to my friend, its size completely overshadowing him. *"Steal her saas,"* he purred. *"Transcend humanity."*

Solshek glanced at me. I shivered at the blankness in his eyes. Surely the Dark One hadn't infiltrated him?

"Myrk Maiden," Aadyalbaine hissed. *"Will you stand there as the weak one eyes you like prey? Kill him."*

The Dark One's words were starting to seep in, and my lumensa reflected this. I shook my head and clenched my fists, trying to squeeze more vitality into my convictions, but...

"Go on."

I looked at my friend, but the word "friend" was suddenly alien to me. It did not appropriately reflect our interactions. He'd guilted me back at the compound; that's what he'd done. He'd told me that my majestic, powerful self disturbed him, implying it wasn't the real me.

I ground my teeth.

Of course it was me. The power dark magic had given me...

Inhaling deeply and ignoring the stench of smoke, I remembered how much I'd wanted to kill him the day he'd confessed what he was—an Akristuran. A heathen and a *traitor.*

In his soft brown eyes, I saw weakness to ravage. My mouth watered. I would take him out like that prey thing, Cobi.

"The summer memories, Twilight!" Solshek wailed. "Remember the summer memories!" He grunted and struggled against his baine captors.

The summer memories.

I blinked, and they began to filter through the haze in my spirit.

Our writing. Our laughter. His poetry and kindness, and our serene visits to the starlit lake.

"Twilight!"

I turned toward the voice. It belonged to Father Sein.

"Leave this place!" He wailed. "You must never come here!" He fell as one of his tormentors smacked him with a club.

I turned toward Aadyalbaine and gazed directly into his empty eyes, pale and barely flickering inside his black abyss of a body. *That* face was no comfort, but I wouldn't be deterred by it. Never mind the dark drool sliding between his teeth nor the rich death stench wafting from him. I would forget the urges tugging at my Shadow nature—nay, my human nature as much as my baine genetics—and remember whose side I was on.

"Not yours," I spoke in a trembling tone.

Murderous thoughts sprouted in my mind. I swatted them away; Solshek wasn't my inferior.

"You forsake Me again?" Aadyalbaine snarled. *"Fool."*

The Dark One rose from the surface of the lava, preparing to crush us with magic. Instinctively, I thrust my hands forward. Aadyalbaine was too preoccupied with indignant rage to notice the magic when it flowed forth.

I knew it wouldn't work, that faint stream of light leaking from my palms.

So small. Too feeble and spineless, much like its owner.

Hopeless, I thought miserably. *Aadyalbaine is seconds away from destroying us.*

I should have panicked. The Dark One was—

Too much. Can't... handle it.

Gritting my teeth, I maintained my position and kept heaving at Aadyalbaine, though I knew he could feel it now and was surely about to smite us. A thin tendril of belief dangled before me. I grabbed it, not letting go, as I struck the Dark One with an increasingly bright beam of lumensa.

The magic washed over Aadyalbaine's formless body. A cacophony of howls and shrieks tumbled from his blackened mouth, and his shadowed fist began to descend—

"Stop!"

One voice soared above the thousands of others wailing in the abyss. It was enough to seize Aadyalbaine's attention.

"Sein?" I whispered.

"Go, Twilight!" My grandfather gasped before his baine attendants clubbed him again.

Something collided with my skull, and I fell into near-complete unconsciousness.

I heard Solshek shouting somewhere around me. I felt his anger at seeing me fall, though I couldn't quite grasp what was happening or why the heat around me was so intense. Where had I gone? What sort of horror was I living through in the dream dimension?

Arms wrapped around me. I looked blindly for them, seeing none, but I knew the heartbeat against me was not mine. The comforting arms gave way to a sudden pain as I fell onto something. Rousing from sleep, I remembered where I was and saw that I'd been thrown up onto a rock ledge surrounding the lava pool.

Solshek had thrown me, and he now sought to climb out himself.

"Help me, Twilight," he pleaded as baines stalked toward him. "Give me your hand."

My hand wasn't long enough to reach him, as he kept slipping down each time he thought he found a foothold in the stone. I looked at him with breathless horror and a strange satisfaction. The Void's wickedness became me again.

I started to cry. My spirit clanged and clashed against the darkness, but the darkness was seductive and clever, and it made my friend into something he was not: the enemy. I watched him beg for my help, soundlessly observing his bitter cries of, "Twilight! Twilight, my friend... please *help me!*"

Friend.

I gulped down a sob and fashioned a stick out of lumensa, sliding the end of it over the ledge.

"Grab... it," I grunted.

Before I change my mind, nay, before the beast makes up my mind for me.

How my hands wanted to pull back. The Zyvienkt should die there and be consumed by baines.

"No," I wept, pulling as Solshek took hold of the stick.

Let him go, my humanity begged.

Kill him, my Shadow snarled.

Let him die! They chanted together, filling my head with searing pain.

My tears scalded as I tried to heave him up, all the while deliberating whether I should because he was a *Zyvienkt,* not like me, but *lowly,* prey-like, flesh to consume!

"Akri... stura," I wailed. I sucked in a breath and coughed out tears from the smoke. "God of Light... save..."

Protect him, whispered the spirit.

I forced myself to heave one last time. I drew Solshek, finally, over the ledge.

"Me," I sighed, falling back on the stone.

He seized my hand and pulled me back up, sweating heavily.

"Make for the exit," he panted. "Back where we were. We'll use whatever magic we have to try and open that portal."

Sprinting, meandering between hissing holes in the ground and piles of worms pushing themselves after us, we almost made it to the exit before a new challenger descended to block our path.

This baine was far less intimidating than its cousins. It was emaciated and stoop-shouldered like an aged man and carried no weapons or magic in its hands. We would make short work of it.

We positioned ourselves to strike when the creature spoke. My inner fire lessened upon hearing its words, suffocating under the baine's speech.

"Why do you struggle, little Shadows?" The entity asked. It opened its arms in a peaceful gesture, a deep frown unfolding across its face. *"This is where you are meant to be. There is nothing for you outside of here. Return to where you belong, and cease fighting for the light."*

"I won't," I responded weakly.

The baine shook its head. *"The light god does not love you. Why would it create you only to damn you upon your birth if it did? It cares nothing for you, but the darkness can win yet."*

"It can't," Solshek snapped back. "Get out of our way!"

"This is useless. You are wastes," the baine moaned. *"Traitors of the light god, and traitors against yourselves. Your old nature awaits you, Myrk Maiden."*

Seething, I screamed, "I'm *not* the Myrk Maiden!"

A halo of light flowed out of my chest and plunged through the baine into the darkened portal entrance behind it. The baine evaporated with a vicious howl, and the portal began to open.

"Go," I ordered breathlessly.

Solshek and I threw ourselves into the light, not looking back at the wounded Dark One, and relished the tugging sensation as we were pulled away from that realm of endless horrors and depthless evil.

Deliver us safely, Akristura, I prayed.

It was my final thought before we landed back in the tunnel.

CHAPTER TWENTY-NINE

"**N**EVER DO I WANT to go to that place again," I wheezed.

We had made it through the portal relatively unscathed—our perturbed spirits were a different wound entirely—and it remained open behind us. We raced up through the tunnel until we were a safe enough distance away.

"I wonder if I can close it."

I summoned lumensa and ordered it to close the portal, but it did nothing but ricochet. Worse, the portal seemed to take personal offense to my attempt, making another rushing sound. Neither of us waited to find out if it would suck us back in again.

"I don't think it looks like that for Sharavaks," I explained as we ascended the tunnel slope. "They're blind to Aadyalbaine's reality and their own realities. *That* is their true fate." I pointed behind us.

Solshek agreed. "It was something I worried about constantly when I thought of you." His eyes softened, making me feel guilty for what had just happened.

"I'm so sorry about my deliberation," I whispered. "I shouldn't have felt it."

"You stared the Myrk God in the face and hit him. With your magic." Solshek chuckled softly. "Whatever thoughts you had, you came through, Twilight. I respect you for that."

"And I appreciate you picking me up and throwing me out of that pit." I started to smile at him when he gripped my arm and pulled me to his side.

"What?" I cried.

He pointed in front of us.

Sakaiah was still unconscious, but worse than this were the two bodies around her that seemed more than asleep.

"No," I gasped.

Solshek lowered his head, and my heart followed suit. We both tried to ignore the slash marks across the sentries' fronts and how one of their necks was bruised and crooked.

"Killed each other," said Solshek softly. "Driven to madness."

"You're sure it's not Zemorah?"

I smelled her perfume again. It seemed fresh and led past the portal.

"She would have eaten them," Solshek pointed out.

I nodded. "Right, after she'd done other things to them first."

Grimacing, I stooped to the princess and inspected her, breathing with relief.

"She's okay! Oh, if they had taken her out, too..."

I shook my head and jerked her awake.

Sakaiah coughed and opened her eyes. "Did you get it done?" She rasped. "Did you kill them?"

"Well..." I glanced at the fallen sentries. "No. Things are worse than we thought, I'm afraid."

Sakaiah noticed the sentries and hissed between her teeth. "Gods above *and* below!"

"We really should go," Solshek said. "The power here is so potent that it eventually corrupts or destroys anything in its presence." He flicked mournful eyes at the deceased guards. "And Zemorah is still on the prowl."

"At least Karvo is dead," I muttered. "That's one less pair of evil eyes in the palace."

Sakaiah blinked at us. "Karvo died?"

I nodded. "We'll... we'll show you the memories a bit later, Princess. I'm just too empty right now."

"Yes, and we need to go," said Solshek urgently.

We made our way back through the forest, grateful for what we'd learned on our journey but horrified all the same.

Sakaiah, to no one's surprise, was livid when she learned the Sharavaks had "installed" a portal in her homeland. Her parents were, too.

"Is this what I recover to?" Her mother fretted, finally back on her throne.

"What is the purpose of this portal, Twilight?" The prince asked, his tone taut with concern.

Finally using my name, I thought. *That's a win.*

"Highness, our guess is it's been opened to let monsters or something through onto the island," I explained. "We didn't see any small beasts in the Void while there, but it's likely they were elsewhere, resting. If the Sharavaks want to punish you for rebelling, all they need to do is call forth the monsters and start an attack."

The prince seethed. "They must have made this portal, what, back when the pact was formed?" He looked to his wife, who shook her head.

"I don't know, dear. It doesn't quite matter, though, because we have a wide-open portal to the realm of the damned in our land. We must deal with this swiftly."

The prince agreed. "And you say the Shadow woman, "Ze-more-uh," is still at large?"

"Correct, Highness."

He hissed and rubbed his cheek with his palm. Solshek took a moment to propose something.

"There is a portal in the Caligin behind the Sharavak dwelling. I'm of the belief that there may be one or more of them in all three regions on Aash so they can effectively subdue the world during Myrkraas."

"Lovely." Prince Seraphina threw up his hands. "Demon people, spiritual torment, and portals to places full of fire, monsters, and death... have you any more good news, guests?"

"Father, they bravely fought for their lives down there—"

"I am not saying they didn't, Sakaiah," the prince interrupted. "In truth, I am impressed by the both of you." He nodded appreciatively at us. "My concern is over our army. We need to train them well and quickly, because we live on short time. A *portal* has been opened. I will send a group of my best magicians to try and close it, but if that fails, you know what's likely to follow."

Everyone nodded.

The Sharavaks' retaliation.

"So." He clasped his hands together. "What I need from you all is to train as much as possible. The army may occasionally request some of your magic expertise, so please lend it when you can. Sakaiah? Are you still planning on hosting the Sun Festival?"

Right. The Bronze celebration festival she'd told me about near the beginning of my stay.

Sakaiah looked away uncomfortably. "I would like to, Father, but it seems unsafe. However, the people have been looking forward to it. We have more citizens participating this year than ever. I..." She sighed and gazed guiltily at the prince. "Don't want to let them down."

The prince chewed his lip and thought about it. "It may not be the wisest idea, indeed. Not with all this going on." He gestured widely. "But if you get some of those soldiers trained up—the new ones, mind you, not the sentries and reservists—I believe we'd have adequate defenses. We can send a third or more of them to guard the festival. How does that sound?"

Sakaiah beamed. "I'd appreciate that, Father, and I know the people would, as well. You know how much we love to do this."

Prince Seraphina nodded. "Yes, and it's why I don't want to deny it to you. Well, everyone, you have your tasks. Twilight? Solshek? I have a request for both of you."

We bowed and invited him to share it.

"Seeing as the Sharavaks are probably not done with us, I would ask that, in return for our pledge to help you in the event of a mainland war, you would remain with us here for an additional month in case the Sharavaks attack."

I bowed deeply. "A perfectly fair exchange, Your Highness. I am flattered you want us to stay behind."

He grunted. "I know you're one of the stronger ones, girl. Sakaiah doesn't need to tell me, though she often does, because I feel it in you. I will admit this... I would not want to endure a conflict with the Sharavaks without you on our side."

Touched, I bowed even lower and said, "Thank you, Highness. I'll keep these kind words close."

"Mm. Do that. Now, go train."

We hurried off, grateful that the royals finally accepted us. Unfortunately, that meant they were now desperate, too. The situation had grown dire enough for them to see it for precisely what it was—a disaster waiting to happen.

CHAPTER THIRTY

W E TRAINED AS WE never had before for the next week. Most of our waking moments seemed occupied with magic strengthening, practice with Cobi, and helping Solshek effectively wield what magic he had when he wasn't whipping up potions. Sakaiah and I also dueled; this time, I did not resent her natural abundance. This time, it was necessary.

We dueled in the field where the Bronze army received its combat lessons, and she did not hold back on me. Explosion after explosion of magic bounced off my lumensa barrier, and I struggled to keep pace with her.

"Come on! This is not your best, Twilight. Enthusiasm would suit you well."

She chucked more magic at me. I ricocheted the orb and almost hit her with it, but she slammed it back at me. The lumensa fizzled against my face like a gentle drizzle of rain. Valdur would not feel so gentle in comparison.

"Again!" Sakaiah cried.

I studied her motions, noting the twist in her torso when she drew her hand back and how that brief moment of posturing time could be exploited. I fired. The lumensa nearly struck her, but she again deflected it. This time, though, I returned it to her, and we were tossing the orb back and forth for at least a minute.

I finished the match by casting the magic to the side. To protect myself, I formed a hasty barrier and then fashioned a rapid magic sword in my free hand. Sakaiah made herself a shield and mace. She advanced first, slinging the mace's spikes in my face. I blocked with my sword and drove her off, nearly unbalancing her, but she danced away so quickly that I never anticipated the lumensa coming at me.

In one breath, my defenses were gone, and only the sword remained. Not good. It seemed to be my instinct to do two things at once.

The princess attacked. I swung in every direction to try and block her orbs. I succeeded once she'd ceased firing them at me, but it left me depleted.

Sakaiah noticed my weakness and caused my sword to sputter into non-existence with a stream of magic, which then contacted my chest. I staggered backward, useless. She had won.

We were both panting from the physical and magical exertion. It had been a solid match, but I still feared I would be nothing in front of my father.

"You started exploiting my weak points too late in the game," Sakaiah explained. "Hesitation won't reward you in combat. Your enemy will not hesitate to kill you."

Korbin had said something very similar once.

"So think ahead, then," I said, sighing. "Got it."

"Think ahead," answered Sakaiah, "And think vicious. We play to kill, as they do."

You really do sound like Korbin right now.

I swallowed the sudden lump in my throat, thinking of him and my father. Damion had to be put down, but I didn't want it. I didn't want to watch the life slip from his gaze as I had seen in others before.

"I know it's tough," said the princess softly. "But so are you."

I didn't answer aside from a mild "Thank you," and I switched to training with Cobi.

Cobi continued his weapons work, which Sakaiah and I participated in at least once daily. When she was off tending to royal business or the festival, it was just him and me training together. Cobi liked to test his reflexes against my magic as he'd done with Sakaiah, deflecting the power off his blade where he'd send it hurtling into the wall.

His hand grew stronger every day. Consequently, so did he, and he was succeeding against even my more aggressive magic attacks with increasing ease, which nourished his starving confidence.

"How's that for weak?" He asked after I'd teased him and then bombarded him with twelve orbs at once, which he successfully ricocheted.

"Eh." I shrugged. "I still think you can do better. Let's up the ante. If you can drive off *fifteen* of these, I'll stop "emotionally abusing" you. How's that?"

"Ooh, that's a bargain," Cobi replied with a grin. He seemed happier with me after I became more encouraging of him, which didn't surprise me. "No emotional abuse means no more making fun of me for making fun of you! Sounds almost sad, though. I don't want to say goodbye to our banter."

"Trust me, I don't want to stop mocking you, either," I told him. "So how about you fail and satisfy both of us?"

"Mm. It's tempting, but I'd rather make you eat your words."

He swept the blade out in front of him to prepare for my attack. I dealt out the magic with a merciless hand, tossing one orb after the other and watching, impressed, as Cobi struck almost every one.

Almost.

"For the love," he panted, "Of mankind and magic-kind. I hate you right now."

I laughed. Cobi groaned loudly, sheathed his sword, then held his hands and sighed.

"You win for now. You may continue castrating me for the time being, but mark my words; you will be eating your own words come tomorrow. I need to come up with some more nicknames to torment you before I make it to where you can no longer be evil to me."

"Wonder when that day will come?" I asked.

I slapped him on the shoulder and flashed him a cheeky grin.

He rolled his eyes. "Soon. You can at least give me props for my firearms handling. I'm working toward being a marksman; do you realize that?"

Looking over his targets, I had to agree.

"You're doing well, like with the sword. That's ideal. A lot is happening quickly right now."

"Yes," Cobi agreed. "Not to turn serious, since that's not my style, but do you feel the tension? Like we're about to landslide into something bad?"

I grimaced. "Odds are, we probably will. We can't preoccupy ourselves with it, though. We have to trust that things will unfold as they ought to."

He agreed and took up more attacks against his dummies. I wandered into the field and restlessly tossed my magic at my own targets, grunting from the exertion and wondering if I would ever be ready to confront my father.

"Careful!" Solshek cried nearby. "Watch where you're throwing that." He gestured to my right hand, full of lumensa bleeding purple.

"Sorry," I muttered.

It was a wonder it hadn't turned purple all the way from my angry thoughts.

"Why don't you rest for a bit?" Solshek suggested. "You've been working all day."

His warm gaze brimmed with concern. I wanted to bask in it, but I had other things to do.

I shook my head and raised my hand to fire another projectile at my dummy target. Once I'd cast the magic and slung the dummy across the field, Solshek said, "Twilight."

"What?" I snapped. "Solshek, if I don't keep on top of things, I'm going to die, don't you get it?"

He came to my side and gently took my magic-wielding hand in his. "Look at me, please."

I glowered at him, and he smiled.

"Let's go back to the palace and spend the rest of the day in the library. Would you like that?"

Of course I'd have liked it, but I more liked the idea of surviving the coming war. Solshek's smile, however, overpowered my critical thoughts.

"Okay."

He nodded approvingly and handed me a potion. "Drink," he ordered softly. "You need it."

I grinned at him and took a swig. "Okay, Sir Korbin."

Solshek chuckled. "Sir Korbin? Nay, I am not at his level, nor do I think I can achieve it."

I rolled my eyes. "It's the way you look out for me. He would do the same."

"Ah." His eyes darkened with what resembled grief, but not as deep. "I miss the man. I hope to see him again."

"I'm sure you will."

Back in the palace library, Solshek and I settled into seats beside the large windows to resume an old activity of ours.

"I haven't written anything since I left," I admitted. "It felt wrong to do when so much was going on, and when you..." I trailed off, trusting he knew what I meant.

He nodded. "That is okay, Twilight. Never force your writing. Those who do so compromise themselves and the art form." He bent over his paper and began to jot his likely beautiful words across it.

"Maybe I can try it," I suggested, taking a paper, ink well, and quill for myself.

I just had to think of something to write—but what?

Solshek seemed especially introspective, throwing himself into his work with greater vigor than I'd yet seen, and when he would finish each piece, he set it aside face-down.

"You don't want me to see?" I asked.

"No. Not yet." He smiled and moved on to the next page.

"When?" I pressed.

Solshek chuckled and pointed at my paper. "Work on your writing, Twi. You'll see these pieces when the time is right."

I rolled my eyes and huffed, "Fine. I thought these writing sessions were about sharing our work, though."

"Not necessarily. Sharing comes after the art has been put together. I am not finished yet, and neither are you. We still have to tell our stories to ourselves."

I hid my smile at the way he made these statements. So serious, but in the most endearing way.

"Thank you, though," he added softly, glancing up at me from his page. The fading sun rays caught his eyes, making them frolic with gentle gold. "This," he said, indicating his writings and mine, "Is priceless. I never thought... "He gazed at the floor before continuing, "I never imagined I would have this."

I knew what he meant. Genuine human connection over a shared interest. Unlike Solshek, I was no philosopher. He would probably remain my smarter and better half forever, but this didn't threaten me. I respected him for who he was and how Akristura had made him. The artist was not so different from the art he created.

"Neither did I," I answered slowly. "You don't know how awful it was during those months, wondering what happened to you. I was so angry at Korbin." I shook my head. "It was agony."

Solshek nodded. "I do know. I know it very well. I had the same concerns about you." He flicked his gaze back my way and handed me a sheet from his pile of literature. "You can have this one now."

He busied himself with looking out the window while I read.

"Light and shadow war for her mind, yet light embraces her in time," I read, finishing.

He worried about me. Him and everyone else.

"This is pretty, Sol. Your work always is," I told him.

He started to beam with pleasure when a servant entered the library and called us to the front of the palace.

"Her Highness Sakaiah wishes to go to town with you," the servant informed us quickly.

Solshek and I smiled at each other and headed out to the waiting carriage.

"Hi!" Sakaiah greeted, looking breathlessly excited. "I thought we'd take a break from our training and see what the Sun Festival is looking like these days." She winked and ushered us into the carriage.

It was impossible to be in a sore mood around the Valechkans and hundreds of colorful displays. Thousands of citizens chattered in the square as some worked on their floats, and others pitched their items while wrangling in wanderers when they spotted some.

There was also tension, though. We heard frequent whispers about the likelihood of a coming war and Sakaiah's urgent request to make weapons and armor. Sakaiah promised them she would reveal the reason behind this after the festival ended. This seemed to appease some of their concerns.

In the meantime, we admired the Valechkans' creativity.

"That one," I said, gesturing to the biggest float yet, "Is amazing."

Sakaiah beamed. "Yes, it is. It's the most important one, too. We run an entire fireworks show and a dance with it, but I won't spoil anything more."

I took one last peek at the float and a gorgeous woman practicing some kind of dance in front of its skeleton. Several onlookers applauded her while an older woman made adjustments to her traditional Bronze attire.

"Just a few more days," Sakaiah said. "Everyone will be there."

I frowned, not wanting to dampen her mood, but I couldn't leave my concerns unspoken.

"I'll be honest, Sakaiah. I'm a little worried about what may happen at this festival."

She dismissed me, saying, "You heard what Father said; many of our sentries will be here enforcing the law and ensuring safety. I understand your concerns, Twilight, but it's been so dark and heavy recently—can we not just enjoy a good time?"

I feared she would say that. In any case, she and the rest of the Bronze seemed incredibly enthusiastic about the event, so it couldn't be all bad, security issues aside.

Besides, the Bronze army and sentries weren't terrible with their weapons. Most of them had entered the service in fine shape, and they only continued to strengthen with each passing day.

Once we'd finished viewing the festival set-up, we returned to the palace in higher spirits than we'd left it in. Before we reached town, we came to an abrupt stop near one of the small farms.

Sakaiah frowned and hopped out of the carriage, going to the front to see what the holdup was. I left to join her, leaving the others inside.

"What's going—" I started to ask.

Then I saw it. A dead cow laid upon the stone.

It was not merely deceased. Its entire middle had been split apart, emptying its intestines and a heavy lake of blood onto the road. Long gashes and black lacerations laced across its decimated corpse.

My breath stopped in my throat. I slowly stepped up beside Sakaiah, gazing down at the brutally murdered creature and wondering what native Bronze beast had committed such an act. The slashes were everywhere, including across its disturbingly empty eye sockets.

Sakaiah shook her head. "We do not have violent animals in this land. No bears. No wolves. Nothing of the sort."

"Whatever it was, it liked the eyes," I noted. "Do predators normally eat the eyes?"

"I don't know. I don't think so."

"Hey!"

We were startled as a rancher sprinted up to us. He pointed at his cow and cried, "She was my best! My best!"

"I am sorry," Sakaiah replied softly. "Here." She handed the man a few gold pieces from her purse. "For your loss."

The rancher accepted the money, but the frown didn't leave his face.

"I want to know what did this. Otherwise, it may happen again. I cannot afford losses, Highness."

Sakaiah agreed and promised she would investigate the incident. I glanced again at the cow. Sinister energy clouded around it.

Zemorah?

Or the Void monsters?

"Let's go," Sakaiah said.

She, too, was perturbed. I took one last look at the empty-eyed cow and thought she had every right to be.

I took some time to myself the evening before the Sun Festival to decompress. The tension and nonstop magic practice had exhausted me. Sakaiah, knowing my state, offered me medicinal body washes and lotions to help ease my muscle aches.

When I thanked her, she said, "Consider it payment for when you helped soothe my hurts with your magic."

I was glad to have a friend in her after the whirlwind that had been the last few weeks. After working some healing lotions into my skin, I prayed for a long time, letting my mental and physical pains release together.

While I did, I reflected on the work we'd accomplished with the Bronze army, helping them navigate magic whether they had it or not. The generals appreciated my and Sakaiah's input from time to time and implemented it into their training routines.

I sighed at my past accomplishments and failures and took in my face in the mirror. It had been a while since I'd stared myself down, and I wondered if I'd find anything new in my reflection.

As it always was, every inch of my skin gleamed pale like I had been clothed in the pelts of skinned stars. The black shimmer of my eyes and hair looked to be harvested from the vacuum of space. Muscles peeked beneath the stark pale since my training, clinging to my delicate bones and giving me a more distinguished form, but I would always be small. My frame size was beyond my frame of control. The magic inside me, golden and conscious, could be my only rescue from death.

"Twilight?"

I snapped out of my staring and left the bathroom. Sakaiah was standing there, worry on her face. Was she embarrassed, too? Her blush revealed that she wasn't about to discuss something pleasant.

"Sakaiah. Thank you for the soaps and lotions. They work well."

She smiled and nodded. "We make everything from nature here, so I am not surprised. But listen, Twilight... there's something I need to tell you, and I feel it's best to explain now so you know where I stand."

"Of course," I said.

She took a seat at the edge of my bed, draping one leg over the other and crossing her arms. "I think you'd noticed when I seemed a bit skittish around your friend Il. In truth, I don't much like the thought of any Akristurans." She sighed. "Now, I wish to explain why." She averted her eyes. "One day, while visiting my people in town, a devout Akristuran man came to me and begged me to help him heal his injured wife."

Her slight smile curved into a bitter tendril. "Of course, I wanted to help him. How could I not?" She shook her head, scowling. "So I followed him down one of the side streets to his home. Afternoon was fading into dusk, and I'd ordered the guards to remain in the carriage. There was no one left on the street but us."

Breaths were starting to pile up in my chest. I sat rigid, not wanting the next words to come. Sakaiah's bitter smile deepened into a grimace oozing malice.

"He attempted to do the unthinkable to me: that activity that rests at the top of the heap of unforgivable actions. As we tussled and struggled, I ended up killing him with a shot of magic to the head. At the time, I felt two things: sickened and justified. Most of the ill feeling I had centered around his proclamations of being a strong man of the Akristuran path."

She huffed a quick laugh and fell back against my bed, sprawling her toned limbs. I was silent, unsure of what could be an adequate response. Finally, I settled on, "So that's why you hate Akristurans."

Sakaiah nodded against the quilt. "Yes. It is a considerable portion of my dish of distaste. In truth, I've never been fond of your religion, but Cleric Halakor settled the issue for me. Akristurans can only be hypocrites. All of them poisoned to the core."

Considering some of the exclusivity of our beliefs, I could understand people's distaste for Akristura and His followers. Sakaiah did not know what Akristura had done for me and the changes He had brought about in my life.

In a sense, I was grateful for being so entrenched in darkness because without it, I may have never known light. The stains tarnishing my mind and spirit were ghastly, but did they not serve a grander purpose?

I would never forget what I had once been, what I'd done to the innocents in Orsh, nor the Akristurans during the battle.

I had decimated them. Oppressed them. Commanded their minds and turned them on each other. With each exercise of power, I'd slipped lower into the unending well of despair, consumed by shadows and an intensifying lust for death.

These were not feelings I could cast aside as if nothing. But if not for Akristura and the slowly growing sense that I was worth more than my mistakes, I would not have survived. Not the baines. Not myself. And certainly none of the entities in the Void.

Sakaiah... could she ever understand this?

"I understand," I said. "It makes sense. But—"

"No," Sakaiah whispered. Moisture clouded her eyes and blossomed against her cheeks, dribbling onto the quilt. "My hatred may seem justified... but is it? I think not. I cannot condemn an entire people for one man's actions and my pre-existing prejudice. You, Twilight, were the one to show me this."

I blinked gratefully, and she raised herself up from the bed.

"I have thought more about your beliefs over time. I still have problems with some of them, but you and your story are genuinely compelling. The fact that you went to the literal Void!" She laughed. "You and your friends amaze me, Twilight. You, especially, as a former Shadow. Never forget that."

She stood to leave, and I could swear that she took my lingering aches away with her.

CHAPTER THIRTY-ONE

THE PALACE WAS BUSTLING the following evening as everyone prepared for the Sun Festival.

This was it. Princess Sakaiah's big event of the year.

She sent half a dozen servants to each of us to prepare our outfits and makeup, appearing and disappearing randomly throughout the afternoon into dusk. When evening came, she had as much energy for the festival as she'd shown earlier in the day.

"My servants will collect you shortly," she told us breathlessly as Cobi, Solshek, and Norva had congregated in my room to talk. "Mother and Father are experiencing delays. Father blames it on Mother's vanity, but Mother insists no one wants to see her "like this." No one knows what that means because she's always very lovely." Sakaiah laughed. "But I'll be seeing you all soon." She looked us over and said, "You look wonderful, by the way."

She dashed off, leaving the rest of us to chuckle at her enthusiasm.

"She's not so bad of a lass after all," Norva said. "She's actually quite sweet."

"Quite," Cobi agreed.

Solshek fired an amused look my way. I rolled my eyes and made a last-minute adjustment to my robe collar.

"I do worry about this festival, though," I said quietly. "Cobi, maybe you ought to bring your sword and shield. Just in case."

"You really think something's going to happen?" He asked.

I shrugged. "Don't know."

"Well, what are your predator senses telling you?"

I paused and glared at him. "I don't know, Cobi. I can't see into the future; I can only work with what I've got. Just bring your stuff, okay?"

"Easy," Solshek warned. "We are all a bit nervous, Twilight, but we have a deity smiling down on us from high."

I sighed. "Maybe so, Sol, but that doesn't guarantee bad things won't happen. Do you have potions on hand?"

He nodded and patted a small satchel over his shoulder.

"Good." I took a deep breath and released it. "Now we wait."

"I want to warn you," Sakaiah murmured when we climbed into the palace carriage, "About how this festival opens. It's a tradition."

"Oh?"

She nodded, grimacing slightly. "Before we play the *Anthem of the Sun,* our national theme, we have a ritual that celebrates the Bronze's national pride and religious identity. Not that we really have one of those these days beyond gems and the like."

"Okay," I said. "And?"

Sakaiah rubbed her arms in discomfort. "It involves some chanting and... summoning of things. Mostly ideas and concepts like fortune, wealth, and well-being. At this point, though, I don't know what I really believe in. It doesn't seem like we receive the things we pray for when we ask for them from the gems or just... project our thoughts into empty space. When I prayed to *my* gems, I got a dark thing in my body that took me over." She sighed deeply.

I nodded. "We can talk more about that later if you like, but I'll just cover my ears for the festival." I grinned at her.

She smiled back. "Thank you for being understanding."

"I try."

The vastness of the festival began to unfold before us from a mile outside town. Hundreds of lights and paper lanterns illuminated the darkening city, and several dozen parade floats lined the streets. Also notable was the presence of numerous sentries and army recruits.

I gaped at the displays, most of them larger than life, and was practically pressed against the glass when the crowds parted for us on the plaza road and let us through.

Sakaiah chuckled at me. "You look like a child."

I looked away from the glass at her and frowned. She laughed harder, then gestured to their biggest float in the center of the lineup.

"Remember that one? It's a lot prettier finished. That's the opener after the anthem and ritual."

My mouth dropped. So did the mouths of everyone, even the princess, as her eyes glided up the length of the piece. It was a sun, painted in shimmering gold, complete with wavy sun rays and the closed-eyed countenance of a lavish woman. Rouge, eyeshadow, and lipstick blushed from the sun-woman's face.

"Lovely," I whispered. "And you said there's a dance with it?"

"Yes. Another tradition for this festival."

We pulled up into a cleared spot for a front-and-center view of the sun float. Dozens of citizens greeted us, gushing over my healing work and wishing me an enjoyable time at the festival.

"The fireworks show is incredible," one woman exclaimed. "And just wait until you see the dance!"

I could see why Sakaiah didn't want to cancel this. It brought the Bronzians great joy. If it wasn't evident by her actions and mile-a-minute speech, Sakaiah loved it, too.

"The show will commence when the royal carriage arrives," Sakaiah explained. "That is, Mother and Father. As soon as it comes to a stop, the people will cheer, and the event will begin."

We passed the time by talking with the citizens, which made Sakaiah's guards nervous. Everyone I knew was on edge. When the royals arrived in their carriage, though, some of the tension lifted. Sakaiah didn't look happy, though.

"Is Mother having one of those days again?" She wondered aloud, peering at the carriage.

No one could see inside it as the windows were draped.

"What sort of day?" I asked.

Sakaiah scowled and turned away from it. "Never mind. If she wants to be vain and not show her face during the damn Sun Festival, she's entitled to do so. Here, everyone, have a Bronze pastry."

We settled in our seats for the opening display while she passed them around, and I took one nibble before deciding I'd rather not eat it just yet. I needed to keep my senses sharp. I looked around for signs of any unsavory characters before directing my eyes forward.

"Don't worry," Sakaiah urged me. "Half of law enforcement is here. I'd like to see your grandma try something."

I nodded, casting my nerves aside, and listened as the *Anthem of the Sun* began. It was a lovely song, with the performers' beats, flutes, and choir effects ringing through the plaza. When it finished, the illuminated area suddenly plunged into darkness.

Whispers broke among the people. I was seized with dread for one moment before a great fire flared to life off to the side of the float, surrounded by several dozen Valechkans in traditional dress.

Flutes and harps began to play. The citizens paced slowly before the fire until the drums came in fifteen seconds later, accelerating their movements. I watched with breathless fear, uncertain if what I was sensing were baines, as they twirled around the flames, their heads back and their chants soaring into the starlight.

Sweat shivered along my temples. I clutched instinctively at my collarbone, only to grasp my starstone instead. Gasping, I dropped it. It was warm. A faint light pulsed inside it.

"Sakaiah," I tried to whisper to her.

She was too engrossed in the performance. I swore softly and fell back against my seat, trying to put the music out of my mind.

It's okay, I told myself. *You're safe.*

The chanting grew louder. I shivered when the Bronze citizens' forms began to morph into memories from the past. In place of the Valechkans, Shadows danced. Instead of

Bronze robes, black cloaks rippled in front of the flames. Chants for good fortune twisted into demands of the Dark God, and my starstone was really starting to burn—

"Hey."

Sakaiah looked at me.

Are you well?

I shook my head. I was going to explain when the ritual music ended with a bang, and multiple display lights fell upon the sun float. A hush covered the crowd.

"Here we go," the princess whispered eagerly.

Fireworks exploded from the top of the float. A platform slowly ascended from inside; on it was the dancer we'd seen the other day. She strutted across the square of space, with no rails to guard her safety, and performed the Bronze curtsy in her colorful robes. The woman's grace was entrancing.

Everyone went silent.

My fingers involuntarily hooked over my starstone. I gasped at the heat that suddenly seared them and peered more closely at the elegant figure prancing across the platform, showers of fireworks spraying behind her.

Her robe cord had been tied in front. Sakaiah and I shared a frown, as we both noticed this, but no one else seemed to care.

"Is it supposed to be like that?" I shouted to the princess.

She vigorously shook her head.

The dancer held every pair of eyes fast... including mine, but not in the way she held the others. I gnawed my lip until I tasted blood. After sucking out the sour flavor, I closed my eyes and tried to "feel" the dancer.

Was it her that had my starstone hot enough to melt flesh or others nearby?

In the crowd, watching, waiting for a signal?

Drums began to play around the base of the platform. Flutes shrilled. Strange incense poured through the air, clouding around the sun float and sheathing the dancer in a silhouette of smoke. With each flash of fireworks, her wisp of a body, shadowed and lithe, struck a contrast against the smoke's delicate gray.

After the smoke settled in, I noticed that her robe had come off. The dancer was clearly naked, her nude breasts and every curve highlighted against the brightness. No one could see the details they so desperately wanted to, but this didn't stop whistles and awed whispers from following her provocative moves.

"Here it comes," Sakaiah breathed. "The glorious finish!"

One set of fireworks after another blazed through the darkness. Thousands of gasps followed while they broke the sky, and the dancer's hair shifted into lengthy curls.

Lengthy curls?

My heart lurched. No one else had that second's warning. None of the others were prepared when the smoke cleared, and multiple four-legged beasts snarled out from inside the float, black saliva slobbering from their jaws as they threw themselves at anyone near them.

"*Sentries!*" Sakaiah screamed.

Cries exploded from the throng. Citizens tripped over their chairs and stumbled over one another, trying to escape, but the Shadow monsters were already tearing through them like Void worms through the flesh of the dead. I ignited my lumensa barrier and pulled Solshek inside it with me while Sakaiah did the same for Cobi.

We looked toward the sun float platform. The woman—Zemorah—had vanished.

"Void below!" I cursed. "She must have killed the original dancer and orchestrated *this!*"

Sakaiah wasn't listening. Her eyes were on the carriage, Solshek, Cobi, and her people. Over a dozen sentries took position around the carriage, but they were going to need help elsewhere.

We saw a few Shadow men preparing to shed their human skin and join the hunting party.

"Tonight," the leader growled, "We feed."

He shifted into his beast form and threw himself at the nearest citizen, opening her neck before I could attack. I slung lumensa at him, but he dodged it, dark liquid slithering from his lips. Snarling, the beast bounded off. A dozen or so of his followers trailed him from the darkness, snapping at legs and slashing holes in stomachs as they went.

The familiar death stench wrapped itself around us. It billowed from the warm entrails unearthed from their protective torsos, and it stung in coriusg's bitter bite as the harsh liquid gobbled bones and screams in its path.

I choked on the odors and stumbled away from the blood and filth. I had to stop this... the slaughter and the assault on my senses. There were too many Sharavos' to take at once, but we had to try knocking *some* of them down.

How did they all get here? I thought desperately, but I was not able to think long.

Fires from toppled lanterns consumed the tents and floats. Flames clawed across each object in their pathway, and even more panic enveloped the town. The wailing Valechkans were everywhere, their bodies torn asunder. Limbs were shredded from torsos, blood was thrown into the air like confetti, and I could see them all as a Sharavos for a moment.

That was me out there. I was the one conducting the killing. Me slurping up the juices, the remnants of human energy, of *life,* that was unnatural of me to claim.

It was me who was the brutal butcher. These were not Valechkans; they were Orshians. Kind, innocent residents of my hometown.

And I'm the reason they're dead.

"Twilight!"

Four Shadow monsters prowled in front of us. Their hatred lent them this unnatural power to transform, an ability I'd never know again. The first beast flung itself at us. Sakaiah and I knocked it back with magic, but the others moved in to surround us.

Cobi slashed at two with his sword. I felt grateful almost to the point of weeping that I'd told him to bring it. His monsters gnashed their teeth and tried to pry his weapon out of his hands with their mouths, resulting in their jaws being split apart.

Gasping, Cobi pointed the blade at six more that stalked from the darkness where the fires had not yet spread. I hurled magic at his admirers, and I shouldn't have. It was the last mistake before the Void that had broken loose broke loose anew.

Suddenly, all eight of them were on top of us. Bites and scratches erupted everywhere on my flesh. I could feel the warmth of blood and coriusg leaking from each wound and coughed at the horrid stench assaulting my senses.

There were too many of them. They had my arms, legs, and neck, no... not my neck...

I flailed with my magic, slinging it wherever it would land. At least one monster toppled off me, but another dragged me to the ground. From the shrill sounds around me, the others were in the same position.

A highly vulnerable one.

Teeth snagged at the base of my neck. I panicked. Purple light blasted out of my hand, which was now being clamped in the jaws of one of the monsters. More teeth scraped for my throat.

If those fangs slipped any deeper, I would slip away to Araveh.

I didn't want to go there yet.

A female voice shouted above me, and golden light flashed. The monster struggling for my artery was fired away, whining, into its brethren. I devoured a quick breath before kicking off the last two beasts fastened to my boots, and I dragged myself back to my feet.

Numbness was unfurling in my wounds, and for a moment, I wasn't sure I could stand. But my protector, Norva, was under siege herself. I whipped my magic into a blade, slashed at every offender trying to corner her, and then turned to help the others.

Sakaiah and Solshek were both on the ground. Cobi was about to end up there himself, struggling to stand with the creatures jumping at him. One gazed intently at his sword, hoping to steal it from him. He'd die in an instant if that happened.

"Return to the Void!" I screamed.

I launched lumensa at the monster eyeballing him. With his hand free, Cobi sliced at his remaining offenders and hobbled over to help Norva and me with Sakaiah and Solshek.

At least fifteen sentries had already perished. I tried to push this cold thought away and focus on freeing my friends. I booted one of Sakaiah's attackers in the head, and it latched onto me.

Swift and impossibly nimble, the creature threw me to the ground and snapped for my neck when a blade was driven through the place its heart would have been and out the other side. The creature hadn't even uttered a yelp before Cobi, my newest defender, retracted his blade, pushing away the impaled carcass.

We shared one brief look before ridding our friends of the rest of the dark herd.

Cobi lashed out at a monster struggling to burrow into Sakaiah's stomach and whipped off its head. I couldn't restrain my grin, knowing he had gone from dummies to monsters with that technique. I did the same with my lumensa blade on Solshek's tormentors, and black blood littered the street.

The Sharavos' nearby, who had seen their brethren's fates, leaped away from their victims. They dashed off between the flames slathering themselves across the buildings like paint, an excruciating heat not unlike the Void pressing around us.

Sakaiah and Solshek were helped to their feet. Cuts and blood marred their faces.

Once everyone was back on their feet, we worked to rapidly heal each other, but the healing magic did not remove our drowsiness from the creatures' poisoned mouths. Solshek offered potions and took some of his own, then offered to douse Cobi's blade with poison.

I looked out over the square and noted the many casualties. That had taken minutes. All those heads torn off the bodies... mere minutes, and a fire was claiming the entire plaza and everything it contained.

"We need to put out this fire!" Sakaiah cried. "Use magic, water, whatever you can find! Use the fountains!"

We dispersed across the plaza and utilized everything we could to vanquish the flames. Void be damned, the heat was intense. I summoned a barrier to protect me as I had done in Toragaine and worked quickly, smothering as many flames as I could reach with lumensa streams. Cobi did the same with buckets of water, but the fires were too large.

We were losing.

"The beasts weren't enough for you, I see."

A group of Shadows materialized from the darkness at the edges of the buildings. They marched quietly toward us, their dark cloaks breezing over the stone. I shared a look with my friends, whose magic and weapons were already positioned for a fight.

The male Shadow in front grinned under his hood and taunted, "Go ahead and strike us. We won't bite anymore. We'll save that for the citizens." He withdrew a piece of a mangled corpse from his robes, which he sank his teeth into before stripping away a line of flesh.

Sakaiah bared her teeth.

"Where is my grandmother?" I demanded. "And how did you get here? Through the portal?"

"Of course. And you thought it was just for monsters?" The Shadow grinned and licked his bloody lips. "Well, you were half-right." To the princess, he said, "Thanks for lending Zem the sacrifice. I hear he was fun while he lasted." He laughed.

I lashed out with magic. The Shadow waved it aside and smirked.

"We're going to burn this country to the ground. Just like yours, Myrk Maiden, except this won't be figurative. The Bronze has made its alliance clear." He smiled before turning with his brethren and disappearing into the darkness.

CHAPTER THIRTY-TWO

W E DIDN'T HAVE TIME to respond.

    We were distracted by something massive stepping out from behind the churning wall of flames that had already reduced much of the market stands to blackened skeletons. Something that towered above the buildings, bringing swirling darkness in its wake.

If I could describe it, I would call it madness. A jumbled, malicious amalgamation of Shadow beasts, now with too many tangled limbs protruding from a mass of writhing black flesh and spines.

Was this the Shadows' gift to us while they laid waste to the Bronze?

I glanced at the fallen beasts we'd slain.

They're all gone. Which means...

These weren't living creatures. This thing was being controlled, like my mother's body after Father "resurrected" it.

Each of the entity's different bodies pulsed to their own life rhythm within the stitching of sinew and muscle. Multiple mangled heads jutted from the spindly arms, legs, and bones, giving the figure a hunched posture.

Sakaiah, Solshek, Cobi, Norva, and the remaining sentries gathered together, and I sprinted to join them as the chaotic entity scraped toward us on twisted legs. It parted numerous jaws and shrieked, unleashing a noise from Toragaine.

Sakaiah looked at me. I looked back, and I caught Solshek's eyes, too. Cobi faced forward, his sword trembling in hand.

Any drowsiness we suffered from the Sharavos' venomous maws melted away as adrenaline flooded our veins. The entity, which I decided to call the Manglin, swung one of its arms at us.

Sudden sharp pains exploded across my body. I gasped and nearly fell, realizing the Manglin had loaded us with poisoned spikes shed from its flicked limb. We didn't have long to finish this thing.

Everyone threw up their barriers. I pulled Cobi into mine and spared him from another onslaught of spike showers. When the Manglin saw our light magic, it screamed and stomped toward us, backing us against a building.

Get behind Sakaiah's barrier, I thought to Solshek, *And make a bow!*

Solshek seemed to have heard me. He swept behind Sakaiah, protected inside her magic, and hastily tossed together a weak magic bow and arrows. It wasn't much, but it would do.

He loaded the weapon with fumbling hands and fired at the charging monster. The first arrow completely missed. Movement swept across one of the far rooftops. The shape appeared human. I narrowed my eyes, expanding my magic barrier and preparing to dodge.

The Manglin was almost upon us. We dodged its swinging arm before it could knock us away and reassembled on the other side of it. Solshek fired another arrow and punctured it in one of its heads. The head made a sickening splatter sound, black blood shining from the ruined part, and then it started to regrow.

Don't tell me this thing is indestructible, I thought frantically.

"Fire at the body!" I shouted.

If the heads restructured themselves, maybe those weren't the creature's powerhouse. The Manglin spun on us and roared again, lashing out with a spray of dark liquid.

Coriusg.

"Shields!" I screamed.

One of the sentries, who had no magic and hadn't gotten behind one of us who did, unleashed a howl. Coriusg seared through his flesh and ate it down to the bone until he vanished in a fog of vapor. The Manglin was not playing for prey, much like its monstrous components when they had been alive. It had come to destroy.

Solshek notched another magic arrow and aimed it at the thick sheet of meat that comprised the Manglin's main body. Mouths and clawed hands snapped from the mutilated assembly, and the monster advanced on us again. Solshek released.

Light magic detonated inside the Manglin's flesh. It squealed and thrashed, fluids flowing from the gash. Solshek prepared yet another arrow.

The Manglin lunged at him and Sakaiah. It caught them in one of its long-fingered fists, snarling as it prepared to devour them.

By placing them inside its torso.

So that *was* the powerhouse. The many bodies squirming inside the tendons and strings of muscle were the main mouth, the main event.

And my two friends were about to die inside it.

"Let's put our magic together!" I screamed to a bewildered Norva. "We'll combine forces and fire at its mouth!"

If Sein and I could combine our power for evil, she and I could do so for good.

The Manglin's insides split apart to receive its prey.

This is it.

We raised our hands to expel our magic, aiming at the cavernous abdomen salivating for our friends' flesh.

But we never got to release it.

Before the jaws could close on her, Sakaiah screamed and grabbed the Manglin's mismatched "lips" with her hands. Light flared inside it. For a moment, there was only the brilliant shine stabbing through the darkness, Sakaiah's feral cry, and finally, bleeding over the top of her notes, the monster's ear-shredding screech as the princess pried its jaws apart.

An explosion rocked the town. Light, darkness, and chunks of ruined bodies rained down around us. My ears rang. I could no longer hear.

Have we lost them?

I ran toward my friends, desperate to know they were okay. I couldn't lose them then, not when we'd already survived so much. Surely they'd escaped alive?

"Twilight, look!"

A wisp of Cobi's voice faded through my ringing ears. He pointed to the smoking wreckage of the Manglin. Two bodies were rising slowly from the mound.

My heart floated into my throat. I choked out a laugh and ran to them. I dragged them both into a crushing hug, wanting them to feel all my love for them at once. When I pulled away, I saw they were exhausted, especially Sakaiah, but her eyes still burned with a deep thrill.

"That thing was disgusting. I *loved* that." She gestured excitedly to the beast's blackened remains.

I was relieved she was alive. Unfortunately, our victory was short-lived...

And incomplete.

Swooping down among the wreckage of ravaged flesh was a human body. It was lithe and slender, with a torso that curved like curled letters in formal signatures. Dark energy scintillated in the entity's hands, and a crackling cloak of shadows sheathed their feminine form.

Dear Akristura... those red "lengthy curls" from earlier... was that...

"Zemorah," Solshek said quietly.

The woman, her face marred in white lines, slowly approached us with a swing in her hips and entirely too much madness in her eyes. Her dark red lips peeled away from those pristine teeth she loved to bare for zyz males and then sink into their throats.

Light curse her; she *had* changed her hairstyle during the dance. Those crimson coils were Mother's. At least I'd damaged her face during the mirror incident. The scars were brutal below her eyes, etched haphazardly across her cheeks. She was also wearing that ridiculous red suit she'd had when we'd escaped the palace.

"I want to dance, Twilight!" Zemorah called. "Since I didn't get to have fun with you last time, and you made short work of my friends, we should definitely do it this time." She nodded at the Manglin's remains.

"You reanimated them, huh? Like Father did to my mother, to Aubri, whose hair you're wearing?" I clenched my jaw and ignored everyone's looks of horror.

Zemorah shrugged and smiled. "Who else?"

She stretched out a hand flowing with magic and wriggled her fingers. They glittered with their numerous gems and rings. I stepped forward from the others and readied my right hand for smiting her, maintaining my barrier with my left. This would be quick.

"Might I have the first dance?" I asked.

Zemorah chuckled and struck the ground with her hand. Valdur rippled across the stones. My lumensa weakened against the attack, but I kept to my feet. Solshek came to my side and prepared his own hands for an altercation.

"What are you doing?" I hissed.

He glanced at me like I was a fool. "Helping you."

I shook my head. "I'll handle this. Thanks."

Solshek flicked uncertain eyes at me and stepped back so my grandmother and I could have this dance to ourselves. Zemorah lashed out with another magic wave. This one was more aggressive and nearly toppled me. I gritted my teeth and drew out more lumensa to feed my suffering barrier.

"Come out from behind that magic, sweetie," Zemorah taunted, "So we can dance properly. You're making for a very poor partner."

I tried striking her with a wave of light magic, but it was swallowed up in Zemorah's shadow cloak. Curse her! She should have at least staggered from that. Energy buzzed in the air as my grandmother's cloak suddenly dissolved, rendering her vulnerable.

I chucked a few potent spheres of lumensa her way. One went for her head. She ducked. Another angled toward her ribs. She twisted gently out of the way, unfazed. The third was aimed at her navel. Zemorah's torso whipped back with inhuman flexibility while she almost lowered to the ground but never lost her footing. Instead, she snapped back up and blasted me with valdur.

My lumensa shield deflected the magic and sent it her way, but she only threw it back at me. It was the match Sakaiah and I had participated in during training. She had won. Zemorah could not win. She was capable of killing some, but she wouldn't kill me.

I was better than her.

Gnawing on this anger and familiar sense of superiority, I shoved the dark magic at her again. She heaved it back with a smile. The dark power slammed into my shield and drove me back a few inches, unbroken but still dying.

And that, I realized, *Is the point. She can do this all day with no barriers. I need to get rid of this thing.*

It was the same move I'd tried with Sir Korbin, and I'd had to change tactics then.

As soon as I projected the valdur back at Zemorah, I dissolved my barrier and released a fresh explosion of light magic. Preoccupied with the valdur and unprepared for my lumensa, Zemorah was finally toppled when the two magics detonated against her.

She cried out and collapsed on the stones. A sentient mannequin, indeed. Zemorah had always thought she was better than me, but it wasn't true. She had to come to terms with that now.

"How'd you like that move, Grandmother?" I taunted. "Still sure about dancing?"

"Don't be proud, Twilight," Norva warned, about to join the fight herself. "Pride precedes one's humbling."

I ignored Norva and started to form a much larger gathering of lumensa to take Zemorah out with, no longer concerned with preserving her life. She had killed one of our own. She had stolen my mother's own scalp and flaunted it. She was willing to use her own friends' bodies to make monsters, and she was responsible for the Shadows presently lighting up the nation.

It was time for my grandmother to go the way of her mate.

"Hey!" Cobi shouted.

A dark blade sailed toward me from the ground, and my hands were too busy with magic to stop the inevitable. The valdur sliced into my leg and slammed me onto the ground. Red leaked onto the stones around me and gathered in a puddle.

Solshek swooped to my side. I tried to cover him with my barrier while he looked me over, my damaged body, fallen because—

Pride precedes one's humbling.

"Watch it!" Norva cried.

Zemorah was back on her feet, dodging every ounce of magic thrown her way in twirls and twists of such innate grace that she really did appear to be dancing. Solshek quickly came to his feet and ordered me to stay with Sakaiah.

"I need to fight!" I protested, ignoring the pain in my leg.

Solshek shook his head and glanced forlornly at my crimson-coated clothes. "You've done enough."

He stepped forward with Cobi and Norva to finish my grandmother. Biting back a harsh retort, I let Sakaiah ensconce me in warm light as she worked to heal my wound and let my friends continue without me.

"It's okay," she soothed, but we both knew it wasn't.

Her city was in ruins. Probably her entire nation. The Shadows had retaliated against the revolting Bronze, and now Zemorah was going to murder the rest of us.

Akristura, I thought miserably, *I have little faith right now.*

Solshek and Norva took to Zemorah's front while Cobi circled from the side. Solshek was cautious with his weaker magic, but his recent training had bettered him. He stabbed at Zemorah with a small lumensa sword. She parried briefly, narrowly avoiding taking the blade in her ribs, and threw him to the ground. Before she could give him a taste of her own blade, Norva intervened.

Zemorah laughed and cooed, "Let me make you ugly, Pious One."

Norva growled and whipped at her with her sword. Zemorah easily fended it off. Sakaiah and I screamed when her blade whistled across her hip, sending her, bloodied, to the stone. Zemorah quickly turned to Solshek. She prepared to impale him, her dark eyes flashing malice when Cobi yelled and leaped in front of the blade.

"Not him," he hissed. "You can kill me, but not him."

"Our little hero," she mocked.

She drove him back with her sword and nearly overpowered him, not yet finished with her taunts.

"I know you don't want to kill me," she chuckled. She thrust her blade forward and came inches within driving it through his stomach. "And a part of me doesn't want to kill you, either. But I will. I'll kill all your friends if you don't take me out first, including the boy you're so jealous of." She grinned and nodded at Solshek. "What," she gasped, "Do you think of that?"

Cobi didn't reply.

"Does it anger you?" She hissed. "Knowing I'll run you through like a quill through ink, writing your tragic story across this ground?"

"Finish her, Cobi!" I cried. "She means what she says!"

Cobi continued to block Zemorah, his blue eyes wide and wild.

"Listen to your Aaquaena," Zemorah laughed.

Cobi surprised everyone when he whipped out his gun and shot Zemorah in the leg. Zemorah hadn't anticipated this. None of us had. She stumbled onto the stone as Cobi loomed over her, ready to plunge his sword into her throat. I hoped he would because if he didn't, what else would we do with her?

Zemorah beamed, her leg spitting red. *"Do it. Put it right into my windpipe, little boy. Show us who you want to be."*

Her baine had taken over. When she became like that, she grew almost untouchable.

Cobi deliberated for several seconds. One could read the conflict in his gaze and feel it in his trembling energy. Would he go for the throat, quite literally, or spare this beastly woman?

"She has a baine in her, Cobi!" I gasped, "Take her out while you have her down!"

Zemorah laid flat on the stones and tucked her hands beneath her. She was surrendering, though her baine had commandeered her mind. That was why she was doing it, I realized. The baine in her wanted to seduce Cobi into murder, even at the expense of its host's life. After all, if the host died, it would simply find a new one.

Cobi, I thought desperately. *Maybe this isn't a good idea. Maybe we—*

"By the authority of Akristura," Cobi chanted softly, his blade still angled at Zemorah's neck.

She snarled and slithered back from it, crawling to her feet. She fell back down again when her leg didn't allow her to rise. Once he uttered the opening line, everyone joined in. Our voices echoed across the flaming plaza, gaining volume and intensity with each succeeding word.

"We..."

Zemorah shrieked and ground her palms against her scarred eyes, tottering to her feet. I stood myself and advanced on her, maintaining enough distance so she could not strike me. Norva stood, too, limping.

"Cast..."

Cobi crept in behind her and positioned his sword to stab her, should he need to.

"You..."

Norva joined him at his side.

"Out!"

My grandmother fell again, this time with a low and miserable scream. She twirled at the same moment in her last gust of bainic power.

The planet seemed to slow, time itself subdued, as she whipped through the air, a stygionyx blade in hand. It was the same blade she'd used on us weeks ago, and there it went, while the world stilled, while no one could gobble a breath to prepare themselves... plunging through Norva's neck.

She fell. The blade continued on its path, slashing through Cobi's arm. He struck the stones next, followed finally by Zemorah. Once she dropped, a dark presence howled from her lips and manifested before us. It was a whisper of the entity it could only ever be in the Void.

The baine locked gazes with me, a silhouette of smoke. It grinned and laughed.

Xanactyzaas. Father Sein's baine mate had been released.

"Leave!" I screamed at it before stumbling to Cobi's side.

His arm laid at an unnatural angle and was coated in red. Zemorah had cut him just below the elbow.

"Good dance, mortals."

I glanced up at the lingering Xanactyzaas who leered.

"I'll reclaim this body soon, and we'll do it again."

"Away from us!" Solshek ordered.

Xan chuffed at him, then glanced at Sakaiah. I knew what the thing wanted.

"Return to the Void, abomination!" I commanded.

Xanactyzaas moaned and turned away, finally vanishing. Looking at what she had made Zemorah do, it was my turn to moan.

I didn't know if Cobi was going to survive. His pulse was faint, and his wound was so unique that I wondered if lumensa would even fix it. Norva had definitely not survived. She rested in her life fluids, which poured from her ruined neck. Zemorah had removed her head from her body.

I choked on a sob. Solshek and Sakaiah hurriedly ministered to Cobi, who wasn't yet a lost cause. I was about to join them when fingers closed around my wrist.

"Twilight," Zemorah croaked.

I gasped and pried my hand from her. Her own anguished sounds trickled out, accompanied by a slew of tears. She coughed, and blood bubbled from her lips, which were also faintly scarred. I found myself pitying her like I never had before.

"I... don't like you," she whispered through the blood. "But..." She found my hand again and gave it a squeeze. "I'm... sorry."

She disliked *me?* She had no place to say that.

I was about to scream at her when I noticed how bright her eyes were. They'd never been so clear before. Uninhibited. Without the baine inside her, she was aware of herself and likely hadn't been since Xana inhabited her. To live alone and trapped inside one's own devolving mind for centuries must have been brutal.

But I wouldn't feel sorry for her.

"Zemorah," I wept. "You *killed* my friends. You *murdered them!*"

Zemorah nodded dazedly. "I know." Her eyes fluttered. "I've never been... a good person, but I... truly am... sorry. For now, anyway."

I found it difficult to believe until I looked into her eyes again. Something really was there that hadn't been before. How long had she been stuck with that baine inside her?

"Too long," she gasped, clutching at her breasts. "Alive for too long."

I blinked away my tears and shook my head. "Zemorah..."

Her nails dug deeper into my wrist.

"Kill me," she whispered, "Before the Void thing comes back. Don't want to be... in the dark again."

Xanactyzaas *would* return, too, if my grandmother was left unattended. Next time, it would bring friends.

"How can you regret what you did," I asked, "When you *chose* to do those things? No matter what influenced you, you still did what you did!"

Zemorah's lips opened and closed once before she croaked, "I never said... I was good. I had... my fun." She smirked. "Xana h-helped me get what I wanted. Kept me... young. But I don't want what I wanted anymore."

I dropped to the stones and wept, unable to face her. She was what she was, but she hadn't done it alone. Neither had I.

Not everything—or everyone—has to end in violence.

I looked at Solshek. He sent me a fleeting glance before returning his attention to Cobi, who wouldn't have been in mortal danger if not for Zemorah. I gritted my teeth and hissed.

"You don't deserve this." I took her hands in mine. "But I didn't deserve it either, so... hear me out, Grandmother."

As soon as the words started to come, I was at peace with them. There was little conflict or anger. I felt this receding the more I spoke, draining my pain into my pleas.

"Sever your ties, Zemorah. Denounce Aaksa. Embrace the Other in his stead, and you'll be free, as..." I stifled a sob. "As I am. You don't have to die."

Zemorah smiled faintly, her gaze grazing over me, and her fingers slipped from mine. She dropped softly to the stone as fires she and her friends created raged around us.

"Is she...?" Solshek asked before trailing off.

Zemorah's lips shifted silently as if uttering a prayer or perhaps a final curse she wished to bring upon us. No one knew, but as soon as the last breath hissed between her lips, her skin started to fade to an ashen gray.

"What is that?" I cried.

The gray color spread as it climbed from her feet to her torso, specks of the material fluttering into the smoky wind. Zemorah smiled more broadly and sealed her eyes when veins of gray streaked across her cheeks. Her face began to disassemble into a fine powder that drifted past her and through the town.

We watched it go, awestricken. No one knew what to think. When Zemorah's crumbled remnants finally faded into the burning backdrop of the dead city, Sakaiah whispered that it was time to find her parents.

Dozens of sentries were dead. Norva had been killed, and Cobi was severely wounded. We'd been spent.

There was nothing more we could do for Valechka now.

CHAPTER THIRTY-THREE

S AKAIAH'S IMMEDIATE CONCERN WAS locating her parents. She asked Solshek to stay behind with Cobi and take him to the city infirmary while we searched the burning city for any sign of the royals. I grimaced at all the bodies we had to step over. What a horrible mess. I couldn't say that it surprised me too much, though, because everyone had worried the festival might end like this.

I only wished the citizens hadn't had to suffer the brunt of the extermination. It was so... systematic, I thought nauseously, looking over the many bodies.

"They're not in the carriage," Sakaiah cried, "Because it's been burned." She pointed to its black, melting skeleton. "And I don't see anyone else who looks like them." She turned desperate eyes on me. "Twilight... we must go to the palace. It's possible they were taken there for shelter."

I didn't have a good feeling about it. I didn't have a pleasant idea about most of what we were seeing or would see soon, but I agreed to go with her. We raced up the road to the Bronze Palace on foot, as any carriage drivers in Valechka were likely dead or hiding. The road along the path was strewn with bodies of dead people and farm animals.

Sakaiah made a disgusted noise at them, her gaze brilliant with tears.

"Gods, I hope they're okay," she breathed as we continued our trek.

I glanced back at the city at one point and felt my stomach turn at how the entire countryside seemed ablaze. Araveh above, had the Shadows burned *everything* in the Bronze?

The smoke I was starting to smell didn't seem to be coming from below. Indeed, fires raged everywhere, but this new smoke seemed... sharper and more defined.

Sakaiah yelled when we rounded a bend into full view of the Bronze Palace, and I saw where the fresh smoke scent came from. Daggers of flame shot across the palace, piercing its magnificent skeleton with pops and crackles. Its oppressive orange glow ravaged the quiet night sky.

"Gods," Sakaiah gasped.

She sprinted toward the burning structure. I ran with her until we paused in the circular driveway to gaze upon the many figures scattered across the bronze and cobblestone paths. Every sentry in the vicinity had been unceremoniously slaughtered. Their clothing was more red and black than pale, and their faces loomed curiously empty under the firelight.

Bite marks and scratches striped their eye sockets. The Sharavos had pried them out and eaten them, leaving bloody-faced husks in place of men.

Sakaiah's sob cut through the snarling flames and smoke as she dropped to her knees on the ground. "Gods," she wept. *"Gods! Where are you?"*

I said nothing, as there was nothing to be said in this dark moment while shades of light danced and mocked us. I knelt by Sakaiah's side and placed my hand on hers. She continued to sob, and I let her. The Sharavaks had won. They'd accomplished what they had intended, leaving us, their victims, to reel and stagger from the despair.

As I knelt with her, I noticed the statue of Princess Dokor in the fountain. I tensed when I saw the bloody lettering scrawled there. *"ALLEGIANCE NOTED"* was painted across her forehead.

Seething, I rose up... and then dropped back down when the blood hit my head. The smoke... I coughed and decided that maybe Sakaiah and I shouldn't stay at the palace after all.

What remained to mourn? If the royals had been inside, were they not already lost?

"Sakaiah, we should leave," I whispered. "It's not good to stay here."

Sakaiah flashed a fierce look at me. "Then you're no true friend." She rose, trembling from the smoke herself, and toppled into my side. I caught her and held her. She started to cry again, digging her tears into my shirt.

"My parents were in there," she sobbed. "I'm sure of it."

A pang touched my chest. Maybe she wasn't wrong.

Seconds after this thought, as though someone watched us, the memories of the burning palace incident and what had taken place beforehand reached us. We both watched, with quiet horror, Princess Seraphina operating under bainic control. Her languid movements and hollow, unbroken stare guided her toward her husband.

"We won't be going to the festival," she said flatly.

He asked why, and her reply was a stab to the neck with one of the swords in their bedroom. The prince fell, gushing, and his wife completed her wicked task by taking a candle from their dresser and using it to ignite her surroundings. These were a Shadow's memories, and they ended with hearing the elder princess's tortured scream as the non-stone elements of the palace crumbled around her.

Sakaiah ripped herself from the memory and screamed. *"I'll kill you, you bastard! I'll set you on fire before you burn forever in the Void, monster!"* Her voice cracked from the smoke, and she fell again, wailing, before the statue of Princess Dokor.

"Oh, gods," she cried to the smoke-sprawled heavens, "What did I do wrong? What was it?"

I settled beside her and wrapped an arm around her. She continued to weep. Spots were beginning to threaten my eyesight, but still, I held her, unwilling to leave her alone. The smoke continued to swarm around my head, though; before I could stop myself, I was nodding off into a hallucination.

The fire on the palace, devouring what it wanted, seemed to take the form of a tall, robed man. Bainic eyes, with their cold luster and knowing depths, pierced me. The man unveiled a beautiful, hideous grin and hissed, *"Myrkraas is nigh, Myrk Maiden. Not all will survive. Indeed, some have already gone."*

The man's form shifted into what appeared to be a memory. I recognized the brown skin and tight black curls in front of me as Sir Korbin's features, frowning as he thrashed inside a black fire.

He was alive for every second of the flames devouring him, writhing from the pain ravaging his bones, wailing, and—

Have you had enough, daughter?

Father. Father had done this to my friend.

My eyes suddenly slipped closed, and a haze darkened my mind. Father drifted into view. We were alone in the empty dream dimension where Mt. Amber was a distant memory. Only a lonely gray shadow surrounded us. Father smiled at me from the darkest recesses of the realm.

"Miss him?" He asked.

I bit down on my lower lip and suppressed a growing scream. He had not just done that, taken my friend from me. It had not transpired.

"That wasn't real," I responded.

Father exhaled quietly and folded his arms across the front of his robes. "The first stage of grief: denial."

I laughed savagely and snapped, "How could you do this?"

Father smiled. "The second stage: anger."

"Tell me why, Damion! Tell me... you didn't do this.*"*

He chuckled. "Already on to "bargaining." You process grief quickly."

"You're disgusting," I spat.

Father shrugged. "The Akristuran's time has come. I fulfilled Aaksa's wishes. Sir Javari Korbin is gone."

I clenched and unclenched my fists, wishing I could deliver one of them swiftly to his jaw.

"Did you do this... to hurt me?"

Father smirked. "Not everything is about you."

"Clearly, it had something to do with me," I hissed, "Because you showed me his death."

Father waved me off and had the audacity to reply, "Such ingratitude. I gifted you with the last few moments of his life. The same will not be true for little Solshek."

"Solshek?" I whispered.

Father crafted the faint shape of a cat with his magic.

"The pet," he said softly, "That I so graciously allow you to keep for a time. But like all pets..."

He crushed the cat in his palm, its form collapsing into dark dust.

"He will perish before his owner does. Come now, daughter... remember Sunshine?"

I gasped as the magic swept through me, spinning me into a new dream.

Footsteps echoed from the shadows behind me. I turned to face my mother, whose sweet expression had soured into a grimace. She raised her chin, her scarlet spirals breezing gently behind her, and locked eyes with me before speaking.

"We have much to discuss, daughter."

GLOSSARY

A guide to Braekos for Mortalmouth tongues.

Aadbaineos *(ad-bane-ose)* – the Sharavak language

Aadyalbaine (ad-yawl-bane) – the Myrk (Dark) God

Aafyrira *(ah-fee-ree-ruh)* – the most powerful known form of Sharavak

Aakira Fadain/Madain *(ah-keer-uh fah-dane/mah-dane)* – the High Father/Mother; term denoting the highest Sovereign male or female in the Sharavak society

Aakonsa *(ah-kon-zuh)* – a Sharavak king

Aaksa *(awk-suh)* – God

Aaquaena *(ah-kee-nuh)* – a Sharavak queen

Aayalvak *(ah-yal-vock)* – a Sharavak of exceptional power, but lesser than an Aafyrira

Alash Vokar *(ah-losh voh-kar)* – the highest advisor of Sharavak Sovereigns

Baine *(bane)* – demon

Braekos *(bray-kose)* – the Brethren Code

Coriusg *(core-ee-usg)* – Sharavos venom

Excribur *(ex-crib-eer)* – Exchange

Lumen *(loo-men)* – light-magic person

Lumensa *(loo-men-suh)* – light magic

Maktas *(mock-toss)* — the middle realm between mortal life and everlasting death

Mitya *(mit-yah)* — a Sharavak of middle or average power

Myrk *(murk)* — dark/darkness

Myrkraas *(murk-ross)* — the supreme darkness, denoting the Dark Hour

Nashk *(noshk)* — an afterworld of nothingness

Raefsa *(rayf-suh)* — "the steal"; an action that involves the consumption of a human saas

Saas *(sass)* — a term for both a soul and a soul's residual energy

Sharavak *(shar-uh-vock)* — shadow man

Sharavos *(shar-uh-vose)* — shadow monster; "other Shadow"

Spirnyx *(speer-nix)* — demon spider

Stygionyx - *(sti-jee-on-ix)* — a black, stony element that enhances dark magic ability

Toragaine *(tore-uh-gane)* — the Void; Sharavak afterlife

Valdur *(voll-der)* — dark magic

Zyvienkt *(zee-veen-kt)* — a Sharavak of below-average power

Zyz *(zeez)* — non-magical human

Other Aashian terms:

Akristura (ah-kris-too-ruh) — the Light God

Araveh (ah-ruh-vay) — the Akristuran afterlife

Non — a non-magical person (not derogatory)

Acknowledgments

We have officially done it—my middle child has been born.

She was pieced together all across the world: on the East and West Coasts of the United States, my hometown in Washington state, Idaho, Montana, on an airplane gliding thousands of feet over the Pacific, and in Yokohama, Japan while looking out over the lovely Cosmo Clock 21 ferris wheel.

I have the following individuals to thank for helping with the writing and encouragement process:

Kyle Schena, my best friend and the original fan of this series. Your suggestions and enthusiasm have never steered me wrong; my mother, Alicia Winningham, whose objectivity and support have bolstered my books near and far; Donny Winter and Daniel DiManna, two incredibly gifted writing friends who have sharpened my storytelling and blessed me with their wonderful friendship; my Grandma Bev and Grandpa Gary for their love and generosity; my Grandma Teresa for being my cheerleader, and finally, my editor, Mark Justice. Mark, you are the writing mentor every author wishes they had in their corner—insightful, spirited, and deeply well-read, I am forever grateful to have you evaluating my work!

Now I would like to thank these treasured supporters for their kindness and generosity: Daniel DiManna, Jose Beltran, Luis Ramirez, Nathan Marchand, Jack and Amy Jones, Kyle Anderson, and Stephen Garcia. Your support of the launch campaign was touching.

Last—but very much the opposite of least—I must thank God Almighty, the original Author, for guiding every step of this story from its conception to its revival. Thank You for Your faithfulness and for writing the greatest Story ever, in which I am honored to be a character!

Blessings to you all, family and friends, and to you, dear reader. If you are reading this, there is light to be found and wonders to enjoy around every corner—if you doubt that, look no further than certain fictional characters.

Until next time!

ABOUT AUTHOR

Alyssa Charpentier has always been enchanted by fantasy and things unseen. She is a dark fiction novelist, poet, and the author of the Myrk Maiden Trilogy. In addition to publishing her own original work, Alyssa regularly contributes articles to Daikaiju Enterprise's G-FAN magazine. She is currently a Sailor in the U.S. Navy, and when she is not writing, she is composing digital music, making YouTube videos, and pondering the themes in her favorite Godzilla movies.

Made in United States
North Haven, CT
06 August 2023

40006982R00193